20

"Not all who wander
are lost..."
J.R.R. Tolkien

*The*
WANDERER

Judy K. Carlson

# *The* WANDERER

A man,
a mystery,
a mission,
and a maiden

*A novel by*
Judy R. Carlson

XULON ELITE

Xulon Press Elite
2301 Lucien Way #415
Maitland, FL 32751
407.339.4217
www.xulonpress.com

Unless otherwise indicated, Scripture quotations taken from the King James Version (KJV)–*public domain*.

Scripture quotations taken from the Holy Bible, New Living Translation (NLT). Copyright ©1996, 2004, 2007 by Tyndale House Foundation. Used by permission of Tyndale House Publishers, Inc.

Printed in the United States of America.

ISBN-13: 978-1-54567-752-0

# TABLE OF CONTENTS

## PART I

## PART II

## PART III

# PROLOGUE

Author's apology for her book

"When I at first took my pen in hand
Thus to write, I did not understand
That I at all should make a little book
In such a mood; nay I had undertook
To make another; which, when almost done,
Before I was aware I this begun."

John Bunyan
The author's apology for his book,
Pilgrim's Progress

# INTRODUCTION

The story started from nothing. Not just the typical 'blank page nothing' as the writer stares at the page, praying and hoping for an amazing beginning to strike him for his story idea. In this story's life there wasn't even an idea, much less a page of any kind.

It really started when our evening party had moved to the 'Gathering Room' at our cottage, here in the Ozarks. The night was rather like Winnie the Pooh's words to Christopher Robin, "Doing nothing can lead to something," as some of our children and grandchildren sat together, trying to relax.

I offered what I thought was a fun idea. Except for card games, I was the self-appointed 'fun' planner'. For cards, my husband was the chief gamer. My word 'fun' was the word that hung in the air of the family's 'after dinner, sleepy time, feeling half-drugged evening'.

"Let's all write a story together!" (This was spoken joyfully by a storyteller, of course.) I went on to say, "You know; it's how that group game thing works where someone starts telling a story, then stops and the next guy has to pick it up, and so on until you have a story—kind of. But let's each write ours down instead of just telling it. That way I'll make a copy, after everyone leaves, and we'll each have it so we can remember the story! I've got the perfect notebook." (Of course!)

There wasn't quite 'complete' silence. Here's a sampling.

"Well... that 'could' be kind of fun" or

"It might take a while" or

"Do we have enough pens?" (That was a joke as most everyone knows I keep an arsenal in my purse, 'just in case.')

Or, "I have really bad handwriting."

Lastly, as I recall, a loud snore came from one of the men. Only my thirteen-year-old granddaughter lit up, who was already a writer, and quite a precocious one at that.

"Such a great idea, Mor Mor! I'll get the pens."

She jumped up but I could see that the vote was not unanimous! It passed by default. Normally I would just fold to the will of the group, but not that day! And so, the writing began. I was first and then came Lydia. It was just like that, right out of the blue, and the story began.

"It was a cold night, not the kind of cold...," and then Lydia took over a few short paragraphs later. That was it! No one else wrote a word!

So, before you is that story, now a book. Did it have a noble purpose, or years of careful research? (Only 70 years!) Was it a mandate from God? (Who knows?) Or, was it born out of a close family gathering with all of us just loving being together, enjoying Dad's hand-built fireplace and a cozy fire? It was just a November night in the Missouri countryside.

"Heh Honey," it was a few days after everyone had left and the quiet was a balm although a bit of a sad and lonesome sort of balm, but nevertheless a balm. And this I said to my husband Tim. "Listen to the story Lydia and I started that night in the gathering room. I think it's pretty good, considering its unheralded, unorthodox beginning."

I had written a few more pages as I couldn't resist adding more drama to the **very** short tale. In addition, the man who was my introductory character had captured my imagination. I was embarrassed to admit it, in case Tim dismissed the whole thing. I read the few pages I had. He really surprised me by saying, "Heh Jude, I really like that. You should keep working on it; I think it has real potential!"

"Are you kidding..., seriously," I replied. "You know I'm not going to work on another book."

"Whatever you think Jude."

That annoyed me, although I was quite pleased that he liked the little tale. But it was not enough for me to even consider writing more.

Extraordinary Pooh how "Something can come from nothing." Well at least what appears as 'nothing' from our hazy view can become something.

"Do not despise small beginnings." "Strange are the ways of Providence!"

January 25, 2019

Judy R. Carlson—Huggins, Missouri

THANK YOU TO: Harold T. Carlson, Chaplain (COL)-R, U.S. Army, husband and (Editor-in-Chief) and to my Son-in-Law, Justin Rex Schamberger (Word Processing and Technology Advisor). A big 'Mange Takk' to Liz Carlson (Our battle buddy daughter, par excellante,) and Lydia Sharon White (whose creative writing helped the whole thing begin.) Thank you to Annalisa Noelle Schamberger for designing the front cover of this book.

# PART I

# Chapter 1

# The Meeting

You number my wanderings;
put my tears into your bottle;
are they not in your book?
The Psalmist

It was a cold night, not the kind of cold where one thinks of cozy fires and hot chocolate, but a terrible cold, forlorn, damp and penetrating. At least so it seemed to the man who walked rapidly on the cracked sidewalk, shoulders hunched in his poorly fitted coat, bare hands jammed into his pockets seeking some unlikely refuge. Drawing out a slip of paper he stared at it and walked headlong into a young woman. She carried a box of some size which flew from her arms on impact. Secretly annoyed she bent to seize her parcel but was overtaken in the task by the man. Bending awkwardly, he looked at the brown gloved hands and straightening saw clearly in the light of the streetlamp, the face of a very young woman, her crystal blue eyes looked unwillingly into his. Unable to recover her composure she was peevish in her demeanor. She fully meant to take the box with complete indifference from her dull champion. Feeling worried for her father's sake, the girl was tired and anxious as she had already missed her first bus and knew he would be uneasy.

As the man held out the package, he looked dully into her eyes. Something she saw changed her affect and made her start. An unnoticeable gasp escaped, and it felt like her cheeks flushed. *Thankfully,* she thought, *he can't see me in the night.* His eyes, deeply set, were dark with suffering from some desperate inner plight which she saw in an instant. Even in her annoyance his distress could not be missed by one such as she.

Unable to think of something appropriate to say, stemming from the look in his eyes, she stammered out, "Thank you". When she received no polite reply, she continued hurriedly, "I'm sorry to have bumped into you; but you do seem in a dreadful hurry."

The man looked around, like a lost child, desperate to see someone or something familiar. Linnea was both distraught and confused by her apology for clearly, he had been the offending party. And yet the look in his eyes held her fast, like the refrain of a song she couldn't recall. It crowded her senses like a tonal memory, familiar but illusive, full knowing she had never looked into those eyes. Still their depths demanded a response, a naming of the tune they carried, but no understanding came to her. *Why did it seem she must have known him; or did she just wish to?*

"Forgive me; somehow I have missed the correct street for my meeting place. But the fault is entirely mine. Please excuse the inconvenience."

It was then that Linnea thought she detected a very slight accent. In an impulsive rush of sympathy, and with some curiosity, she found herself unable to resist saying, "It is perfectly all right Sir, but is something wrong? You seem distressed or perhaps lost?" Something, like a flash of anger, came into his eyes but then quickly extinguished, like turning off a light in a well-lit room. She couldn't be sure it had really happened.

"Do not distress yourself Miss. I am new to this city and am a bit lost; but I wonder, could I trouble you to ask if you know the location of this address?"

He held out a small slip of paper. She looked closely at it, under the streetlight, and glanced up quickly.

"Oh, that is the Saint Robert Street Cemetery."

His body stiffened noticeably, she thought. His voice was emptier than before if that were possible.

"Pardon me, but are you certain?"

Looking steadfastly at him she said softly, "Yes Sir, I am very certain. I have been there many times for services."

"Cemetery services..., you? But you are too young to have such solemn pastimes." He spoke with some doubt or perhaps denial of her disclosure.

"Yes, it is true; I am young; but my father is a minister and I am often needed for these sad duties."

"It is a sad business..., death," he murmured.

The girl nodded. Her mind drifted momentarily to a very recent scene which related well to his statement, *"It is a sad business...".* Isabella was a girl she had befriended several months earlier. Her friend now lay beneath the frozen earth, a baby cradled there in death with her. 'They shall rise together on the last day, mother and babe, at the sound of the trump of

God!' Those words were engraved on their tombstone. Tears formed at this fresh grief; but she willed them away. *The duty of commissioning the engraving had fallen to her. Yes, it was a sad business.* Glancing back at the silent man, he was shaking his head, as if in denial of some dread thought. Drawing his coat collar higher under his chin and bracing for the cold walk ahead, he tipped his head.

"I must detain you no longer. I was in haste and now I am sorry to have troubled you Miss." He held out his hand for the note.

Handing it back she said, "Linnea, my name is Linnea; and surely you will not go to such a dismal place now, and on such a night?!"

Jamming the paper into his pocket he said nothing. Then, again touching his hand to his head, as though he wore a hat, he brought his heels together, bowed and walked away. His pace was unhurried. The girl, for she wasn't much more than that, watched the unorthodox stranger as he now clasped his hands behind his back, heedless of the cold and seemingly staring at the sidewalk moving beneath his feet. There was no map written there but perhaps he hoped it would show him a better path than the one he seemed destined to be walking.

Quickly following, Linnea caught up and touched his arm. "Sir, please do not think me annoying or impertinent for detaining you."

He stopped and spoke in a kind but subdued voice, "No, young Miss, but rather perhaps you are not quite safe to be shadowing one such as I."

Did the lady detect a very slight smile as she glanced under the streetlight? She smiled a little. "Perhaps the cold night is

what you should see as unsafe." Suddenly, self-conscious at her
boldness, she continued hastily. "Sir come with me on the bus.
I am here to catch it and it will be here very soon. You could
ride and be warmed. Then, I could tell you where you need to
connect for your destination." The man said nothing.

"You see, I am going home to my father and I would like to
invite you to stay the night since you are a stranger here. But
even if you do not want to come, you can at least warm yourself
on the bus. If you are willing to at least stop and visit a while,
perhaps my father can help you. You are new to our town! He
knows a great many people from various professions."

He stared at her with a bewildered expression and then
replied, "But why should you or he show such kindness to me?
I could be a dangerous man. Are you in the habit of taking in
wandering strangers?" He queried her in an unsteady voice, his
tall, lean frame chilled to the bone. So little nutrition, in recent
days, erased any stamina he might have had to combat the cold.

Linnea looked at him unblinkingly. "Sir, I think I must
care for you, a little bit, as you seem lost and unable to care
for yourself. Besides, I fear nothing when I am on a lighted
bus!" She said this cheerfully, as if it were a well-known fact
explaining everything and eliminating all possibilities of any
personal jeopardy.

The man was amused at her simple solution to safety. He
smiled and said, "True enough, no doubt the bus driver knows
you well and would do me a harm should I act with anything
but the utmost decorum towards you."

"Here it comes!", she cried, tugging his coat sleeve and hurrying to the curb. He took her package and acquiesced, like
an obedient child.

As they boarded the lighted transport, the girl turned and whispered, "Don't worry; I have tokens; but ask for a transfer; they are good for four hours, just in case." She dropped the tokens, with a little jingling sound, and they seated themselves halfway back. The bus was quite occupied.

He heaved a shuddering sigh, put his head back on the seat and closed his eyes. After a few moments he queried, "Can I ride all night Miss?" She laughed sweetly, very pleased at his relaxed posture.

Linnea gestured for the package, and as he handed it to her, she said, "You see, I told you that a bus is a very wonderful place to be on such a night, especially for a 'wandering stranger.'"

She smiled and then looked away, not quite certain of how to act now that they were seated next to one another. They were still very much strangers. She didn't even know his name. But one significant thing she did notice, in the lighted bus, was that he was quite a young man. That seemed the saddest thing of all to her. He spoke again and she turned his way.

"Please excuse my poor lack of a salutation at our odd meeting. My name is Renuel, and I thank you for your care. Perhaps you are correct in your reasoning that I am not in a place to care very well for myself."

She nodded, and glancing his direction, said quietly, "I think not Sir, and my name is Linnea."

She offered her hand and he took it gently and quickly released it. Linnea, her face reddening, folded her gloved hands and looked out the window at the passersby. Her thoughts were troubled as she mused on the traveler beside her. Shivering slightly, Linnea adjusted the package under her seat and wrapped her wool cape more tightly around her. The air, near the floor, was cold. She rubbed her gloved hands together and soon began to chatter, covering her discomfort at the closeness of his broad shoulders, pressing against her.

"Your hands are cold, Miss?"

"A little bit, and I should have worn mittens; they are much warmer for this cold. But a special friend gave these to me. So, I like to use them."

"Yes, Miss, mittens are better than gloves. You can make a fist inside them and that keeps warmth in the fingers." She looked up surprised.

"Why that is exactly true; but how do you know since you are new to this part of the country?"

"I did indeed come in great haste from a southerly clime and am unprepared for winter's chill. But I have lived in a cold", he paused, "area in earlier times in my life." Linnea thought, *you must have been a child since you cannot be more than twenty five now.*

Instead she declared, "Oh, but that can be easily remedied. My father has extra gloves and hats. She looked at him smiling, "But I fear he has no mittens, Sir."

He thought, *she has no fear in her eyes, only a bit of shyness. It was quite unlike the fear he had seen in a different young woman's eyes not long ago.*

He replied, "Does your father often house and outfit strangers in the night?" His features had relaxed in the warmth of the bus and a wry smile tugged at the corners of his mouth. Still his eyes remained sad. He looked at her momentarily and, once again, leaned back his head.

Linnea spoke softly, "Only if he sees the need before him."

He looked over at her and stated more than asked, "Or, if you do, Miss?" The girl looked down, her fair skin again reddening.

He perceived her discomfort. "Pardon my manner; I am often too direct. I am a rather rough fellow at present. I fear I am ill-mannered due to the rarity of such fair company, especially of late."

Linnea said nothing and the man also grew silent. After a while he looked discreetly at her reflection in the bus window wondering, *How did he ever meet such a beatific savior and that on this 'dark night of his soul'?*

# CHAPTER 2

# A RICH MAN AND A PAUPER

"His eyes were bright with intelligence
And trained powers of observation;
And they were beautiful with kindliness and
The well-bred habit of giving complete
attention."

Juliana H. Ewing

Deep conversation had passed between the older man and his companion. The visitor leaned back in his chair and stretched his legs.

"Thank goodness for a fire on such a night."

His host smiled. "Well said, my friend. Goodness should be acknowledged in all things great and small."

"Is that goodness with a capital 'G', Sir?" The guest commented with a bit of cynicism.

The pastor replied sincerely, "Most definitely Evan." And then, taking out his pocket watch, he exclaimed, "But where can Linney be? Her bus is past due by an hour."

His companion queried, "Delayed by bringing home another stray? Perhaps some poor drowned rat this time?"

"Only if it has a chance of being revived," the older man kindly replied.

"Well, perhaps your tardy daughter just tests your faith in God Pastor?"

Smiling, the pastor agreed. "Well-spoken again Evan. One must always be subject to examination by the Almighty; for the motives of the heart are often suspect. Even an agnostic, such as you, must acknowledge the fickleness of the human heart."

"Ah yes, but I comfort myself that there may not be a God who tests my heart."

"Did you not just suggest that my daughter is God's agent to test my confidence in Providence? What a bold proposal for such a dubious fellow!" The elder gentleman chuckled and then, at the expression on his friend's face, a fount of laughter spilled over.

Then he said graciously, "I venture, friend, that you often find yourself dialoguing with this God whose existence is so under your scrutiny."

His questioner answered in a subdued tone, "I would be a liar indeed not to acknowledge that; and I would hate to add such a sin to my already long list. Just in case, of course, that you are right and I am wrong." He smiled, but not with any heart.

The pastor arose and clasped the shoulder of his guest. "I respect an honest doubter as opposed to a chronic skeptic. We must talk again Evan; I enjoy our discussions and am not yet certain which position you represent."

The devious debater leaned forward speaking quietly, "Talking of rescued strays, what finally became of the young woman your daughter befriended a while back?"

The older gentleman looked surprised. "I assumed that had become town gossip." Clasping his hands, his eyes were fixed on something; something that Evan could only surmise. His mentor spoke again, "She and her infant babe have entered paradise together. Their spirits have flown; and she made confession for her sins. But there remains no surcease from sorrow for the ones she has left behind."

"So then, there has been no word of next of kin or at worst the brute who abandoned them?"

"No, I fear there has been no discovery of anyone connected to her." The Pastor spoke quietly, almost to himself.

"So, she was with child..." Evan looked up quickly, with a slightly defensive tone to his voice. "I had heard it rumored so months ago. But I always shrink from idle talk without proof of its veracity."

The Pastor nodded solemnly, "Do you, Evan? That's most unusual." Evan looked away. "Nevertheless, truth will raise its head and often, only in part. The whole truth will only be found by those who seek for it. Others are well satisfied with a comfortable measure of the truth, only too willing to think the worst of their fellow humans; though they themselves have doubtless done far worse."

The visitor coughed and was silent for a few moments. "I presume then that not all was known of her situation. Well, your Christian belief of paradise should be a comfort to you; but I can find no such happy ending for such a wasted, damnable end. I would prefer that the villain enter a hell in this earthly domain, for his calumny, since you know I doubt any retribution comes beyond the grave."

The elder shook his head, looking into the eyes of his student. "Is this your belief or do you speak what seems the current thought? Be not in haste to pass judgment friend; albeit on one who appears quite guilty. The girl herself would not condemn nor reproach the babe's father. She declared she could not speak of what had transpired but that her true confession was not of a moral nature. Whatever it was, she took it to her grave. Sadly, even a seeming villain can be much less of a sinner than you or I; if all were revealed, and someday all shall be laid bare."

The younger man felt a chill run up his spine but remained silent, keeping his discomfort to himself.

"My Linnea gave all her heart, once she discovered the girl's guarded condition; but Providence was already enfolding them and would not allow them to be parted."

The young man shook his head angrily. "How strangely you speak of your God! I wonder you should either blame or defend such senseless death in so young a person. Both the mother and child had their whole lives before them. What sovereign cruelty to be greedy of them so soon, especially when you Christians believe that your God will house them eternally. What was the 'Great Hastener's' motive, I ask you?"

The minister shook his head and spoke softly, more to himself than anyone. "Do you not know why the good die young? But is it not to spare them from something far worse?"

Out of confusion the dissenter said nothing. Those words the Pastor quoted seemed impossible for him to accept but equally impossible for him to dismiss. And, so it was with the tutor and his pupil, junior to him by only two decades.

As always Evan left the presence of this 'God defender' with more questions than those which he brought to the table. At times he wondered if it was not as much being in the presence of this singular, honorable man more than what was debated, that brought him back. There was warmth and a comfortable repose that seemed to emanate from his person and to fill Evan's vapid soul with an indefinable longing for something more. This 'something' was far from his understanding, or at least he dared not allow himself to think that it could have been 'someone' rather than something. He sensed Deity in the Pastor's presence. That kind of Christian mysticism, should he embrace it, would place him in great peril of changing his long-held views. Such a crack in his beliefs he could not afford; the result of which would overturn all the tables of his mind and the bent of his personal direction.

*'Does he think I can be so easily persuaded?'* This was his final thought. Of course, he was not the first to think such things in the aftermath of Christian dialogue. It began two thousand years before.

Moving silently toward the door Evan took his proffered hat and coat. Extending a large warm hand, the Pastor grasped the cold one of his pupil's, squeezing his forearm with his other one.

"Goodbye, my friend. Come again Tuesday next, if you have the mind. We will discuss Mr. Milton's view of Lucifer; since you seem to doubt his existence as much as you do his Maker's."

"Whose maker? Don't try to tell me you believe that your God created that mythical villain?!" His voice was not angry but annoyed and incredulous.

Once again laughter came from the Pastor to the debater. "Have you given up on your reading Evan? You still possess your copy in hand, do you not?"

Evan shook his head and thought rather than spoke. *He means his book which I try to hide from my colleagues probing eyes.* But instead he replied glibly, "Yes, yes sir, I guard it well, tawdry and aged as it is."

"Perhaps methinks you guard it too well, my friend", the older man replied, a sparkle in his eye coupled with a wry smile. "You could procure your own better copy from the library."

"Yes, but then it would feel like 'paradise regained' instead of 'lost'. Besides your old marked copy gives me your insights into what has to be the world's longest rhyme."

The minister smiled and added, "By and by friend there is a new study coming out which is a preface to the book we are reading. But perhaps it may be a bit too academic for our purposes."

"You mean too difficult for a simpleton and doubter like me?"

"Doubter yes, simpleton... no; indeed, though the author is a revealer of truth, he is profoundly simple in his impeccable logic."

As he opened the great outer door Evan noted, as before, the slightly thread bare cuffs of his tutor's suit jacket. The white shirt sleeves and collar were clean and starched but had a slightly yellow color. They were aged from long years of wear as the oils of the skin will do. Glancing down he stepped past his master (for so he acknowledged him his superior in all matters

14

of thought and religious knowledge) and observed the polished but worn tops of his black shoes. *He is not a poor man but clearly keeps a humble and sparse closet, why,* he wondered.

Tipping his hat, he moved purposefully through the open door and almost knocked over the minister's daughter.

"Begging your pardon, Miss!" He spoke loudly, reaching to grab her. But behind her stood a tall, very thin looking fellow who had his arms out and steadied her. He wore a fixed, bleak expression. All this Evan took in very quickly.

He turned and nodded to the Pastor, while mouthing the words, "Drowned rat", and moved past the young people.

His exit was rapid but not before he locked eyes with the stranger. Penetrating, intelligent eyes were fixed on his; they were wary, but indifferent. *Not quite drowned and possibly able to be revived,* was Evan's last thought.

Evan Reinholdt desperately needed to see himself as drowning in pride and denial. Both were making him inaccessible to that breath of Divinity that patiently waited to grant him life. The choice Evan had set before him was becoming a perilous one to ignore. "They had made a deal with death to dodge the grave." Evan too had tampered with such a deal by choosing his own pathway. It was a high-risk game; and he had played it far too long. His soul's eternity was teetering at the edge.

# Chapter 3

# Hanging by a Thread

"A flickering flame he will not extinguish;
a bruised reed he will not break."
"Hope springs forever eternal in the human breast."

"Excuse me Sir," the girl cried, avoiding Evan's eyes. Then, allowing him to pass, she thanked the man behind her. Taking her reluctant guest by the coat sleeve Linnea drew him into the house.

"Come, make haste Linney", her father called. "The air has a deathly chill." As soon as the tall visitor came into the light of the foyer, the Pastor exclaimed, "But how now, young man, out in such a night devoid of hat and gloves!? Here, come into the sitting room and warm yourself by the fire whilst you still live and breathe!"

He further thought, *He has left somewhere in a great hurry to be so ill clad.* "Linnea, ring the bell for Marthe, tell her to bring hot coffee. Then come back and warm yourself, tardy child." Her father looked tenderly at her and smiled.

Weary though he was, being somewhat depleted from the conversation with his protege, he nevertheless quickly ascertained the condition of the man before him. It was a gift, this recognition of human need. It required neither time nor assessment in the usual sense; it simply came to him unbidden, but not unwelcome. Within his aging body there lived a vigorous, ageless man, ever renewed and informed by the divine spirit within him.

"Sir, I do not wish to trouble you; I will just warm up a bit and be off."

"No trouble here, young traveler; please be seated. I hear Marthe's footfall already." The housekeeper entered the room with the tray of coffee. "Thank you Marthe. I see you have brought cream and sugar. "Ja, Pastor." "But this man needs some cheese and bread as well by the looks of him."

"Father", his daughter reproached gently, "You will frighten our guest away."

"Nonsense child. Sit over there, young man, in that chair closest to the fire. I don't believe it is close enough to scorch." "Thank you, Sir." He moved toward the chair and seated himself.

Linnea spoke quickly, "Pardon me father; this is Renuel." She paused slightly, her face reddening. Realizing she didn't even know his last name it all now sounded too familiar, even to her." A...a friend I just met this evening who had lost his way." Suddenly the whole circumstance seemed very foreign.

Her companion looked at her and stood, quickly extending his hand to her father. "My name is Renuel Breech, Sir. But please do not inconvenience yourselves; for I am truly soon off."

"Off to where friend, and on such a night as this for a lone soul? For what is of more value than a human soul, especially with a chilled body?" He smiled with such a genuinely kind expression that Renuel could only smile back. "Take his coat Linney, he will warm soon enough and not feel like a visitor needing to depart."

Their guest looked at the girl. "It will still be here in the morning," she said, smiling at him. Walking to the side of his chair, she waited as he hesitantly unbuttoned his overcoat. She eased it from his shoulders as he raised himself slightly, gently protesting.

"Thank you, Miss, but..."

Her father interjected, "Come now; we have much space and gladly welcome visitors as often as we can. You are safe and in good company."

Linnea folded his coat and said reassuringly, "There, you see, I will lay it over this bench, and you can retrieve it tomorrow." Shaking his head, he looked from the girl to the father.

"You are both most kind; but I cannot impose on your hospitality. Your daughter has shown me well the workings of public transport and I already have a transfer in hand. If you would direct me to an establishment, along the bus route, I would be grateful."

The older gentleman replied firmly, "Young man, you have already been directed to an establishment by a power much more persuasive than I. This is your inn; I am your innkeeper and there is room in the inn!" He smiled at his allusion. "Now, we are ready for the best part of the evening!"

Just then Marthe returned with a plate of cheese and bread as well as pastries. This time the stranger looked up and saw an older woman. She had once been quite attractive, no doubt, and was aging well. Her dark hair was streaked with white and she was of medium height with a frame that was strong looking beneath her apron's cover. The man looked into her eyes and saw compassion, if just a bit of wariness also. He thanked her; at which she nodded, but turned away, stared momentarily at the host and left.

The host saw their guest's hesitation as he raised his hand. "Don't even think of saying no to her small repast friend. Marthe enjoys serving her delicacies, especially kringle".

The stranger fought the emotions that were threatening to overcome his calm demeanor. Events of the past few months, of which these people could never know, bombarded his mind. Yet, here they were, caring for a needy traveler. He did not grasp that they were walking in the footsteps of that Good Samaritan who helped a desperate traveler long ago.

Renuel held the cup of coffee in both hands, letting its warmth seep into his fingers. He occasionally lifted the cup and carefully drank of the hot, creamy brew, like a soldier in the field, losing himself in its familiar comfort and putting away thoughts of the battle to come.

Linnea and her father chatted amicably with each other, hoping that their guest would give himself over to the food he so obviously needed. The dark bread, slathered with soft butter and cheese, was very appealing. Although he gladly partook of what was offered, he ate sparsely and declined a second portion. While doing so, he looked at the remaining food as though it were odious in some way and began to act detached, almost in a trance.

The stranger had been able to smile, nod and eat and even visit some; but now he was no longer fully present in their company. Wherever the man was, and with whomever, the host determined it was in another place and time, much different than this pleasant environment.

Rev. Johanneson spoke rather quietly, "Linnea," She looked askance at him and then at the traveler. She wore a tender expression, like one would give to an injured creature found by the roadside, as her father continued. "I believe our guest is quite weary. Let us call Marthe to show him to his room."

"Of course, Father."

The minister, sparing the dignity of their guest, stated, "We are all weary; conversation can wait for a new day. Are you ready Mr. Breech?"

Upon hearing his name, the man stood up stiffly and said in a strong tone, "Yes Sir, present and accounted for Sir!"

Linnea again looked at her father, now puzzled even more by the man's strange response. The minister stood, walked over and placed his broad hand on the shoulder of the traveler.

"Yes friend, you are here now and accounted for and we are glad of it. All will be well. Your mission can wait for morning light. Perhaps I can help you in some way. Come, I will show you to your quarters. Our housekeeper is apparently a bit occupied. Their visitor looked directly into his benefactor's kind eyes and tranquil face. Both were etched with pleasant signs of age.

He sighed deeply, "I thank you Sir; I thank you."

It was as though he had now awakened to his surroundings. He said goodnight in a distinct voice, glancing slightly at the girl. She nodded, smiling only a narrow smile. She could see he was beyond any social graces; all he needed was rest. Marthe entered the room at that moment and nodded towards the master of the house.

"Come vit me young man; all has been made ready. Even t'e foot varmer is between t'e bed covers."

"Thank you Marthe." The patron smiled. The visitor gave a slight bow and followed the housekeeper as she led him to the guest room.

As they walked away, the pastor put his arm around his daughter and squeezed her gently. "Well done, my girl. A fighting man, or even a former fighting man, needs care sometimes since the welfare of so many has been laid upon his young shoulders."

"You think he is a soldier then Father?"

"Is, or certainly was in some kind of military lifestyle."

"Here in our country?"

"Quite doubtful, his accent denotes he is from another place, perhaps a movement or a revolutionary force. But we shall see if he chooses to share any personal information. He is a private, reserved man; but wants to trust us, I believe."

"He was on his way to the Saint Robert Cemetery Father. Is that not strange?"

"One cannot always know the whys child; but in any case, it will not be deciphered at this hour." Ushering her towards the stairway, they passed by the chair their guest had occupied.

"Look there, Father!" Where Mr. Breech had been seated lay a gold chain with an oval locket attached. Linnea held it up and looked toward the hallway to where their guest had gone. Then she looked at her Father.

"Not tonight Linney, he is likely already retiring. Place it here on the buffet and return it tomorrow."

"Of course, Father." As he walked away her curiosity overcame her. She clicked open the locket which had a picture inside. Bringing it closer, Linnea gasped and covered her mouth. "Ohh...," and shot a look of shock and confusion at her father who had looked back.

"What is it Linnea?!" Walking over, she handed the open locket to him.

# CHAPTER 4

## LOSSES

"...And then she lost her losses,
  her aching and her weeping,
  her pains and griefs and crosses,
  and all things not worth keeping."

George MacDonald:
'Gifts of the Child Christ'

The 'guest' awakened to the warmth of a feather quilt engulfing him. Confusion from sleep blocked his memory. *Where am I? What hostel is this?* His eyes snapped open. *No, no I am in a house, their house. The girl, her father..., how can I be swaddled in such comfort and feel safe, and warm, so warm? Could there be a plot? Will they betray me?' His heart began to pound! 'Trust so many lies, so much deception..., could he really trust them?*

He sat up. The smell of coffee wafted from below. The stranger fell back on the pillow speaking aloud softly. "I must relax. They asked me nothing. I've betrayed no one. She remains safe—for now. I am certain our enemies are unaware of where I am." He sighed.

Looking at the wall he saw a plaque which he read in the dim light. It was stained with age; but the letters were very large and dark against the tan background. 'God is my helper; what can man do to me? The Lord is the strength of my life.' He sat up and read it again. *The words were slightly familiar. He must have heard them in an old catechism.*

As a youth the man enjoyed hearing the words read by the priest, even though the chanting tones seem detached, much like the detachment of those who occupied the pews. Occasionally he had a question for the priest; but the man always disappeared through the side door immediately after the last liturgy.

"God is my helper." It seemed more recently he had heard them. Then he remembered. Isabella had written those words in her last letter. 'Renuel, God does care for Oleksandr and me, even with all our sorrows. He is your helper too.'

He shook his head at the memory of those shining eyes set in her pale, sickly face. Again, speaking softly, he said, "Perhaps, Isa, perhaps."

A month in hiding had followed her letter. His memory haunted him. The hunted man tried to shut out the screams that had awakened him in their secluded place many months earlier. That was the night she had disappeared. He could still hear the men shouting, "Whore!" There immediately followed the sound of their heavy boots stomping down the stairwell, and Isabella's muffled screams.

Renuel had beaten madly on the door until his fists ached. Then he'd kicked it again and again in utter desperation. *How did the soldiers find them?! Was Olek captured too? Was Isa dead?* These questions ran mercilessly through his mind, torturing him in the night hours and continuously reminding him of her eyes. They were so hopeful of life, so true. They had even dared him to hope when hope seemed gone.

Olek came later that morning to check on them. He had finally jimmied the lock with a tool he carried. Head in his hands, Renuel barely looked up from his chair.

"She's gone; they took her in the night. I am so sorry Oleksandr Skoropadskyi."

His friend stood staring in horror, disbelief on his face. Then sobs slowly convulsed Oleksandr's body as the terrible truth sank in. He went forward and grabbed him from the chair.

"How, how could you...? and she with child!" Renuel remembered moaning in low tones and shaking his head. There were no more words to be spoken at such a moment. Even now grief washed over him again for the hundredth time.

His sad reverie was broken by a voice, "Mr. Breech". It was followed by a knock or two and again, "Mr. Breech, are you avake? Breakfast is in half an hour at eight o'clock."

"Yes, thank you; I will be there promptly." The steps receded. He had leapt off the bed at the sound of the housekeeper's voice. His pounding heart slowly quieted.

Isabella had written to him only a few times since that terrible night. Her letters were a lifeline, confirming that she was alive. She could not reveal her whereabouts but had escaped and was underground somewhere. But now nothing could cover his guilt or remorse for not saving her. Isabella assured him, over and over, that she did not hold him responsible for anything.

"We were all very aware that it was dangerous; but we were in it together. It was mutual consent Renny; never forget that. Oleksandr will understand one day."

The troubled man tidied his bed. He found a razor, shaved, dressed and made his way down to the main room. Walking into the area where he had been the night before, he met Linnea. She was so lovely that it took his breath away.

But he only bowed slightly saying, "Good morning fellow farer", and with a wan smile, "Are you true through life?" She nodded, but with a confused smile. "It is just an old poem, Miss".

She approached him and handed him something. "Here Mr. Breech, you left this on the chair last night. I hope that makes me true." She smiled a bit shyly. He looked at her and then at the locket which she handed him. His eyes grew wide.

With voice trembling he replied, "Oh yes, how can I thank you Miss! This is a keepsake from which I would be loath, beyond words, to part."

The lady was silent but looked up at him in a puzzled, beseeching way. Their eyes met and she tried to look away but remained locked in his gaze. Renuel's thoughts were dark and racing through events she could not have imagined.

*What would they think if they knew? Should I tell them? No, it would not be right, even if Isabella really is gone.* He swallowed, with difficulty. *I will not assuage my sorrow by telling her this tale of woe. But perhaps, I might disclose it to the priest.* Renuel found himself staring at the girl.

"Forgive me, Miss; I do not wish to cause discomfort; but I am somewhat distraught by the circumstances which brought me here. Thank you for your kindness and that of your father.

I have not been accustomed to being in the company of people, such as you, recently.

I am a poor guest that has not only has lost his way, but his manners as well. I must be gone now."

"Oh, but you must stay for a little breakfast", Linnea chided.

He replied in a strange, faltering voice, "I think I…" To Linnea's shock, he slumped forward. Had she not caught him he would have fallen. He was a tall man and his weight against her caused her knees to buckle. With her arms grasping him tightly, they went to the floor. His head drooped forward, with his face pressed against hers. His breath was so close that she nearly thought it was her own. At that moment her father entered the dining room and saw the whole drama unfold.

"Marthe!" he called, "Bring some wine!"

Linnea gently released her burden and he slumped to the floor. His breathing was so light that she put her ear close to his mouth to determine if he was still breathing at all. "Perhaps he is dying. But no, I feel air on my cheek." She whispered in a panic. Her father strode over rapidly. Looking up she cried, "Is he dying father?"

"No child, I don't believe so." He knelt feeling the man's pulse.

"What is wrong with him then?" Still looking at the stranger's face, she saw him trying to open his eyes. "His breath is sweet; why is that", she asked.

"Half starved, I would say. The breath is cleansed when food has been withheld for a time."

"But he did eat a bit with us last night," Linnea replied, unable to mask her worry.

"A very little bit, I noticed. Trust in us is not yet established and food is only good to the palette in the absence of fear."

27

Marthe came with the wine and took a pillow from the couch. "Here, Miss Linney, put dis under his head. Ja, poor creature, scared of everyt'ing and everyvone." The girl did as she was told and then edged away, remaining near to her charge.

Linnea felt he was her charge since she had brought him home. So now she continued to feel his distress quite keenly. Having taken the wine from Marthe, her father handed it to her.

"Lift his head and see if he will come to enough to take a sip." With trembling hand, she slid it behind Renuel's head.

"Mr. Breech, Sir, will you take a small sip of this wine? It will help you."

The man's eyes labored to open but closed again as though they were denying the light that was calling him from his stupor. Linnea lifted his head a bit higher and he attempted to raise his shoulders from the floor. She placed the glass to his lips. He took a sip and lay back down with a groan. His eyes fully opened, he stared into the frightened countenance of his benefactress. Looking up, he saw her father wearing a concerned expression. Breech sat up and struggled to stand. The minister grasped his arm.

The man did rise, but his voice was shaky, "My apologies Sir, this is most unworthy of me to bring such a burden upon you." Looking uncomfortable, he saw Linnea kneeling where he had lain. "I must trouble you no longer. Here Miss, take my hand, for I fear I took you down with me."

She shook her head shyly. "Oh no, Father will help me; you aren't well."

"I am well enough, Miss." Looking over at her father he nodded. Then, taking Linnea's hand, he firmly helped her to stand. "It seems that the longer I remain here, the more I am indebted to you. I must leave soon; or I will never be able to repay you." He smiled, ever so slightly, at his hosts. The minister took his arm gently and offered his daughter his other.

"Yes, I understand. But come, we will delay your departure only briefly so that you can first taste some breakfast." The pastor guided them into the dining room. After all were seated, he put his hand upon the shoulder of his guest. "Sit a short while and eat; it will give you strength for the day's demands. You are safe here, friend." Renuel looked up quickly and saw the kind eyes of his host and knew that it was true. He relaxed and acquiesced.

"Perhaps you are right; just a few moments to steady myself and I will trespass on your hospitality no longer."

"Let us pray and partake together." Seated at the head of the table, the Parson offered his hand to Linnea and the other to his guest. Linney, in a natural gesture, reached across to offer Renuel her other hand as well. The man was obviously uncertain but took the proffered hands.

Her father then prayed these words, "Bless this food to our bodies, oh Lord, and our bodies to your service."

Their visitor ate a bowl of oatmeal, with a generous handful of raisins, adding butter and cream. He then enjoyed a steaming cup of coffee. He smiled at their conversation, commenting on the age of their home as being quite like his childhood dwelling. Rising, he thanked Marthe for the excellent breakfast. She had brought in a plate of cinnamon rolls and pressed him to have one. When he politely refused; she quickly disappeared into the kitchen. He had already arisen and was speaking words of farewell.

"Perhaps someday I may find a way to repay you and your daughter for entrusting me with your home. It is a trust I find little of in my world today." When he said the word trust he looked directly at her father, glanced at Linnea and, with a smile, bowed.

"Thank you for riding with me on the bus, Miss. I won't forget to get a transfer." Touching his hand to his head he stepped back and turned toward the door. Marthe came back and handed him a brown lunch sack, a scarf and some gloves. He shook his head; but the housekeeper gave him a stony look. Then, with a sturdy motion, she grasped his arm and steered him toward the door.

Whispering, or more nearly correct hissing, she said, "Do not insult t'e master of t'is house in my presence, young man, by offering such a proud refusal. You know t'e bus route back. I expect you vill return anot'er day to show your gratitude. T'ere is time enough t'en, to return t'ese small items."

Looking chagrined, he took the items, bowed respectfully and was gone. Linnea stared at the door.

"Oh Father, such a bleak day for a lone stranger. Do you think he will ever return?"

"I should say definitely, if Marthe has anything to say about it." He smiled at their housekeeper as she walked haughtily by, refusing to acknowledge him. He let out a chuckle and turned his attention to Linnea.

"Do you wish it so much, daughter?"

She looked down and, with embarrassed animation, said, "Why..., yes father, he knows no one and I wish to help..., if I can. Don't you?" She finished her reply with an almost desperate appeal.

"You like this wanderer, do you? You think he is worthy of your care?"

"I trust him Father; though it may seem strange." Her father's eyes had a tender look as he spoke.

"Yes..., trustworthy, I think that is an astute observation of our guest. Better is trust, than 'savoir faire'; is it not?" She knew his words were in reference to Attorney Evan Reinholdt. Linnea's eyes looked solemnly into his. This solemnity was born of the unsought attentions paid her during recent visits.

"Indeed, I find it to be so, Father."

# CHAPTER 5

## CONSEQUENCES

"Getting and spending we lay waste our powers...
we have given our hearts away, a sordid boon."

John Milton

E van paced impatiently back and forth in front of the fireplace. His house was richly furnished. After making his
way in the world, he had married late to a wealthy woman who
was a physician. She contracted a dreaded illness through the
knick of a contaminated surgical knife.

The man had not wanted children and neither had she.
They were too taken with their professions. Not knowing the
latent perils of waiting too long, she began to have an incon-
solable longing for a child. Her disease was such that the doctors discouraged a pregnancy. She conceived, dismissing all
warnings, including Evan's protests that this could seriously
harm her. Her illness seemed to be going into remission as the
months passed; but when her condition worsened, they were
advised to terminate the pregnancy.

She was in her sixth month, but the doctor declared it might give her a better chance of survival. There were no guarantees; but Evan pressed his will. He never wanted the child anyway. He told her it was a last bid for her life. The child was born caesarian and his wife insisted on seeing it, dead or alive. They could not refuse her request and the baby lived for three days. Then, it died in her arms. This was probably the death of her instead of the life extender for which they had hoped. She died, to the shock of the doctors, one week after the baby's death.

Evan shook off the memories. So, what if they had deferred having children? He luxuriated in their pleasures and their additional freedom from unwanted responsibility. He had no regrets. It was only when facing premature death that his wife wanted a child. They had agreed on having no children so they could have the life they wanted. In the end, she was the one who had caved. She broke their agreement. It wasn't his fault. The baby, barely even human looking anyway, was better off. He knew that anyway!

He did miss his wife for a short while. But Evan got over her absence rather quickly. They really were more invested in their happy arrangement and their work than in any depth in their relationship. Now, he was alone and needed to find another wife to make things tick properly.

The minister had come into his life while he was in his most vulnerable state, just shortly after his wife's death. Filled with bitterness toward God, bordering on malice, he declared that he was an atheist and threw himself into his work. How dare some Divine tyrant intercept the perfect life he was living? He chose to chalk their tragedy up to happenstance and dismiss the idea of God entirely. No doubt he would never have begun these talks with Johanneson had he given himself a bit more time. When he overheard the pastor conversing, over coffee with a parishioner, he began to question himself. It was disturbing to have his values and beliefs challenged. He was slightly annoyed at his tutor. Still, he kept coming back for more. Perhaps tonight he was starting to understand why.

*It was that young woman..., his daughter!* Her face and form, her capacity to embrace happiness, and her purposeful life of service had destabilized and disturbed him. Mystifying to his ego was the fact that she seemed to regard him as invisible. It angered him, but in a strange way tantalized and seduced him. *'What a waste of an obviously gifted and beautiful girl',* he thought.

For girl she was, and perhaps *her* being twenty years his junior added to her delights. But this lack of noticing him, or at least of engaging him, was unacceptable. To him, she was playing a game that all women he had known often played. There were the high-level society women without spouses: widows, divorcees and even women of low morals having attracting beauty, and most with no boundaries. He had enjoyed the pleasures of many of them but never with any hint of a responsible future being offered to them.

This image of Linnea Johanneson, daughter of the minister, kept coming before him on this night. He had to face it. Why now was it so clear to him? Perhaps it was the man at the door that had aroused his latent passions and fascination. Linnea was young, without a fortune, and in her naivete, utterly captivating. She wasn't beautiful in a sophisticated way.

His first wife had certainly been that, as well as being very sensual. She always caught the eyes of men with her allurements. Of this, she was quite aware. He reveled in her making them feel virile and wanting. He enjoyed the jealousy of other men's lusty gazes.

No, this young lady, for she could be referred to in no other way, took his breath away in a totally new way. Her eyes haunted and taunted him in their ice blue softness. She lilted her way through life as though some unseen, sweet zephyr lifted her above others. Was it her aloofness that captured him and made her so appealing?

He often stared at her, with desire, as she served the two men. He would brush her hand when she offered him a sample from a plate of cookies. He even made comments to her father about her attractiveness and availability. Both the Pastor and the girl acted politely indifferent. Evan had decided to ignore their response for the time being.

But her way of living seemed near folly. He observed this during the months he had been Johanneson's pupil. There she was, taking life as it came, not fearing the consequences of her cryptic rescue missions. She was almost reckless, without reason to be, protected only by her parson father who doted on her.

Evan reasoned that she was charged with duties beyond her sphere and certainly beneath her station. He would put a stop to such idiocy. The man couldn't fathom her response to those unworthy persons, like the pregnant woman, and now that pathetic fool she brought home. Nor could he rationalize his own attraction to such a creature. (How could a man, like himself, realize how utterly unworthy his thoughts and desires were toward her? If this girl had a true inkling of his low and dark dreams, she would have fled from any contact with him whatsoever.)

Evan's handsome face moved from consternation to arrogance. How easy it would be for him to capture this bird of paradise. He had everything and she had little to nothing. There was a small place in society where she may have some acclaim. It was in the academic world where her father was respected by many. She was gifted with intelligence and her schooling was quite beyond her age. Her father had taken her under his wing. He had expanded the girl's education in higher level humanities, especially literature and art. Her musical skills were performance quality, but she preferred to use them in the church.

"Bah!", he spat out. "I will place you in society to show off my prize's gifts!" Pondering her father's academic credentials suddenly surfaced an unwelcomed thought concerning his theological position. Like a distant thunder cloud came the faint threat of a pall over the attorney's plans. This dark cloud began to force its way up through his selfish meanderings of possessing his prey. He realized that this pall was not just her refusal, at least in his mind, but Pastor Johanneson. The minister's august face surfaced, with his narrow view of morality, obstinate God awareness and divine laws of life. His practiced calm, his confidence in his salvific beliefs and his knowledge of holy things rankled Evan.

Why should that awareness trouble him in obtaining the girl? Why would her father's regard for spiritual things matter? Surely the man would view Evan's offer to wed his daughter as an honor, and a privilege, from such a worthy suitor. Then it all came into focus to this haughty, fallen man. The young chit, he thought with an oath, whom her father loves better than life, would be denied to him because he was a non-believer, a passive heathen, not even a religious pretender. That was probably the only thing her father would approve of in him and he wasn't pretending to be religious. But he certainly was pretending to be a good man; as in so many of the ways he had convinced himself that he was.

*But had he convinced the old man at all? Johanneson knew about Evan's wife and the baby. Evan had revealed their business in a much earlier conversation. Curse that day!* These thoughts infuriated him because immediately he knew what Johanneson would say to his offer of marriage. *What a fool! He knows I am a rich man! I will always be a rich man! I will never be parted from my wealth! I have influence.*

His imagination, directed by dark forces, caused him to speculate about the girl. *She thinks she can pose as a little usurper of my happiness. But no, I will have her!* An evil smile replaced his agitated expression. *Calm yourself man; you just need a strategy that does not involve the father at all.* His eyes filled with an unwholesome gleam, straight from his tainted heart.

## CHAPTER 6

# TO THINE OWN SELF BE TRUE

"This above all, to thine own self be true,
And it must follow, as the night the day,
Thou canst not then be false to any man."

Hamlet

Linnea helped to bring some of the breakfast things into the
kitchen. For the first time, that she could recall, her mind
was crowded with conflicting thoughts. *I am happy here with
father. I'm not afraid of being different from my acquaintances. I
love my life with him; and he needs me for our work.* Her father
had often encouraged her to consider a schooling option, such
as a nurse or even social worker, either here or abroad. *I don't
wish to be out in the world, on my own; I have willingly chosen
this path.* She sat down at the kitchen table feeling depleted.

The face of the wanderer flashed before her. *It's he. Why do
my thoughts keep returning to him and why do I feel so drawn to
this stranger? Or perhaps he makes me question who I am, being
so comfortable with my life of comparative ease. No, it can't be he!*

*I have known him for such a short time.* Her friend Kati Jo had teased her about her father's words about Reinholdt's 'savoir faire' alluring her, possibly just a little?"

Linney hotly denied it with a flushed face saying, "That's not true. That's why I like Mr. Breech. He's not like that, Kati." But then thought, *that is true, must still just be me. It's his penetrating gaze and something in him that makes me feel this way.* Unbidden came this realization, *I feel that suddenly I am as much a wanderer as he is.* The girl tried to force her mind in another direction, but Mr. Breech's plight continued to surface.

"Vats t'e matter Missy? You haf a bit of trouble you vant to talk about?" Linney looked at the beloved face of their housekeeper feeling caught, like a guilty child, with her hand in the cookie jar.

"Some troubles should not even be thought about Marthe, much less talked about."

"Ja, you mean like t'e troubles of t'at young man you are tinkin' about?"

The girl's face reddened, "I don't know him, much less what his troubles are; so why do you say that?"

"But you vud if you could. Ja', I know you Kristin Andersdatter'." Linnea smiled wanly at this expression she had heard so often.

"Blaming my mother again Marthe?"

"Ja, she never knew a stranger, 'ust like you."

The housekeeper's eyes became moist and Linnea knew she was remembering bygone days when Kristin's home was ringing with the sounds of industry, parish visitors and children's play. Linnea's mother gave birth to her at the age of forty-seven and died when her little girl was only five. All four of her siblings were out of the house before she could really remember much about their living at home. They were more like visiting aunts than sisters. But still, she loved them very much. However, Marthe remembered these days very well as did her father.

"Five years isn't a very long time to be so like her; though I should love it to be true."

"You 'ust remember t'at five years vas long enough for her to put her whole self, inside you. God saw to t'at, Kristin's datter!"

Musing on that remark Linnea thought she heard a distant cry. "Is that the baby Marthe? Is she alright?"

"Vell enough witout her own moter holding her close. Ve need to give her up soon child; you are getting too close vit her."

"I know that; but let her sleep with me, just tonight, in case she still has the croup. I fear she may have died had I not had her with me. I slipped away after father went to bed and gave her a bottle so she would stop crying. She was so sweet; and I hated to leave her alone in her cradle."

"Dat is 'ust vy you should not have her vit you again tonight. For if she loves us bot so much, especially you; how vill she ever love anoter mama?"

"I know you're worried about me; but if I love her so much, she will feel it and be able to receive love more easily from her new mother."

Marthe shook her head slowly but her voice was gentle, "Maybe so Missy, maybe so."

Linnea's eyes filled with tears at Marthe's kind words. They had taken in orphaned children and discarded babies before and been able to place them in homes of people they knew. It had been very difficult with the babies but Linney always knew they could never be her own. This baby was different; and she knew that her attachment was very strong. She couldn't help it since the circumstances were so different from the very beginning. She had come into her care just a few hours after she had been born.

The young woman gave a deep sigh of unidentified longing. This was unusual for someone who always endeavored to believe God was enough and could be trusted. No matter where it took her, 'You have been the music of my earthly life', was a Hebrew psalm she loved. Her sisters claimed her mother had often quoted it.

Nevertheless, Linnea Johanneson also had feet of clay and those mortal feet were a bit dried and fragile, just as the earth becomes in a time of drought. Yes, her attachment to the baby was fixed; and it was obvious to those few who knew her well that a storm was coming. The girl sensed this also but was unable to comprehend what it would mean. She felt helpless to avoid it; even if she could. Such was the pathway that Linnea Kristin Johanneson had chosen!

Laying her head down on the table, she felt the hand of Marthe pat her back gently and then listened to her footfall as she walked away.

Her lips moved in a whisper, "Please help me Jesus; I feel like I am sinking in a mire but; you are there. I must not give way, for even in the depths; you are with me."

# Chapter 7

## Dark Suitor

"He who advances a mile towards God,
through doubtings dim,
God will advance a million miles
in blazing light to him."

The bus route was often taken by Linnea and she could be reflective, or just watch the people passing and not miss her stop. This time her thoughts were very distracting.

As the bus slowed to a stop she heard, "Miss! Miss!'

From out of her reverie she jumped up, realizing it was the bus driver calling to her. He well knew her point of departure. "Thank you", she called back, hurrying out the rear door as it slammed behind her. Within seconds the conveyance rolled rapidly past her on its noisy way. "Whew! I had better wake up or I will forget my head the next time", she said aloud.

Pulling on her mittens, against the cold, she heard a vaguely familiar voice behind her. "Miss Johanneson, how have you roamed so far from home? It is a frosty day for sightseeing."

Looking back inquiringly, she saw Mr. Evan Reinholdt, her father's recently acquired student, better described as his questioner. He had come up beside her and taken her elbow in a familiar way that made her heart to beat slightly faster.

"Oh Mr. Reinholdt, how are you?" Linnea knew that her face was red; but she tried to cover it with a cheery voice. "It would be a silly day for sightseeing; I have an important duty nearby." She had no intentions of telling him where she was headed; for he had earned no confidences from her whatsoever. "I hope you are well, Sir."

He still had a firm hold on her elbow, which was both pleasant and disturbing. She casually transferred her purse to her other shoulder as she turned more toward him on the sidewalk. He smiled in a very engaging way, with a slight chuckle.

"Better by far than I was five minutes ago. The day warmed up very nicely just at the sight of you."

Linnea couldn't help but think how easy his manner was, making her feel happy and carefree. It was quite different as compared to the feelings generated by Mr. Breech, who acted so forlorn and bleak. He made her feel almost guilty for feeling glad. Linney wondered if perhaps that bleakness was part of her own forlorn mood earlier in the day. Such emotions were not foreign to Linney; but she quickly turned away from anything gloomy. She thought it was faithless and self-centered to pout or be in a rut, especially around others.

"So, what is your secret formula? You seem often quite happy."

"The world is so full of a number of things, I'm sure we should all be as happy as kings." She said it quite glibly, even more than she felt, because it wasn't personal information about her.

Evan chuckled more loudly this time. "Well, at least we should be if we have as much money as a king!" He said this in a resolute, confident voice until he thought he perceived a slight shadow cross her face. "Well, how else can a king be benevolent to his poorer subjects?"

The faint cloud left her; and she smiled happily, "Of course, Sir. All will love a benevolent king. But do you not think his subjects would be happier if they could earn their own way?"

"Perhaps some might think that. But, have you not heard of the fine solution to enlarge the welfare system and have the government respond to the needs of its less fortunate citizens? In so doing, all will share the wealth of our industry and there will be no need for the free market system. We want to help the lower elements to be relieved of their burdens."

"But surely, Mr. Reinholdt, you would not want to reach into your own pocket to distribute the wealth to these 'lower elements', as you describe them?

He flashed an indulgent, confident smile. "Surely not, little lady, that is what the federal budget is for. Sometimes you must borrow from Peter to pay Paul. It just takes a bit of shuffling the money around."

He winked at her and squeezed her arm, moving a bit closer as if they shared a lover's secret. Linnea was quite undone by his intimate manner and uncertain of what his last monologue meant.

Turning towards him she stopped and stepped away. "Sir, you seem very knowledgeable about government matters and I am not. My father believes an old adage, 'He that shall not work shall not eat.' He also says that people are much happier and successful in all areas of life if they work hard and create their own opportunities. In this way, they profit from their resourcefulness rather than leaning on charity, especially from the public trough." She had a resoluteness and formality in her manner.

"I must leave you here, Sir. My business of the day takes me in another direction." The girl stopped and turned toward him. She extended her mittened hand in a purposeful farewell gesture. He smiled a magnanimous smile, removed his glove, took her hand and kissed it firmly.

"You are a most fascinating conversationalist, Miss Linney. I hope you and I can meet soon in a more planned manner and place. I should like to hear more of your ideas about how the world should be run."

Linnea withdrew her hand feeling very flummoxed by his bold words and by his use of her personal family name. "I fear I have little to say that would interest you; but perhaps I could sit in and listen the next time you and my father dialogue on matters of faith and culture."

With that she smiled and turned quickly, crossing the street and going in the opposite direction, but choosing not to walk toward the cemetery. *There was no way she wanted that man to know that 'it' was her 'duty' destination.* Her heart was pounding from the kiss on her hand and the familiar way he postured himself about a 'next' meeting. A subtle warning in her mind advised her that she was no match for his masculine, worldly way. That much about his behavior she comprehended for certain. He frightened her with his good looks and obvious interest.

Linnea had noticed, with discomfort, that his eyes had often been upon her whenever she entered the room during her father's sessions with him. Sometimes she was asked to bring refreshments when Marthe was not present. It was a fine feeling to be admired in a safe place where her vanity could overcome her discomfort.

Evan had nodded amiably enough at the girl's suggestion, which was an obvious turn from his offer of a private meeting. He turned, with dignity, replaced his glove and strode away with a relaxed gait.

"Demure little temptress," he whispered as his dark eyes flashed. *I have unnerved her; she trembled at my touch. Those blue eyes are awakening to my advances! That shy demeanor will soon be swallowed up in my sensual embraces. He threw his head back and laughed aloud, speaking in a low and unnatural way.* "We shall meet again soon, Miss Johanneson, or should I say 'Linney.'" Glancing back, he watched her retreating figure fading from his view.

He spoke aloud, "Fie on that father of hers! I shall indeed devise a plan that will not involve him. I will lure that girl!"

# Chapter 8

# The Cemetery

"The Lord is close to the broken hearted,
and those who are crushed in spirit."

Psalmist

Renuel knelt by the small stone, wiping away the snow and ice that blocked the engravings. The words on it startled him with their fierce hold on eternity. They were filled with the hope of immortality, even to the point of being proud in death. 'Death, be not proud...' *Why must those words come to him and from where?*

He shivered; but he was past feeling. He also realized how frozen his hands would have been without the gloves from Marthe. The sun warmed his back, like a friend's comforting hand; for so it was. Indeed, it was a friend from the 'Maker' of the sun. Even his tears were 'kept in a bottle' by this Caretaker he had not personally met. The same One was He that lingered at another tomb, long ago, and spoke comfort to a mourner there.

*Isa, Isa, can you, from your cold domain, still forgive me? How could your babe tiptoe out of this world, with you, never to be seen by Oleksandr or me? But I am glad that the 'little stranger' had his troubles end before they began. Perhaps they both saw Olek as they passed through the veil. Oh God..., where are you in death? Here it is so cold! Are there no winter flowers to dress their frozen bier? Thank you, Isa, for loving me, even in your dying. I must live higher than my heart permits with the horror of your being betrayed. I will do this because you wish me to; that I know. You have forgiven your enemies; but can I forgive my enemy, even I, whose name is Renuel?* He arose, wiped his cheeks and stood silently for a time, staring at the stone marker.

Some moments later a form moved toward him and knelt at the grave quite unobtrusively. She looked up slowly, and as if in a dream, he saw the face of Linnea Johanneson. She reached into a small bag and took out a few handfuls of red rose petals. The girl gently scattered them over the white snow and glanced up.

"I am so sorry, Mr. Breech. I knew and loved Isabella. She was so kind and trusting; but I know she suffered a great deal. In it all there was a sweetness about her which spoke of God's presence. This was also true as she lay dying; and many felt it! All of us were made better for knowing her."

Linnea arose and shyly stood by Renuel, casting her eyes downward. He looked at her from pain filled eyes. She offered a blushing, living face, full of tender sympathy and girlish sweetness. She was alive, yes, so alive. The grief-stricken man removed his glove and gently took Linnea's hand and held it. She pressed it to her cheek, tears falling. He was so glad to be standing there with someone who also loved Isabella.

Wordlessly they lingered at the graveside of the mother and infant son.

After some minutes had passed Linnea slipped her hand from his and replaced her mitten, feeling strange to be that familiar and yet, sensing an inexplicable tie. *What was it about him that made her so unguarded,* she pondered. *He had a genuine and kind manner. Maybe their kinship, in this loss, made her feel closer to him than she really was. But to compare her grief to his, having been a husband to Isabella, was impossible to comprehend.*

Thus, there emanated an even greater sympathy as Linney repressed her own sorrow to make place for his. From her tender heart came a benediction on Isa's life and his loss. Renuel felt this in a spiritual way, not recognizing its source.

He looked over at her and spoke softly, "Ah me, the day has grown cold again without your warm hand in mine. How Isa must have been warmed by your care." Linnea looked down shyly as he continued.

"But don't be cast down, kind lady; my heart is much warmer than it was before you came. Perhaps it is because you loved her that I can still feel her life so real and present here today."

Linnea cried out earnestly, "Oh no, Mr. Breech, Isabella and the baby are alive and that is why you feel her so strongly. But they are not alive with us. They are in a new country now; but it truly is her life that you feel. Death is only a darkened hallway that leads to God's light and a new life! It is in unbearable light for us, Mr. Breech. But if we believe in Jesus, like Isabella did; then we will see them again. They are with God now! She is living Sir, not in some dark, dismal place of death."

That phrase and more came again unbidden to his mind. 'Death be not proud, though some have called thee mighty and dreadful; for thou art not so...' Again, it was something from his studies...; yet now so pertinent to this moment.

Linnea's eyes were shining with a hope that what she had spoken had reached the sad stranger. "You must clearly understand Sir that I speak of Jesus, the Son of God. My father says that even devils believe in God and tremble. You must believe in Jesus." Her face reddened and she looked down.

The man stared first at her and then down again at the snow covered grave. The red petals, bedecking it, were to him like great drops of blood. The engraving was clearly legible. He thought again of Isabella lying coldly there. *At what 'trumpet?',* he mused sardonically. *This is the 'last day.'* Renuel shook his head, speaking with finality.

"This talk of Jesus, God and immortality seems only to be enjoyed by the delusions of the living. Is it possible that I am also dead in a grave, even while I live? Even if that is not so; I can find no joy here."

He looked up at Linnea and what he saw imprinted his mind with an unforgettable image. *She was exquisite, beautifully adorned, a 'nouveau enfante', freshly exuding life and hope. 'Encantada...', she almost makes me believe that mankind was not meant to die but should live on and on into infinity. I would gladly take her hand and walk straight into the jaws of hell or, a sinner into the terrors of heaven, whichever would guarantee my immortal state with her by my side.*

Knowing none of his thoughts, Linnea felt tears welling up within her from his denial of a life forever. This was the only truth which could give him hope of seeing Isabella and her baby again. Looking up into his face, her blue eyes were glistening with tears. She saw his eyes leap with hope, past his dark words, as he looked at her with focused ardor and longing. It pierced her with a sweet desire for something she had never known. Linnea felt light-headed and disconnected from her present.

Renuel turned to kneel by the grave, which drew her from the dreamy ecstasy of his gaze and back to sorrow and loss. "I am sorry to sadden you Miss; but I fear I have looked into death's face too often. I am jaded by her shroud. Most certainly I have not looked enough into the face of God as I think you and your father have. Perhaps these two faces have the same visage to a lost soul like me." He shook his head. "God help me."

With a surge of tenderness Linnea leaned down and took Renuel's hand. "Come, Mr. Breech; you are cold. There is a small café nearby. We can warm ourselves with something hot to drink. I have a bit of information I must tell you about Isabella."

The man's eyes darted to her face, showing alarm. "What more needs be told? Her grave tells all I wish to know of her woe."

"Mr. Breech, I will tell you nothing grievous. Please, you must trust me yet again." Renuel nodded, saying nothing. He stood, and before they stepped away from the scene, keeping her hand in his, knelt again and kissed the stone marker. He then spoke. Linnea did not hear much; nor did she try. Already she was feeling like an interloper; but he said something about a sister, she thought.

Walking in silence, Linnea led them from the cemetery to a small café a few blocks away. She kept hold of his hand. It was a gentle hold, closed on his, as one would use when leading a child who was uncertain of the direction to go.

Entering the café, they were seated. Linnea ordered them hot chocolate. He had never partaken of it and declined at first. After several cautious sips, the chilled man, in body and spirit, sighed deeply, "This is much better than tea on such a day Miss. You have won my approval of hot milk and chocolate!"

The girl laughed a gay, sweet laugh. He smiled back at her and felt the world seemed a brighter and warmer one than it could or should be on such a day.

Linnea took a deep breath. "Mr. Breech, please prepare yourself. This is not a bad thing at all; although it may come as a shock, given the circumstances in which you find yourself. It is true that Isabella was joined in death by her baby boy, but...," the young woman paused, looking cautiously into his face.

"Go on Miss, don't be afraid."

"Well, you see, Mr. Breech, your wife Isabella had another infant, a twin, who survived. She still lives to this moment." Renuel stared at her in total, shocked silence for fully a minute. She paused and then continued. "I felt this needed to be said before we parted today. The baby is in our home and Marthe and I attend her. She is a beautiful, healthy baby girl. You see, Mr. Breech, placing her hand on his arm, "God has left to you a living child, even amidst this great sorrow. Isa named her Bella Rene."

He looked up then with such a start that her hand jumped in a reflex action. He said softly, "Do you know what she named the deceased child? Did she give it a name?"

"I don't know; but she left you a note and may have written the child's name there. She did ask that no name be engraved on the tombstone."

His head in his hands, he kept moving back and forth, saying in a tone the girl couldn't make out, "Oh God, what shall I do, what shall I do? Oleksandr, please forgive me." He then began to murmur quietly. Linnea thought it was in a different language. But she felt no right to invade his thoughts at such a moment. Finally, he looked up at her with the most inscrutable expression she had yet seen. He had not spoken to her again when a voice called from the door of the café.

"Having teatime conversation without your father, Miss Linnea? How juxtaposed this seems. What will the good pastor say?"

Renuel looked over blankly as Evan approached their table, realizing someone had spoken to Linnea. He looked inquisitively at her, "You know this man, Miss?"

Feeling the color rise in her face she nodded, "Why yes, he is my father's pupil."

Evan interjected quickly, smiling roguishly, "Oh, but I wish to be much more."

The girl's eyes grew a darker shade of blue, or perhaps it was her flushed face in contrast. Renuel was already on his feet. Linney spoke nervously, "Mr. Breech, this is attorney Evan Reinholdt. Mr. Breech is a new friend that my father and I are helping so he can become acquainted with our city."

Evan smiled but his eyes were hooded. "What a keen man you are Sir, having this charming lady as your personal tour guide."

Then, dismissing Renuel with a disgusted glance, he turned directly to Linnea. "I see now that your father can be quite generous with his treasure."

With this, the stranger looked again at Evan, bowed briskly and remarked, "A good day to you Sir." And as he rose to leave, he remarked, "Greet your father for me, Miss Linnea, and thank him for his hospitality. Tell him I will return his articles shortly."

Linnea was very distressed and put her hand lightly on his arm, "Oh please, Mr. Breech, keep those things. You know father wanted you to have them; and besides, he is expecting you tonight. Marthe will be quite put out if you are late for the six o'clock dinner hour, you know." She stepped toward him, looking beseechingly into his eyes, with her back to Evan. Her hand still resting on his arm, she smiled and said with emphasis, "I'll tell father to expect you before five."

"You are certain all is well now Miss, with your new escort? He said this, nodding boldly at Evan. Linnea barely smiled. He continued, "I thank you for sharing the treasures of your time today. I am the richer for it, as well as the hot chocolate."

Renuel dropped a five-dollar bill on the table, clicked his heels, bowed and was gone. Linnea gasped, knowing that he was near penniless. She knew the drink was only 25 cents a cup. She took the money and hurriedly paid the bill, leaving a dollar tip, determined to return the rest to Mr. Breech. *What was the man thinking*, she wondered, as she reluctantly took her escort's arm. As Linnea left the café she was still wondering, *what was the man thinking?*

Evan said, "You seem quite taken with this stranger; or is he a stranger? What can you tell me about him? From where has he come? Does he have some special reason to be visiting in our city?"

Reinholdt was annoyed. *The girl acted as though she hadn't heard a word he had just spoken. She seemed more interested in that 'drowned rat'. Well, he would take care of that.*

# Chapter 9

# The Bride Price

Still as of old,
men by themselves are priced.
For thirty pieces,
Judas sold himself, not Christ.

Mr. Breech's behavior continued to puzzle her. But for the moment she was focused on her newest escort. *He was so much older than she. What was his interest in her? Why did she agree to go with him from the café and why did he make himself uncomfortably near?* Somewhat distractedly she had these thoughts. But then, how could a girl, such as she, ever conceive of his pitiless, degrading plan? He was, no doubt, reveling in this unexpected opportunity to blindside the unsuspecting parson and get next to the girl to boot. He believed she was naïve enough for anything.

Turning towards her, he gave his most engaging smile, "Glad I happened along again just when I did, Miss Johanneson. One never knows what such desperate types of men are capable of doing."

"Hmm," answered Linney, in a distracted response, thinking only of having given Mr. Breech such a false picture of her social life.

Reinholdt was furious at her, once again, for ignoring him but thought calmly, *Nothing, nothing we can't deal with later.* He then placed his hand firmly over hers in a supposedly caring gesture. She trembled slightly at his touch. It was not with desire, as he presumed.

But then, how could this egoist begin to comprehend why the man in obvious penury was the one of whom she was thinking? This stranger, whom Evan despised, thought almost nothing of Evan Reinholdt but was only concerned with the safety of the girl. Renuel's payment of the bill was a small token, to be sure, like an ancient gesture of a bride price. Or more in the present, maybe it was an attempt to show an ignoble man the worth of the lady in his care. Perhaps neither of these, nor any others, resided in the heart of this man from another place.

In any case, as he walked out of the café, his head was reeling from Linnea's image. Even so, thoughts of her intrusive companion also troubled his mind. In it was an all too familiar recognition of a wolf in sheep's clothing.

"God help her," he mumbled aloud, surprising himself at the intensity of his concern for her protection. *From where that prayer came, he could only surmise. Could it be from the company he had been keeping for the past twenty-four hours?* Or is it always within a goodly man's soul that there is a wish to protect an unguarded lady?'

Renuel found himself drifting back toward the cemetery. Arriving, he walked through the gate and sat on a stone bench. This place was the only link to his purpose in coming

North. It had been Isa foremost, then the deceased child and now, a living child, whose existence had totally destabilized him.

A sweetness he had not known, like the scent of honeysuckle at a distance, slowly crept up from his subconscious, shy of surfacing too quickly. *Bella Rene...*, it seemed like a dream that there could be a living extension of Isa and Olek. He both feared and longed to see this child who was untimely born.

His mind shifted suddenly to the baby boy who was laid down with his mother. She left him unnamed on the tombstone. Surely, she must have granted him a name! He knew Isa would name her baby though he breathed no earthly air and glimpsed only celestial light. No inscription on the stone might be a fear of jeopardy for her living child, at least in her mind's desperation. Someone could trace the last name Isa would have been required to give on the birth record.

He shook his head. *My poor, poor Isa. She was with child, alone and unknown, and at the mercy of the deeds of evil men.* His thoughts grew dark and hostile. *Men, like the one whom he had just met, educated men, posing as defenders of the masses who were an elite oligarchy with motives to subdue and to conquer.* This was the land of the free; but no country could free the hatred in Renuel Breech's tortured soul. *Why did he walk away from the café? Was the girl as safe as she tried to portray or was that fear in her eyes as he deserted her. She claimed Isabella was freed from her fear of death at the end; but Isa had feared dying all her life. What could have given her that hope now?*

Renuel found himself also wanting to hope, much like a drowning man clings to anything more stable than the watery abyss beneath him. Yet strangely his thoughts kept drifting back to the girl Linnea and her vulnerability.

"Keep movin' along now, Mister. We don't allow no loi-
terin' here."

Renuel turned a wary eye to the man speaking who must
be a warden or grounds watchman. He was a rotund man with
a bulbous red nose and a low, mean look. He replied with a
sting in his voice, "Excuse me, Sir, but I had understood that
lingering here, in grief's hour, was a large step above common
loitering."

The man looked Renuel over with a critical eye. "You ain't
from here so's I doubt yer grievin' a U.S. cit-e-zen, fancy words
er not! Let's have a look at yer identi-cation."

Moving aggressively towards Breech, with his hand out,
the smell of alcohol was strong. Renuel knew his ID was a
passport and not a driver's license. This man was looking for
trouble. Maybe it was to turn him in to the police and justify
his job placement. But this mourner had reasons not to have
his passport studied closely; and it wasn't only for his own
protection.

He had come across such men before, swelled with their
meager power, and yet menacing in their own domain. Renuel
had already arisen from the bench and then, to the surprise of
the caretaker, approached him quickly in an intimate, secretive
manner, as though they shared a common bond.

The young man leaned in closely, turning his head this way
and that as though someone might be spying on them, saying
in low tones, "Good watchman, I duly respect your attention
to duty here on these sacred grounds. I myself have stood guard
on many occasions but none as vast as your responsibilities
here; and you have no comrade by your side. The hours must

grow long in such a tedious, but noble tasking." The man's eyes bulged a bit at this speech, but he remained immobile.

Renuel continued, "'Tis such a frigid day, even with the warming sun; one sometimes needs a bit of a jolt to keep warm and attend to duty, eh?" Here he nudged the ample shoulder of the guard. "Smells like a rich man's brew; you wouldn't want to share a shot or two with a cold and grieving soldier beneath your station, but in need of your benevolence?"

Here the guard grew defensive. "Whaddya mean, I got only enough drink for me today and you beggin' for my comfort?!"

"Well Comrade, only just a sip or two before a policeman should stroll by and smell the strong, expensive liquor and start asking uncomfortable questions. If you get my meaning friend. You know, being intoxicated, while in the line of duty, and all that legality stuff. These law keepers can be rather narrow-minded when you have the smell on your breath as you do. Of course, maybe we could bribe him with a shot or two." Here Renuel pushed up against the beefy man, crossed his arms and leaned against him pretending to scan the sidewalk up and down for the police.

"Now look here, you ain't goin' to say a word about my stash to no police or I'll tell them you were 'uncorkin' in public too."

His tormentor replied, "Well, I am able to pass the breath test; but I doubt you would! And I can walk the line without fear of reprisal. So, I must advise that they would find you as the guilty party and I would walk away a free man. But I would not say a word about your little habit. We men on guard duty have to stick together."

"Listen you, get your skinny arse agoin'! I don't want you round drawin' 'etention to the ceme'try grounds attractin' the po-lice; you hear?"

"I fully comprehend, Watchman Sir. When I return here, another day, I will not even speak to you. I will not detain you for even a small sampling of your comfort and I shall guard 'our' secret well. We will act as indifferent strangers."

The man starred furiously at Renuel. "Jist get outa here and don't come nudg'in up on me agin! Next time you come, do your prayin' or cryin' or whatever and mind yer own business and I'll do mine. Yer makin' me more nervous than them fresh corpses in thir graves!"

Renuel Breech tipped his hat, the one lent to him from the good pastor, and walked through the gate trying diligently to keep his face turned to hide the smile he couldn't control. Nevertheless, he was fully aware that, though he had perhaps not made an enemy; he certainly had not made a friend. It might occur later to the man, who was a brute, but no simpleton, that Renuel had not shown him any ID.

Perhaps the next visit needed to be with the Pastor or better still, the father and the daughter. They would be a respectable and safer cover for his final visit to the graveside. He couldn't risk going alone again but he knew he must return one last time. Surely that would be acceptable to them. But he would have to tell the real story about his past with Isa. He owed them that much before he left the country.

That Reinholdt man, her escort of today, did he detect some discomfort in her introduction of him? The man had been at their home and was obviously trying to lure the girl. The gigolo would not approve of Renuel becoming intimate with the Johannesons. He had noted the despising look in his eyes at their brief meeting.

And now Renuel's stricken thoughts grew dark and an old hatred begged to surface. A surge of physical desire came over him as he thought of the girl and the cad escorting her. *Fool, as though you have the slightest prayer or a gambler's chance for such a creature of delight and holy intentions to ever consider you! Put your lustful thoughts away; she is unworthy of what they will lead to.*

His mind raced to a saying often quoted by his grandmother, 'I have made a covenant with mine eyes, how then could I gaze upon a virgin?' "Renny, you are a handsome boy and many ladies will dally with you. You must practice this discipline often as you struggle with the lust of the eyes, as did Job of old, and men before and after him."

Suddenly, he was young Renny again, hearing her words. He smiled slightly. Kicking a rock into the street he shoved his gloved hands into his pockets and walked rapidly on into the adjoining park. His hand felt the bus transfer in his pocket; and he thought of his ride with the girl. His dark musings lifted and the day grew brighter. Renuel glanced ahead at the walkway and smiled wanly as he mused. *A stroll here in this pretty park may encourage thoughts of new beginnings with little Bella Rene.*

# Chapter 10

# Quit, Quit

Quit, quit for shame; this will not move,
This cannot take her.
If of herself she will not love,
Nothing can make her...

Sir John Suckling

Evan drew Linnea's arm even more closely so that his frame further crowded her. Still distracted by her thoughts of Renuel, it took her a few moments to realize that an unnamed fear was surfacing in her mind. When she fully tuned to Evan's continuing closeness, and tight hold on her arm; she recoiled. Linney tried surreptitiously to ease away.

"Come now, my Lady Love," he spoke in a jaunty way, while continuing at a brisker pace, but not releasing his grip. "Surely you have some need for warmth! We can afford that by staying close and moving at a strong pace. I believe your father would totally approve of our 'tete a tete'."

He laughed and held her even more firmly. At his mention of her father her heart calmed, thinking that perhaps it was

63

safe to be with him. Still, she felt a strange dread. They arrived at the street, across from the cemetery, which was bordered on the north side by a walkway. It led into a large city park having various species of fir, evergreen and birch trees. At intervals there were stone benches for those on a ramble needing some reprieve. He guided her immediately across the street, onto that walkway, saying how the day had warmed considerably and truly was perfect for a continuing bit of exercise and conversation.

"But, Mr. Reinholdt, I...."

"Tut Tut Miss, surely you have some space and time for a man of distinction, such as I, compared to the one by whom you were just attended." His voice retained a controlled pleasantness; but there was an edge to it that she disliked even more than his words.

Linnea balked as her thoughts grew angry and jumbled, so she murmured, "Yes, I have a bit of time, Sir." She also bit her tongue because Mr. Reinholdt was her father's pupil and respectable in as much as she was aware. After conversing with him for some weeks her father had confided that he hoped the man's questions were not those of a skeptic, but of a seeker.

"Linney, my prayers for him are that I can address the deeper matters of the soul and allow time to soften the bitterness of his grief. He has a heart of stone. I shall invoke the Almighty that it might become a heart of flesh."

Given these thoughts, the girl did not want to create a barrier for her father by refusing Mr. Reinholdt as an escort. She smiled slightly, but disengaged her arm, as well as she could without dropping his arm completely.

"Ho, Ho," he laughed. "Such a lady you are..., dignified and proper. I shall give a good report to the Parson; but indulge me and commit to being more friendly."

She barely looked up at him and kept walking, anger welling up again. She replied formally. "I am as friendly as I ever am with someone of such little acquaintance, Sir. After a short walk here in this lovely park, I must turn around and go back to the business of my day."

"And what might that business be? Is it returning to your guided tour with that very shady acquaintance?" They had already walked a distance, with their brisk pace, and their conversation was stilted. By walking rapidly, it had covered some of the need for speaking, though not enough. Linnea was not shy, and words were something she was keen on; always eager to share her thoughts. Restraining them at this moment was the challenge; but nonetheless she kept her words measured.

"Mr. Breech needed our care. My father and I were offering him hospitality as the Holy Scriptures command. If you knew anything of our home, you would know that this is not an unusual gesture. Today was an extension of that when I found him alone at the cemetery. I thank you for your concern, on my behalf, but both my father and I have found Mr. Breech to be a gentleman." *Hmph...gentleman, what an outrageous notion about that tall, thin hobo.*

He thought these things but simply said, "Hmm, is that so," and smiled benevolently. Evan's thoughts raced, keeping pace with his heart rate. *There was no question that she was an unusual girl. Her powers of speech, composure and use of language, coupled with her ability to defend herself were commendable for one so young. It was an obvious tribute to her father and their habit of academic pursuit. Along with this was their social circle.*

He smiled inwardly at the trophy she would be in intelligence, charm, and beauty. Her unsophisticated style of dress would be discarded as he changed her look into one of sophistication and allure. Yes, what a prize! Her command of language would be impressive at his cocktail parties and high-level entertainment. She was already used to frequent guests and running a large home with a housekeeper at her bidding.

Evan's satisfaction was written on his smiling face. But Linnea Johanneson was not interested in any messages written there. She did not glance his way but continued to walk. There was a small path leading to a park sign, of some kind, about fifteen feet off the walkway. The predator's pulse was racing with his whole self, aroused by thoughts of the girl belonging to him and being at his command. Without warning, he steered Linnea onto the smaller path and said in an intimate voice, leaning close and smelling the fragrance of her hair.

"Here, let's go in and read what the park has to say about itself. That is innocent enough, is it not, my Lady Love?" He laughed as he saw the color rise in her cheeks. She was trembling and he was sure it was with desire. This was his moment and he would grasp it. She could not resist his charms; no woman ever had. Linnea was so confused by their sudden turning off onto the path that she did not protest at first. As soon as he spoke, she stopped, instantly dropping his arm.

"Sir, I think I must immediately return to my own duties for the day. Mr. Reinholdt, it is getting late."

He urged her on. "Certainly Miss Johanneson, but let's just have a look at the sign posted over there." "We may learn something that we haven't experienced here in our city." He spoke quietly, with an intimate inflection.

Terrified, she looked at his face. His eyes were smoldering; and he was desperately aggressive. Yet, his expensive clothes, debonair scents and actions only frightened Linnea more. She looked directly at him and turned to face him, speaking in a louder, but quavering voice.

"You must not detain me further, Sir; I will turn around now and go back the way we came with or without your company!" She turned to leave but the man only interpreted this as timidity, and her naivete.

"Come, young, alluring girl, I won't hurt you." At this point he took her face in his hands, looking into her frozen blue eyes. "My intentions are entirely honorable; I want you for my wife. You will be the jewel of my world, my bird in a gilded cage! Everyone will be at your feet and I will be the envy of my fellows."

Linnea cried out, "No, Mr. Reinholdt! No! This is not...", she screamed and tried to push him away.

But he just laughed, pulling her near and bringing his lips close to hers. She smelled his stale tobacco breath and felt nauseous.

At that instant something tore him away. He shouted aloud and Linnea saw a blow to his face as another man leaped upon him. They both fell to the ground. As Linney looked on with horror, she saw that it was Renuel Breech, pounding and being pounded! In his weakened state he was no match for the strength of Evan, who was older, strong and well-fed. He had been a boxer in his school days. They both leapt to their feet. Evan gave several wicked blows to his assailant's body, knocking him to the ground.

Linnea screamed loudly when the fight began and continued crying out. Running towards them, from the walkway, was a policeman. He was followed by the caretaker of the cemetery who was pointing and shouting. Both the fighting men were bleeding from their faces. Evan was still on his feet and had wiped at the blood smears with his handkerchief. He then straightened his tie and gave another brutal kick to Renuel. Linney screamed again and covered her face.

The policeman ran over to Renuel and pointed his revolver at him. "Is this the man!!??"

"Yeah Officer, that's the troublemaker, tryin' to rob the gentleman there and terrify the little lady he was escortin'! Now, there's a bad one fer ya!!"

Linnea was hysterical and screaming, "No! No! Don't point that! Don't shoot him!"

At that moment she felt everything drain out of her and her mind wouldn't function. The color left her face and she felt her knees shaking, not to the point of fainting, for she was still able to stand. Her entire constitution was assailed. She folded her legs and crumpled to the ground, half sitting. From her daze she looked into the deep brown eyes of Renuel Breech. He was staring at her. He was now half sitting on the ground, with a weapon still pointed at him. They were those same tormented eyes in which she had first been lost, only a day ago. Now again, she found herself lost in them.

He spoke quietly, "We have exchanged places today, and I was hoping to aid you Miss."

"Shut up you bum," shouted the caretaker.

Crying, and shaking uncontrollably, Linney tried to speak to the policeman on behalf of her defender. "No, No, you don't understand..."

Renuel raised his voice, speaking forcefully to the officer. "For God's sake man, help the young lady, call an ambulance! She is in shock. Can you not see that?"

Still trying to speak to the policeman, a terrified Linney looked once again at Renuel. He glanced at her, barely touching her hand, which no one saw and gave a small shake of his head, as if to say 'no'.

Evan gave yet another wicked kick to Renuel, knocking him over. "Ignore the tramp! Never mind the medical call. I'll take charge of her Officer." Shouting at the caretaker he demanded, "Quickly, you idiot, call a cab or I'll have your job!" Turning to the policeman, he changed his tone completely, "Have no fear, my good man. I'll bring her home to her father. He's a Reverend and I am intimate with the family." Here, he winked at the officer. "I don't think she's in any shock or jeopardy, just frightened by this brute and all the blood."

Linnea heard a scream when Evan kicked Mr. Breech again but never realized it was her own cry. She knew nothing else, after that, until now. Looking up, she gazed into Marthe's kind eyes; her father was also sitting beside her. The loyal housekeeper was holding her hand.

She grasped his hand and cried out, struggling to sit up. "Where is he Father? Where is Mr. Breech? Is he alright!?"

The mother figure pushed her gently back down, clucking her tongue in disapproval. "Vel, did ja ever hear such a question? Poor creature, she is more worried about him t'en her own self. "He is in t'e city jail, vere he should probably 'ust sit a vile, and as for t'at ot'er philandtropher, he should be right in t'ere vit him."

The pastor cleared his throat, and said softly, "Philanderer, I think you mean Marthe."

The housekeeper looked at him with fiery eyes and nodded fiercely. Although quite concerned for his daughter, he could barely cover a slight smile.

Linnea covered her face and began to sob through her words. "He tried to help me and now; who knows what will happen to him?"

"Rest now Linnea; I will try to help Mr. Breech; but you must try to calm yourself." The pastor/father was fighting a battle of his own with deep, but controlled anger from what he had deduced from Evan's depiction of the incident.

The smooth talk of Evan Reinholdt did nothing but reinforce Johanneson's awareness that this was a case of mistaken identity of the real culprit. One look at Linnea's terrified glances at the man told her father the sordid story. Yet, always the gentleman and pastor, he managed to graciously encourage Reinholdt's departure as quickly as possible. He spoke with an outwardly calm demeanor but within, he struggled mightily lest he forsake his Christian grace and bloody the perpetrator's face for a second time that day.

# CHAPTER 11

# JAIL MATES

"Stone walls do not a prison make nor iron bars a cage,
Minds, innocent and quiet, make that for a hermitage."
Richard Lovelace

It was different from other prisons he had known. Once he had stayed in one, as a child, when his father was arrested. He was released the next day; but they detained his father. There were many prisoners jammed into that cell. Inside were the high and low, the politicians, entertainers in fancy clothes and the middle-class. That place was no respecter of anything, or anyone, but only required an arrest on suspicion of whatever the state determined.

When his mother came for him, he resisted leaving, holding on to his father tightly and crying, "No father, I must stay. I am afraid for you!" His father knelt, detaching himself from his son's iron grasp. Putting his hands on his small shoulders he looked straight into his eyes. "Do not be fearful, my son. Fear only God; for men can harm the body, but the redeemed are eternal.

Remember, the Almighty One will watch between us until we meet again. Help your mother to care for little Isa."

Galena embraced his wife fondly and kissed her. Then Renny and his mother were pushed away by a surly guard. He could never forget that moment and his father's eyes; they were serene and brave. Renuel never looked into those loving eyes again, except behind bars. He was eleven years old and his father was never free again. He was a writer and had exposed the corruption and brutality of the government.

"We must not side with the strong against the weak Renny. We must have courage and expose evil when we can and destroy it in God's name."

Though his writing was in the form of essays, short stories and poetry, he was identified as a dissident and silenced, as were all whose voices cried out for justice amidst tyranny. Their accusers were subtly clothed in the garb of socialism. Again, it was equality for all, protection for the impoverished and distribution of wealth. But the government lived in lavish waste and everyone else became poor. This lowly group wasn't just poor. They became even poorer *and* were also increasingly oppressed. Especially targeted were the Christians. Their lot was grave indeed!

"God has set us an example, my son; we must give no less than our lives wnen necessary."

And so, they had, all of them: Grandmamma, Father, Oleksandr and now Isa and her infant. Indeed, only he, his mother, and now the infant remained. His thoughts were despairing and angry. *Why not me? Why must I be alive to breathe, know what I know and live in torment and guilt? My mother lives in constant danger of her life. Is that a merciful God and Father, 'a Savior like no other?' How can I believe, or want to give myself to such a divine tyrant?*

"Heard you gave that guy what he deserved. Looks like you got what you didn't deserve! My name's Pace."

The huge, tattooed man clapped Renuel on the back, making him wince. He then guffawed good-naturedly, as did a few others in their jail cell and the next one over as well. The new prisoner smiled wanly and glanced over at the surprisingly young face of Pace, whose eyes were a-twinkle. An unexpected feeling of warmth spread through him and Renuel realized it was comfort. Yes, he felt comforted. What a strange comforter in a strange place!

"I'm Renuel, glad to meet you."

"Was she worth it," another man called over. There was more laughter.

His cell mate nudged him kindly, "Now don't take a quarrel off of that; he's just ribbin' you a bit."

Renuel rubbed his jaw and covered his black eye. "Must have been!" he called back.

Several shouts and hearty "Yeahs!" followed and then someone said, "She must have been a lady; her kind is worth a beating'!"

"Aw hell Pace, everyone of 'em is worth a few black eyes, the good or bad. Damn those hot shot p____ks! I think even the Almighty Hisself would have throwed a punch for a good woman. Of course, not takin' her for Hisself, being God and all."

"Yeah Jeb, you'd better say that; or you'll get struck by lightnin'!"

More raucous laughter ensued. Renuel's smile broadened with each comment. *This was the kind of theology he could approve of. Even these men, from low places, know right from wrong.* Maybe they had been beaten down so low and for so long they looked up a lot more. Certainly, more than the high and mighty who set out to save themselves and no one else. Another thought came to mind from the past. *Odd words of wisdom he was hearing that were calling to him from the city streets via a jail cell.*

"She was worth it!" he shouted unabashedly and chuckled. Groaning suddenly, his hand went to his face as his jaw gave a shot of pain from the effort to laugh. Renuel started as he heard a loud slam of the huge outer door leading to their cells. Voices in the other room were muddled, but audible.

"Yep, he's in here." There came a muffled response from the jailer, "ID? Yep, he had some kind of worker's visa; but I didn't bother to read the thing. He's legal 'til Spring; that's all I care about." There followed another request by the person. "No, can't show it to anyone without a legal document, sorry." A threatening tone by a second voice was followed with silence. "Well..., maybe I can make an exception in your case, you being a lawyer and all."

The door opened. "Renuel Breech! Someone's bailin' you out. Do you accept?"

The prisoner stood slowly. "Would you be good enough to ask the man's name?" A curse followed as the door slammed. It partly opened again, "Says he's Att. Evan Reinholdt."

It hit Renuel with a force almost as bad as one of Reinholdt's punches. With barely a few seconds of hesitation he replied in a firm, hard voice, "Tell the man, no thank you. I would much prefer my present company." Then he sat down.

The cell's occupants exploded into laughter, cheering and clapping. The big man Pace spoke, "Our man's got taste. What do you think of that, fat pocket?!"

"Yea, fat pocket," called another.

The large door slammed again and then opened slightly. The jailer's voice was loud and derisive, "Said to tell you, 'Now you are going to pay big time for this day's work!' "You know..., TIME—. Got it stranger?" His loud, cruel laughter echoed throughout the jail.

The cells grew deadly quiet then with a few coughs and a couple of obscene gestures directed toward the slamming door. Renuel said quietly, "It will not be the first time." He thought, *perhaps I did learn something from your imprisonment father; but for you, being jailed was a divine mandate for me today; I'm not sure why I chose thusly.*

He looked up smiling and said, "But she **was** worth it Father." The stranger, who was often a stranger to himself, was still a stranger to this God of his father's; for God does not patch a good or bad man up. He remakes him from the inside out. They are reborn, incredible as it seems. They can't enter the womb again so they must be reborn in a different way. This is a divine 'fantasma' beyond human and natural experience. Whoever even thought of such a thing? Who, but God?

Sometimes the journey to the Celestial city is long, arduous and uphill much of the way. This pilgrim was being pursued by the 'Hound of Heaven'; he would not get away! A couple of hours later the loud slam of the outer door once again jarred his nerves.

The grating voice of the jailor called out, "Renuel Breech! Someone else is here ta see you!"

# Chapter 12

# The History of Renuel Breech

"If you can bear to hear
The truth you've spoken
Twisted by knaves
To make a trap for fools."

Rudyard Kipling

After the Rev. Johanneson had posted bail, and Renuel was released, he entered the jail's anteroom where his benefactor was waiting. There was a space for visitors to sit down and the younger man made a gesture toward the bench.

Johanneson placed his hand on Renuel's shoulder and said, "Come, let us have our conversation in a friendly environment." He nodded to the jailer and they exited the building.

Arriving at the house, the Pastor requested coffee and a light snack from Marthe. Renuel, however, took hold of his host's arm. "Please Sir, may I speak first, and allow me to tell you my history before you offer me hospitality again." The older gentleman nodded and they both took a seat. The host's eyes were kind but his expression serious.

He nodded, "Certainly, go ahead Son. But you must remember that hospitality has very few conditions in our home."

Renuel was agitated and sitting seemed impossible. He also felt a surge of energy at being called 'Son' by the man. The pang of grief he often felt, when hearing others referred to in such a manner, was assuaged for this moment in time. *Would that it could last, the security of that title of 'sonship'. But for him, it could only be for an instance, a momentary state of being.* Yet, the kindness of the words and the soothing voice of the man calmed him. After a slight hesitation he sat down.

"Thank you, Sir. I assume that your daughter is recovering, or you would not have come and posted my bail."

"She is and she hoped you were not too injured by your defense of her." The strange champion shook his head, looking down at his bruised hands.

"A brawler deserves few good wishes; I fear." Looking straight into Renuel's eyes the parson said nothing. Instead he grasped Renuel's hands. "Thank you, Mr. Breech."

The younger man responded, "Forgive my harsh response. It was ingracious of me. Please be so kind as to thank your daughter for her words."

"I will, young man."

Rev. Johanneson spoke little. He did not trust himself. He knew he must withhold private information concerning Evan Reinholdt's life. In not doing so, he would break a confidence, grieve the gracious spirit and re-ignite the young man's anger.

As Renuel disclosed his history to the pastor, an unexpected thing began to play before Breech's eyes. The face of Linnea appeared here and there in the expressions and reactions of her father. An indignant frown, an occasional gesture or a chuckle danced before him like the face of the girl, but only for an instant; and it was gone. She was very like her father, but of course a feminine version, yet wholly herself as well. Renuel had observed her with the keen eye of espionage training. Without this discipline, the facial recognitions may have escaped him. She was indeed a pretty edition of the parson!

As he continued his history, Johanneson understood the young fugitive's past was laced with terror and personal tragedy. Still, he was careful to speak of the charm and beauty of his country of origin. Scarred by the tumult of childhood, he also described a life filled with family gatherings and relatives in their stately homes. Beautiful pictures of scenic places and city life, with bustling outdoor cafes and traveling musicians singing their tales of love.

At this, Renuel paused and looked momentarily away. But soon he continued with descriptions of wintry scenes and snow-covered houses, on lighted city streets, that were dotted with white birch and pine trees.

But then, the frightening arrests in the night began, sandwiched in between concerts in his town square where the people had danced and laughed and talked. All of that was silenced in a few short years.

"My mother is an artist. She has kept the beautiful scenes and the ancient architecture still present in the paintings from her gifted hands. And so, you see Sir, though evil men have cost me my citizenship and my freedom, nothing can rob me of the memories of what once was beautiful and good there."

Here, he paused, his hands clenched while staring ahead. "What the fiends have taken from us is hope, hope of returning someday to such scenes of home. Now there is no beautiful city that beckons me to come back, no goodly place where I can bring Isa's child. My mother's arms would enfold this little one; but instead, she is forced to live underground for fear of losing her freedom or her life."

"Isabella", he cleared his throat, fighting the emotions that threatened him. "Isa was not my wife, Sir; she was my sister and her husband Oleksandr was my closest comrade. You must understand that the infant is my niece. I failed to protect her mother the night she was arrested by the police. Oleksandr is dead. He was seeking to escape with my sister but was caught shortly after she left the country."

Stian Johanneson's voice was grave as he leaned forward and clasped the hands of the young sufferer. "Dear God in heaven, how you have suffered these past months not knowing her whereabouts! You are Isabella's brother then and your mother is still there in danger. We must pray for her safety and or her departure."

Breech nodded but sat quietly keeping his emotions in check. He was feeling drained from the retelling of his story but also relieved. He reached into his pocket and pulled out a small wallet, flipping it open.

"Here, Sir, is my mother's picture. My suffering seems small by comparison; and she bears it without bitterness." He handed Johanneson the leather wallet.

"What is your mother's name?"

"Natalyia, Sir."

The pastor looked upon the face of a woman, probably less than fifty years of age. She looked younger but the dark circles under her eyes and forced smile gave an impression of a life of struggle. He thought her lovely. He noticed that her eyes, though sad, had a tranquility that may have accounted for the impact her face had on him. Even her slight smile made the photograph come to life.

"Your mother is a beautiful woman, Renuel; you bear her likeness, except for her smile." Here Johanneson smirked, with a bit of mischief, as their young stranger rarely smiled.

Renuel nodded. "Well, she does get angry sometimes; but never allows it to remain for long. Such is not the case with me."

The parson smiled and glanced once more at the picture. Her hair looked black, like her son's, and her olive skin had a bit of a sallow look, no doubt from malnourishment. She was too thin, but her eyes captivated him even though ringed with fatigue. They shone with something like light or energy. A feeling leapt within Johanneson at the resilience and tenacity of the woman pictured. Although certainly burdened by her trials, she looked alive in her soul. What could be more appealing in a person than buoyancy and hope amidst struggles? He hadn't had such a feeling rise in him since Kirstin died.

There would never be another woman like Linnea's mother. The old thrill and the old sorrow of her memory washed over him again. He handed the picture back to Renuel.

At sixty years of age Stian Anders Johanneson was strong and steady in mind and body. He had a bit of a stoop from too much study and writing. But he also had a zest for life, and a fire in his soul that burned for God and truth. The woman he had loved ardently, with whom he had shared five children was gone. All this, and so much more, still lingered in his heart. She had brought to Stian her love and all other beautiful things as well. It was a profound loss of friendship and camaraderie. "Everyone who loves is born of God and knows God. He that loves not, knows not God, for God is love." The next words came to his mind and with it, a smile. 'With the breath, smiles and tears of all my life.'

"And the fights," Kirsten would always add laughing.

Renuel's voice brought him back. "My mother is a bit fatter now than in this picture." The youth had such a serious look as he said it, staring closely at the photo.

At this, the parson gave a hearty laugh. "In this country, my friend, that word isn't quite the compliment that I am sure you meant it to be to your mother."

Her father was still smiling when Linnea walked into the room carrying the babe in her arms. Marthe was following close behind, looking annoyed and muttering in Norwegian loud enough to be heard. Renuel stood up abruptly.

Johanneson turned around in surprise stating firmly, "Linnea Johanneson, you are supposed to be resting upstairs this entire day."

Marthe spoke adamantly, "Ja vell, I told her t'at Pastor, but she vud be 'ust like her mot'er."

The young woman cooed tenderly to the baby, kissing her repeatedly on the cheek. Walking up to Renuel she looked up kindly, but purposefully, "ReyRey, you must meet someone who already loves you before he knew what a sweet darling you are."

She didn't hand him the baby but turned her little face and body so that she was in full view of the uncle. He looked at the child in Linney's arms, her tiny face speaking wordlessly of Oleksandr and Isabella. It was a poignant scene for Renuel! It was also a discipline not to gaze, with admiration, at the girl holding the creature. Indeed, he felt a confusing ardor, not certain if it was for her or the infant, and momentarily forced it away.

But the feeling for her soon returned. Linnea's fair face was framed with her light hair and the curve of her neck. Her eyes were looking up at him, full of trust and tenderness that was almost too much to endure. It suddenly all seemed sad and hopeless. His eyes looked toward her father for some counsel.

"Linnea dear, there is something Mr. Breech has told me that I think you should know."

"Excuse me Sir, I would wish to tell the young lady myself."

He looked back at Linnea and the baby. Lifting his hand, he stroked the baby's soft cheek somewhat warily. Then, looking down into the girl's eyes with that same deep stare he had displayed earlier in the park, he paused. How could he have known how undone she was by that gaze. She dropped her eyes, bending slightly to kiss Bella.

He began, "Miss Johanneson I..."

But the girl kept looking straight at the baby and said, "Dear little Bella, this is your Uncle Renuel after whom your mama named you. Wasn't that a nice thing for her to do?"

Marthe interrupted indignantly, "She vud not be stopped from coming down vit t'e babe and listening t'e whole time, vit out a single bit of conscience for eavesdropping on a private talk vit da young man. Hmph", and she folded her arms in frustration.

Both men looked at each other a bit speechless. Renuel suppressed a smile. It seemed comical to him to see Marthe so upended.

The father replied, "It's alright Marthe; Linnea will have her way when she deems it right to do so. You are not responsible."

Marthe turned to go but looked at her master firmly. "Vel, I must fetch some lunch now! But some day t'at girl might hear somet'ing about herself she von't like too much." With an offended air she turned briskly on her heel and walked away.

"Poor Marthe, I am such a trial for the old dear. Won't you hold little Bella just for a moment, Mr. Breech? She isn't afraid of men; she loves my father dearly." Renuel had been standing when she entered the room. "There, sit down now, Mr. Breech."

Before he could voice a protest Linney pressed him to sit, and immediately handed him the baby.

"Besides, I am getting weary as she is quite an armful after a while." With that cunning comment there was no protesting and he received the baby awkwardly into his arms. The little infant looked up at him and reached for his face.

"Linnea, how you do press your will onto Mr. Breech." The girl laughed with an unself-conscious delight. "Oh Father, he must get used to Bella; he is her own true uncle. After all, I haven't asked him to change her diaper..., at least not yet!"

She broke into laughter again and plopped down on a large hassock close to the child and her uncle. Still holding the baby's hand, Linnea made certain that Bella could see her and not be afraid. She didn't want Renuel's feelings to be hurt. "You see, she is quite content with you, Mr. Breech."

Seeing tears forming in his eyes as he held the child, she busied herself, cooing to the baby and arranging her little booties and clothing. Much like her father, she was not nearly so detached from the emotionally charged moment as she pretended. Her greatest desire was to see their stranger glad. It would seem she had succeeded, at least for the time being.

# Chapter 13

## Awaken Not Love

"Love look at the two of us,
Strangers in many ways..."

Old Song

It had been a few weeks since the encounter with Evan Reinholdt in the park. Early on, Renuel had been urged by the pastor to remain as a guest. He came over to explain why he strongly protested, but when Marthe spoke up, she was adamant. She would brook no opposition to his taking up residence somewhere else.

"And vere vould you go ten? Propaple vind up back in jail for loit'ring all night on t'e city bench someveres!"

The pastor shrugged his shoulders and patted Renuel on the back. "The matron of the house has spoken, Son. There it rests." Stian walked away knowing Marthe would easily win that small coup.

Edging closer to Breech, the older woman spoke kindly, "Ja sure, and how many times has your family given shelter for ot'ers who vere vitout a place to lie t'ere heads? Ja, I know a t'ing or two about t'e underground during var times. My parents and us older shildren, ve had some secrets from t'ose Nazis before t'e invasion. 'T'en, some years later my husband..., vell nefer mind, you ust stay here. Ve ALL vant you to."

She looked slyly at him after emphasizing 'all'. Renuel looked at her, all defenses rebuffed. Marthe's tender, firm look made him drop his formed and unformed protests. It was true; Miss Johanneson had begged him to stay "for Bella Rene's sake" and as "a personal thank you" for which she had entreated, blushing.

"Thank you, Marthe. Unfortunately, I am still a wanderer; but having Bella Rene here does influence me. Also, I am waiting to hear from my mother. She is in a precarious position and may need to leave the country soon. Yes, and to respond to your question; my parents have, in times past, housed many, shall we say, 'displaced persons'. In fact, it is part of my mother's danger at present. She knows where I am staying as I gave her this address, with Pastor Johanneson's permission. She does know of Isabella's...;" it was difficult for Renuel to speak the words, 'place of rest'. "In any case, I may need to suddenly leave this area for her sake."

"Tsk, tsk," Marthe responded, touching her eyes with her apron. She patted him and walked quickly into the kitchen.

That had been a few weeks before. Later one evening the housekeeper and the pastor had some dialogue about their former interchange concerning Renuel's mother.

That next morning Johanneson took Renuel aside. "Mr. Breech, sometime soon my daughter, Marthe and I will be taking an extended trip to visit with Linnea's sisters. It would be mutually advantageous for you to remain here."

"But Sir, my leaving could be very sudden." The host held up his hand.

"If you must leave quickly to aid your mother's safe exit, there is only one place we can abide your bringing her. It must be here. From what we have grasped from little Bella, your mother is a longed-for person whom the child is anxious to meet". He winked at Renuel slyly. "You would do us all a great kindness by coming back again. We hope you will see it as your home, for however long it may be needed. It is also possible we will not have returned ourselves." The pastor's eyes sparked.

"Marthe is not the only one who can keep secrets and house 'displaced persons!" He went on. "We will also speak to the church board of your being our caretaker and that you may also bring to us a dear friend."

Hearing a sound behind him Renuel turned and saw Miss Johanneson sitting on the bottom stair. "Linnea, you could have let us know of your presence."

"But Father, then you and Mr. Breech would have had to go over the whole plan again with me."

Stian laughed. "Just like her mother, she never allowed secrets."

"Father, after breakfast Mr. Breech is taking the bus to the cemetery. He has invited us to go along. Stian looked at his daughter's shining eyes and felt a sudden fear emerge. He had observed that Linnea was losing her heart to this wanderer from almost the first night she had brought him home.

Strangely enough, the pastor himself was also drawn to him. *His fear for Linney, he quickly identified. It was simple. Renuel was a 'goodly' man in whose short-term care he entrusted his daughter. But the man was wrestling against being a 'godly'* man, tho' he claimed it for his own father. Until the new birth in Renuel's soul occurred, his attempts at goodness were vain. So, the pastor surprised even himself with the suggestion he was about to make.

"I fear I am steeped in parish duties this morning. Why don't you go with Mr. Breech, Linnea, or he may forget to get a transfer." He smiled at their young guest.

"Oh Father, you will insult him." But she smiled too.

After breakfast the excited girl quickly helped Marthe to clear the table. She then proceeded to head upstairs. Bella had awakened from her morning nap calling out.

Marthe intervened, "No shild; you took time early vit her bottle and ot'er duties. Go off now vit' Mr. Breech or it vill be lunchtime!"

Linnea shot the housekeeper a happy smile and went to fetch her sweater. The spring air was still quite cool. Marthe sidled up to Renuel as he waited,

"Do not go to t'e cemetery today. Vait for t'e gud Parson to go along vit you anot'er time. You take our girl and go on to Como Park. She knows t'e vay. It is a nice place for a girl and young man to valk. Ja, and t'e policeman valk t'ere too." She had spoken in low tones but emphasized the last sentence.

Their guest looked puzzled. "But I have told Pastor Johanneson..." The woman interrupted in a firm voice, "I vill tell him. He listens to me. It vill be 'ust fine."

Linnea came quickly towards them. She had pulled on her sweater and was tying a small print scarf, which she had folded into a triangle, on her chin. "It's the style!" She laughed and pulled Renuel by the arm. "Come on, Mr. Breech. The 10:00 a.m. bus may not wait for us."

When he told her their change of destination and Marthe's words she exclaimed, "Oh the dear thing. She knows it will be so much more fun and there will be a song fest later in the big pavilion. See, I have brought a little lunch." In her hand was a black lunch box. "It's Father's. He won't mind today. Here, you can carry it!" The girl laughed as she handed him the box.

"Alright Miss, but you must carry it home," Renuel replied smiling.

"We'll see about that!" She flashed him a cunning look. He opened the door and they left.

As they walked the man pondered his last words. *He had said, "home." Why did he not say, "back to the house" or "back to your place" or simply "back". It was not his home. Home..., such a place had long been absent from his life. He had no expectation it would ever return. He had died to such things.'* Renuel looked down at the girl walking beside him chatting and pointing here and there at various things.

She suddenly tugged at his sleeve, "Look Mr. Breech! There's the bus! It did wait for us! Kind old Mr. Slater. Hurry! I know you will love Como Park!"

*Even the bus driver knew her. Then it came to him. Wherever that girl did abide was **home.*** He shook his head, smiling at the revelation.

She looked back as they climbed on. "I am glad to see you smiling. You really will love it there, Mr. Breech!"

Renuel mused, *here or there, anywhere, as long as I feel her warm body nearby!* Still smiling, he climbed aboard.

# CHAPTER 14

# HAPPY TIMES AND THE CALL

"And there I will keep you forever
Forever and a day,
Til the walls shall crumble to ruin
And moulder in dust away."
Henry Wadsworth Longfellow

That outing was somewhat of a continuation of the short time he had with them following the Reinholdt debacle. On some evenings they would sit and read aloud, with Pastor Johanneson, and even Marthe joined them on occasion. There was a mystery writer whom Renuel particularly enjoyed for his detective intrigues. One night a discussion followed.

"But Mr. Breech, I think if you retraced some of his steps you would find his clues were farfetched and not so well connected to the outcome."

Renny smiled saying, "You are very keen, Miss Johanneson, but Mr. Holmes might take offense." He glanced at the Pastor. "Sir, do you not think that his plots are more worthy than, say, Miss Austen's?"

Linnea broke in with a cry, "Surely not Father! One cannot compare these two types of stories for one is sleuthing and the other Victorian Romanticism." At this passionate outburst the girl's face reddened.

Renuel responded, "Yes Miss, that is true, and very adroit of you; yet I do believe that Mr. Holmes is a bit of a romantic in his own, how do you say, 'careful' way?"

The good parson chuckled and leaned forward, "Well, Mr. Breech, as for my part it depends on if I am in the mood for mystery, sans romance, or as is often the case with Miss Austen, an intriguing combination of both. So, I conclude you are both correct! What do you say Marthe," he queried hoping to tease her a bit.

"Vell, I like Mr. Vatson te best. He does not teas!" she declared, staring at her antagonist with a very slight smile. At this, they all laughed.

There was some agreement with her father's observation in the end, but Linnea shook her head and stated, "Come Father and Mr. Breech, let us go outside and walk a bit. The night air will clear our visitor's poor confused mind." She laughed mischievously.

That evening stroll and the 'chance' sighting of a certain lawyer staring menacingly in their direction disturbed Renuel; but he remained silent. He was glad his companions hadn't noticed the man.

And so, the days and nights passed in much pleasantness. Sadly, it could not last. A dark force was at work, partly in the person of Evan Reinholdt, but also in something much larger in scope and even more sinister. Renuel knew it was tied to Bella and the destiny of his country.

Fading in and out of his thoughts was a statement the Ambassador's sister Iiulia had made as they parted from Oxford, not long before all the danger began, "Renuel, our country cannot survive long-term, even if we defeat this present tyranny, if all we look to do is reinstate the monarchy. We must urge and educate the Resistance to look to a parliamentary system of government; or all is lost."

As the sister of a man whose ostentatious lifestyle was fully supported by the Russian Oligarchy, he knew Iiulia spoke the truth. His father had written of it often.

"Look at Russia; socialism was only thinly veiled tyranny which had as its goal the rule by the elite rich. They have succeeded. The people are worse off than before the monarchy fell. It is not that our people lack intelligence; they lack the truth. We must tell them the truth!"

Although at present his major concern was the ambassador's threat to his mother's safety, Renuel knew he would have to come face to face with Iiulia's reality one day.

But the first threat he had felt on that evening walk became his present jarring reality which concerned both Linnea and Bella. Renuel had been growing more and more uneasy about his feelings for this girl, Linnea Johanneson. They were bordering on hopeless obsession. Her very presence in a room was both exquisitely painful and delightful. If he missed a reading night to avoid her presence, she would search him out and, without caprice, put her hand lightly on his arm saying, "We missed you tonight, Mr. Breech."

Her touch was electrifying to Renuel and yet, it was filled with hopeless pathos. Then something happened, quickly terminating all contact between them.

91

It was after 2:00 a.m. when Renuel heard a repeated knocking at his door. He roused himself and felt the old panic arise at the unexpected sound. He walked across the room, bracing himself, and opened the door to Pastor Johanneson.

"Son, you have an overseas phone call. Do you wish to accept it?" The expression on his host's face was concerned but his voice was steady. It slightly quieted Renuel's pounding heart.

"Ahem, um, yes Sir, thank you. I have the money for the call. As you know I gave my contacts this number."

"Have no concerns about the cost."

Renuel was unnerved but had also been aware that this call could come at any time. He kept in close contact with informants concerning his mother's well-being; and all was tenuous.

Dressing quickly, he found the pastor waiting just outside his door. Stian led him to the library where he could take the phone call. Renuel was relieved. He knew that knowing the details of this operation could place the Johannesons in jeopardy.

Offering his hand to his host, he shook it and looked painfully into his eyes. "Thank you, Sir, I trust we shall meet again one day. Your help to me and little Bella has been incalculable. I can never repay it."

"Son, I know you will remember that the intent of our hearts is that our 'family friend' be brought here when it is opportune for you to do so." Renny was already heading into the library as Stian called, "We will be praying and awaiting your return Son."

Renuel looked back and nodded, "I will try. It is a long and perilous journey Sir." Then, just before he closed the library door, he turned back and said firmly, "Please explain to Miss

Johanneson and kiss little Bella for me as the hour is late for farewells."

"But surely you will have time for this in the morning."

"Tomorrow is uncertain, Sir."

And with that, the door closed behind him. When the household awakened, Renuel Breech was gone. They heard nothing from him during the month they visited Linney's sisters. But finally, just after arrivng home, a telegram came. Bringing your family friend. [stop] arriving Friday. [stop]

# PART II

# CHAPTER 15

# WIDOWED BEAUTY

"God's gifts put man's best dreams to naught"
E.B. Browning

"Are you very certain Renny? My English is not what it once was. I needed to conceal my connections with the West; so, I feel nervous now speaking with Americans."

"Mother, these are generous and gracious people. They have so wanted you to meet Bella; but I informed them of the great risks you would have to take in getting here. They are so happy you have come. They will not evaluate your English!"

The woman smiled at his comment. Her dark eyes looked up at her son. "Risks..., yes, life is full of risks, but God's will is always a fair risk to take; is it not, my son?"

He frowned and said cynically, "Like Father's risks for God and country, you mean?"

Her face grew sad and he was chagrined to speak so darkly to his mother who had lost so much. "Forgive me; I have regressed."

"Yes, Renny, indeed he did risk all and now; he has gained all."

"And you..., and me? What have we gained Mother? Seems you believe he gained it all, but I only see that we have lost it all. Is that what you call a 'fair risk'?"

Natalyia shook her head and looked ahead, not looking at anything in particular. "I don't have an answer for you that will satisfy your quest for a just world, Renuel Galena."

"It's alright; I am not expecting a just world, not even an answer. I am angry at a God I don't presently believe in. I'm probably using you as my scapegoat, dear lady. But let us be glad. Here we are."

Pulling the strong cord, the bus groaned to a stop. Several people got out with them. "It's just a short way now."

As they began the walk to the Johannesons they saw a man fast approaching them. Renuel recognized his stride, as well as his arrogant demeanor.

Quietly he said, "Mother, this man has some power in the city; and he is definitely not trustworthy. Don't say anything; I will tell him in English that you are a close friend of the family, just visiting."

Natalyia was very accustomed to feigning normalcy. She was adept at forced calm in threatening moments, from years of behaving so. Evan Reinholdt strode up to them and stopped in front of Renuel, barely acknowledging his companion.

"I thought I warned you about returning to this city." His voice was subdued but hostility was in his tone. Renuel stepped forward, leaving his mother a few paces behind, beckoning Evan.

"Sir, I ask your respect as this is a close friend of the Pastor's family. He contacted me with a request to help her when she arrived in the city. You know they have been on an extended leave of absence and feared missing her. I am in their debt and could not refuse, nor would I, considering their kindness to me as a stranger."

"Humph," Reinholdt responded, looking back at Natalyia.

She was a very striking woman. Her tall figure and dark hair belied her age. The tailored suit she wore was expensive. It was the only outfit she owned for travel outside of her country. It was from better days with Galena when they had moved in high academic and social circles. She looked at Evan with indifferent dignity, nodding only slightly and pointed across the avenue.

Calling to Renuel she queried, "Mr. Breech, I believe we must be nearly arrived, are we not?"

It was said in nearly perfect English. Her son was shocked and wondered if it were memorized. Since her arrival they had been speaking in their own language. Evan, the intruder, for so he now felt, looked at her uneasily and tipped his hat. *Perhaps he'd better show her some regard, just in case she was connected to the Johanneson's in some intimate way. He was already treading on thin ice in his pursuit of Linnea and had made very little headway. He didn't need a setback now.*

Coming forward he spoke with cordiality, "Madam, I trust your stay in the city will be enjoyable."

She nodded slightly, with a very small smile, and said nothing more. He flashed a smile at Natalyia and turned, giving Renuel a menacing stare as he strode away.

"Such an unpleasant acquaintance, Renny," she said quietly after covering some distance. "Is he a friend of the family?" Renuel's eyes grew dark as did his tone.

"He is a dangerous man who tries to ingratiate himself as a benefactor to Bella. He hates me and has threatened to bring trouble if I connect myself to the Johannesons. I believe he has his eye on the daughter, Linnea."

"Hmmm, the one I believe you also have eyes for." She laughed quietly. "I am looking forward to meeting her. I won't tell Iiulia."

"Mother, you know that can never be. It would be perilous for all three of us." His voice was sober, but he looked back, saw no one and squeezed her shoulder, smiling.

His mother teased further. "Besides, you don't love her. Poor Iiulia..., maybe there would be some hope if she were even five years younger?"

"Mother, she is a very good friend and attractive; but that is all. Now, no more talk. There to your right is the manse."

It was a stately older home, well-kept and set back a good deal from the sidewalk. To the right of the parsonage was a lovely garden with a large arbor which was covered on top with climbing roses. Natalyia was reminded of the beautiful homes around which she and Galena had lived, although theirs was much smaller. It was what an income for a professor/writer could afford.

They had walked to the door; but before the doorbell could be rung, Stian Johanneson opened the front door with a wide, welcoming smile. Immediately extending his hand to Renuel, he gripped it with both of his. "Thank God, Son, you are finally here! Oh, the Almighty is good!" Renuel smiled broadly, almost chuckling aloud as he caught the look on his mother's face. "Come in, come in!" They quickly stepped into the alcove.

Stian stopped and warmly took Natalyia's hand while looking at Renuel. "Of course, this is your dear mother."

"Mother, this is Pastor Stian Johanneson, Pastor, my mother."

Her eyes, dark and serene, looked into his, and on her lovely face was a reserved, but genuine smile. The woman emanated a calm demeanor and Stian felt she seemed more in control of the situation than he.

"Pastor, thank you greatly for your hospitality; we are for all of this much in your debt."

"Please call me Stian and no debt at all between friends."

"Or anyone else for that matter!", added Renuel, smiling.

The good parson chuckled. "Perhaps that is so Son; but don't tell your mother. She may not believe how glad we are for her presence."

Natalyia laughed lightly and released Stian's hand. He felt a nudge on his arm. Looking back, he saw Linnea with Marthe just behind her. Stepping sideways he brought Linney forward. Renuel took his mother's arm.

"Mother, this is Linnea Johanneson, and nodding to the woman behind, "And Marthe, the keeper of this large home."

Linnea had flushed just hearing Renuel's voice again. Add to this, here he was speaking her name. She came forward and embraced Natalyia warmly. This surprised and touched the lady. With someone who was so close to Isabella, it was almost like an instant connection with Isa. She fought back her emotions and returned the greeting in kind.

"I am so happy to meet the person who taught my son public transportation riding. Then she smiled at Renuel cagily.

"Oh..., the bus!", cried Linnea flushing again. "Oh, but Mr. Breech, you did not tell us how beautiful your mother was; did he Father?"

Stian looked admiringly at Natalyia. He was very glad his daughter had given him an excuse.

"Indeed, he did not! She is most lovely." Natalyia said a quick thank you but immediately turned her attention to Marthe. Stepping forward she extended both hands and took the older lady's warmly in hers.

"You must be so hard work to keep such a large house under your care." Then, added, "And I have heard you do so much besides. I hope you will instruct me as to how I can help with your load of tasks during my reside here."

Marthe was obviously quite warmed by this gesture. "Vel, t"ank you M'am. I t'ink if Miss Linney does her part, ve vill be 'ust fine." She smiled benevolently at Linnea.

Marthe took their wraps, telling them to leave their suitcases there.

"Thank you, Marthe," stated Stian and escorted them into the dining room. "It is time for a bit of luncheon. We can visit more at the table," said Stian, with a cordial smile.

He pulled out Natalyia's chair to seat her. But first, glancing over her shoulder, she looked up at him. "Thank you, Pastor; it has been a portion of time since a chair is offered me in kindness." Still looking up, for he was quite a bit taller than she, she said, "I see I will need to look up at you; but my son tells me I must look also up **to** you for all care you have given to him and little Bella."

Stian replied, wondering why he felt undone again when she looked into his eyes. "Oh, think nothing of that; we are much on the receiving end to have you and Renuel here now and here safely." The lady moved to sit and Stian gently pushed in her chair.

"I thank you Pastor and I must also thank your daughter for her gift of love for Isa." The pastor was moved by her efforts to speak in English.

Linnea had disappeared and returned carrying the curly haired baby. Marthe had brought in a highchair and placed it between Linney and her father.

"I know I said she was having her morning nap; but when I ran to check, she was lying with her little eyes wide open."

Marthe murmured quietly, "Ja, ven you openet t'at door she openet her eyes, no doubt!" A few chuckles from the group were somewhat suppressed for Marthe's sake.

"I am only a little apologetic," Linnea said eagerly looking around. "I thought she would love to be here with all of us." The young nanny looked at her father, eyes bright.

"Yes, Linnea." Looking at Natalyia Stian said, "The baby is much like her caretaker, a very social little creature. We best show her off now. Obviously, she has been made ready for our party." He smiled at the baby.

Their guest's eyes filled with tears as she gazed upon the child of her daughter for the first time. The girl brought her over, offering the baby's hand to her grandmother.

"Here Bella Rene, here is your own dear Grandmama. Can you hold her hand?" The baby looked at Linnea and then at the lady who had taken her hand, and now kissed it tenderly.

"Hello little Bella, I have such happiness to meet you." She turned to Renuel and spoke in their language.

He replied, "My mother apologizes for her lack of words but wishes to say how the child's eyes are so like Isa's, large and deep brown." Linney was touched for she had thought the same thing of Bella and her mother. Their guest softly spoke again but only Renuel understood her words.

Stian's voice struggled with emotion viewing the tender scene. "Shall we give thanks?" He took Natalyia's hand and the others followed in kind. Thus, the meal began, in a warm and natural way, with the travelers sharing their story and even using humor in retelling a few harrowing moments. There was still secrecy concerning the actual country of which they spoke.

Johanneson, having traveled extensively in their region, somewhat recognized their language. Learning more and more the years of peril Natalyia and her family had undergone made this caring man wish to create a safe and pleasant asylum for them. He thought of the ancient story of the landowner Boaz and his words to a refugee widow named Ruth.

"May the God under whose wings you have sought refuge protect you." *Of course*, mused Stian; *the story doesn't describe the Moabite woman; but doubtless she had similar coloring to our guest. He believed, or hoped, that Ruth's beauty was at least close to the stunning looks of Mrs. Zupancic, for Boaz's sake! Holding her hand during prayer was quite pleasant. Thank God for tradition.* All these thoughts were rapid and surprising to the widower Stian Johanneson.

With great effort he succeeded in not staring at their visitor every moment during their repast. Though she seemed a reserved person, the lady was so taken with the baby, and with Renuel at her side to translate when needed, that it gave her liberty to laugh and to interact. All of this was showing her to be both warm and loving in manner with an open temperament.

On occasion Stian spoke directly to her and looking into her dark eyes, he saw them alight with humor and intelligence, but also laced with sadness that could not be hidden. The good pastor was somewhat undone with the enchantment of her presence but knew he must appear calm and unaffected. Renuel had explained some of the threat to her from the Russian liaison, Putin, who had made no secret of his desire for Natalyia.

Stian had always lived out being a dauntless protector of the vulnerable. Again, this was evident in his care for Isa and Bella, and many, many others before them. He now felt subdued anger at the ruthless enemy who doubtless had this woman's goodly husband killed to secure his quarry. *The villain*, he thought, especially now, after meeting Natalyia. N*o scheme was too dark to secure for himself this lovely lady who seemed so unaware of her charms.* Stian's thoughts rambled on. *Doubtless all beautiful women must be aware of their power over men but some reserve that force of attraction for only one man.*

Coming suddenly out of his brief reverie, the host smiled and made another failed attempt at eating. *It has been a long time since a lady has stolen my appetite away.* He smiled just slightly at the thought.

Linnea was responding to a question posed by Renuel.

"My mother asks if that gesture by Bella is unusual."

"Not at all, she often wants to hold my hand during our meals. Perhaps it is because she still mainly drinks her bottle and isn't very hungry." Bella's little arm was outstretched, holding Linney's hand. "It is an endearing little thing she does; and I simply can't refuse her. Father sometime tries to relieve me, as eating is a bit of a challenge." Stian took the baby's other hand but she also still clung to Linnea's. "Well, sometimes it works." She laughed sweetly, looking at Bella.

Natalyia dabbed at her eyes saying, "My Isa often wished for me to hold her like that at meal."

There was a small silence when Stian spoke up. "Well, who could have known such a thing could be passed through the genetic line? Just like Jacob and his striped goats!"

There was laughter and a short review of the old Hebrew story by the pastor. Renuel translated but Natalyia had gotten most of the drift as evidenced by her laughter. She shared that her mother-in-law had relayed many such stories and lessons from the scriptures when they lived with her during Galena's first imprisonment.

Their guest remarked, later to her son, that their host was a kind man of great depth. But to herself she also felt moved by his carefully inclusive way with Renuel. Galena would be grateful, she thought. The pastor seemed to avoid much eye contact with her. Such wordless eye contact by men was always a threat to her and she studiously avoided those interactions.

Thus, she was relieved and put at her ease by a man who seemed to equally enjoy all who were present. Yet, there was no denying the personal warmth and congeniality she felt from the pastor towards her. It seemed that it was all joined with the home and those who were blessed to dwell there. Natalyia felt it like a soul tonic, a 'balm in Gilead', reviving her memories of life with Galena. Such memories of past times of tender, familiar associations and friendships were stirred. Natalyia still hoped that she could renew these one day.

*Their host was tall, with very blue eyes and a generous mix of light brown hair mixed in with his white. It was a bit longish and curled some at his neck and ears. No doubt he was too busy and had no wife to pay attention to the finer parts of his toilette. His build was still strong, slightly stooped, not heavy set, but with a fuller physique than he once had, no doubt.* She smiled, her thoughts concluding that between the housekeeper and his daughter, the pastor fared well.

These details their guest took in very quickly. Being keen and observant was a result of the necessity of staying ahead of trouble, or even to avoid detainment facilities. It wasn't just for herself she was wary. It could save others' lives to see and remember details. Carelessness wasn't an option for the likes of Natalyia Zaplavnov.

It had been a most lovely day and Natalyia's daydreams were sweeter than any she had had in a long time; but night terrors always threatened. However, she fell asleep peacefully. Her nighttime dream held no terrors but did leave her curious. She was a girl again, maybe twelve. It was wintertime and she and other children were sledding down a long hill.

Unlike the others, she had no sled and it made her feel that she didn't belong there. She was sad and wanted so much to be part of it all but stood off to the side, a short way down the hill. Suddenly, she heard a voice shouting from behind. She turned, coming down the slope was a boy on a sled.

"Nattie! Get ready to jump on and grab hold of me!" She heard her childhood nickname, and as he got near, saw his face.

It was ruddy and his hair was blond, with crystal blue eyes, but she didn't know him.

"I don't know you!", she shouted back.

"It's okay! I'm safe!" he shouted. She jumped on, grabbing onto the boy just as the sled was gaining speed. Suddenly it was a tobaggan and a couple of other kids jumped on behind her. They arrived at the bottom tumbling off amidst laughter and flying snow. Then, fully awake she smiled and realized she was still laughing from the dream. (It was such a lovely awakening; as you will agree if a dream has ever caused this to happen to you.)

## Chapter 16

# The Parson, the Paw Prints and the Predator

"If you can dream—
And not make dreams your master..."
Rudyard Kipling

The good parson had arisen early while the rest of the household slept. That was, of course, excepting Marthe who was singing softly in the kitchen. There was no smell of coffee yet and that was good, as Stian Johanneson hoped to have a cup later in sweeter and fairer company than his own.

"Ah me, how long has it been since I've shared morning coffee time." But instead of Kirsten's image, he was quite undone by the image of their guest. *And quite a sight she was, to be sure, Natalyia Zupancic..., hmmm.*

The memory of her fragrance wafted back from yesterday's luncheon and dinner as he pushed in her chair. *Johanneson was not appalled nor chagrined at these heightened senses, just surprised. His marriage bond with Kirsten had ended years before, with her death. Although an extreme loss, he had accepted, in* time, that their life together had ended. But he was a devout Christian man and believed in eternal life. He knew he would see Kirsten again in a new country and in a new City, whose Builder and Maker was God. That was exciting. But for now, he was still in this world and so was Natalyia Zupancic; and that too was exciting!

The Reverend Johanneson was a strong, virile man, just turned sixty. *In the years since Kirsten's passing, he had not been drawn to a woman in the way of the marriage union. At least not with any strong inclination, not yet; that is.* He smiled, shook off his very pleasant musings, and focused on the day. It was very early spring; and the morning was beckoning for an early walk. The reality was that the parson needed some reflective time, as his sleep had come reluctantly the former night. *That was always the question he asked himself.*

He went to the kitchen, informed Marthe about his walk and left his domicile. As he walked, he began to ponder the possible reasons for a restless night. *There were no troubles in the Parish to account for it. Well, no troubles, other than the elderly Mrs. Robinson's cat.* Johanneson smiled. *The feline had been declared guilty of leaving catty footprints in the newly poured sidewalk of the right Honorable Judge DeVant. His wife wished to 'throw the book' at the deviant creature, or at least throw 'a' book. Said animal had also been reported to have been dropping unseemly deposits and digging up dirt, then covering it, in Mrs. DeVant's potted geraniums.* Chuckling to himself, the parson mused further. *The geraniums should flourish nicely in the newly fertilized soil. But he had thought it best not to mention that to the Judge's wife in the church narthex. Her husband was not a church attender.*

Johanneson continued walking briskly and found himself at the main avenue. He was going to turn back but felt he hadn't pressed his mind quite enough. He still needed to discern the why to his sleeplessness. *After all, it was partially the purpose for this morning pilgrimage.* Looking across the arterial, he realized he wasn't more than a block from the Judge's house. Curiosity drove him forward to ascertain the true 'calamity' of the paw prints.

He also said under his breath, "I really ought to pay the Judge a pastoral call. From what I hear; he is quite a pagan. Well Lord, we could certainly use a 'saved' judge. Doubtful that he'll be about at this hour; however, the cat might be!"

Stian crossed the street, and after observing a few homes, quickly recalled that this side of town was decidedly richer than his own neighborhood. Walking past the mansion-type dwellings, complete with iron gates and lush grounds, he soon saw the Judge's 'estate'. The walker remembered that his student, Evan Reinholdt, also lived in this area. The attorney had been quick to mention this. Johanneson wasn't sure that Evan hadn't spoken in a louder voice than necessary that day as Linnea served them coffee. He shook his head, knowing full well that his daughter had no notions, nor did she care a thing about the man's status, nor about him, save perhaps his soul. It was as though she was oblivious to such types; though it wasn't beyond her notice when the delivery boy flashed her a smile. "He's a nice boy." She defended herself on her father's comment about returning his smile. "Handsome too!"

He laughed as she blushed saying, "Father!"

Evan Reinholdt was fortunate to get so much as a nod from Linnea; and that was before the incident in the park. He scowled slightly, *that girl is an excellent judge of character, just like her mother.* Johanneson approached the imposing edifice. At that moment, he noticed a man going into the Judge's house.

The parson had to admit more than a little curiosity about the paw prints in the cement. The story was reminiscent of his father's freshly poured barn floor. Stian was a young boy, at the time, and had surreptitiously put his whole flat hand in the cement. When his father discovered it; he got a paddling. Not because of the handprint, but because he sneaked and did it without asking permission.

The next day his father said, "I would have told you to also put your initials and the year in it," as he tousled his blond hair and hugged him.

The old Norwegians were thrifty, as well as strict, and did not hold with foolishness. Johanneson wondered if his imprint was still there. *Would it be that he could so easily imprint the lives of lost people, people desperately needing God, but running in the other direction. This lostness was no respecter of persons nor of social-economic status, not even for the likes of Evan Reinholdt. They were 'ever learning, but never coming to the knowledge of the truth,' just like the caretaker at the cemetery who had been so uncouth and rude to Linnea.*

"Bring him a bag of Marthe's cookies next time Linney." He shook his head; *I need to pray more* and dismissed his meandering thoughts.

"Paw prints", he murmured, "That's what I'm after", smiling at his clandestine mission.

Mrs. Robinson had stated, in defense of her cat, that it was probably the Judge's nasty little chihuahua that had made the prints. Walking up their private walk, off the public sidewalk, the sleuth stooped down upon seeing the evidence. Before a proper evaluation was possible, he heard a door open and subdued voices coming from the Judge's porch.

Although it was a bit of a distance away, Johanneson recognized Evan Reinholdt immediately. Something made him straighten quickly, return to the main sidewalk and step behind a tree. Maybe his caution was seeing the attorney look furtively around, shake the Judge's hand and then leave hurriedly by a private gate. The pastor glanced at his watch and saw it was before 6:30 a.m.

"Rather early for a visit", he murmured, somewhat intrigued. He knew Reinholdt hadn't seen him. *Wonder what he's up to?* Still, not wanting to be suspicious, he determined it must be a legal matter for which Evan was seeking advice.

Then he said softly, "Hate to be ungenerous, but I trust it isn't concerning a current case in court, which is against trial law."

*His trust in the Judge was moderate at best, and in the attorney, even less. Normally, if the Judge had emerged, he would have greeted him in a friendly way; but this little subterfuge made the parson turn around, glad to be leaving.* He sought to dismiss his uncharitable thoughts. The other muse, that wanted to surface, *was why the restless night and the uncharacteristic destination of his walk this a.m.? Was there a connection?*

The troubled parson began the homeward trek, with long strides, eager to be out of that neighborhood. He crossed the busy avenue with a relieved sigh. The truth was that he was still disturbed over the Attorney's arrogant, crude manner with which he had approached his daughter in the park. She had relayed to her parent the entire debacle.

The man had since sought permission to visit the Johanneson household so he could make up for the former 'misunderstanding'. Some weeks had passed and after profuse apologies to Linnea, he softened his approach from suitor to caring friend. Her father was convinced that Evan was simply pressing his suite through some other means, perhaps even devious. In the beginning, not only was his daughter put off by him, but was frightened at times. Her father determined to end the visits, but by that time, unknown to him, Reinholdt had often begun to mention to her the 'peril' of Bella's non-family-member status.

He stated to Linnea that, at any time, the authorities from the social work system could call on them to determine whether the child should be a ward of the state. The warning had credibility, as all their other infants had been privately adopted when they had reached Bella's age. She kept this threat from her father. *He could not understand why his daughter continued to allow the man to visit. Was it a miss-direction within her Christian heart?*

In Johanneson's eyes, Reinholdt was not even a contender as a suitor. His spiritual condition was as decidedly below hers as his social condition was decidedly above hers. The attorney's chances were bleak indeed. A marriage between them, without the man's redemption and a rebirth of heart and soul, was untenable; and her father would never give his blessing. Linnea surely would not go against this beloved parent. Even if this suitor confessed such salvation, he would have to prove its authenticity for a noticeable amount of time. The pastor had seen too many 'fox hole conversions' gone bad, just to secure a desired end.

No, Stian Johanneson was a vastly long way from approving the joining of his precious Christian daughter with the likes of Attorney Evan Reinholdt. *But what*, he wondered, *what hold did that man have over Linnea? This was very disturbing; and he must pray for discernment and for truth to surface. His soul felt darkened and his instincts were on high alert.*

As he continued walking, with thoughts of arriving home, a sweet visage came before him. *It was, once again, Renuel's lovely mother. His heart began to pound with anticipation. Reflections on his insomnia reminded him that he enjoyed, in his sleepless-ness, musing about their captivating house guest. Her face, form and manner of being drew him in immediately. Her laughter, her leaning against Renuel in a shared moment, or touching his arm in a tender link to a memory they shared from their narrow escape;* all of these played upon his mind.

Stian had found himself envisioning the lady leaning tenderly against him, like that, and touching him in intimate trust and devotion. He noticed her hands, strong and somewhat work-worn, with a simple gold band on her right hand. She would twist it 'round fairly often, and Renuel would squeeze her hand caringly as if to say, "It's alright Mother."

When they had come to the dinner table that evening, the lady had changed out of her traveling suit. She wore a white blouse, with a khaki skirt. It gave her a girlish look; yet she still projected a womanly grace and poise. As he moved toward her, and pulled out her chair, he again caught the same light fragrance as before. The good parson tried diligently to block the image of giving her a loving embrace. She looked up at him with a smile, and a nod, which made him want to invent any even slightly plausible excuse to remain in her company indefinitely.

Nataylia Zupancic radiated something that felt almost divine, and perhaps those that have suffered deeply do have the presence of the Master clinging to them. "She has the touch of the angels about her." It was a line from a book they had been reading with Renuel. Bewildered by these thoughts and feelings, the host had avoided looking at her lest she become aware of his tumult and be uncomfortable in his presence.

All in all, it was disconcerting in a most amiable way. As Johanneson arrived home, he climbed the steps and, with his hand on the doorknob, said aloud, "Well, I'm too old for a mid-life crisis; it must be love!!"

# CHAPTER 17

# OUT OF TIME

> "...But a smooth and steadfast mind,
> Gentle thoughts and calm desires,
> Hearts with equal love combined..."
>
> Thomas Carew

Back within the house Stian Johanneson sank into his chair, leaned forward and clutched his head. It was still early; and when he had poked his head into the kitchen, Marthe had left the room for other pressing duties, giving care to the baby, no doubt. He returned to the living room and busied himself, building a fire, and then sat down.

"Oh, Father in heaven, I should feel quite guilty! How can I have such feelings for one whom I have barely known; one only just come here and under great duress; entrusting her very life to us." The man spoke the words quietly; but it was more of a declaration than a prayer, and any guilt seemed absent.

He was filled with a zeal akin to his most intense moments when sermonizing. Often truths that blazed out at him, from the scriptures, set his heart on fire. He was only slightly contrite that he felt a similar zeal for Renuel's beautiful mother. *Remember, you are not a schoolboy. This is 'a temporary madness', not love; it will doubtless pass,* he mused smiling.

The Parson stood and as though he were speaking to someone else said aloud, the smile still pulling at his mouth, "Gather your wits, old man. You have been alone too long. Think of Linnea and see what an example young Renuel is. Although in constant peril of letting his emotions for Linnea surface, he yet regulates himself. You can do no less."

Nevertheless, Mrs. Zupancic's reserved demeanor, her dark eyes and beguiling face remained. Again, thoughts of Renuel and his daughter surfaced. *Yes, he feels deeply for Linney but controls his ardor and he, for the present, is likely an unregenerate soul.* The Parson felt chagrined and yet buoyed at the tender dilemma in which he found himself. Then he said aloud, "Well, it's a great deal better than deciphering paw prints!"

Stian made his way back to the kitchen where he smelled the coffee brewing. Poking his head into the door, he saw Marthe busying herself. Looking up at him, a bit piqued, she said, "Vel Pastor, you are still too early and t'e coffee is not finished yet. I t'ink you should go read t'e Bible."

"Dear Marthe, just what I was 't'inking' about."

"Tsk tsk, such a man!" Stian smiled at her. She was a good soul and took his teasing well.

"But, instead of the Bible, I will go and see if the newspaper is here now. It wasn't a few minutes ago." He grabbed a sweater out of the closet, in case he had to wait for the paper boy and went out. In less than five minutes the paper had arrived and Stian went quickly back up the steps and opened the door with a brisk movement.

At the same moment he opened the door their lady visitor fell forward, towards him, with no door to brace her. "Oh, oh, I am sorry", she cried as Stian deftly caught her. Easing her back gently, so she could stand on her own, he released the surprised woman while smiling broadly.

"Mrs. Zupancic, you are awake! So good to see you this morning. It is well that we are not strangers, given such a friendly greeting!"

Natalyia laughed lightly as Stian closed the door, stepped back, turned and offered his hand to assist her.

"You are being in humor this daytime, are you not Pastor Johanneson?"

"Yes, I am teasing you."

She replied, "I was just leaving for the morning breath of air and walking some."

"That is very good as I need more air to breathe, that is, if I may join you? I was just thinking how I would like to enjoy a second walk if only the right person should chance along; and here you are! It is an answer to an unspoken prayer, Mrs. Zupancic!"

She laughed, in delight, quite certain he had not prayed such a thing. Still, it touched her knowing that he was willing to spend time with her, a stranger. Natalyia was quite aware of other kinds of men wanting to take up with her, stranger or not, but this man was of a different caliber.

Nevertheless, thoughts and images of Ambassador Putin flashed before her, making her feel sick.

The lady was thrown back instantly to another place and a very recent trauma. She began to step away saying anxiously, "Oh no, Pastor Johanneson, I could not trouble you as you have already been out. Doubtless many in your parish will be needing of your time this day!"

Stian rubbed his chin thoughtfully. "Speaking of' 'them', I believe you could do me and 'them' a great service."

"Sir," she asked totally bewildered, "What is this service?" Natalyia could see a slight smile playing around the Pastor's mouth and a twinkle in his eyes.

"Well, you see, dear lady, my neighbors and parish friends think I have lost all social graces and no respectable woman, under seventy, would accompany me on a friendly stroll. You may even save me from being dismissed by the bishop entirely."

Now that Natalyia was beginning to understand the direction of his words, her features softened, and a smile began to surface. She felt herself relaxing and remembering where she now was. She realized that the pastor was surely a safe escort.

"How terrible to think that you should lose your position here! You must take dear Marthe for healthy stroll for she is well under years of seventy!" She laughed and remembered the delightful time they had spent with Renuel and the family last evening. Yes, they were in a safe place and she was with a safe gentleman.

Stain chuckled, "I am not certain Marthe would agree to that proposal!" It thrilled Stian to see her affect brighten and her fear dissipate. This touched him, in his pastoral heart. It was always a great joy for him to bring a smile, a laugh or a word rightly spoken to a burdened heart. Was it not said that "a smoldering flame He will not extinguish, nor a bent reed He will not break?"

And so thusly did this man of God conduct this holy business, even at this unplanned moment. More than any words of pious counsel that he might share, he preferred the light in her eyes, and the smile and humor which they brought.

Was not part of his sacred duty to bring hope to the downtrodden, the sad, and fearful heart? How could he think of extending less to her who had suffered so much? And then he thought with a boyish smile, *what an intriguing, lovely lady with whom to share a sacred tasking.* Lifting his eyes heavenward he almost believed he could see the Almighty winking at him. (If such a thing were possible of course!)

He offered her his arm. "Come, Mrs. Zupancic, let us offer the ladies something to reassure them. Now they can see that their parson is not beyond hope of social dialogue nor beyond the hope of their prayers!"

Smiling, Natalyia took Stian's arm in courtesy of the moment. Moments later, she had completely forgotten her reserve toward men. Her fears and her recent jeopardy were gone! She felt so comfortable in his company. Images of his kindness, Renuel's high regard, his daughter's love for Isa and little Bella played in her mind. These bolstered her trust and regard for the man beside her.

As she took his arm, the pastor briefly covered her hand with his, patted it and quickly removed it. It was only a caring gesture she told herself; but the warm feeling of his touch sent a shock wave through her for which she was totally unprepared. A few minutes later Natalyia gently removed her hand from his and looked up at Stian.

"We do not want to trouble people's viewing of proper expectation of their Pastor; now do we, Sir? Also, it mayst frighten away ladies between age of six to seventy", she quipped mischievously.

The Parson chuckled but looked down at her with some surprise at her teasing manner. Again, he felt a bit befuddled in her presence and even slightly embarrassed.

And so, their brief walk was filled with conversation, some parts humor, some pathos, and some sharing of their history. The conversation flowed as though they were simply renewing a previous friendship. Both felt the ease of it; but both felt that to speak of it was to tread on sacred ground. In the course of their interchange some dark days were alluded to as life brings to us "the thousand natural shocks that flesh is heir to." Soon they turned to talk of lighter things, and some jesting about two ladies, in particular, in the neighborhood who had stared shamelessly at Natalyia.

He informed her, "Yes, the Lord knows that Berthe and Ebbe are his watchdogs for Linnea and me. Nothing gets past them!" Natalyia nodded and smiled, remarking that she thought even more ladies were out sweeping their sidewalks or shaking rugs than on their first pass.

"I must think those two ladies have proven their care of the Pastor's well-being and even told others of some danger to him!" She spoke, with a teasing smile and, as they were nearly to the door. She ran up the steps, like a girl, laughed lightly and turned around. "Come Pastor; it is time for coffee!"

He watched the lady so happily smiling and thought, *a cheerful heart does good like medicine. Well, she certainly is a tonic to my heart*!

He took the steps quickly and opened the door. They entered the house, parting ways inside the alcove. Stian was relieved that no one in the family had observed them come in or go out, especially Renuel. He didn't wish the young son to have any fears for his mother on his account. Johanneson headed for the kitchen and saw Marthe working.

"I'm back, any coffee for a double time walker?"

"Ja sure, Pastor. Such a long promenade deserfs two cups, I t'ink." Marthe was smirking and set down two cups of coffee.

Stian shot back, "Vell, aren't you 'ust a sleuth!"

Just then Linnea walked through the door and saw the two cups on the table.

"Oh, that other one must be for Mrs. Zupancic!", and she and Marthe laughed together.

Stian replied sardonically, "Well, such nosy intrusion is the nature of the Pastor's life!"

# Chapter 18

# Legal Evil

"You shall not side with the powerful
Against the powerless."

What had appeared to Evan Reinholdt as a minor road-block to securing the girl's acceptance had now become a viable threat. Renuel Breech was a wrench in his plans. His foray into the Johanneson family was growing daily. It had to be terminated and the attorney knew he had the power to effect it. Watching him leave the parsonage, on a day when Evan was stopping for a visit, gave him his opportunity. Parking his car, a half a block away, he waited on the other side until Renuel passed by.

Getting out, he followed the man for a couple of blocks; then closing the distance to a few feet, he called out, "Breech!" Renuel spun around instantly. Reinholdt was upon him. "You transient, immigrant bum, your game playing is over. You're in the way of my plans and no one ever gets in my way for long. I have drawn up papers to have that bastard baby removed from the Johanneson's into government custody. That will be final unless evidence of paternity can be placed before the court. Either you leave now, or I will file these documents. Why don't you admit your dalliance with the girl? Hoping for some action, aren't you, fool?"

Renuel felt a horrific rage surging; but his regard for the Johanneson's surfaced and caused him to quell it.

"Only a man, like you, has such low thoughts. That girl does not 'dally' with anyone." Renuel wouldn't give any other words of defense lest in anger, he disclose something about his connection to Bella.

Reinholdt's threats continued. "We both know that the Pastor and his daughter have no legal rights to that child. She is a ward of the state, just like any other abandoned infant."

The accused was silent but stared unflinchingly at his enemy. "You say nothing because you know there are no adoption papers. Did that woman ever write a letter signing her child over to them? Some have even charged that the 'no-name' child is the baby of the Parson's daughter!" He laughed wickedly as Renuel took a step forward with eyes that were black and threatening.

"Oh, I'm so afraid, Breech. You incriminate yourself by your silence. There is no possibility of such an accusation by me against the daughter. Everyone knows she wouldn't look at you twice, much less consort with such a low life. Don't be misled by her charitable nature; she knows your status and pities you. But taking pity on the likes of you will soon change. She'll learn better at my hands when I get her away from that parson father.

"Speak up idiot; or are you too ignorant to know your own defeat? You'd better be out of this city by Friday." He laughed again, but this was an unnatural laugh without humor.

They were cruel, strange sounds that seemed to come from a different voice than Reinholdt's. Renuel stood staring at him, stock still, hatred filling him. The man held all the cards in his hand. Fearing his own fury and knowing it would be of no use in fighting him, Renuel held his tongue.

Renuel turned sharply on his heel. After a few steps, he stopped, turned half around, speaking in an ominous tone, "I am leaving. But I give you counsel. From this day onward, look to your back, whether in the courtroom or out of it. I am not as friendless here as you might suppose."

Reinholdt guffawed again but a cold chill covered his body. Breech walked away at a slow and deliberate pace. His tall figure was indeed imposing. He would not flee nor would he utter another syllable to so unworthy a foe. Renuel knew that for now he was beaten, as were all ruled by power hungry men with no moral standards.

This time the despair was draining him of all hope for any future happiness. Linnea would believe he had turned his back on her and Bella. But Renny was also aware that either way, he would lose them both. No doubt that blackheart would contrive to gain her hand by manipulation with some dark scheme connected to his niece. Bella was safe now, if she stayed with Linnea, who would fight for her. He had to focus on that fact. He had to leave. He was out of options.

Renuel's head was pounding from the rage he felt. All he could see was the mocking face of Reinholdt. He kept walking, then turned onto an arterial and saw a bar on the other side of the street. Crossing over, he stepped into the doorway. The first form that he saw in the darkened room came sauntering over and slipped her arm through his.

"Well, if it ain't the new guy in town, looking for his true love; and here I am. Want a drink and some social life, handsome?" He stared dumbly down at her. But the loud music and brash voices within were strangely welcome, drowning out his tortured thoughts. His 'companion' led him to a table.

"I've heard about you stranger, right Pace?" He glanced over and saw the tattooed man from the jail. She added, "Heh, stranger, will you take a punch for me too!?" The woman laughed, giving a seductive lean into his body. "I've been longin' for a good man like you." She was dark-haired and very easy to look at but instead, Linnea's face flashed before him.

As Renuel sat there, barely hearing her flattery, thoughts of the Johannesons brought some semblance of calm. Those brief moments shamed him for his murderous thoughts. He had been reared better and his father would be saddened.

"Be angry and sin not Son," he often quoted.

He returned that evening fully intending to tell the Johanneson's that he would be leaving the next day for 'an employment opportunity'. A phone call from Pace that night made it imperative. His rugged friend tipped him off that two mafia types were asking about him at the bar. Early the next morning, after kissing his mother goodbye, he went in search of Linnea. He found her reading in the sunroom, which was her custom.

# CHAPTER 19

# THE WANDERER'S LOVE

"Fear it Ophelia: fear it my dear sister
And keep you in the rear of your affection..."

Wm. Shakespeare

Renuel stood stiffly and spoke in a formal tone. "I must tell you, Miss Linnea, I cannot remain here any longer. These weeks have been restorative for Mother and me. I will miss our times with Bella; but it is imperative that I leave today."

With maddening resolve and a slightly darker tone he replied, "You must remember, Miss, no one knows about my mother and me. It's part of our agreement. I was simply an agent for reuniting you with a dear friend."

"But we won't ever tell anyone who you are!"

"If I stay, there are those who may be watching, even now. Soon they will start asking questions, dangerous questions. These would almost certainly lead to disaster that would endanger both Bella and my mother. It could also threaten you and your Father."

"Of what danger do you speak, Mr. Breech, and from whom?"

"My mother's connection to our country cannot be revealed to the American authorities."

"Is she here illegally?"

"No," he replied, "Not exactly. But Zupancic is not her legal name. She has used it as a protection.

"Is Mr. Breech your real name then? No Miss Linnea, it is not." She knew that this spelled danger, serious danger, to Bella as well.

By this time in her life Linnea could usually control her emotions. It had always been difficult, and hard to keep herself in check. Since her earliest recollections, her runaway feelings had hurt others with her angry outbursts. Parental discipline had trained this youngest daughter to achieve much success in her struggle of the will. But today was not such a time! Where the baby's well-being came into question, she was combative and emotional. And now there was another layer, fear for a man she had come to care for in a way unknown even to her.

"What is it!", she cried. "Why would anyone care about a woman visiting our home? Is Bella Rene in danger because you two are in danger!" Her pitch grew higher and higher.

The fear and the passion in her voice lit a different sort of fire in Renuel. Linnea's flashing blue eyes and flushed face were intoxicating. They seemed directed to him personally. He had thought of her over and over in the months since he had arrived. Now, these past few weeks, his feelings had grown into a kind of enchanting torment.

They were in the sunroom, at the back of the house, facing the garden and the alleyway. Standing a small distance apart, Linnea approached Renuel, her eyes brimming with tears, anger now giving way to a fear of unknown danger. Greatly agitated she cried out, "Why are men so cruel?! Don't they fear God? Who would want to hurt a baby? Do you know who they are? Can't you protect her? You're her uncle! And now you're leaving again. It's your fault. I hate you for leaving me, and us! Why is God letting all this happen?"

Linnea had come closer and closer and was now staring into his eyes. Renuel was quite overcome with her nearness. He could smell her skin..., her hair! He wasn't thinking about Bella, his Mother, the present danger or where they were.

"Oh God, Linnea," he said, as he took her face in his hands. He wiped the tears and kissed each cheek. Through bleary eyes Linnea gazed into Renuel's deep, brown ones. She felt an abandon and a longing, such as she had never known. She threw her arms around his neck and he lifted her off the floor. They shared a tender embrace. It left him reeling, feeling something so real and eternal that it touched his tortured soul as nothing ever had. *Is this holy love?* This was his first thought but certainly not his last.

He held her briefly, his face against hers. Then gently he set her down. She lingered a bit but dropped her arms and blurted out,

"I am so sorry to have flung myself at you just now. Please understand that I am upset about the baby and I know that you also love her dearly. Forgive me for what I said. Bella is like my own baby and...", putting her hands to her face, she began to sob.

Renuel had said nothing as she spoke but stood gazing at her sweet face. His heart was still pounding from holding her and feeling his lips on her soft skin. Words left him, as they often did, in such intense moments.

*You are beautiful upon the mountains, my lovely one.* His grandmother's words surfaced but there was no time for Jewish love songs. *Or, was there? It seemed now or never.*

He took Linnea's trembling hand. "Dear Miss Linnea do not berate yourself. I was the one who acted first. We are both tied to the baby; and I took liberties with your strong feelings for her. Please accept my apology." Kissing her hand, he released it.

He would do anything..., lie, cheat or steal if at this moment he could assuage her grief and ease her tender conscience. He recognized he had taken liberties with this infectious girl. She was such a true heart. This he would never betray. He swore that he would make certain that she would feel vindicated in her own eyes.

Linnea had calmed down. Renuel's gentlemanly words and tender kisses were a healing balm. As a child would, she dried her tears by wiping them on her clothing. This touched Renny, remembering Isa's being scolded for it.

She spoke quietly, "I can only allow you to share part of the blame; for I needed comfort and you were there, at just that moment, doing your duty as a friend. I too took liberties and...; well, I had better check on Bella."

She was looking down, obviously disconcerted at her unfinished speech. She didn't dare look at Renuel.

"Miss Linnea, I am not as sorry as I perhaps should be. That was one of the high moments of answering 'duty's call.' May it please your God for me to be very near if you should ever need such a friend again."

Linney looked cautiously up and saw the playfulness in his eyes but felt certain there was also more. She smiled, stood on her tiptoes, and kissed his cheek.

"Thank you, kind Sir, for answering the 'call'." The lady laughed sweetly and then soberly said, "I fear you will be too far away should I need such a friend again".

Tears welled in her eyes. Renuel nodded slightly as his smile also faded. Shoving his hands into his pockets he turned to leave and thought, *God, keep her from loving me. I am a hopeless exile, a wanderer, a man without a country who is far from God. But, oh Christ..., how I love her!* He turned and looked once again at her beautiful face and form.

He shook his head. Staring straight ahead he walked out of the door and into the garden. He had never uttered that name before in an oath. But he did, however, remember voicing it in his youth as a prayer. His mind couldn't process why now he had used it profanely. It was such a sacred name to his parents and to her. Something moved in Renuel's heart. Even later it was something he could not fully explain. Perhaps it was sheer desperation but then he had an even more desperate moment.

Stopping and turning on his heel, he strode back through the garden and into the sunroom. Linnea was still standing there; she had been watching him. He noticed that she was trembling as he approached. He could not know that he had wooed and captured her maidenly heart. Renuel stood very close and, staring down, he pushed her hair back slightly and spoke with deep passion. "Linnea Johanneson, I love you. Never forget that. This fallen, damned soul will love you forever... even in Hell!" He kissed her passionately on her tremulous lips.

The girl cried out and pulled away, covering her mouth. He took her in his arms and held her tightly before releasing her. He could still feel her heart beating and the warmth of her body pressed against him. Renuel knew his passion had frightened her badly. But for one eternal moment; she was his. Linnea was afraid, but lifting her face, she said in a trembling voice, "I fear I may love you back, Mr. Breech; but you must trust God with your whole heart, or my heart can never be yours."

The would-be lover looked gently into her eyes and said, "Pray to your God for my hard heart, for Bella's safety and my mother's too. I fear you are lost to me now, my lovely Linnea." He looked longingly at her and left.

As Renuel strode out of the door and into the garden he thought wildly, *I know I betrayed her maidenhood with that kiss. But that moment with her was worth all the meaningless days of the past and, all of the ones which are to come. Even in perdition, with the vengeance of God that I deserve, I shall never cease wanting her.*

Then, again unbidden, these ancient words came to him..., *Enjoy the wife God has given you all the meaningless days of your life.* He shook his head and said bitterly, "But not for me, I can never have her, Grandmama."

# CHAPTER 20

# THE JUDGE

Evil men constantly stir up evil
plans, like the foam of the sea

"So, how is your little twit resisting the veritable charms of the 'Great Attorney Reinholdt'?" The judge enjoyed goading Evan because he held control of the man's upward mobility to the Judge's Bench. The right Honorable DeVant could risk a bit of the younger man's wrath. Although masked, there was plenty of it to be had. Wrath, waiting to be unleashed on the powerless, was well within the grasp of Reinholdt's legal control. Evan looked up with hooded eyes; lest he betray his fury.

"Oh, I'm just keeping her at bay. Don't want to show more than I feel…, may find her tedious rather than reserved."

"Her alacrity and wit may be her undoing then?"

The Judge laughed, without true humor, at catching Evan in his lie. The younger man cursed himself for revealing too much to DeVant, in the beginning, about his desires and Linnea's appeal.

He hated the truth and would accuse her of ignorance and naivete if it wouldn't make his choice of wives look bad later. Image and power were everything to Evan Reinholdt. The man was devoid of natural affection. For years he had exempted himself from all family connections with his own siblings and parents. They offered him nothing of what now mattered most to him.

"Cursed be to all women, a damnable gender, are they not? Isn't that what King Solomon said? He couldn't find a worthy one in a thousand." Now it was Evan's turn to laugh. The account of the ancient king crept back from a distant past of spotty church attendance. As a teenager he had wooed, with false pretense of piety, a lovely young girl that he was able to despoil. Then, leaving her with his child, he abandoned her and left religion far behind, never looking back.

"So, you'll have her by hook or by crook. Have had a few of my own such ladies, but why the damn marriage, man?!"

"You have had Judge, how about the present?" There were more snickers from both. "Of course, I must marry. It's the Christian thing. I do have a form of religion...; it serves me well Sir. You know her father is a religious man."

"Marry her then! Once you have legal control of her, the Parson is helpless." Evan had already descended to that depth but was pleased to have the judge in agreement. DeVant went on, "Humph..., and why not, there's no power behind it all. It's just a ceremony in a courtroom or a church. There's nothing to worry about and no one to answer to afterward. You do me justice, Reinholdt! Heh, heh, get it man..., justice."

More guffaws from the judge followed but barely a smile from Evan. *Stupid ass, it's he whom I'll soon replace. This is the charade that I play while biding my time.*" Evan further thought, '*His lifestyle is good heart attack material. DeVant is fat and self-indulgent.*

"Say Sir, here's that box of special fudge that you wanted."

"So, Evan, what of this other issue with that child you're protecting from the state? I can't indulge your whims indefinitely."

Attempting docility, Reinholdt replied, "No, of course not, you've been most generous, Sir. I think it's almost nailed down as to who will step in as the guardian of the child. Even I like to perform my civic duty and see justice prevail for the innocent."

The Judge looked askance at Evan. "Just remember, we want a lot of publicity on this; once I award custody. Too much suspicion of the system exists right now; especially by upstart lawyers who are trying to expose our foster care ineptitude. This is big money, top down, and we must keep it up and running. Yes, keep these 'no-name' kids in the system for life. Hold them 'til they're of legal age and then cast them out. They'll come running back, once they start breeding their own brats, and so; the dance goes on. It's money boy, and lots of it...; you hear? We must let a few infants and young kids trickle out for adoption. Makes us look like government benefactors of the less fortunate. It keeps the adoption façade up and running. Got it? I expect the same action from you with this kid; if you ever want my bench!"

"Got it...;" a strange smile and a look of malice came over the face of Evan Reinholdt as he thought of the power that he planned to possess one day. *But then he felt a chill come over him and a sudden terror. He shook it off as some nightmare, half-remembered, recalling only the feeling. Was it a warning of some kind? He had felt it before but neither knew nor cared, at least not at that moment.* For the likes of Evan Reinholdt, there would needs be a greater threat than just a bad feeling

Now, there was only one barrier left; and a sense of 'sudden terror' was not it. Only temporarily, of course, it was the Parson by whom he was bedeviled.

# CHAPTER 21

## SUMMER STOCK

"...And so, we strut our hour upon the stage..."
Wm. Shakespeare

Unable to resist the ad in the newspaper, Renuel found the address. The sign on the door read, 'Tryouts for Abraham Lincoln Show.' Acting was not the job he was applying for. He hoped to be behind the scenes for many reasons; but Renuel had to have work. They needed a stage manager which seemed manageable for him.

The advertisement had captured his eye because he was quite taken with Abraham Lincoln, the subject of the show. His father had often spoken, with admiration, of Mr. Lincoln and, as a young scholar Renuel had read quite a few of Lincoln's writings which were translated into his language.

The man's words had created a great thirst in him. Much of this stemmed from the integrity and humility which the President showed during a most challenging and difficult time in history. Being familiar with most of Lincoln's major addresses also drew Renuel to this production. Yes, he was qualified enough and at least it was a labor in which he could believe.

Knocking briskly on the stage door, it opened to a very uptown looking city girl. She wore heavy make-up (probably stage make-up) but was still pretty enough to wear it well. She looked vaguely familiar. Grabbing his arm, she pulled him in.

"Well, Handsome, don't just stand there; come on in." She looked critically at his face. "Don't know if we can damage you enough to look like Honest Abe; but at least your face is honest looking!"

She laughed and could tell that he didn't remember her. But she, on the other hand, certainly remembered him from the bar that night up North. It wasn't every day that her favors were turned down. "Abe", she called him, "We're desperate to fill that part. Our other man just dropped out, said the Gettysburg Address was too hard to memorize. And I'm your crazy wife; think you can handle me?" She laughed again, this time with a sideways look. "Come on; I'll take you to the boss. I'm Sophie."

Renuel hadn't said a word but suddenly; it looked like he was going to be an actor. His guide had long curly hair, almost black. On the side of her mouth she had a beauty mark which was not at all unattractive. The woman reminded him of a gypsy girl, like many he had seen in his own country. Those girls were beauties too and had certainly caught his boyish eyes. Sophie was no exception. She had a wild, untamed manner.

Some years ago he had read a story about a couple who took in a gypsy baby that was left on their doorstep. The story claimed they could never take the wild strain out of her. A feral creature she was; and this woman seemed much the same. He found his pulse a bit elevated.

He heard his own voice, "I think I can manage the speeches, Miss, but what other requirements come with this? I had preferred to be employed behind the scenes."

Sophie stopped dead and stared at Renuel, "Where in the world did you get that fancy talk?! Was it acting in Shakespeare or somethin'?" She shook her head. "Oh well, probably jives with the role but you'll only have 'til tomorrow night to learn your parts, tonight is the dress rehearsal; like my look?"

She put her hand on her waist and struck a pose, not a very 'President's First Lady' one either. He mused, smiling at her,

"Nice Miss." "It's Sophie, honey." She whirled back around to the door in front of her, opened it and smiled back seductively.

"Heh Ted, look what I found starving on our doorstep..., a fancy Aristocrat down on his luck. Think we can make this 'Handsome Abe' ugly in a hurry?"

The man, sitting with his feet propped on a trash can, had once been good-looking. Dissipation had taken its toll. His appearance, although he wore a suit, was mostly disheveled. His eyes were blood shot and he sported a beard of several days. The tie around his neck was loose. He kicked over the trash can and arose with some energy.

"I can't believe it!" He spread out his arms and looked up. "Maybe God cares about Ole Ted after all! Looks like Abe himself!" He leaned in, "Running from the cops..., pimp gone straight, hidin' from the 'old lady'?" He laughed roughly. "No matter, we'll make you up, so those honest eyes are all that's left of you.

So then, you're in?" Renny nodded, slightly dazed. "You get paid $25.00 bucks per show and you'll be doing three a day. Also, you will bunk here in the theater to help with stage props and scene changes. I can't afford a manager too!" "Sophie, he's even skinnier than Abe; get him some chili from the kitchen."

Sophie sauntered over and took Renny's arm. "I'll get him fed and cozy, Ted." She smiled coyly and Ted glared at her. The girl just laughed. "Come on, Sweets, I'll be nice, no charge this time."

Renny wondered what on earth he had gotten himself into. Amazing what desperation can bring forth! Still, he felt a bit euphoric as he didn't expect that he would get a place to live too. Looking at the appealing figure leading him, he thought with irony, *like a lamb being led to the slaughter.*

His father's words could be such a leveler at most inconvenient moments. "Okay, okay Father," he said under his breath with a smile. The girl stopped at a door and opened it, "Here's your room honey. I'll get you some supper."

The word 'room' was a bit of a stretch. He looked around. There was a bed with coil springs and a very thin mattress. They boinged when he pressed on the mattress. He had passed a latrine on their way. Sophie had pointed at it.

"Buy your own soap and towels after today." She looked at him, "Keep them in your room gent or they'll be gone," and she left.

The room was dark but there was a long, narrow window. He tried to raise the folded shade, but it leapt uproariously to the top. There was a small desk, with a chair, and a narrow closet with a curtain, half drawn. The chair was rickety. His legs didn't fit under the desk.

"Just like you, Mr. Lincoln," he smiled. "Need to get some glue," he said. "Well, home is home, be it a mansion or a hovel; make it yours."

These thoughts echoed his mother's words. She had lived in both types of dwellings and had made an appealing home out of either kind. But what he needed now was a broom and a dustpan, not flowers.

# CHAPTER 22

# CURTAIN CLOSES

"When one does not do what needs to be done,
there is very little else to be done."

Geo. MacDonald

Weeks passed and Renuel began drawing in full crowds for each performance. Perhaps only in this performance would he have shown so well as an actor. For indeed, he played the role so convincingly that it was difficult to separate him from the historical figure he portrayed. Even Ted was often spellbound and would stand, staring at Renuel.

The actor was believable not only because he looked the part but because he truly believed in the life of the man he portrayed. The lines he had memorized by Abraham Lincoln were filled with 'living words.' These words were shaping and molding him.

Also, mainly from his attentions, the theater, including the halls and latrine, were now clean and orderly. Ted began coming in shaved and having his tie neat and snug up to his neck. Renny also made sure that he kept the bathroom supplied with towels and soap, as well as toilet paper. The cloth towels were kept clean from his frequent trips to a nearby laundry mat.

Sophie shook her head one day and said, "Sucker, you are such a sucker Abe. Why do you do it? Nobody thanks you; they don't care."

He shrugged his shoulders, "Mr. Lincoln haunts me at night if I don't do it." He laughed at her incredulous expression as she walked away.

The summer season was nearing its close. There had been one fly in the ointment for Renny all these weeks. It was Sophie. She never let up. Sidling up close to him she would say, "Come on; let's make a dishonest Abe out of you tonight. I am your wife, after all!" Laughingly she would continue, "You know you want to. I see it in your 'honest' eyes."

She would then smile provocatively, her own black eyes snapping with the fire of desire that she had. She continued even further, "I know you don't have a lady love; you're here almost all the time. Well…, except for your 'holy day', huh?" So, how about some 'holy love'? After all, I don't have a lover right now either."

In soft tones she would say, "Savin' myself for you. You're the best; it's only the best if it's going to be Sophie's man! One man at a time, that's been my motto; but now you're my 'man for all time'! I'll help you forget whoever yer pinin' for. I know men like you. Let me be your 'one woman'. She doesn't want you, baby, and I do!"

That statement affected Renny the most. *She doesn't want you,* played over and over in his mind. Linnea's image was a motivator to bring beauty to his stark surroundings. He tried to avoid thoughts of her. It was an impossible fantasy. *But, oh God, how he loved her!*

One afternoon he was sitting on a wooden bench at the back of the theater. He had just returned from a long Sunday walk. Some Saturdays he attended a local synagogue. Afterwards there was often an empty feeling and he felt cast down.

"It's those dry bones, Renny; they must have flesh to live. And then, they'll need the Spirit in order to live forever. Never forget that Renny." Almost like a mantra, his father had said this to him.

Sophie found him there. Wrapping her arms around his neck, the beautiful temptress softly said, whispering into his ear, "Come, sleep with me. No one will ever know. Everyone's gone for the day."

Renuel looked down on her beautiful face and brash expression. She was seductive and intense. Her lips brushed his; they were soft and warm. The blood pounded in his chest. *Good thing we aren't in a more private place*, he thought with his eyes glancing around.

Kindly, but firmly, he unwrapped Sophie's arms. Touching her lips with his fingers he spoke, "But I would know Sophie. I fear your comforts cannot last. You know that new song you sang, 'When I fall in love; it will be forever?' Thanks anyway Soph, best thing that's happened to me all day."

She stared at him, tears in her eyes. "Whoever she is, she is one lucky b____!"

Renuel squeezed her hand and walked away, his whole being fighting desire. Coming to his room he locked the door and wished he could throw the key out of the window.

Renuel Breech left a week later when the show ended.

# CHAPTER 23

# DREAMS AND VISIONS

"Let your reach exceed your grasp;
else what's a heaven for."

Robert Browning

One evening, some weeks after Linnea's confession, Stian could not resist Natalyia's companionship any longer. She had entered the living room, with Linney, chatting about Bella. He waited a few moments, and approaching her, he queried, "Mrs. Zupancic, the night air is quite mild; and I see on the ground the snow still sparkling. It is most unusual to have snow already and it will soon disappear. Would you consider taking a short wintry walk?"

This struck Linnea as a bit odd as she had not observed his being interested in their guest that way. (Oh youth, too taken up with self to see pain or delight in others.)

Natalyia looked at the girl and then at the father with a playful expression. "Only if the pastor give promise to find an icicle to eat and also form a ground angel." She laughed lightly at their surprised faces. "You have not done so here?"

Linney smiled and nodded, "Oh yes."

Stian responded with a grin and a twinkle in his eye. "We Americans only know how to make 'snow' angels; but if that is acceptable, I will readily agree to your terms Madam. But only if the icicle is not yellow!"

It took Natalyia a minute to process his words; and she smiled at Linnea." "Father," the daughter rebuked, "That isn't a very proper comment around ladies."

Their guest chimed in. "Oh, do not worry Miss; if my son were here, he would give a great laughter!" Everyone became momentarily quiet but Johanneson was not to be put off from his intent.

"Well, shall we brave the elements then?" Stian and Natalyia quickly bundled up and Linnea found boots for their guest. Her father had saved an especially nice pair of black leather ones from his wife's things. Kirsten had loved winter so much and he couldn't quite part with them. Now that their daughter was grown, they were too small for her as she was taller and larger in frame than her mother. Mrs. Zupanic slipped into them easily, even with thick socks provided by her young hostess.

Her father winked and smiled over Natalyia's bent figure. Then he put his finger to his mouth, shaking his head. Linnea understood and nodded, with a slight smile, feeling a sudden "sadness not akin to sorrow" pass over her mind.

The lady's mention of Renuel had already played into her thoughts as well. Immediately his face and tall form came before her like a motion picture. She felt jarred by the strength of the image. Renuel..., it was always he that she saw at unexpected moments and in her dreams.

These images filled her with longing and a pining, like homesickness. It had been like this ever since their first encounter; as though she already knew him and now, with his being gone, something was no longer right in her soul. Something was missing, an empty spot, but why..., what was it? To be truthful with herself she knew it wasn't 'something', but rather 'someone'. That 'someone' was her 'Wanderer'. It was the haunted, hunted man who had invaded her girlish dreams and emotions. It could not be denied; but should he be allowed to remain?

"Oh, dear Lord, have you brought Renuel here only to trouble my foolish heart? Is it a test? Or, have I ceased to know your voice, to be your friend? I feel so alone. You are so silent; and I am so sad. Are you mad with me?'" It was an expression she had used as a child which her father and mother had adopted.

Walking to the window Linnea brushed back the linen curtain. She watched her father and Mrs. Zupancic walking and talking, laughing like two old friends. The girl sighed deeply and let some tears fall. Linnea knew her father thought highly of their guest but still had no notion of the depth of feeling he held. Stian had never given any indication that he would remarry but neither had he stated he would not. It had made his offspring a bit sad for him. But inwardly, they were mostly relieved. She and Marthe had talked about it and had agreed that it would take a mighty unusual lady to get past Marthe. She guarded her 'master' like the Viking warrior she was! Linney smiled at the thought.

The two walkers had rambled off. Leaving the scene at the window, she made her way to the music cabinet. It was a song she had often played on their old piano. She took out a piece of aged sheet music. It was a sweet old song she had liked; but the words were now sharp as a cold wind in her face. "When I grow too old to dream, I'll have you to remember." She hummed the tune and finally sang the lyrics of the last phrase. "...Your kiss will live in my heart." She blinked back tears and said softly, "Probably good I don't have a piano anymore..., too sad."

Marthe stood by the doorway, just back enough to be hidden. She shook her head sadly. "Poor 'ting. Vell, she vill ust haf to 'gar hjem' to her God for t'e comfort of t'e Holy Spirit."

It has been decreed that sadness can be a comforter; the enchanting melody and the words wove a sweet spell over her. Linnea Johanneson's dreams were tender and happy that night. But those dreams would be put to the test much sooner than she would have wished.

# CHAPTER 24

# PERDITION'S PATHWAY

"But him being often reproved...
Shall be cut off and that without hope."

E van Reinholdt had carefully chosen his path to power; but his present destiny was a pathway leading to perdition. So far, that downward way was hidden from him by his own will. He had subjugated nearly all reproofs that disagreed with his agenda. His past conversations with the Pastor were the one thing that still plagued him. He had blanked them out so repeatedly that if they surfaced; it was barely in a whisper. Those visits were now like a long-forgotten dream, hardly even an impression remained.

And so, in his obsession to possess Linnea, he had stilled the voice of conscience and he was cut off from even guilt. The vacuous feeling troubled him, for a while; but then he cursed even the memory of self-reproach. Slowly, masterfully he worked at his concern for Bella's future, and had crept into the inner circle of the parsonage. He also feigned, with conviction, his alarm over Renuel's disappearance.

"I have alerted several of my law enforcement connections here in the city and have even crossed state lines to keep on the watch for your missing friend. I know they will contact me should there be any news of his whereabouts. But most importantly, let us continue to work at securing your legal guardianship of little Bella."

He thought distractedly as the dark-haired guest passed by the doorway to another room. *That woman, is absolutely impenetrable!* Though he kept his countenance, his frustration was mounting. Even in all these weeks he had not so much as cracked her sober veneer with a smile.

It really wasn't as odd as he surmised; since she rarely came into or remained in the same room he occupied. Nevertheless, he felt it more because of being dismissed by her. No woman had permission to dismiss the charismatic powers of Attorney Evan Reinholdt!

His hostile mind went on. *Only the Parson seemed to have her confidence. Were they lovers? They demonstrated none of the usual signs. But doubtless she was his cagey, long-time paramour, now boldly in residence as a 'kept' woman. But why not marry her? Johanneson was a priest and it seemed a bit risky to dance around mores. Oh, of course, it made him look pious; that was it! Well, let the 'good' parson have his 'dirty little secret,* he sneered. *Might come in handy,* and he filed it away in his reservoir of evil intents. *She is beautiful and not much older than me. The woman might do for a 'one-nighter', now and then, especially if he threatened to expose their unholy secret.* Evan smirked. His eyes were hooded; and he thought, *I'm not soon to be a judge for lack of savvy.'* He almost licked his lips as he thought of their illusive guest.

"What makes you smile that strange way?" Linnea's look was questioning and her voice troubled.

"Oh, nothing for your feminine ears, little lady; just a bit of legal wrangling. Always working on a plan, you know, for the baby's well-being, of course."

Linnea turned away, still with a frown, and spoke something to Bella who was playing at her feet. The woman, in question, entered the room with a message for Johanneson. Acting very proper, she spoke to him, but in an undertone.

*Oh yes*, mused Reinholdt, *the woman acts guarded even around the host, but in her voice and eyes is a softness that bespeaks trust, and more, no doubt. Fools, do they think they are getting away with their insipid affair.* His desire for Natalyia was based only on lust aroused by her attention to another man as well as her continued indifference to him. He was thusly mastered by his passions, a slave to them; not a free man at all, as he perceived himself to be.

Available women were a bore to him and therefore Linnea was also simply prey. Reinholdt saw himself as a conqueror and that included any women who challenged him. An indomitable spirit or inscrutable superiority, no matter the reason, was intolerable and he would have his way. What he could not know nor comprehend was holiness and its power. That would undo him. It, one day, could be his undoing but also his only possible road to salvation.

Are men, like Evan, nameless debauchers, drunk with power and wealth, beyond redemption? It was said by one who knows men's hearts, "How difficult it is for a rich man to enter the kingdom of heaven...but with God nothing is impossible."

He turned, with a benevolent smile, to redeem himself with his young quarry. "Don't fret yourself, Miss Linnea. My plan to secure Bella is developing nicely."

The visitor's voice was calm and confident, with an almost intimate ring to it. The girl had now become accustomed to his visits. He always came under the guise of giving free, legal counsel concerning the custody of Bella. Her nanny was desperate; and he seemed their only option to settle this critical matter.

Linney's father seemed detached and even unconvinced that there was any immediate danger. He told his daughter privately that he would go and talk with Judge DeVant, if it came to that.

They were loosely acquainted through his wife who attended Johanneson's services. Even with her place in society, she was a sad, lonely kind of woman. But Stian knew Linnea was not assured of anything when it came to the baby.

Evan held out his arm, "Here, let me take the darling thing. I have treats for her."

Bella took somewhat to Evan once she grasped that he would always bring her something nice to eat and sometimes an expensive toy. He had done so that day, much to the protests of all, especially Marthe. Evan gave her another treat which brought a frown to Linnea's face.

"Poor little fatherless child. I talked with a judge friend of mine and, and with some difficulty, secured a stay of hearing. That hearing will determine her placement into foster care. Then, an investigation will be made first into any suitable surviving kin, of course. After these legal efforts have been expended; she will be open for adoption."

"But no kin have surfaced." Linnea spoke anxiously, "We are her caretakers. She wouldn't be taken from us and given to just anyone, would she?!"

Evan replied blandly, "Well, that is a great concern, of course. Let us hope it will not come to that." He then smiled, like a knowing benefactor.

Stian asked calmly, "Who is this judge? I know a great many in local government here. Perhaps I can speak with him." Evan replied quickly, too quickly the parson thought. "Oh well, good Reverend, professional courtesy you know. No revealing of names in the judicial world. Kind of like the church, no doubt."

"Not exactly, we share the names of professionals who have influence and may be able to aid one in need."

"Yes, of course, in the church", Evan mumbled. He kissed Bella and held on to her. She reached for Linnea and he offered the child yet another cookie settling her back into his lap. Marthe had entered the room with a tray of drinks and Natalyia was still present.

"Worry not, Miss Johanneson. I have the judge in my back pocket, so to speak." Here he winked at Johanneson whose expression remained unchanged. Evan changed his affect to a serious one then. "He will respect my plan to provide a suitable place for our dear baby girl that is close to home."

He smiled knowingly at Linnea. She smiled in return and could not help but feel grateful to this man for keeping Bella with them and out of the court system. His attentions toward the baby seemed excessive, but genuine. And now, his hint at her future 'close by', felt like a lifeline.

Marthe let out a less than quiet "humph" and came over and took the infant saying, "Enough treats for t'e shild, time for a rest." She turned suddenly, leaving the room and carrying the baby with her. Evan saw a look pass between Johanneson and their guest and a there was a slight smile on both faces. It only added fuel to his fire.

Stian had noted that Mrs. Zupancic did little and said less, other than the correct social amenities, whenever Evan stopped. These she did with grace and a pleasant affect, and as now, after saying to him, "Good evening to you, Sir"; she left the room.

The Pastor thought wryly, *no doubt that lady is also an experienced judge of character.* Natalyia never spoke about Reinholdt after his visits but wore a clouded expression at any mention by Linnea of his plans for Bella's care. This caused Linney to inquire one day about her opinion of the attorney. She demurred by saying, "I do not know him, Miss Linnea, so my opinion is of no importance. I will trust in Pastor Johanneson for this knowing of him."

Linney had already observed that their guest never sought any audience with the lawyer. It annoyed her and troubled her as it mirrored her own repressed cautions.

However obvious his failures with Natalyia were, Evan tried another tactic to ingratiate himself to the family. He attempted many forced interactions with Marthe. He would enter the kitchen, speaking large flatteries about her pastries and breads, telling jokes and laughing loudly. The housekeeper spoke mostly in monosyllables as she served him dutifully, then excused herself to household business.

"One day 't'at man", as she called him, brought her very expensive perfume and she accepted it with a dull "takk". 'Only for t'e baby's sake', as she said later. After he had left, she stuck it behind the kitchen curtain, near the outer edge of the windowsill. "Vell, ve'll see about t'at!"

Linnea thought, at the time, *that eighty-dollar bottle of perfume isn't long for this world!* She left the room, shaking her head and giggling softly.

# CHAPTER 25

# WEAVING OF A SWEET SPELL

"...Say I'm weary,
say I'm sad,
Say that health and wealth
have miss'd me..."

Leigh Hunt

The almost mythical scene before her cast Natalyia back to a faraway place. But it bespoke the present as well as the past, bringing with it an unnamed wonder. The lady breathed deeply and long of the crisp air, uttering words in her own language. Looking back, seeing her companion, she lifted her arms with hands outspread, catching the snowflakes.

"Oh bellisimo...!"

Stian was so taken with Natalyia exclaiming about the beauty before them that he could only gulp slightly and smile. There was a sparkle in her eyes and she looked into his, and then, she turned in a circle. The snow, falling and glistening under the streetlights, floated down on her dark hair, shimmering like a jewel-studded veil. She stopped turning, still enraptured by the setting.

He gazed at her. *Take a deep breath, old man; she isn't seeing you through eyes of love. It's the snowfall that's bedazzling her!* Stian had known well another woman who had a childlike delight with winter. Natalyia's ecstasy took him back there, but in a sweet and touching way, very unlike the sense of aloneness at other such moments, without his wife. *This lady fills my senses with such gladness, there's no room for sorrow,* he mused. *Ah Kirsten, you would have loved this too*

Natalyia's voice broke into his brief reverie. "Pastor, my country is also beautiful, like this, in winter season". She was slowly turning again, her gloved hand catching the snowfall. She laughed and cried out with delight. Stian enjoyed her abandonment. It was at that moment he realized Natalyia had a defined lilt in her affect.

He commented on her statement. "Someday, Natalyia, sometime, I would very much enjoy seeing your country; when it is safe again for you, of course."

She stopped abruptly and stared at him. He feared he had overstepped. But instead, his caring words excited an unexpected response. She clasped both of her hands around his tightly, her eyes alight.

"Oh Pastor, I would so ask the Great Father of good gifts to give such a request an answer of "yes". You know Pastor Johanneson, God is the maker of each of careful snowflakes. None is same in beauty or form though millions of millions fall. Surely, He could give to us the good thing your words have offered. I will pray for that being His will and Divinity gift to me and in some time, you meet some of our people."

Natalyia was so happy. It seemed they had stepped into a world that was all their own. He was afraid the spell would soon be broken. Still, a peace pervaded him. She had been able to think on the beauty of the life that she had lived in her country. Obviously, those memories included her life with her husband, Isa, Renuel and others that were joined in their struggle. Stian well understood this strange juxtaposition of love lost, yet still most endearing in memory.

After her words, which were more like a prayer, they began walking again, this time more in earnest.

"Eye hath not seen, ear hath not heard, neither hath entered into the heart of man the things that God hath in store."

Something about this moment must have brought that sacred script to his mind. He had spoken them quietly enough, he thought, but Natalyia must have also heard and recognized them.

"Do you believe those words, Pastor?" She asked this in such an unguarded way that Stian overcame the temptation to answer back with a question of his own. Often, this was his way of helping a seeker to look within themselves. But instead, he answered sincerely just as she had asked him.

"Yes, Mrs. Zupancic, yes I do. The time of unknown worlds and dominions is yet to come. Still, even now, there are wonders already in place for us right here." Looking at Natalyia's upturned face made him muse, *Lord, I am not awaiting the 'trumpet call' quite as much I was before Natalyia came here. I am not in quite as much of a hurry for the end of time Lord; still lots of lost souls, correct?! I hope to enjoy the here and now for a bit!* Smiling guiltily at his self-oriented thoughts, he turned back to their conversation.

"Oh...," she had responded to his answer. She was quiet for a few moments. "Galena used to say that also too, even inside the prison wall." Stian was silenced momentarily by her words. The image of her husband's detainment left him somewhat undone and feeling much beneath this slain Christian man.

His lovely companion looked over, slight tears in her eyes. "Would you do a small thing of request for me?"

"Of course, Mrs. Zupancic, anything...," and he wanted to add, *up to half of my kingdom!*

"Would you say my name please?" He was puzzled at her request, wondering if it were a test or if he had misunderstood.

"Your whole name? I am not certain that I know it, Mrs. Zupancic."

"No, just Christian name, given me."

He smiled kindly, "Most gladly." He paused, unexpected emotion surfacing. Natalyia," he said evenly and then, in a tender voice, repeated "Natalyia."

"Ummm...," she responded. "I do like hear you speak my name. It makes me feel still a person with name and life of history, spoken by a friend true and good."

(She had heard so many guards and interrogators shout, "Natalyia Zaplavnov!", in her face, demanding information or with lechery in their eyes, or even just yelling it out for prison roll call).

These were not her thoughts, at present, even though they were often in her subconscious or in her nightmares. The longer she stayed at the Johanneson's, the more distant would these sinister visitations become.

The woman stopped walking. "I have lost so much; I sometimes feel lost even to myself." She spoke those words in her own language. Then, to Stian she simply repeated, "It is good to feel I am Natalyia in this place and company."

The trust in her eyes, as she looked up at him, filled her companion with emotion. He resisted expressing explosive words of love. Instead, he placed a strong arm around her shoulders. Without releasing her, he looked down and kindly said, "I am so sorry, Dear Natalyia, for all your suffering. You are very brave. You are also very beautiful in God's eyes and in those of many others I hope to meet."

She did not return his embrace but remained close and said something that he did not understand. Someday, he might ask her. He imagined it was, *Stian, you are so strong and handsome. I wish to stay this way forever, and then kissed him!* "Umm," came from Stian with a half chuckle.

Natalyia heard him and said, "What is of humor?"

"Oh, I was just thinking how the icicles will taste."

She pushed away, laughing and grabbing his hand, and said, "Come then."

# Chapter 26

# Snowy Night

"...Say I'm growing old, but add
Jenny kissed me."

Leigh Hunt

They walked on and the snow kept falling. Stian had desperately resisted his longing to tell her, *"I love you Natalyia Zupancic and I would love saying 'til death do us part." Didn't the Brits also add, "With my body, I thee worship?" Better not go there, Old Man,* he mused with a smile.

Instead, he remembered her recent plight. Not only that alone, but also the death of Isabella, the disappearance of Renuel and now her present insecurity; all of this must weigh heavily upon her. *No, now was not the time; God would not bless this yet. He had felt it, with certainty.*

They had walked in silence, but it was a charmed, glad silence. Now, he spoke. "Natalyia, my dear friend, of course I will gladly speak your name whenever you wish it; and it would please me greatly if you would call me Stian as well, if I may be so bold."

She smiled, thinking, *he was bold, but in a strong and honorable way. Then she shuddered, thinking of how Boris had stared up and down at her. His lust was not even hidden. Did he not know she saw his evil intentions and was repulsed? This man had never looked so at her. In fact, he often avoided looking at her at all, for which she was relieved.* But she was a bit curious, being a woman, of course.

"Thank you Pastor Stian."

"Just Stian," he interjected.

She smiled saying, "I will, but perhaps not in the presence of others. That could offend or..."; she stopped there. *"Stian", he was elated to hear her speak his name without the 'Pastor'. It felt so real and intimate. Even more exciting to him were her words, "Not in the presence of others". This gave him hope that there would be more such walks, 'not in the presence of others', but just with her. He felt the old giddiness come over him again. For so many years that feeling had been absent, but recently; it was quite frequent. What was it,* he mused, *A crush, excitement, anticipation or could it be love? Whatever it was; it surely didn't hurt! Smiling, he was just glad for it.* What Stian Johanneson did not then fully know was that the weight of his grief was lessening in her presence.

He pointed ahead, "Look, there are some icicles. I think they are high enough." She laughed with delight as he broke them from the street sign. They each began to lick theirs.

"Very good and cold, but why must they have taste of dirt?" Stian gave a hearty laugh. He had just been trying to identify the taste himself.

"Heh, this was your idea, young lady." And so she was to him..., and young at heart as well.

They looked at each other and, almost simultaneously, threw down their icicles, she, with a "Yuk!" Continuing, they came upon an empty lot. By now the snow had gotten quite deep. It was at least four to five inches. On a boyish impulse Stian grabbed her shoulders from behind and she started going down.

She called out a, "Heh!", laughing. He lowered her gently onto the snow.

"Okay, dear lady, it's snow angel time."

She was a bit shocked but looked up, smiling while she lay in the snow. Natalyia watched him lie down, a few feet away, giving them room for flailing arms and legs. After making their impressions, they lay very still; both trying to figure out how to get up without disturbing their snow angels.

Looking at each other they laughed, realizing their predicament. She was ten years younger, tall and rather agile. She started the delicate process of rising. She was careful.

When turning and groaning to rise, Stian laughed as he felt the full sixty years of his life while pushing to get up. She was smiling indulgently and offered her hand.

"Here Pastor, or I mean Stian. I will be kinder than you and give you help in rising."

"Oh, thank you, madam." He took her hand but mischievously grabbed her arm and pulled her down again.

She squealed, "Oh..., you ruining winter angel."

She turned and scooped up two wet handfuls of snow and threw them.

"Oh good, a snowball fight; this is where I will be the victor!" He thrust a quickly formed snowball at her. Natalyia grabbed more handfuls and pitched them. "Alright, now I must do penance, dear lady." He offered his hand, which she gingerly took, smiling lest he trick her again. He began brushing off his coat; then turning her around said, "Here, your back is covered; I'll help!" As gently as possible, he brushed the clinging snow from her shoulders and back.

"My turn now Stian!" Turning his big frame around, she began beating off the snow, crying out enthusiastically, "I will help you!"

He laughed, "Heh, are you trying to get even?"

She called over his shoulder, "What is even?"

"Never mind, dear lady, you've given me what I deserved; I guess."

"Yes, you do have deserving of a beating!" They continued to brush themselves off chatting good-naturedly about their ruined snow angels; but Natalyia's was still quite intact.

"Natalyia, let's go and warm up with some hot cocoa at the café near here. Would you like that?"

"Yes," she happily replied. I would like something warm but this drink...; I do not know of it."

They walked there quickly and hung up their coats. Natalyia was delighted with the warm cocoa. They spoke of many things, and in some depth. Speaking of Renuel's whereabouts brought tears to her eyes.

"Would you mind if I prayed for your son?" She nodded and Stian prayed a brief entreaty for Renuel's safety. They grew silent and Natalyia spoke.

"Pastor Stian, I am trying to believe that those times of joy that "eye hath not seen, nor ear heard" are for now, as well as the time to come. You are helping my doubts to grow small with the days passing by. Thank you for prayers."

She smiled a lovely smile at Stian as they left the café. It seemed a bit chillier now as their coats were damp. But the Parson's heart was warm. He asked if he could put an arm around her as she was shivering. She gave him a grateful nod. They walked briskly now, the snow glistening under the streetlights.

Pausing at the front door, Natalyia raised herself slightly, put her flat hands against Stian's chest and kissed him on the cheek. Her lips were warm on his cold face and lingered there just slightly.

She spoke, "Thank you for happy times and being winter friend, even if pushed down in snow." She smiled. "I am glad for this place of home, Stian." She spoke his name distinctly. He smiled broadly.

Looking into her eyes he said, "You are most welcome Natalyia. With such a reward as you gave me, I will endeavor to make two winter angels next time Natalyia." She laughed gaily, fully grasping the meaning of two kisses.

Her expressions of being glad for their home were simply said in her version of English. It all seemed fresher and dearer than if she were fluent.

As they entered the house they were greeted by Linnea and then Marthe. She immediately scolded him for getting their guest wet with snow.

"Vell, dis is t'e vay to catch pneumonia for t'e bot of you!"

Natalyia smiled at the housekeeper as she remonstrated Stian. Then, she thanked Marthe for her care, in a slightly pathetic voice, but with a twinkle in her eyes. Stian shook his head at Natalyia's theatrics but left smiling and feeling very happy as he felt again Natalyia's warm lips on his cheek.

"Then she left a kiss..., and it was better still for ripening in that air." Those words kept running through his mind.

CHAPTER 27

# UPON JULIA'S CLOTHES

"...Next, when I cast mine eyes and see
That brave vibration, each way free,
Oh, how that glittering taketh me."

Robert Herrick

Pastor Johanneson had observed the ministrations by Evan
Reinholdt towards his daughter and Bella. Being a forgiven man, he hoped, more than believed Evan's words as he
claimed regret for his former behavior.

That he was seemingly tireless in his work on their behalf
was evident. At times he thought the truth of his past had
broken through to Evan; but then he would see that hardness
of heart return. He may have had regrets, but no true repen-
tance. Stian wondered also who had reported little Bella's presence in their home to the welfare bureau. Reinholdt had now
been placed in a position to protect them from her removal;
or so he said.

In addition, there was also the pall and mystery of Renuel's
sudden disappearance. Stian couldn't shake the sense that

somehow it was tied to Reinholdt. Renney's last conversation with Linney deepened his suspicions. He could see clearly that his daughter had been very emotionally affected. He wondered what things about her and Renuel's talk she had kept to herself.

They had a ground rule in their home as well. It had been there with her sisters and now; it was also with her. This rule underscored no romance with anyone of differing beliefs concerning salvation. Their parents believed it was a certain road to unhappiness. "Don't be unequally yoked...," was somewhat of a joke in their house and they all knew it referred to would-be or real suitors.

Stian had studied the man and had communed with his mind and soul. He was very taken with Renuel and saw qualities that he would want for his daughter. His reluctant embrace of Christianity, if an embrace at all, did concern him deeply but somehow; he would not remonstrate Linnea for her affection for him. He had spoken enough to her on the topic for now.

His mind shifted to Natalyia. It grieved him to see the lilt she had begun to demonstrate recently falter. But today was different. She came out of the kitchen wearing an amused expression. She began to set the dining room table, humming a happy melody. Linney called out something to her that made her laugh. But quickly she returned to her duties and her song.

Natalyia was unaware of the pastor's careful eye as she moved from buffet to the table, humming as she placed things in preparation for the evening meal. Of her tune Stian caught only snatches, but thought, *how beautiful are the simple movements a woman has, preparing a table; but how much more particularly I admire this woman's grace and style!*

Smiling, he dutifully lowered his eyes and began his own work of outlining a sermon, lest he forget himself. A while later the Pastor felt a gentle hand on his shoulder. It brought him back from a particularly poignant passage in the Book of Ruth. It was about a game changing night on a threshing floor. Ruth and Boaz were the characters. Ruth was the widow in penury and Boaz, a bachelor, was her nearest kinsman redeemer. This scripture text was the passage for his Sunday's Sermon. What an irony for him now, as he looked up into the face of their own resident widow. Natalyia's dark eyes stared into his, showing concern.

"Here Pastor, I have brought your afternoon coffee. Dear Friend, you look so weary. God will bring you what you so desire. You must rest now from your thoughts and visions." She smiled indulgently, with a sweetness that pierced his heart. Patting his shoulder lightly, she turned and walked away.

Stian watched her go and whispered to himself as his shoulder tingled, "Lord, may 'what I so desire' be just as she has said." A broad smile covered the aging, but handsome face of Pastor Stian Johanneson.

# CHAPTER 28

# LINNEA'S HEARTACHE

"...But Colin only looked at me,
and never kissed at all.
Strephen's kiss was lost in jest,
Robin's lost in play,
But the kiss in Colin's eyes,
haunts me night and day."

Sara Teasdale

Not so sweet were Linnea's daily emotions with Renuel Breech's sudden departure. After several months she was growing more and more distracted. She realized that she was grieving over the loss of his presence and couldn't shake it. Many times, over and over, she replayed their last minutes together. His dark eyes and haunted expression filled her with confusion and longing. His words and caresses troubled her, making her heart pound. Words like, "Oh God, how I love you, Linnea Johanneson!" *Was that a swear word that he used or was he some sort of semi-religious guy who called on God that way?*

"Unequally yoked...," these were words with which she often grappled. Now, thoughts of Renuel made her feel strangely desperate and ecstatic at the same time. Often, she had thrown herself on her bed, begging God to take away her feelings for him, but at the same time; she was terrified of losing him.

Marthe was her confidante. "Love shouldn't torment a person, should it Marthe? That seems wrong." This she entreated without using Renuel's name.

Her old caretaker only shook her head in pity and patted Linney's face, "Poor t'ing."

This terrible love had built such a fortress in the person of Linnea Johanneson that all other 'crushes' seemed empty. This was a totally new dimension of passion and desire. It rivaled her love for God. That was a frightening thing for the Christian heart of one like her.

Speaking out of desperation and despair one day, her voice became elevated and demanding, "Father, where is Renuel? I keep asking God to bring him back, but nothing comes of it. Why did he desert Bella and even his own mother? Can't you make him come back? How could he disappear without even a note or call regarding his whereabouts so we would know where he is! I do hate him for that!"

She shocked herself with those words; but it was out of her mouth, just as she felt it. By then she was crying; but even that angered her as she savagely wiped her tears.

"Dear Heart," she heard her father say as he handed her his folded handkerchief.

She shouted, "I don't need that! I'm not really crying! I won't cry! He...", she paused a full minute speaking quietly, "Doesn't deserve my tears."

Now her voice had a dark and ominous tone. Hardness was threatening to steal into her soul. The girl's head bowed. Her patriarch spoke gently but firmly; for he knew his daughter well. "Love and hate are strong emotions, Linney. I felt those more with your mother than with any other human being."

Linney jerked her head, "Father, how can you say that? You loved her more than anyone else in the world!"

"Love and hate can often be close sisters Linney. Are you sure it is only anger or hate that you feel for Mr. Breech? You have been a different girl since you met him."

In an empty voice she responded, "I promised God I wouldn't love him if he would just bring him back. Bella needs him Father."

"Only Bella?" Linnea looked up with the saddest blue eyes he had seen since her mother's death.

Taking her hand, he turned Kirsten's ruby ring round and round on her finger. "Do you think God disapproves of your feelings for Renuel?"

"Don't you disapprove of him, Father?" Stian was silent. Linney continued, "I don't know Papa. My heart…, my heart seems to be a part of his; like I've always known him!"

Her father flinched slightly, quite touched that Linney had regressed to her childhood use of 'Papa', without realizing it. His words were tender as he took her hand. "I don't object to Mr. Breech as a person; in fact, I am quite attached to him. However, that would not mean I think he qualifies as a husband at this time. What is evident is that he is in a spiritual struggle and he has much potential to be a godly man one day. I know that God's love for you and this 'wanderer' can be trusted, dear Linney."

"I don't know what God thinks about anything anymore, but I know what Mr. Breech thinks about God and it isn't very good. I don't even know what I think about God. Is He real? Does He even care about Bella and all of us?" She stood up, still holding her father's hand. Bending, she held it to her hot cheek and then gently released it.

"Remember, Linnea Johanneson, God already knows your thoughts. He is not shocked nor remote from your feelings of loss and confusion. Talk with Him; He is your friend, brother and father."

She nodded. "Goodnight Father, I shall try." The sad-faced girl kissed his cheek and walked away.

# Chapter 29

# A Word Arrives

...As old Time makes these to decay;
so, his flames must waste away.
But a smooth and steadfast mind,
gentle thoughts and calm desires,
hearts with equal love combined,
kindle never dying fires.
'The Unfading Beauty' Thomas Carew

The nights were slightly cooler so Stian sat before the fire in the drawing room. He had only a small lamp lit and was reading from a little book. It included the seven 'Divine Poems' of John Donne. He often reread them in the old English dialect just to bask in their antiquity and spiritual power. Johanneson was deep in thought when a quiet voice entered his consciousness. It was a voice he loved hearing.

"Pastor..., or Stian, excuse me; I do not wish to disturb your reading. But I feel it necessary for just some moments of speech with you."

Natalyia so rarely sought him out and it was all that he could do not to jump out of his chair to make certain she wouldn't slip away, like some phantom. *She was a phantom of delight...*; these words rushed through his mind. The powerful, but subdued man had immediately begun to rise; but the lady quickly sat on a chair near him.

She put out her hand. "Oh no, please sit. This conversation will be of a short space of minutes. I have concern about Renny; or I mean Renuel, my son."

"Dear Natalyia, Mrs. Zupancic, your presence is never disturbing, except perhaps to my heart." He smiled and touched his chest. "You always leave too quickly; and I fear that it will be some time before we talk together again, just the two of us."

"Thank you, you are always so amiable to my words, not quite properly spoken." She laughed slightly, "My husband used to incite me to practice my English so my many words would be fewer. He was a man of many words, and I, a woman of few, except with him."

Stian's blue eyes were dancing as he looked straight into Natalyia's brown ones and quipped, "He was a blessed man to enjoy much conversation with such an enchanting companion."

She smiled and looked down briefly, recalling how enrapt he had been as she told the tale of her escape from the clutches of the government. Of course, she omitted the fury of the love-crazed Russian Ambassador when she disappeared. Renuel had translated her story, as it was a bit long for her English to navigate.

In a private discourse Stian questioned Renuel as to how his mother had ever been released from imprisonment; for she had a death sentence hanging over her. He was then informed of the Ambassador's obsession.

The man had known both of Renny's parents for over ten years. He begrudgingly admired Galena for his courageous stance as a writer; for he always told the truth, no matter the cost. Though the Ambassador had him killed; he knew that with Zaplavnov's death went a trusted source of advice and counsel that would hinder his own traitorous work. Such strange bed fellows are villains and truth tellers!

Natalyia spoke in low tones, looking towards the dining area, as though some source of betrayal might be hanging about. "Renuel contact me through code letter with a return address only he and I know. He applied for worker visa and it denied. He then again did and risked use of true name, Zaplavnov; and it accepted. Pastor, someone notify authorities and they watch for a Renuel Breech. Who would do this?" Her face was drained of color and fear showed in her eyes.

Stian drew his chair a little closer, "Firstly, thank you for entrusting me with your real name, Zaplavnov. I will take great care to keep it secret and safe. I am also very grateful that you have heard from him. And yes, it is a bit strange that anyone would object to his applying for a simple work permit. Perhaps it was just a mistake and they would have taken his request a second time without any change of last names. I know that he has no record with the authorities under the name of Breech."

The lady looked up quickly, "How do you know Pastor..., er, Stian?"

"Because I know, having checked and seen nothing this entire past year. I paid for his bail when he was put into jail for a skirmish he had encountered. It was with a scoundrel who deserved a beating that he did not receive. The perpetrator withdrew all charges because he wanted no part of it on his own record; guilty as he was. Renuel's record with the police is clear; trust me for that!"

Natalyia looked puzzled with the story but smiled in relief. "Thank you for help to Renny; you always are good."

"No Madam, I can be eager or impulsive for others' good, but I'm not good; only God is good. I just wanted justice to prevail where justice was due. Renuel is a stalwart man, even if a bit of a skeptic. He'll come to the new birth in time. The 'hound of heaven' is in pursuit; and there is no escaping him."

"Yes, I know this poetry," she smiled sadly. "But then, why have this happened? I do not believe it mistake. I believe he has danger." Tears filled her eyes. How Johanneson wished to take her in his arms and comfort her. He grew more devoted daily. It had been many months since Renuel disappeared. Stian continued to have his suspicions about who was behind it. But the fact that her son had applied for a work visa was a good sign that he wished to go through proper channels and be legal in this country.

He did not wish to alarm Natalyia who had good reasons for her fears. As these thoughts surfaced, he quickly stood and offered her his hand. "Renuel is doing the right thing. He is acting in an honorable way. I am sorry for this incident that has caused you such concern. But, at this point, I believe that we can trust that it was a government error, since your son's record is clear. Tomorrow I will go to the Police Station and ask to recheck his file. I'll use some excuse about my having posted his bail and that I am still concerned lest he be attacked by the villain again."

She squeezed his hand tightly, "Oh thank you in a large way; that would relieve my mind to not be worrying. I would be happy to know of no record." As Stian heard her words a thought crossed his mind, *she has heard from Renuel before but has kept it silent. I am in the inner circle now. Thank you, Lord.*

He smiled and said gently," Let's pray for your son." Natalyia placed her other hand over his. It was such a tactile delight that Johanneson could barely concentrate on praying. He managed a short, but sincere petition for safety and the defeat of any plot that might be aimed at Renuel.

The lady sighed deeply and looked up at Stian. There were tears in her eyes, but also a smile.

"Let's trust Him together."

"Yes, thank you, Stian."

"Now, my dear lady, I believe it has been some time since we had a walk together. Coffee or hot cocoa would be a great tonic at our little café. It is early but it is still open. This is a fine month for a stroll; is it not? Besides, we must keep the neighbors guessing!"

Nattie laughed in relief. "Alright Stian, I believe right. It would be tonic in pleasant season. I am certain about ladies are still many to observe walk on the way." Her dark eyes looked up at him. He thought he saw a spark of something more than trust in them. Could it be? He then did something on impulse. Laughing, he drew her close and kissed the top of her head.

"There, that is in case either Berthe or Ebbe, my self-appointed caretakers are peeking through their windows and need some conversation points."

Natalyia laughed slightly, trembling at Stian's caress. Feeling this, he gently released her, but not before squeezing her hand again. She went to fetch her coat. As he assisted her with it, she spoke, "Oh Dear Pastor, I think passing shadow is out there!" She uttered these words with a lovely laugh.

Stian thought as they walked away, *now it's my time to tremble. Is she a marvelous creature sent by God to me; or a 'phantom of delight'? Can she be real? Oh, Dear God, let it be!*

# CHAPTER 30

# FUER ELISE AND THE SLOUGH OF DESPAIR

"...Has found out thy bed
Of crimson joy;
And his dark secret love
Does thy life destroy."

William Blake

And so, the conflicted thoughts of Linnea Johanneson continued. During the ongoing weeks her prayers for Renuel remained constant, but as to hopes; they were despairing. A certain resolve had taken hold of her. Perhaps Renuel Breech would never return; but she would not lose Bella, no matter what. Under that growing determination the attention to their plight, by Evan Reinholdt, made her feel more and more confused about her feelings for Mr. Breech.

One day a persistent knock came to the parsonage door. Two delivery men pointed to their truck and inquired about her name. They claimed to have a delivery for Linnea Johanneson. Bewildered, she called for her father and they walked out together. The men threw open the back doors of the truck and pulled off a large blanket. There was a beautiful, small grand piano. It was black and gleamed in the daylight. Linney gasped and her hand flew to her mouth as she looked to her father.

"No dearest, it wasn't me," he said, shaking his head.

One of the men smiled saying, "The buyer asked to remain anonymous. But if you are Linnea Johanneson; this is yours!"

"Oh, my word," was all she could say.

The men rolled it off the truck and into their living room. With Stian's instructions, they placed it where their other instrument had stood, but angled slightly outward. It was a lovely addition to an area quite unchanged since Kirsten's passing.

Two years ago, they had given her mother's piano away because of a cracked sounding board. A small church had been without one and Stian hoped someday to replace theirs. To date, funds had been needed elsewhere. Sometimes Linnea would walk to the little church just to play it.

Before the delivery men left, Marthe served them cold lemonade and cookies. Linnea sat down at the piano. Stroking the black, lacquered board, she raised it carefully. Looking over at her Father she smiled and began to play a song she had memorized…, 'Fuer Elise'. As the beautiful, familiar melody sounded forth, Stian Johanneson raised his eyes and whispered, "Thank you."

Marthe stood in the kitchen doorway, dabbing at her eyes. "Hear t'at, Kirsten?" she whispered.

The next time Evan came over Linney was at the piano. He queried as to the donor but after hearing the story, smiled. Then, with a knowing wink, he acted nonplussed.

"Hope you like it." He left them believing strongly that he indeed was the benefactor.

Walking out later he swore aloud, "Damn that hobo; it was he who gave that piano to her! Hope she never finds out. By God I can make sure that never happens. I'll put the 'fear of God' into him." He smiled at his sinister irreverence.

The next day he brought an expensive doll for Bella. Along with it was a tiny toy piano. They were both much beyond her years and Marthe gave a great, "Humph," and stalked into the kitchen.

"This is only the beginning of what I hope to do for you and Bella," Evan quipped. The baby was delighted with the doll and held up the little piano to Linnea, her eyes shining. Naturally, her young nanny was touched by the baby's response.

Evan knew this was his moment. He took Linnea's hand, while whispering to her, "Oh, how I wish to help our dear Bella. I want her to have all the things she deserves in life. Just trust me to care for her; whatever it takes to make that happen."

Withdrawing her hand, Linnea stared at Reinhold in confusion. He stood, kissed Bella's cheek and swept confidently out of the door, leaving Linnea emotionally torn. His words held out some measure of hope, but even more, a lingering, sick feeling from the touch of his hand and the phrase, 'our Bella'. Across her mind flashed an image of Renuel Breech. That image made her heart pound and her eyes fill with tears.

It was less than twenty-four hours when Reinholdt returned. Stian, Natalyia and Linnea were seated before the fire in a conversation concerning Bella. As soon as he stepped through the doorway her companions saw the look of distress on Linney's face.

He strode confidently into the room, but with a look of consternation. Taking Linnea's hand lightly, he spoke, "I am deeply grieved for you, poor girl. I have done all that I could to secure Bella in this home; however, I have just heard today that the state will not extend her stay. It has been six months since the informal hearing and no next of kin has stepped forward. There is a fully qualified adoptive couple who is close to the court and have influenced the Judge to allow them to secure the child. It will, of course, be a closed adoption, as is the law. I deeply regret being the bearer of these ill tidings."

Linnea had stood by, this time, withdrawing her hand. Her face was white and her body stiff, her voice deadly cold. "Well, they can't have her. We are the ones who knew her mother and cared for her. It was her greatest desire to give the baby over to us. This is Bella's home now; the state has no right to take her!" Her voice was becoming agitated and her words desperate. "I'll run away with her or, you're a lawyer; you can get me papers stating that I am her mother and was afraid to say so. Say she was born to me out of wedlock! I don't care, Father!"

Stian had come and put his arm around her. "People gossiped that she was mine anyway; they would believe it!" She stepped away from her father and grabbed Evan by the arm. "Yes, that's it!" She kept looking back at her parent, in desperation, for his approval. "She would be legally mine, Father! No one could take her then. Isa would want Bella with me; no matter what others thought. You have to help us Mr. Reinholdt!"

Evan had stepped back when Stian came forward. The lawyer then moved closer and put his arm very lightly around Linnea. "I have an idea that may work." She was repulsed, as always, by his touch, but other than a shudder, she barely felt anything but terror over Bella.

Stian looked back at Natalyia. She stood as still as stone; her face drained of color and staring at Evan with a look that chilled his blood. She said not a word; her expression was implacable. Johanneson stepped closer to her but said nothing.

Linnea had stayed still, allowing Evan's arm to remain, with a confused hope that somehow this would help her plea bargain. Dimly she heard her Father's voice, "Linnea dear, let us not give in to despair. I believe we can appeal this decision of the courts; can we not Attorney Reinholdt?"

"Yes, good Pastor, we can appeal but they will still remove the child while the court decides her placement."

Linnea tore herself away and ran to Marthe who was standing in the doorway and fell into her arms. The girl was sobbing convulsively but never uttered a sound, burying it in her body as tears were flooding her face. The agony for her old nanny was terrible.

Evan spoke in a condescendingly saccharine tone. He had the upper hand and played it like the pro that he was. "My dear man, I have appealed, cajoled and pleaded with the judge to no avail. Your custody time with her will simply run out in seven days. We had to report the child's presence in your home, as you remember. Had your daughter declared maternity then; it might have made a difference, even without proof. We cannot lie now to the courts; the birth records would have needed to be altered months ago."

Johanneson looked at Natalyia and shook his head. Linnea tore herself from Marthe. Stian saw her wild-eyed look.

"Yes, we can lie! I will, I will! God will forgive me; He understands. God can't want her to be taken from us and given to strangers. It would break her little heart!"

Evan stood there, shaking his head, his arms folded in an official posture. "She will be a ward of the state until adoption. You would be arrested for kidnapping, should you be caught taking her somewhere without the court's permission."

Natalyia began walking out of the room like someone in a comatose state. "Wait", called out Evan to everyone. "There is a legal loophole; one way to halt this. Natalyia stopped in her tracks but did not turn around. The others stared at him. "As you may know, I am a close colleague with Judge DeVant. He knows of my constant interest and attention in this case. We have kept Bella with you because of my efforts in the court-room. The Judge also knows of my deep affection for the little child."

He stopped and looked at Linnea with a paternal smile. "I can request first rights for adoption. I must be married if I am to obtain the child permanently." He looked over at Linnea in a businesslike, but kind voice, devoid of emotion. "If you and I were to be married by a Justice of the Peace, before the end of the seven days; I could secure firsts rights in view of my longstanding connection to the case. I know the Judge would grant it."

Eyes of all were darting from one to another, incredulously silent at his words. "We would dissolve the marriage a month or so later, when the adoption is finalized. The longest would be six months and you could be back at home caring for the child, should it be a longer time frame. Just a civil ceremony, no other requirements necessary, except for that first month in my house.

Of course, we would have separate quarters." Here, he turned and nodded at Natalyia who had turned around by then. "Perhaps Mrs. Zupancic could join Miss Linnea for companionship? I would award Miss Johanneson full custody; when we dissolve the marriage."

There was a formidable quiet in the room. No one spoke for fully two or three minutes. Linnea's voice broke the silence, cold and hard. "I will do it. It is the only way to save Bella. I must do it." She looked at her father, almost daring him to disagree; but the torment in her eyes screamed, *Stop this!*"

Stian Johanneson was disturbingly calm and his voice was very firm when he finally spoke. He walked to Marthe and patted her shoulder, "Marthe dear, will you bring us some coffee and refreshments?" He then passed Natalyia, looked into her eyes shaking his head, just slightly, and touched her hand.

Almost ignoring Evan, as though he were not present, he stood between Linnea and their dastardly antagonist. "No Linnea, I will not vouchsafe this arrangement. This is not the purpose nor the motive behind sacred matrimony." Here he turned partially and nodded at the lawyer. "I will invite Mr. Reinholdt to return soon. Then, we will discuss Bella's future, after looking at all the options."

The girl stared a moment at her parent and stated with an angry edge, "You heard him, Father; there are no other options. I am of age; you cannot stop me." He heard Natalyia gasp slightly and saw her hand cover her mouth.

Still his affect and disposition remained stoical. Turning fully to face Reinholdt, he spoke firmly, with some grace in his manner, "Sir, please allow us to contact you with an answer. As you know, we are a Christian home and we will seek to solve this weighty matter in our way. We will respond soon."

Linnea walked up to Evan. The man then spoke, ignoring Stian; but his anger was barely disguised as he said darkly, "Remember, Miss Linnea, what I said about removal of the baby while the court decides on an appeal."

She replied, "Mr. Reinholdt, I have given my final answer. Bring the marriage license and any other requirements for the... the event. I can sign them myself."

The vile man looked at Stian with a strange expression. Then, taking his coat in hand, he said in an indifferent tone, "Your daughter is of legal age. I will return with the necessary documents. You need not be present."

And then, like announcing a picnic plan, he said, "Goodnight, the weather looks to be quite fine all week."

He took Linney's hand, without permission, and kissed it; but, as he turned to leave, Stian called out, "Yes, He is the Master of the wind and the weather, as well as our soul's destiny, goodnight."

Evan never even turned around; and he was gone.

# PART III

# Chapter 31

# The Return

"Tell me not sweet, I am unkind,
That from the nunnery
of thy chaste breast and quiet
mind, to war and arms I fly..."
Richard Lovelace*

As Linnea turned the corner to leave the cemetery, she passed under a large chestnut tree. Someone grabbed her from behind! She would have screamed but a hand quickly covered her mouth. Instantly a hissing voice came, close to her ear and said, "Shhh, it is me, Renuel Breech. I am sorry to have frightened you; but you were walking so fast I feared you would leave the cover of the tree. I will not hurt you Miss."

Linney was gasping as she had been trying to tear the hand away. She turned and looked straight up into the face of her accoster, not believing it could be Renuel. She had dreamed and prayed for this. In a near involuntary reaction she threw her arms around his neck, a safer haven than any she thought possible, in this her most desperate hour. She held on for some moments and he put his arms around her as well.

"Oh Renuel!" she cried out. "Where have you been? How did you know to look for me here? Does my father know?" She blurted out questions, gradually releasing her vice grip.

The frightened look in her eyes began to abate and Linney suddenly felt vulnerable. The girl released her hold, trying to step away but Renuel's arms were slow to let her go. I am sorry Ren...or Mr. Breech; I was just so glad you finally came back and you're safe and...but now...Oh, I think it's too late for me and..." Linnea fell silent for a few moments. She looked down as tears filled her eyes. "It seems like it is the end of all things happy and good and right." Linnea Johanneson's despair had been beyond tears with others, but not with this man.

She dried her eyes as she sank down on the bench beneath the tree looking up at Renuel, bleakly fearing even he could not be the savior she envisioned. "I know I sound dreadful; but if you only knew." Renuel looked soberly down at her, his voice quiet and grave.

"I know." Linney's eyes darted up at him. There was silence between them because the knowing was too terrible a thing of which to speak. (Have you ever been told something so grim that neither the teller nor you could speak of it?) Saying it aloud would give Linnea's fate a reality neither could abide.

The Wanderer glanced at her with those same dark, haunted eyes as at their first meeting. But there was a difference. The hardness was now tempered with knowledge of her that he didn't have before, and coupled with that, a special care. This something she saw made her heart pound; but there was also anger and an expression of desperation. This terrified her and filled her with dread.

"What is it Renuel; what are you going to do? Will you kidnap Bella? They will surely catch you and put you into jail! Please let me save her. I know I can! I have a plan to...; you know." Linnea flushed, looking down.

Staring straight, he replied in a subdued voice, "Surely your father disagrees! But, I'm here on another urgent matter. My mother is in grave danger. The Ambassador..., but never mind that! They have found her location here in your city. These people never give up. They will soon arrive at your house. Please listen to these instructions. Firstly, she must leave your house tonight, by herself."

Linnea was stunned. "What?! Your mother? Alone?! Who is after her..., and why? I thought Bella was..." Renuel took her by the shoulders. The intensity of his grip spoke loudly.

"You must listen. If she doesn't do exactly as I say, they will find her. Eventually this could lead to the identity of Bella, Oleksandr, and the..., then, to discovering all the others."

His last words trailed off as he released his hold on her. "Without my mother, they have no link to any of us. They will be forced to presume that they followed a false lead. They do not know anything else. They just want my mother for other reasons."

"I don't understand." "You will one day soon; I can promise you that at least. "You must give her these exact instructions tonight. It's not if, but when they come; tonight possibly, or for sure, by tomorrow; there must be no trace of her in your home. They will come with a search warrant you can't refuse. They may be genuine policemen or ones with false identification."

Renny proceeded to give to Linnea the plans for Natalyia's public transportation route, which stops to make, and which transfers to take. "This must be communicated to your father as well. I know you can do this secretly and accurately. It is vital! Can you trust me in this?"

"I will try but...", Renuel turned, looking furtively in both directions.

"I must go."

"No!" Linnea grabbed his arm. "What about Bella, and Evan Reinholdt and..., me?" She was almost shouting. He turned toward her and cupped her face in his hands.

"Listen now," he said grimly. Do not believe any or all of that saboteur Reinholdt's assertions." He gazed into her eyes, "But go along and pursue your plan of marrying him."

She was certain that she felt him shudder as he spoke those last words and dropped his hands. "Delay it as long as possible. I pray it will not be necessary to go through with this ceremony. Perhaps it can be annulled." This he said darkly. "Bella will be safe if he thinks you are complying with his plan to marry him; but you must be convincing! Now it is your turn to be on stage, Miss Johanneson."

Her thoughts began to race, *On the stage... but you must be convincing, and there is so much at risk and for so many...'* and on and on her thoughts replayed his words. Then, she spoke, "But I think Mr. Reinholdt really is trying to save Bella and maybe the other thing about me is true too. This is the only way I know that I can keep her."

"It is the only way, at present, but that villain has no idea what really is at stake. He knows only of his own sordid plan of having you for himself. Bella is the bait to catch you. I hope he will fail; but I fear many more will fall if we don't play out this charade. If only there were another way."

"Who?! Who will fall?! What does that mean? Fall?" Linnea was feeling frightened, desperate and confused.

He replied, "I cannot divulge these things now. I must ask you again to trust me. Will you believe that all of this is to protect Bella? It's not for our sakes, but for hers. Try to believe me." Renny thought, *I know now why my father was silenced long before his death. He knew too much; a great deal more about Olek and the goals of the resistance. It was his father's own words that sparked that realization.* "No matter our end, my son, God cannot be silenced by evil men's schemes. He controls the end from the beginning." That familiar tome seemed surreal to him now.

Renuel arose to leave and so did Linnea. She stood very still and, staring at him, spoke slowly and with difficulty, "If there is no other way to keep Bella, tell me that you want me to marry Evan Reinholdt. I know now that he won't let me go after..., after." She looked at him with a fearful expression and continued, "After... we are married."

Renuel looked solemnly at Linnea. Pulling her close he brushed her cheek with his lips. He could feel her heart pounding. "Some things in this life are worse than death. For me, this is that thing! But, yes, you must do this because I cannot risk so much only upon the strength of my love for you. It doesn't seem there is any other way."

He held her at arm's length. "I believe that God is on our side Linnea." She looked at him with surprise. "You do?" Strangely, Linnea had trusted Renuel from the beginning; but she was afraid of his anger at God and his melancholy.

As he had done for others before her, God had given her a vision of the real Renuel Breech. Behind his desperate façade she saw something that he would be and could be if he would choose life. Something had changed in him..., a metamorphosis of his soul.

Renuel brushed aside her hair and began wiping tears as they ran down her face. "I would take you away from all of this right now; but I could never live with myself. Besides, you would despise me for what I had done. Only God can protect you, my mother and Bella. "He never leaves us and is even in the depths of our deepest despair. I remember that my father wrote that in his last letter."

He held her again so tightly that it literally took her breath away. Then, saying something to her in his language that sounded fierce, he released her and rapidly strode away.

Linnea ran after him. She had seen desperation in his eyes but also the beginnings of something new and good, there and in his words. Calling his name, he turned around. She came to him. Her face was flushed, her blonde hair askew and her blue eyes despairing. She exclaimed, "No matter what I must do, I love you Renuel Breech and always will."

"Play a song for me on your piano, dearest Linnea."

"You! It was from you? Oh, Renuel!"

Then she stood on her tiptoes and touched him softly on the lips. "Goodbye, pray for us." She turned and hurried away.

He watched her lovely form go and whispered, "I think perhaps I have betrayed her. But if it please you God, take care of her. I give Linnea Johanneson to you."

# CHAPTER 32

# THE BUS RIDE

"Of all sad words of tongue or pen;
The saddest are these,
'It might have been.' "

John Greenleaf Whittier

Linnea had rounded a corner and was out of sight. Renuel was still partially hidden as a Plymouth Sedan drove slowly by, jarring him to his senses thinking, *I must get away from here, before I'm seen!* He stared at the vehicle as it turned left and was gone. Just then he heard and saw the bus rumbling from a short distance away. Crossing the street, looking around furtively, he jogged to the stop, barely seen in time by the bus driver. He jumped aboard, fumbled for his transfer and nodded at the driver. "Thank you for stopping."

"Riding alone today, I see", he said with a wink. Renuel looked at him more closely and noticed that it was Mr. Slater, the same bus driver who had taken them to Como Park and knew Linnea.

"Sadly enough, I am Sir." The driver handed back the transfer to him and commented, "That one is no average 'run of the mill' gal. Better not let her get away, young fella. I saw her walking by herself just a few minutes ago."

Renuel was so taken aback by the driver's candor that he nodded, replying in the affirmative. "No Sir, I hope not to," but his affect was melancholy.

"Hopin' and doin' are pretty far apart Sonny." Renuel looked, with resignation, at the man, nodded his head and walked to his seat.

*Hopin' and doin, they were horses of a different color;* he pondered. *One horse was held back, chafing at the bit, and the other one was charging forward into the battle, or the race soon to be run.'* Renuel shook his head, speaking softly, "Well God, I guess I am the 'hopin' deadbeat horse."

The wanderer felt himself back in his exiled status. He stared out of the window as the bus bumped past city streets. Some minutes later, it stopped with a jerk at a busy downtown intersection, startling Renuel from his sad reverie. Looking disinterestedly across the street, he was suddenly riveted! There was Evan Reinholdt, closely escorting a sensually attired woman to the rider's door of a shiny blue Packard. Showing a great deal of leg, she got into the car and looked up, blowing a kiss to the attorney as he closed the door.

Renuel spoke aloud, under his breath, "That charlatan. I could kill him. And he says he is marrying Linnea Johanneson this week?!"

The bus took off. The rage that consumed his thoughts, toward Reinholdt, was murderous and vengeful. *Guess I'm not so holy as I deem myself to be, Father,* he thought guiltily. The would-be lover's dark musings were threatening to envelop him. They were quickly pushing aside everything he had resolved to do for Bella.

Renuel felt backed into a corner with seemingly no way out. He knew he couldn't let the baby's real identity be discovered. Pushing his hair back and leaning forward, his head between his hands; he mumbled in despair, "God, you are supposed to help us!"

The bus had left the city center and now had come to the end of its route. Everyone else had gotten off.

"Heh bud, this is the end; you better get off," the bus driver called. Renuel looked up, confused.

"The end?"

"Yeah, I turn around now and go back the same route you've been on."

"Oh sorry, I will get off then. Thank you, Sir."

Renuel was about to disembark when the driver said, "Look, it's none of my business; but I really like that little Johanneson girl. I've seen how she's had that spark in her eye for you, from that first night, and ever since. Do ya love her boy?"

Renuel was stunned by his question. Suddenly he felt either unhinged or jubilant..., or both.

"Yes, yes, I love her," he said, speaking fervently to the driver.

"Well then, why don't you marry her and make the best of it. What have ya got ta lose, buddy? She's worth the risk, I'd say." Renuel stared at him.

"Do you think I should...just marry her? Really, you think I should just do it?" No comment came, just a strong look.

"So, are you 'staying on or getting' off?"

Renuel knew he wasn't ready to get off and a plan was flying through his head, like a jet picking up speed on the runway.

"I think I will stay on awhile. Here is some cash; I don't have any tokens."

"Can't take cash fella. Gimme your transfer. After all, you haven't gotten off the bus. I'll just punch it again." Renuel, in a daze, thanked him, gave him the transfer and sat down.

By the time they neared the stop, near the Johanneson's, Renuel had been formulating a plan.

# CHAPTER 33

# BICYCLE EXCURSION

"How do I love thee,
Let me count the ways...
With the breath, smiles and tears
Of all my life..."
Elizabeth Barret Browning

The following morning, still disturbed by the events of the past evening, Natalyia took a solitary bike ride. It went against all her past habits of no risk taking and even her own instincts; but ride she would.

Coming closer, she saw the welcoming graveled area by the waterway and parked her bicycle. Sitting on a bench, at least twenty feet up from the gurgling, surging waters of the falls and rapids, she breathed deeply. The sounds of the river, with the bright sky overhead, made it all so invigorating to her weary spirit.

She looked down and saw that the sun had lit up the waters in a crystalline extravaganza that took her breath away. "Oh, dear Lord, is this extravaganza just for me today", she said aloud. "Thank you."

Smiling, she looked around, happy to not have to translate her thoughts into English words. Two or three men, a full twenty-foot drop down from her, were standing on a large flat rock and fishing upstream.

The rushing river blocked out any conversation sounds, except an occasional faint shout of success! Just the sight of them casting out their lines seemed so worthwhile for a pastime. She felt glad. Galena and she had gone fishing for their supper in the early days of their marriage. Those memories were distant, but sweet.

Natalyia had borrowed Linnea's bicycle and rode the three miles down to the Waterway Park. The Pastor had asked if he might ride down, after a time, and accompany her back. "Just for a bit of exercise," he said. "Sermon writing is rather sessile work. Besides, one cannot be too careful with such a charge as was given to me by your son."

"What is charge?"

"What he said was, 'Watch over my mother; she can be a bit careless in her need for solitude.'" I replied, "Sounds to me like you also have 'wandered' a bit dangerously, Mr. Breech." The lady gave Stian a serious look.

"Yes, this is so of me, and of my son." Natalyia queried Stian, if that conversation took place the last time he had seen Renuel. He confirmed that it was, but she felt there was more he didn't say.

At this tranquil place she was feeling a much-needed peace come over her. She knew that she greatly needed to calm herself after the events of the past evening. *To think of Linnea's marrying that falsifier, that evil conspirer, not to mention him as Bella's father, makes my stomach turn. It is unthinkable with the child's legacy; and I know he will not keep my grandchild long, once the marriage is legal.* "It is the girl he wants, poor thing, and anyone else he fancies for himself," she said with disgust; having observed Evan's wandering eye. Natalyia had spoken the last sentence in whispered tones and now felt chagrined. *I am sorry, dear God. These fears are not from you. Imprison them and I will trust again in your goodness.*

She sighed, but her heart lightened quite soon after. Standing up, the lady walked a few steps forward and leaned on the banister. The breeze was light and refreshing. Natalyia was perplexed by her new identity in this foreign country. She had believed it would be short-lived after obtaining Bella. It was such a charade, in so many ways; yet certain strong feelings she had were no charade and could not be denied. Pastor Stian Johanneson had totally blindsided her with his tender words, his companionship and his manly appeal. These emotions surfaced but did not coalesce with her purpose in coming here. She felt so glad, but also guilty.

Smiling, she looked to the east at a narrow bridge spanning the river. It was downstream from the water intake area. The river wound in another direction and she could not see beyond the bend of it. It was much like arriving here, as only God could have arranged this safe place for her and Bella. She could not see beyond life's bend either. Renuel barely got her out of the country safely and here she was, living in a household with the kindest, most God-fearing and principled people she could have ever envisioned.

*Who am I? My pulse races whenever I am around this pastor, as it once did with Galena. I am not a girl; but this man commands my heart. I thought myself forever immune to such 'crushes.' I thrilled to his kiss of friendship on my cheek. I must not presume it to be anything more.* She could almost hear Galena's teasing voice, "Do you really think so, Natty?" Gal had known of her suspicious nature. But it was not true, in this case; she was certain. *He is a trustworthy man. I am Bella's grandmother and I can see Renuel is also dear to him, just as Renny is to Linnea. I fear my son is quite enamored of the girl. Poor Renny, such a hopeless affair it is. And I, I will not suspect the Pastor's feelings for me as anything but worthy, still how it warms my lonely heart to be surrounded by his friendship and care.*

These were her thoughts, but aloud she whispered, "Gal, you are so far above and removed from these Earthly things. Our covenant is no more. We are separated by three heavens; and when we meet again, we shall be dear friends, no more."

Natalyia could almost feel Galena patting her on the shoulder saying, "Don't fret Nat, you will know the right thing; but you must pray." She chided herself that no doubt she was really saying this into the empty air. *I know the Lord can hear me from the highest heaven; but can you Galena?*

The woman smiled. Her thoughts returned to Stian. *How many ladies in distress, have loved this Pastor whose eyes spark with godliness and largeness of life. Oh me, I am just another one drawn to him in my need.* A sudden, trying thought overpowered her. *I must leave or my heart will betray me! He must never know. But how can I go and take Bella before Renny returns? Where would I go? No, I must remain; but the pastor must never suspect my feelings for him.*

Just realizing she couldn't leave yet made her heart skip with girlish delight as she mused happily, *I will see him at supper. Maybe we will sit afterwards by the fire and we will read aloud. Dear Miss Linney can be my alibi for staying in the room with him and perhaps Marthe and Bella too. Oh, how that girl loves the baby. I don't see how Isa could attend her with more devotion.*

Natalyia could see the fear on Linnea's face when 'that man' hinted at the baby's peril in the courts. *She recoiled, thinking of the deviousness of wicked men in high places who were holding lives in their grasp. They were villainous usurpers of the safety of decent, God-fearing people.* How often had she seen it; but she reminded herself that God was indeed seeing it all, as the Ancient of Days. *He will be the just judge of all wrongs.*

She thought again of Galena's last words to her, *"Do not despair Natty. Remember, God elevates Kings and those in authority and he also takes them down to nothing. He is greater than all earthly powers."* She sighed.

As part of the underground she was always watched, with even her conversations overheard. Galena never doubted God's goodness, but his anger would ignite if Natalyia was ever detained for questioning.

Without Ambassador Putin's influence, she would never have been released the last time. His infatuation with her made her shiver with dread; and he was relentless. It began many years before when she rejected his pursuit in favor of Galena's. The ambassador was handsome, rising in power, and sought after; but he was a Communist, and no match for the tall, skinny Galena Zaplavnov. He was godly and intelligent, with winsome ways, and in Natalyia's eyes, a prince by comparison.

Gal was humble but lively and fiercely outspoken regarding the evils that were threatening the country.

After being widowed, her revulsion of the ambassador intensified; and she openly rejected Putin's advances. *He was a self-aggrandizing power monger who had no place for God or people in his life, not even his own sister, Iiulia. He was bent on Natalyia; but she had escaped. He was not a good loser.* The lady shuddered at these thoughts.

Enter now a new rival, Pastor Johanneson. Now, there was a contender for her Christian soul and heart. Masculinity and meekness joined together in a divinely centered man. This was an irresistible combination for Natalyia. She had grown to love him, her depth of feeling unknown, even to herself.

# CHAPTER 34

## STIAN AND THE ABDUCTION

"On a starred night Prince Lucifer arose...with
memory of the old revolt from Awe...; he looked and sank."

George Meredith

Natalyia felt a warm hand on her shoulder as a voice said, "Don't be alarmed; it's just me, Stian." She flinched slightly, feeling like a young girl caught by her parents while reading a story after bedtime.

She looked up, "Oh, hello Pastor", her voice a bit tremulous. The man sensed her alarm.

"My apologies, I tried not to startle you...," he paused. Looking straight at her, he queried, "Where were you in your reverie just now? Far away in another time and place, I'm thinking." As usual, Stian tried, with less and less success, to disguise the intensity of his feelings for Natalyia.

The lady looked cautiously up at his tender expression. *Oh, why must he look at me in such a way? I feel so found out, so disconcerted.* She looked down briefly and took a deep breath to gather herself. Then, glancing back with an attempt at sincerity she said, "I believe somewhere in the third heaven."

"Ah, most of my parishioners wouldn't know what that was, nor where. That's my fault. I need to whet their appetites more for God's dwelling places. So, what was it like up there? I've often wondered and even wished for just a glimpse of it." His voice was teasing but his expression warm and sincere.

She smiled. "Look there...," and she pointed at the river. "You can catch a small glimpse, as you say, from shimmering waters."

Stian was often taken aback by her vocabulary and English usage. *Perhaps that too needed to be hidden and coded from others. Who knows how many terrible scenes she had been forced to witness, wishing desperately to avoid them? Perhaps that is why she dreamed of God's abode. What a life of faith and courage!* "Did you see anything more?", he cajoled.

She laughed in a whimsical, but sad way. "Well, Pastor, since the apostle who visited there could not find his words, even with many tongues, how am I to? Besides, it was so bright I could not open my eyes. I believe the dull vision of mine is not made to gaze upon a world of such brilliance."

Stian replied, "But how intriguing and enchanting to think that we are creatures made for that other world; otherwise, we would not long so for it." Natalyia's eyes were shining as she nodded in response. Stian continued, "But I must say, Natalyia; it seems to me that your brown eyes grow brighter every day." His face was very, very near, "Don't you agree?" She felt alarm. *Oh no, does he suspect? Does this great fondness show in my eyes?!*

Stian saw a shadow pass across her face. He feared she was frightened or offended. Perhaps she had been thinking of her husband or Renuel's present danger. He changed his tone and affect; chagrined to think he may have alarmed her.

"I believe your eyes reflect your growing hope that Renuel is safe and that you will hear from him soon."

"Yes," she nodded, looking at him cautiously since her day-dreams hadn't been about Renuel at all. Then she thought, *He, no doubt, wishes we would soon leave. We have stayed so long.*

Seeming to read her mind, Stian gently touched her arm. "You know, friend, how we love little Bella and hope you won't think of leaving any time soon."

She spoke quickly, "But I fear we must. We have trespassed on kindness long enough time." The lady noticed a slight frown cross his face.

"Well, Natalyia, you surely have noticed that we have no signs posted saying, "No trespassing here!" He chuckled, taking her hand as she arose. Natalyia felt his large, warm hand enclose her cold one. The river's damp air had chilled her. She was swallowing against the rush of feelings she had towards this intoxicating man. Avoiding his eyes, she stood up and released his hand, her thoughts racing.

*Yes, truly he is a man among men, but not for me. I'm just a fugitive, a woman without a home or country.* Natalyia fought her emotions, biting her lip slightly to hold back the tears. She must resolve to put aside her longings for Stian Johanneson. Smiling, with forced bravado, she got astride her bike. He did a slight salute back at her and they rode off.

Stian did not realize that she had fallen so far behind. He had climbed the hill much faster than she. He stopped to let her catch up with him. Just then a car slowed alongside her. Natalyia turned to look as the driver rolled down the window.

"Ma'am, can you direct me to the City Zoo?" Still pedaling slowly, she saw that the voice belonged to a young woman with sandy blonde hair. She also had blue eyes and a bright smile. But something in her eyes, a hooded look, alarmed Natalyia. She had seen that look before.

Natalyia stopped, as did the car. Trying to keep her voice steady and her words free of accent, she replied, "No, I do not. I am a visitor out for a bicycle ride."

The woman answered, "Thank you" as the car moved forward. Then it abruptly stopped, the back door opened, and a man jumped out. Kicking over her bike, he grabbed her.

Natalyia screamed, "Stian!", her eyes darting up the hill. She valiantly struggled but the man was already pushing her into the car. Johanneson was forced to see Natalyia being shoved into some stranger's car.

"God, oh God, he shouted, jerking his bike around at a dangerous angle and surging down the hill. He ran a red light only to see the car screech around a corner and disappear. It was a dark blue Plymouth Sedan. Stian knew the year; but that was all.

As he careened around the corner, staring frantically down the street on which her abductors had sped, there was nothing in sight. Stian felt horror, unlike any he had ever experienced since the day of Kirsten's fatal accident. Natalyia was gone!

# CHAPTER 35

# THE CENTER CANNOT HOLD

Things fall apart; the center
Cannot hold..., mere anarchy
Is loosed upon the world.
W. B. Yeats 'Second Coming'

Stian parked the bicycle without thought of his action. He was greatly affected by the terrible ordeal but walked calmly up to his house. Entering, he immediately called out, "Marthe!" Heading to the kitchen he called again but concluded that she was upstairs.

Hearing a sound at the front door he spun around, just as it opened. It was Linnea. Stian sighed in relief. He was on high alert, expecting almost anything. He stepped quickly towards her, with a sober expression. "Linnea, I fear I have some desperately bad news."

She cried out, with a terrified expression, "Bella, is she gone!?"

"No, my daughter, the baby is safe."

"What then! What's wrong?!" "Is it Natalyia?" Her father's voice was grim and deliberate. "Natalyia has been abducted."

Linney covered her mouth with both hands saying, "Oh Lord Jesus! Father, you have called the police?"

"No Linney."

"We must. I have just seen Renuel. He warned me of his mother's great danger but thought we had more time before..., oh, how terrible!" Linnea moved toward the telephone.

Her father quickly stepped over and put his hand on the phone. "I think not."

"But why," she protested with a cry of panic. Stian's voice was solemn, imaging again the scene of Natalyia's abduction.

"I fear we would be placing Mrs. Zupancic in a different kind of peril of which we are ignorant. Her abductors must have been watching her movements closely. This was the first time she had left the house alone." To himself Stian thought, *Natalyia must know something politically or be a link to Renuel and some information he has. Something more was going on here.*

Then aloud Stian said, "Renuel may be the one for whom they are searching."

"No Father, they wanted his mother. He told me so. But I am afraid for Bella too. I must quickly tell you what Renuel's instructions to you were." Linnea explained everything Renuel had told her to tell them. Now, it seemed so pointless. He had also told her to inform Natalyia to take Bella with her, out of the house.

Stian nodded, and then replied, "Though it may not matter now, I want you to do just as Renuel has requested; even though Natalyia is gone." His voice caught, and Linnea stared at him.

"What happened Father?"

"There is no time. I will tell you later." Marthe was now in the room listening fervently. "Marthe can gather all of Natalyia's things while you ready Bella Rene and yourself. Take her to a friend's house, just for a social visit. Then, ask to spend the night, using some credible excuse. You do have such a friend in Kati, don't you?"

"Yes, of course Father, I will take her to Katie Jo's. She and I work together at the Emporium. I often stop at her place after work or on walks with Bella. I have shared some personal matters with her; and this will seem normal. You've met her a few times."

"Oh yes, isn't that your atheist friend who always complains about God?"

"Yes, that's she."

"That is ideal. A good cover for the child."

Very quickly they set to work. Marthe finished clearing and hiding all Natalyia's things. She then gave the room a clean and emptied look. A short while later Linnea had gathered what she needed and held Bella out to her Father. He took her in his strong arms, and they prayed together. He hugged Linnea and soon, the two of them were out the door and gone. Linnea's last look was a bit frightened, but she smiled, seeing her father's confident expression.

"You are both in safe hands, my daughter, come what may." Stian stood in the silent hall after the flurry of their departure. He felt fully now the strain of the past hours. The shock of losing Natalyia in such a drastic, few moments of terror played over and over in his mind. He stared vacantly.

"Vud you like some coffee Pastor?"

It took him a few moments to respond. Marthe's voice was soft and caring. She stood with her hands folded, not certain of what to do next. Service was her way and her simple offer was a tonic to his troubled soul.

"Yes, yes, thank you Marthe; that would be good I think." He looked at her kindly. "Thank you for your assistance today. You must feel distraught yourself. But this is not a time to doubt our gracious God is it. We must trust him in this."

"Ja Pastor, He is gud haver dag." She left abruptly, dabbing at her eyes and not knowing she had lapsed into her own language. Stian sighed deeply as he walked to his leather chair. As Daniel of old, the man knelt, his hands folded, head down and prayed, "...In words that cannot be uttered."

# CHAPTER 36

## UNWELCOME VISITORS

"...Thou'rt slave to fate, chance,
kings and desperate men..."

John Donne

Within a short time, there came a loud knocking on the front door. It was more of a banging than a knock. Stian had arisen from his knees only ten minutes before, waiting for Marthe's coffee. He arose, signaling her to wait. His body tensed but he went at an unhurried pace and opened the door. There stood three police officers; or so they appeared to be. He was quite certain that he recognized the youngest.

"Can I help you?"

The older ranking man spoke abruptly, showing his badge. "I think yes."

"Well then, come in officers." They walked stiffly into the sitting room. It was obvious that the other two men were surprised by the courteous and unruffled affect of the minister. Perhaps they were even somewhat embarrassed at his kind, though formal tone. "Please, sit down. Now, how can I be of service gentlemen?"

Marthe entered the room with Stian's coffee and some cinnamon rusks on a tray.

"Thank you, Marthe, would you be so kind as to bring some for our guests?" The senior officer immediately declined, stating they were on duty. They would need to proceed with their business at hand. Stian smiled as he lifted the cup to his mouth, taking a sip. "I trust you won't mind, Sirs; but it is my habit this time of day to indulge in a cup of coffee and a small treat."

The officer blustered something like, "Fine then."

Stian gestured to them, "Come, sit by the fire; it is warm here." The two younger men sat on the davenport facing Stian and the other policeman, nearest him, sat near the fireplace. "Now," as he sipped his brew and tasted his rusk, "What exactly can I help you with?"

Johanneson was stalling to give Linnea and the baby as much time as possible to get settled at her friend's house. He desperately hoped that Renuel was aware of his mother's disappearance by now. A cold chill ran up and down his entire being as the scene flashed back, yet again.

There was a loud, "Ahem." The two men on the couch looked at each other nervously. They were obviously uncomfortable with their mission. They kept eyeing their captain for some cue.

Stian spoke to the light-haired officer. "You there, friend", nodding kindly and continuing, "I believe I saw you at Iverson's Café on Payne Avenue a bit ago. I was there with a visiting friend. You aided an older waitress who was being bullied by an unwieldy customer. I do believe the man was or is the day watchman at the cemetery. He was slightly inebriated, I gathered. Our visitor was quite impressed by your calm, but firm, command of the situation. She has since left us."

Stian continued, "Robin, Robin Hood was your name; was it not?" The blonde officer turned red but nodded, with a smile. Stian winked at the fellow.

He smiled again, but replied, "Robinson Sir, Noel Robinson." The senior officer cleared his throat again, loudly.

"Enough talk. Are you quite ready Reverend Johanneson?" The younger policeman had snapped back into his former posture.

"Sorry Sir, sorry!"

Officer Wrench, or so he had identified himself, spoke, "So then, your lady visitor has left? Gone back from wherever she had come?"

"Yes," said Stian, "She will be travelling some and will then return home."

Wrench, in a demanding tone, said, "Home..., and where is that?" Johanneson replied calmly, "Now you wouldn't expect me to reveal a lady's travel itinerary, would you, Mr. Wrench? That would be unseemly of me, or even of you, to ask."

Wrench then produced a search warrant. Stian invited them to look wherever they desired. The younger men continued to be uncomfortable with their ignoble task. Wrench arose and sent the two younger men to search upstairs. He then proceeded to the kitchen and out to the dayroom, under the steely gaze of Marthe. Returning, the officer declined Stian's offer for any further searching. He met the others coming down the stairs and seemed frustrated with their report; but he had no other questions.

They were about to leave the house, apparently not finding reason to linger, when Stian spoke. His voice was even, but his words carried a chilling message. "I am so glad, Sirs, that here in our land, true justice can prevail. Officer Wrench, our guest was a person of upstanding character and quite highly connected in her country of origin. She is now a widow. For her own personal sanctity, she has kept these sad facts personal."

He paused, staring hard at the men and spoke in a grim voice. "I know that there are unjust judges, governors and even presidents here in our land. Yes, my friends, there are even unjust policemen. But there is coming a day of reckoning. All shall feel it. I trust that we are all careful with the demands of evil men. By defending the innocent, we may escape that Great Judgement Day, wherein comes to light all deeds done in the body, good or evil." Wrench mumbled something about their following orders and doing their job for God and country.

"Yes, Mr. Wrench, your noble words are our greatest aim, as engraved on our Lady Liberty, 'Bring me your tired..., your huddled masses yearning to breathe free...' Seeking asylum or refugee status is a sacred trust we have always granted for those going through the proper channels; as did my parents. We welcome their presence; do we not?" The man's affect was sullen. He said nothing and the others were looking quite uncomfortable; one averting his eyes, the other staring at Stian. Suddenly the 'host's' voice changed to a friendly tone.

"By the way, officer Wrench, please greet Judge DeVant when you next see him. Tell his wife that her geraniums were 'like a picture'!"

"Judge DeVant?", blustered the man. The two young men looked wide-eyed at each other and back at Johanneson. Wrench turned first, leading the way. But the other policeman, Noel, walked the few steps back, extending his hand.

"Thank you, Sir, for your cooperation. I am quite certain there will be no more trouble now." He spoke firmly, looking steadily at the Pastor.

"Robinson!", shouted his superior. (Superior in rank only.)

# CHAPTER 37

# INTERLUDE

"And there was silence in heaven
for about a half an hour."

St. John the Revelator

Earlier Renuel had contacted his rather unorthodox band of helpers to assist in guarding his mother and protecting her from foul play. He would later return to their meeting place at the bus stop to allay any suspicion about the house. He would get off the bus at the Johanneson's stop. This sometimes freedom fighter, lately wanderer, now had a fire in his heart for making things right with Linnea, if he still could.

The bus driver's words played over again in his mind, *Marry her boy and make the best of it.* He felt his blood boil at the thought of her marrying that philanderer. *What if I can't stop it?! was his torment. I have to, I will...I'll kill him...I...I,* and then it happened! In that moment he knew his choice was between giving up the powerful 'I' of his own will over to God's will. The instant was upon him. His father's oft quoted words returned forcefully, *"God does not patch up a good man,*

*Renny. He makes an entirely new man. He is a gentleman. God knocks, but only enters in by invitation."*

The struggle within him had been loving the treasury of bitterness and revenge. But now, it was time. The long-held rebel in him had to die and he said aloud, "God, please forgive me. I need you."

Renny felt a feeling like death; then an ecstatic relief, as though everything angry and spiteful had drained out of him. He knew something had irreversibly changed. There were tears in his eyes, but glad tears.

It was then that the plan began to take shape in his mind, and he knew it was not of his own devising. It was a bold plan but a riveting one. Renuel saw the bus lumbering toward the stop nearest the Johanneson's home. He pulled the buzzer string and walked to the front. "Thank you, Sir, for your advice."

The bus driver again tipped his hat and said, "Remember, she ain't no average girl." Renny smiled and squeezed the man's broad shoulder.

"I know that; I hope she will have me." He climbed down the steps and walked away as the bus 'clackety clacked' down the street.

There was a phone booth on the corner, by the stop, and he went in and dialed up his secret contact concerning his mother's safe arrival.

"What?", he shouted into the phone. "When did they take her! From where!" Renuel's voice went deadly silent for a full minute. "Yes, I'm still here. Listen, I think I know who is behind this and at least they will protect my mother or suffer terrible consequences."

The man gave the code name for Boris Putin. Renuel replied coldly. "Yes, that's right. I have little doubt it is he, knowing his vile heart. Now, listen carefully. I have a small band of men who were going to guard her 'safe' house tonight. Instead they can help me try to find my mother. I have somewhere to go first; but I'll be back at this booth later and call you. Maybe you will hear something by then." They had been speaking in their own language so Renuel had no fear of anyone overhearing. His distress for his mother was profound.

His heart was pounding as he walked toward the Johanneson's, trying to act as casual as possible. Yet, he still felt with clarity a new fervor. Renuel had no sudden vision for the outcome of the night's events and his mother's abduction. But, one thing he did know for sure now; he would do everything he could to marry Linnea Johanneson! Evan Reinholdt would never have her or Bella without a fight. *Linney's last words raced back, "Do you want me to marry Evan if it comes to that?" "Yes", he had answered gravely, "If it comes to that."*

His answer was a betrayal and he knew it for certain now. He repeated it aloud angrily. "If it comes to what!!??" His thoughts raced. *No other way? no other option!?* "Fool comment!", he spoke again aloud. "Perhaps she would not have him now." But he felt himself setting out on a mission; not certain it was of divine origin, but with high hopes.

"At least I can tell her how I feel and about her bus driver's challenge. Our marriage could protect Bella from that 'wolf in sheep's clothing.' God may it be," he whispered.

In a forever fraction of time, Renuel Breech had been reborn. He could not know what a change was at work within him and how now, he would be aided by supernatural forces. Of such transcendent powers he was quite ignorant. (Ah, reader, how often do these 'other worldly' forces for good fight on behalf of nations and men? We have heard such fantastic accounts; have we not?) But to this 'wanderer' those had not been accounts, but only made up tales or hysterical visions of religious zealots, like his mother and father, and others like them.

Now it was he who had called upon the 'Mighty One', and in so doing, warrior 'Beings' would be with him in his struggle with dark foes. Renuel's former reckless courage had turned into a moral and spiritual quest. He had been a battle-ready soldier, but now; he was not on his own mission. He would fight, perhaps even lose; but it was well with his soul.

Renuel circumvented the Johanneson's house and came through the alleyway. Looking furtively around, he routed himself through the lilac trees, then quickly stopped by the kitchen. Seeing Marthe at the sink, he tapped lightly on the window. She startled, putting her hand over her mouth. He raised a finger to his lips in a 'shhh' gesture. The woman nodded, eyes wide, and without a sound, pointed to the garden entrance. His lanky form was difficult to keep low; but he hunched down until he saw the door open and her beckoning. Renuel was grateful to this trustworthy woman; for his hurried encounter with the Parson depended on absolute secrecy. As he walked into the garden room, Stian Johanneson came in from the other direction. His was dumbfounded.

"Dear God, Son! When did you get back here? Is your mother...?"

Renuel interrupted, "I have no word on my mother, not yet. I am here momentarily to see you about another critical matter. My 'friends' are waiting for me and we will go and search out some leads as to where she might have been taken or to whom. I have no concerns for her life as I believe I know who is behind this debacle. I am sorry for my uninvited presence and my abrupt manner, Sir; but I must ask you a very presumptuous question."

"Yes, Renuel, I am listening." Marthe started to leave but Stian called her back. "We have no secrets from Marthe in this house, unless it be for her protection."

"Certainly not, Pastor, nor do I." The housekeeper turned and stated that she would prefer to hear any pertinent matters concerning Mr. Breech later. And with that, she left. "She is a rare person, Sir."

"Yes indeed, Son, but please continue as I know you are impatient to depart."

"Yes, well, good Pastor, this is my request and I cannot fathom why you would agree; except for the dire circumstances in which we find ourselves." The youth paused, trying to collect himself.

Stian queried, "We? Meaning you and your mother?"

"No Sir, meaning myself and Miss Linnea. I am requesting the hand of your daughter in marriage. I know I am most unworthy and unfit in all ways a father would desire; but I do love her with all my tawdry heart and will pledge to protect and to love her with my life. The salient point, significant to the urgency of my suite, is related to the custody of Bella. We both know the attorney's plan to secure both Linnea and the baby by their civil union."

Stian let out a long breath, "Yes, Renuel, this is a very unusual request; but I am fully aware of the painful alternative and its present torment for my daughter." He paused and looked down momentarily; then looked up. "Yes, Son, I will speak to Linnea of your offer of marriage. When were you desiring the ceremony to take place?"

"Well Sir, because of the countdown for Bella's court case, if in fact that lying sociopath is telling the truth; it is imperative that we be married within the week. There are other reasons for the gravity of my niece's circumstances that I cannot divulge at this time."

Stian nodded his head gravely, "I accept your precautions and trust that you will share these facts at another time."

Renuel replied, "Thank you, Pastor Johanneson. Although I have not asked Miss Linney this most engaging question, we have very recently spoken of our love for one another. I hope that she would grant my proposal of adoring her for the rest of her life, rather than the alternative."

Stian's face broke into a wide smile and a low chuckle. "I do believe that offer might well please her, Son." His voice now became grave. "Were her desperate choice not so daunting, I would entreat your patience for familial reasons, as well as spiritual. But the other marriage is so base to me, that I give you my blessing. I request only that I might perform the ceremony."

Renuel's face flushed at this unexpected response. "Thank you, Sir, thank you! I am well-aware of the depth of your love for Miss Johanneson. I will not betray your trust."

Stian offered his hand to the stunned suitor and held it firmly with both of his. "Young man, I have one last word for you. You are taking to yourself a Christian girl, not just a religious one; but one who has given her soul and heart to God. She is a true believer. Nothing, no one, man or devil, can take that from her. But a husband who sets his face against her soul's deepest love would slash her heart in two."

Unbeknownst to the parson, the wanderer was a 'spiritual wanderer' no more. Renuel squeezed the older man's hand and said, "Sir, I am glad to tell you that I have most recently bridged that great chasm and the boatswain, Styx, now holds no terrors for me. I have said with the thief, 'Sir, remember me when you come into your kingdom.' No Pastor, I will not tamper with her soul's love, I will encourage it. But it may be more difficult not to tamper with her temper!" They both laughed.

Very quickly Renuel became sober and intense. "As I remarked earlier, much more is at stake than my mother's safety and even my life with Linnea. Bella's life could be in great jeopardy if it were known that she exists. I don't believe that my mother's abductors, or the perpetrator, have any realization of this fact. But other despotic men, in high places, must never know of her birth. Only God can save our country and our people from this perfidy. A very trusted few know of Bella's life here and her need for a safe hiding place."

Stian replied, "We will pray for God's protection for Bella. Let me know if I can aid in your mother's rescue."

Renuel was walking away now, calling back, "Thank you Pastor. If Linnea will have me, we will not marry without your knowledge and presence. I give you my word, Sir!" He was out the door, scuttling across the lawn to his meeting place.

Stian was stunned by this turn of events and by Renuel's words, *"Many wait for Natalyia's release." Who are the many? And what about "Bella's hideaway? Who else were they dealing with, besides Evan Reinholdt plus the thugs who had kidnapped Natalyia? Was her would-be-lover and pursuer Putin, involved?*

*And now there was Renuel and the little orphan child who was no orphan at all and who, it appeared, had many more connections; most of which the Johannesons had no knowledge.* His troubled musings continued, *A nation in tumult, countrymen in jeopardy, a deposed monarchy and a resistance movement in which Renuel was deeply entrenched?* He shook his head and walked slowly back into the main rooms, passing the kitchen.

"Marthe, come join me for coffee. I will share with you some serious matters."

# Chapter 38

## The Dress

"Here comes the bride, all dressed in white."

Linnea Johanneson sat dolefully at the small kitchen table. It was a sturdy wooden structure, painted white, brought years ago from Marthe's old house. It had two leaves, built in. Each was supported by a slat that slid into wooden stops under the table's top. Linney loved that old table and always made sure that a little glass cream bottle, with a stem or two of flowers, was set in the center. Marthe thought salt, pepper and a sugar bowl were decorations enough.

Then Linney, almost to herself, said, "These red placemats were quilted by Mom. They need some holly in the middle, for color."

Marthe looked at the girl with kindly eyes. "Ja, Linney, t'at vould be nice." But she knew it wouldn't happen.

After a long pause Linney spoke, "I need to get back to Bella soon. I just came to do one last thing."

"Vat is dat, shild?" Linnea looked beseechingly at her old nanny and friend.

"I know I won't ever wear it, after all, but I just want to try it on, one last time before..."; her eyes were sad and desperate.

"T'e tress."

"Yes", it required no explanation.

'The dress' could only refer to one thing. They headed upstairs to her father's bedroom. It was stored there, in her mother's cedar chest, under the window. Lifting the lid and removing the dress, from its place among baby clothes and other keepsakes, Linnea undressed and slipped it on. Marthe commenced the task of buttoning each satin-covered button. She attached the train and smiled widely.

"T'ere." Walking to the closet, she opened the door widely, exposing a full-length mirror. Marthe stared into it, taking in a sharp breath. Behind her, to the side of the mirror, was the reflection of Linnea, the blond, blue-eyed image of her mother. Yet, in her face, she bore a strong resemblance to her father. She stood there, tall and graceful, but girlish too. The dress fit very snugly as her mother had been a smaller boned person.

Linney smiled at herself and swept her curly hair up into a bun. Then, she let it fall. Although always intending to wear her hair up for her wedding day, tonight held a different purpose. Taking the veil and tiara from Marthe, she placed it on her head, chasing away all sad thoughts. This was her night to dream happy things. Brushing aside a few rogue tears, she laughed and said, with determined affect, "Come Marthe."

Walking to the stairway Linnea said, "There Marthe, I must descend to my waiting bridesmaids and then, a short walk to the church." Having a flushed glow, she covered her face with the veil and lifted her satin skirts. Marthe held the train as she walked to the stairway. Taking a short breath, the girl began to descend. Linnea had acted out this drama often before, but not lately. Halfway down, the doorbell rang. They both froze. Marthe stared over at the hall door, just visible now.

Linney hissed, "It's 8 p.m. Marthe; who could it be?!"

Then they simultaneously said, "Evan Reinholdt!"

The dread thought had merit. As of last week, Evan had become bolder after Linnea had agreed to his proposal. He had stopped during the day, and again the other night at 9:30 p.m. He fully expected to see her, acting as though it was now his right.

Her father had spoken briefly with him, excusing his daughter due to the late hour. The man's response to Stian was haughty and rude.

"Late? Hah! It's time your daughter grew up and learned the art of being a social presence in this world. Good night, Pastor Johanneson; no fear, she is about to have a new, different kind of teacher." He laughed, turned on his heel and slammed the door. Stian never shared this disturbing scene with Linnea and quieted the rage he felt at this sordid usurper of his happiness.

Marthe dropped the train and edged past Linney. "Vell, you ust stay right here Missy. 'T'is our home and I vill ust send him away!" She navigated the stairs with determination and a set look on her face.

Linnea felt sick to be seen in this dress, by him of all people. *Well,* she thought grimly, *Serves him right. He'll find out soon enough that he will never see me in this again.* Her anger blocked out her fears and drew her thoughts to her father's grief and dissatisfaction. He termed her choice to marry Evan a drastic plan, totally without God's blessing.

It was for that reason she had stopped tonight, as her mind was so troubled over her father's silence. She was determined to see him and try to make him understand. She had tried to act natural with him, in the old way, but to no avail. His affect remained sad and quiet. Linney had rarely, if ever, seen her father so disturbed. Now, with Mrs. Zupancic's disappearance, she feared for his physical health and mental state. *Two shocks could bring even a strong man down, couldn't they,* she thought fearfully.

Linnea had begun to comprehend her father's deep regard for Natalyia, since the terrible trauma. The doorbell rang again, two or three times in a row and she heard the front door open. Evan Reinholdt's voice rang out. With her head held high, she began the remaining descent. Wearing her gown that night had enabled her to embrace again those magical feelings of enchantment. But Reinholdt's sudden arrival left her feeling ill with horror and confusion.

By now she was fiercely gripping the railing as she reached the last step. Linnea couldn't bring herself to take that remaining stair. *She was completely disenchanted now at the idea of 'him' seeing her in her mother's gown. It felt unbearable and seemed enough to make her heart stop! Had she been counting every breath since agreeing to marry that man? No, she wouldn't faint or die; she was a strong, young woman. Remembering Renuel's words that were now too clear,* "You have to appease Evan Reinholdt and make him believe that you will really follow through with this charade."

Suddenly, utmost in her mind was her fierce protectiveness of Bella. Still, Renny's tortured words kept coming back to her, "Some things are worse than death; and this is one of them."

"Please, help me Lord," she whispered.

The time that had lapsed since the first doorbell ring seemed endless to the terrified girl. But finally, Evan pushed past Marthe, insisting on speaking with Linnea. He then glimpsed his prey standing at the bottom of the stairs and he took long strides towards her. Looking his way, she saw him through her veil.

Her words came out calm, but firm. There was a hint of sweetness which even surprised her. "Oh no! Mr. Reinholdt is that you?", and she turned away. "Why, I'm trying on my wedding gown and you mustn't see me. But thank goodness, I have on my veil so at least you can't see my face; or it would ruin all my hopes and dreams. Oh please, hurry away. I shall talk soon of all that must be planned for my wedding day." Linney was shaking all over but stood there rigidly.

"You mean, our wedding day?", he replied coldly.

Marthe broke in heroically, "Vell, you know how brides are about t'is specialist day of t'eir lifes. Please, hurry avay Sir. Ve vouldn't vant t'is to delay t'ings."

Linney had already turned away. She gripped the railing again saying, "Thank you for complying with my wishes. It may make 'our' wedding day the happiest of my life."

Very reluctantly he replied, staring angrily at Marthe, "Alright then, but tomorrow we WILL set the day."

"Goodnight Evan." Linnea never called him by his first name. It had the desired effect. He looked back and smiled strangely at her, but then surprisingly, cast down his eyes. Nevertheless, a cold chill came over Linney and her stomach lurched again.

The door slammed. In a minute or less Marthe called, "He is gone!"

Linney turned around and just stood there, unable to do or say anything, except a weak, "Thank You, God."

In a few moments she lifted back the face veil and sat on the step, too drained to do anything except stare down at the lovely pearl-studded gown. Lifting trembling hands, she looked at them blankly. There was not even a diamond ring to herald something so huge that now lay before her. Strangely enough, Linnea had never even wanted a diamond before; but now, not having one, added to the desolation that she felt.

A short while later there was another knock on the door. About fifteen minutes had passed since Marthe left Linnea sitting on the steps. She was about to encourage her to remove the dress and rest a bit before returning to Kati Jo's house. The fearless woman was mumbling angrily to herself, "It better not be 't'at man' again; or I vill 'ust have to...!" She went and slowly opened the door. There stood Renuel Breech!

Her dour face changed in an instant! She spoke in a low voice but with a huge smile, "Vell, vat a surprise! So gud to see you again tonight, Mr. Breech. I vas 'ust 't'inking how gud it vud be for someone to drop by for a visit. I vas feeling lonesome." She purposely turned him around to help remove his jacket and block his vision.

He protested saying, "I really cannot stay. I talked with Pastor Johanneson earlier, as you know; but I was hoping to find Miss Linney. Is she at home or staying somewhere for the night? Has her father returned yet? If so, did he come back alone?"

Marthe shook her head rather gravely. "Vell, I am sorry to say t'at he is still out vit' a parishioner who vas in distress."

Renuel stared at her perplexed. *A parishioner?* and then thought anxiously, *Did Marthe know anything about tonight's happenings? What about his request to marry Linnea?* Marthe could be as impenetrable as a brick wall with private information but tonight she wore an odd expression. He couldn't read what it meant and shrugged it off with other matters more pressing.

"Miss Marthe, I know Linnea and the baby probably aren't here tonight; but I have something of great import to ask her. If you can please inform me as to her whereabouts and Bella's; I will be most grateful." He bowed formally, in the old Renuel way, looking intently at her with his deeply set eyes.

For some reason that bow always touched her, some vestige of days gone by perhaps. *T'ose eyes, so like his dear mot'er* she thought. "Vell, I don't t'ink t'at house vud be such a gud place to talk vit her." Marthe could hardly keep her countenance looking serious. Renuel took her soft, older hand in his.

"Please, dear Marthe, these things are very urgent. I have obtained her father's good will. I know you are her caretaker; but I love Miss Linnea too. You must trust me." He looked down momentarily and then glancing up, saw her face light up.

"Vell t'en, I t'ink I can help you. Come." They advanced to the dining room and Renny heard a sound and saw movement ahead. There she stood, like a fairy tale come to life, or a creature from another world. He kept walking spellbound. Linnea's golden hair fell about her face and shoulders, and a flush spread over her cheeks; but she still stared straight ahead. He had nearly reached the stairs.

Vaguely Linnea had heard the front door open again and Marthe's voice speaking in low tones..., *surely it is my father, surely,* she thought with alarm. The young woman stood up, not wanting her parent to see her; if indeed it was her father, in this dress and having such a melancholy affect. Putting on her best smile, she straightened her gown, fluffing up the skirts, and waited.

The low voices from the living room grew silent. Two forms were coming towards her. She was about to take the last step but stopped. *Surely it was her father; Marthe wouldn't have allowed 'him' in again.* Nonetheless, she couldn't bear to look their way, just in case. But nothing could have prepared Linnea Johanneson for the scene that was about to unfold.

Hearing her name spoken, "Linnea...! Oh God...". She glanced, in confusion, towards the approaching person. And then..., there he was, tall, dark and rugged staring at her with tenderness.

"Renuel!!", she uttered, with an ecstatic cry and fell into his arms.

# Chapter 39

## The Late Visit

∽୨୧∽

"I would not wish for all of these,
As I would wish for thee."

Anonymous

Renuel had left the Johanneson's house after talking with Stian about Linnea. When he got back to the bus stop, he saw Pace's car and climbed in with the others, informing them of his mother's abduction. As they drove to the area where she had been taken, they saw an old bum lying on a park bench. Renuel told Pace to stop the car. Renny got out and gently questioned the man. He said he had noticed the car chase right away, as there had been a clergyman on a bicycle, racing down that hill after it instead of another vehicle. *That was an odd sight*, he thought. He pointed down the hill to the corner where the car had turned to the right and headed out of town. Renuel knew that route and thanked the man, giving him five dollars for his trouble. He thought sadly *that money won't be his downfall; by his appearance and the smell of his breath it had already happened. Besides, he earned that five bucks.* Renuel jumped back into the car and they headed out of town.

It was getting late and soon it would be dark. They drove for some time eyeing every car they passed. Renuel saw a phone booth on their way through town and told Pace to stop.

"I need to call my contact." He made his call. The man had been reached via telephone by an informer. The informer had a plan; but the meeting place was too far for Renuel to make it in time for the rescue. It was then that he thought of Stian Johanneson and called him.

Renuel felt that the most critical thing now was to go back and speak to Linnea. They had a block of time now, waiting to hear from Johanneson, if his rescue was successful; before they went after the thugs. It was during this interval that Renuel had returned and knocked on the Johanneson's door. Marthe invited him in and took him to the stairway. That was when he saw her!

"Linnea..., Oh God! Please forgive me for staring at you; but you are so lovely." She had thrown herself into his arms, holding on for dear life. Backing away from the stairway, he set her gently down and immediately knelt on one knee. "Dearest Linnea, will you forgive me for betraying your trust, and make my greatest hope to become real? Will you be my wife, beautiful lady; I love you beyond anything. I do not deserve your love and I have only myself to offer." Laughing and crying, Linnea pulled him to his feet.

"Yes, oh yes!", and threw herself back into his arms. He stood there, kissing her forehead, her face; then, very humbly, he took her hand and gently caressed it. He had been careful not to kiss her on the lips this time, having promised himself he would not take advantage of her again.

Marthe took note of it for Linney had shared with her about the passionate goodbye and its haunting affect. Renuel stood a bit taller again in the older woman's eyes as she mused, *young men, avaken not love until it pleases*. Ja, ven it pleases God; t'at's ven t'e kissing vows are spoken. "Ja", she muttered in approval of this love affair.

Renuel lifted Linney and slowly turned around in a circle, her dress flowing out from her.

"Ust like a motion picture," Marthe whispered as she watched. Her own heart was beating faster, remembering the great devotion she and Per had experienced before and during, their short married life. There were no regrets, only a dim longing for more than their five years and their lost baby. Linney's pleading voice to Renuel brought her back to the moment.

"Do you really love me? Do you promise you won't let him take Bella and me away from you, no matter what?!" Linney was babbling on in an ecstatic, verbal maelstrom, which was so her way. "We'll run away with Bella where no one can find us! We can go to Canada or Mexico!" She looked over at Marthe. "Or maybe Norway? Right Marthe? We'll be safe there. We can live in your town that we visited, in some little dwelling there, you have relatives in Vos! I remember how nice they were."

Laughing, Renny grasped Linney's trembling hands. "Yes, we will make plans, my Viking heroine. We will protect Bella; but we won't do it in only our way. Your father has some ideas we have not yet fully discussed. But we must have a wedding first, my lady."

She retorted, puzzled, "What plans? Whose way? You mean God's?" She looked down sadly. "But...God's way isn't always safe."

Marthe interjected, "Tsk, tsk; now shild, ve know t'at He is not alvays safe; but He is alvays gud."

Her tone was serious; but her words were kindly spoken and Renuel looked at her, nodded, but with a flash of something dark in his eyes. He was still compromised with anger which reared its ugly head. Marthe saw it; but Linnea was oblivious. The conflicted man saw that the housekeeper had caught his mood and he said with chagrin, "Linnea, my grandmother used to say that the 'Angel of the Lord' was the commander of heaven's armies and that he fought for us; better not argue with Grandma." The housekeeper nodded but was silent.

Linney looked at Renuel, the fear returning to her eyes. "But what if Evan finds out that I won't marry him and that I am going to marry you? What then?"

"Rest easy, dear Linnea; before He finds out, I have a feeling he will be found out to be the cur he is."

"How?" she pleaded.

"Somehow." He replied more confidently than he ought.

Marthe interjected, "Come now, Miss Linnea; ve must get t'at dress off you and get you back to Bella. You 'ust listen to t'is good man and his Grandmama and trust in t'e dear Lord. God has vays t'at are not our vays."

The girl grabbed Renuel's arm, looking at him like a frightened animal. "But I am afraid he will come and take us away, like in my nightmares."

"No, Linnea Johanneson, you and I must believe that God is stronger than our enemies. I will take you back to Kati Jo's house; you will be safe there. I have some matters to take care of tonight; but I promise to come back as soon as I am finished."

"Oh, dear Renny, you are good and strong and wanting so to trust God. I will be strong too." She kissed his cheek and quickly went upstairs with Marthe and came down again shortly. Her nanny went into the kitchen and came back with her car key, handing it to Renuel.

"I t'ought you vould vant to follow her to Kati's hjem wit' my car and see t'at all is vell before you come back." He nodded, grasping her warning.

"Thank you, Marthe."

"Ve must say a prayer, Mr. Breech." And so he did, to Marthe's surprise, Linnea's awe and maybe to his own also, though prayer had been a constant in his upbringing. The faithful housekeeper bid them well and the young people went out into the night.

# Chapter 40

## Katie Jo's Place

"There are more things in heaven
And on earth, Horatio,
than are dream't of
in your philosophy."

Hamlet

In the morning Linnea looked down and saw that Marthe's car was gone. "You really brought him back last night God! Such a trustworthy 'Father' you are. Marthe was right." she uttered and felt a poignant stab of gratitude, then bliss, then excitement! Linney felt no alarm now in the absence of the vehicle. She knew the daytime hours were safe from Evan Reinholdt. Nothing kept him from his routines of exercise and 'coiffure', in addition to his self-aggrandizing presence in the courtroom. He often bragged to her of his many 'coups' in bringing justice to the beaten down and underprivileged.

"Thanks to my tireless efforts, they will have every need provided, for now, by the welfare system, even without regular employment. In fact, it may be to their advantage not to work at all. Their worries are over, the state is their 'brother's keeper.'"

She shivered at the mere reflection of her knowledge of that man. He seemed almost evil, or at least filled with evil intent. Linnea had kept these conversations to herself knowing how opposed her father was to such government control.

Her mind began to assault her with fears of reprisal by 'that man'. *How could Renuel stop him? I know very well no words of intimidation will threaten his standing in the community. He has too much power and wealth. How was such a man to be stopped!? Renuel Breech knew no one in high places to intercede for them. She knew now, Evan wanted her at any price. Bella was only the bait.* Her thoughts continued to race and her stomach to turn with every hopeless conclusion.

"If I were a man, I would just punch him in his mean face." She said this aloud with some fervor just as Kati Jo entered the room carrying Bella.

"Whose mean face?" The baby held out her arms to Linnea and Linney scooped her away, hugging her close. She looked hard at Kati.

"Three guesses, the first two don't count." Her friend replied dryly, "Oh him, the creep you're going to get stuck with for the rest of your life? The rich and famous one with the fancy house? What a bleak future."

Linney mumbled, "Umhum." She even smiled at Kati's taunt. Kati Jo's opinion was that she was throwing her life away for a baby that wasn't hers and for the love of a wandering green card holder with no money or future?

"This is crazy. But it's your kind of crazy." She said it cynically but laughed and patted Linney. Hugging was not her thing. Linnea looked at her young charge's shining eyes. The young nanny kissed the baby's lips.

"I heard you Bella ReyRey, but Linney was too pre-occupied to stoop and pick you up."

"You came in so late; no wonder you're tired."

"I know Kati, thanks for watching her."

"Yeah sure, really hard, watching her sleep."

"Well anyway," chirped Linnea, "I'm not really tired; in fact, I'm giddy!" Setting the baby on the floor, she grabbed her friend's hands and started dancing in a circle. Bella clapped her little hands as the two girls laughed and twirled.

"How did your terror of marrying that phony turn into giddiness in one night," cried out Kati Jo in the mayhem. Linnea slowed to a stop and stared at her dance partner.

"So, you think he's a phony? No, not just a phony, but a creepy phony?" Linnea dropped her hands.

"But you said he was handsome and rich?"

Her friend shrugged. "I still say that; but what else is there to say about a rich forty-year-old guy who wants to marry a teenager with a no-name baby? But it still doesn't change what I said about his being rich and famous. Besides, what can I say when you say, with fight in your eyes, that you're going to marry that creepy phony for some desperate, secret reason?"

Linnea laughed, picked up Bella and fell on the bed, gently rolling back and forth, holding her little body close. Then she sat up.

"Kati Jo, I know this may be hard to take in but, I am marrying Renuel Breech in one week!" Kati stared at her unblinkingly.

"But but he's still missing!" Pausing a moment, she continued, "Isn't he?"

"He came back!" Linnea chortled.

"You mean the great 'Wanderer' has returned? The 'knight-in shining-armor' that saved your honor and then disappeared? The jailbird? The 'kiss-and-run' strango boy? Baby Bella Rene's weird namesake? What was the deal with that anyway? The melancholy, fugitive green card holder? That mad-at-God guy you almost gave up Jesus for?"

Linnea had been nodding, smiling and laughing at the descriptive, but true, epithets of Renuel. She looked at Kati, her eyes dancing, but her voice and affect serious to the bone.

"Yes Kati! That's the one! And I never really would have given up Jesus for him. I couldn't."

"Well, you were close."

"It's not about my giving 'Him' up; it's He who never gives us up; but we'll talk about that another time."

She placed Bella on the floor, and laughing again said, "I told you I couldn't live without him. God must have felt sorry for me. Besides, Renuel got saved!"

Kati countered with, "Are we going over that 'saved' thing again?"

"No, but I told you; you should talk with our friend, Pastor C.W.; you would love him."

"And get saved?" She smirked.

Linnea hugged a somewhat stiff Kati who continued, with a smile, "Maybe."

Finally, Katie exclaimed, "'Mr. Wanderer' better be saved, because otherwise you'll be living with a pagan, like me."

"Why do you care?"

"Because you might become a pagan living with the likes of me."

"Oh Kati," and Linney began to cry. Then both laughed and Linnea hugged her resistant friend. Suddenly Bella began to cry. All the emotional hubbub had unsettled her, as well as unfamiliar surroundings. Linney flew to her. "I am so sorry, my darling," picking her up, and cooing in her ear. "Let's go downstairs and Mama will get you a nana. Does that sound yummy?"

She looked back at Kati. "I only call myself 'mama' with her once in a while."

"Really."

"Really. Let's eat too while I explain some of the details of what brought all this about."

"That would be helpful." Kati Jo replied sarcastically.

As they descended the steps Linnea stopped and said, "By the way, do you have a bridesmaid's dress handy? Never mind; we'll go shopping."

"With what? Did your 'Wanderer' rob a bank for your dowry?"

"KaKaKaKati, you know I'm fixed for a wedding gown."

"I do know that. I wonder how your sisters are going to take this 'shotgun' wedding?"

"Oh, very funny. They will understand. I told them some about Renuel when we visited. They won't worry about it."

"Well, I don't know, after all, you do have a baby!" They were in the kitchen now.

"They know about Bella too," her hostess droned. "Ah, such naïve souls these Christians are." Linnea threw a wet wash rag at Kati.

# Chapter 41

# The Rogues and the Lady

⁓⦇

"With every haunting trouble then, great or small,
The loss of thousands, or the lack of a shilling, go to God"
George MacDonald

Natalyia felt the old terror grip her body. She felt drained, rigid and deathly afraid. A man was on each side of her, in the back seat, and she was blindfolded. The driver went at maniacal speed to get away from the scene of the abduction and the pursuing bicyclist. As soon as they lost him, the driver slowed to the normal speed limit. He wanted no police apprehension for a speeding ticket or reckless driving.

"Your friend gave worthy pursuit, especially for one of his apparent age." The man on Natalyia's right spoke in her language but his prisoner was mute. She neither looked at him nor spoke. Both men's shoulders pressed against hers. She found herself shrinking away from the one speaking. Her action seemed of little notice to him.

Even with her extreme care in coming and going, Natalyia had been detained in her own country. She had learned to be always on the alert. But in recent months, here in this place of residence, she had become careless, almost carefree. Having broken all the rules for safety, she could only hope that Stian was safe.

The woman in front turned and spoke, not really to her, but not trying to exclude her either. *That is a typical tactic of thugs*, Natalyia thought. The voice was matter of fact and spoke in her language. "Perhaps he was just a bold stranger, this would be savior. You know how these Americans love heroics. Better not tell the Ambassador; he wouldn't be pleased if it were another lover pressing his suite for the beautiful Natalyia." She laughed, as did the other two, save the man on her left.

Their captive felt her stomach turn and felt the color drain from her face; yet, she remained silent and still. Now, the driver spoke, "I heard it said that she wouldn't have him, preferred the memory of her worthy husband over a romp with the pimp Putin, that rich and famous bastard."

The other man, on her left, cleared his throat, rolled down the window and spit.

The driver shouted, "Heh, you fool, tell me when you're going to do that!"

Natalyia's seat mate replied dryly, "Relax Max, you know that slick devil wasn't worthy to clean Zaplavnov's boots with his black tongue!" The man guffawed loudly; but the woman in front was silent. Had Natalyia not been blindfolded, she would have seen her gestures and furious expression.

The strained silence clued the captive to the identification of one of their names..., Max. Their close knowledge of her status unnerved Natalyia, including the unsettling words about Galena and the relentless pursuit of the Ambassador.

Did the captor on her left really believe in the superior worth of Galena? His writings were only available to readers underground. Even most of those were found and confiscated a few years before his murder. The woman in front then continued the taunt.

"Well, I do believe the gray-haired bicyclist was more than a good deed doer; for I heard her cry out his name. It was filled with passionate zeal. Or was it a cry of warning?" Her voice was needling but with a purpose. That purpose was intimidation.

She wasn't finished. "It seems clear to me that Mrs. 'Zaplavnov' has great feelings for this attempted rescuer. I ascertain that he has strong feelings for her as well. He took great risk with his careless abandonment and foray into traffic, even ignoring street signs. The man appeared to wear a clerical collar. Perhaps the lady prefers a priest over her prestigious suitor at home."

The man on her left commented dryly, "The lady has taste."

Surprisingly to Natalyia, he did not speak of her preference in a belittling way. *They are baiting me,* she thought, *taking me off guard, presuming to know my extreme dislike of Putin. They might not know about Stian and where I've been living. This mockery is a part of their tactic to wear me down. I will supply nothing about my benefactors.* She was resolute and her expression unchanged. She would reveal nothing about Isa or the baby. Natalyia believed they were kidnappers in the pay of Boris Putin, not anarchists. But she did fear Stian would get the police involved in a search. This could have frightening consequences if Bella's future role in their country was uncovered somehow.

Suddenly she was terrorized by this thought, *What of Renuel? Had other agents found him? Had he been killed?* Hot tears welled up and began to wet her blindfold. *Was she never to see Bella or her son again?*

*And Stian and Linnea..., would they assault them too? Was all discovered? Surely not. Boris had hired these rogues only to abduct her. But had the government discovered Bella too in all of this?* Her lips quivered and began to move in silent prayer.

Though Natalyia couldn't see, one of the men tapped the woman saying, "Billijae," and pointed at Natalyia.

"Shut up", she hissed. He shrugged but she did look back at the victim. Saying nothing more, she continued to watch Natalyia. Billijae put her finger over her mouth and lifted her arms in a, *what am I supposed to do?* gesture.

Natalyia's prayer was something like this, *Dear Lord, help Stian to protect Linnea and Bella and warn Renuel. You know that I love this man. I know this love can never be, but I thank you for his care. I shall never forget. You are always good. I give this all to you, Amen.*

This was prayer at its deepest level. It was a great balm and gave rest to the captive's tumultuous mind. She gave a great sigh and her whole body relaxed. *Peace, in the presence of mine enemies*, she thought. A continuing calm came over her. Her kidnappers felt it. They looked at one another and at Natalyia, feeling unnerved. The man on her left lifted his hands and then pointed at Natalyia, but no one spoke. There was a holy presence in the car. They didn't understand it; they only feared it.

Natalyia could have told them that their 'it' was really 'Him'; and she was no longer afraid. Not even being blindfolded again could undo her now. Her captors' deep uneasiness was palpable, and it grew into an unspoken terror. One of them would act upon his fear; for his fear was not for himself, and yes it was for their hostage, but for many more as well.

# CHAPTER 42

# THE INFORMER

"There is no pit so deep,
but that God is not deeper still."

Betsy Ten Boom

The police had not been gone an hour when the phone rang. It jarred Stian from the gravity of his thoughts. Marthe brought him the phone quickly; too quickly he thought. Her face was pale.

"Who is it?"

"It is Mr. Breech, Pastor." Stian took the phone.

"Yes, Renuel."

"Sir, I have received a call concerning my mother. It may be a false lead; but the informer's name is known to me. I cannot risk ignoring it."

"No, of course not," Stian responded briskly.

Renuel added, "I am too distant to arrive there in time. May I be so presumptuous as to request that you would follow up on it, Sir? It may be dangerous; or it may be nothing at all."

"I would be willing to risk much for your mother's release," Pastor Johanneson responded.

"Thank you, Sir, but you cannot call the police for backup," the caller warned.

"No?"

"No Pastor." Renuel's voice was deadly serious.

After a slight pause Stian said, "Alright Son, I will not call them." The instructions from Renuel were simple, perhaps too simple, thought Stian. But he replied calmly, "I will leave in just a few minutes. I think I can make it in time, God willing. Let's pray." The older man prayed a brief prayer for Natalyia's safety and his involvement. He handed the phone to Marthe. She was wide-eyed with apprehension and concern.

"But Pastor, ve don't know vat you vil come up against. You must call t'e police too."

"No Marthe."

"No?"

"No..., Renuel warned that he doesn't know who is on the other side of this. Police could endanger his mother even more as well as the informer."

"Ya Pastor, t'at is true, but now bot' you and Mrs. Zupancic vill be in danger."

"Marthe, I have to help her. I don't believe there is anyone else who can. Besides, I confess that I have grown to have high regard for Natalyia. I would do anything to help her."

"I know t'is Pastor." Stian was surprised at her reply and, also, a bit rattled by his confession. Each grew silent, realizing the truth of what he had said. His housekeeper nodded, patted his arm and sat down heavily.

"Ja, she is a fine lady; I vant you to help her." Then dabbing at her eyes said, "Oh Jesu, help us!"

The stalwart man ascended the stairs, two at a time, and went straight to the nightstand beside his bed. Out of the drawer he drew a pistol. Staring momentarily at it, the memory of an intruder flashed before him. Stian had intentionally only winged him; although the man had been holding a weapon too.

Tucking the gun into his belt, after spinning the carriage, he looked up. "Just in case, Lord," he said grimly. "I may need to protect 'my bride' to be." It was a large assumption. The phrase was a modified quote. The speaker carried a pistol and claimed the same intent; except he was married. Johanneson greatly admired his work. He was reputed to also have a blade hidden in his walking stick for the same purpose. *A man after my own heart*, he thought.

Looking up he said, "I know that the wrath of man does not work the righteousness of God; please God, save these brutes from my ungodly wrath." Hurrying back downstairs he called for Marthe. "I'm leaving. Pray for us." She was already at the door, his coat and hat in hand, and he was off into the night.

Marthe knelt and prayed fervently in a tongue of men or was it of angels? Her heart was pounding with images of past war traumas. Now similar images came but with new faces..., Natalyia's, Renuel's, the baby and Pastor Johanneson's. These new fears were evident in her entreaties. She arose, somewhat quieted, though very keen of the danger, and entered the kitchen.

A short while later Marthe heard a fumbling at the front door and a familiar voice calling, "Father, Marthe, are you there? It's me, Linnea!" Marthe had been busying herself in the kitchen, mainly as a distraction, not for any pressing duties. Hurrying, she unlocked the door to Linnea.

"Vell, vat is t'is? Out again so late? You vas supposed to vait for Mr. Breech to return"

Linney spoke soberly, "Yes, I know. I am going to go back and stay with Katie Jo; Bella is asleep. I just needed to talk with Father. It's not that late yet. I'll go back soon." She paused and entered the drawing room.

Marthe interrupted her, "He is not home. Remember, he left on a call a v'ile ago."

"I know, but still out, at night... the hospital?" Linney brushed her hand over her father's chair. "You know Marthe, if Renuel doesn't...make it back, in a few days Bella and I will come here only as visitors."

"I know shild; but t'is vil alvays be your hjem."

The girl dropped into her father's chair and sat staring. "But please can you say where my father is?"

"Vel, t'at I can't say; he vas much too hurried."

Coming back to her thought about imminent change, Linney brushed aside her dismay regarding her father's whereabouts.

"As to this always being my home," she uttered, too quietly for Marthe to hear, "That's only if that evil man lets us come home, if the worst...."

She walked over and desperately grabbed Marthe's hand, "Oh Marthe, has God deserted us?" Looking up woefully, her eyes filled with fear and panic.

"Remember shild, He tells us, "I vil never leave you or forsake you". Dese vords are true, Linney, veder ve alvays feel t'em in our hearts or not. Not'ing can separate us from his love, Kirstensdatter Not'ing, even t'e Devil's plans."

In a subdued voice Linnea replied, "Thank you Marthe; I know, and I shall try to remember that." But then, once again as she walked toward the door, she looked back and queried, "But truly, where could Father be?"

# CHAPTER 43

# JANKEN, MAN ON THE LEFT

"...His action won such reverence sweet
As hid all measure of the feat."

Ralph Waldo Emerson

There was a full five minutes of silence; then the man on the left spoke. "Stop the car Max!"

"What are you talking about? We're not even close!"

"I need to talk to Billijae alone!", he hissed at the driver.

The woman said very agitatedly, "I told you, no names!", pointing at Natalyia.

Janken swore, "To hell with that. Stop the damn car!"

"Pull over Maximillian", she said in a deadly tone. "Then we can all just get cozy and introduce ourselves?"

"Suits me," the man on her left replied. Then, looking at Natalyia, he nodded his head saying, "Why didn't you tell me she was Zaplavnov's widow!" His voice remained angry and demanding.

She replied quietly, "Because I knew you wouldn't help me; and I needed your dominance over the others."

"The car had rolled to a stop by a deserted gas station. Billijae got out. The man shifted toward the open door but stopped, looking at the prisoner.

"Listen Ma'm, my name is Janken. Don't try to get out, Mrs. Zaplavnov. These thugs might panic and do something stupid." Natalyia nodded, with a shudder, but didn't look at him. Then, glaring at the men, he spat out, "Don't touch her!" As he got out, before the door slammed, she heard him shout at the woman, "For God sakes, Billijae, you know Galena Zaplavnov was an underground hero in the Resistance!"

The next words were lost on Natalyia as the woman had lowered her voice. "Yeah Janken, her husband is now a dead hero. I'm not going to see my my father go down like he did..., shot and killed."

For the next several minutes she could hear shouting back and forth, even with the doors closed. The two men left in the car were sullen and other than saying a few things like, "The idiot," or "she's a fool too!" or "What's his beef?"

After more silence and glares out of the window the driver said, "So, what if Janken's got connections; he's too squeamish for this job. She should have known, stupid b____."

The other one spoke, "This whole thing's making me nervous. I hate this political crap."

"Shut up you fool! Damn, I'm hungry."

"Me too, hungry for love." He laughed and stared lecherously at Natalyia. She could feel her flesh crawl.

The voices outside were less animated, but still audible. It was all so terrifying. Natalyia was confused and disturbed by this strange stall and the quarrel.

"Heh, maybe Janken's got a thing for her too and wants to control the loot."

The driver cursed, "I told you to shut your fat mouth. Besides, he's not her type, not religious enough!" They both laughed brashly. Natalia could feel the breath of the man beside her who was leering at her and moving closer. She inched away in disgust and fear. The captive found herself wishing the man, called Janken, would come back. These other two were low lives for hire, and unpredictable.

"Heh lady, move back over by me; I miss the female touch!" He gave a "heh heh" sound and she was sickened even more as he edged closer, putting his arm around her.

At that moment the door opened and Janken saw the scene and said in a menacing voice, "Get your filthy arm off her. I said don't touch her, she's our prisoner, not our property."

"Okay, okay! Just haven' a little fun. Besides, why shouldn't we get our licks in. Putin won't know; we'll threaten her if she tells. You know you want to." His voice was wheedling, and the last words were spoken in low tones.

"You should be shot and put out of your misery," Janken blurted out, staring with hatred in his eyes.

The driver laughed but the woman called back, "Button up or I'll let Jan have his way." That man was obviously intimidated by the man on Natalyia's left; and she felt oddly safer for it.

Billijae spoke in a command voice, "Now listen everyone; we have a way to go and we need to stop for food and a bathroom. Try to act normal, you two fools, like casual and friendly, when you get inside. Warn her, Jan, and tell her what we decided about the blindfold and all." Janken nodded but didn't say anything.

In a few minutes he started speaking to Natalyia in a subdued voice, "I'm sorry about this; but when we stop, I need to
take your blindfold off and put my arm around you, as though
we are a couple. Billijae doesn't want anything to stand out to
curious onlookers. We will stay in the car until they come back
with food and then she'll take you in. I'll go in last and we'll
meet back in the car.

Are you hungry Ma'm?" She shook her head quickly. "I
know this is difficult for you; but it is important that you try
to eat. It may be some time before we stop again; and you'll
grow weak without it."

His voice seemed genuinely caring and she knew he was
telling her the truth as she was already feeling the energy drain.
She nodded and said quietly, "I will try."

Within a few minutes they were at a truck stop with a
restaurant. Immediately the man gently removed her blindfold. As the others got out, he put his arm around her discreetly,
more on the back of the seat, barely touching her.

"We are supposed to talk now as naturally as possible.
Billijae will come back with her food and then take you into the
lavatory and order you something." She nodded, and turning
very slightly, looked at her jailer for the first time. He was a
younger, dark-complexioned man, with a short, cropped beard.
Good-looking was something she couldn't even process; but in
another situation, she might have thought so. What Natalyia
did notice was the kindness in his eyes; and she looked away
with tears forming.

"As you say then," was all she said, trying desperately not to
cry. *If he had slapped her, she would have remained stoical; but*

*his mercy touched her. Lord, I thank you for this strange care-taker; if indeed he is one,* she thought.

A few minutes passed and several people had walked by their car. The man's body tensed. "God, I need to get you out of this mess!" He was very still and then he removed his arm. He squared his shoulders and turned toward her, speaking in a low voice. Natalyia was very unnerved by his words and his affect.

"Mrs. Zaplavnov, please listen carefully and memorize exactly what I tell you. They'll be back in just minutes. Look over and stare at me as a couple would do. One of them may be watching and these were Billijae's orders. I don't want them suspecting an escape." Trembling, with only a few seconds hesitation, she turned and looked straight into his eyes, barely breathing.

"Alright, I am listening; and I will remember."

In less than five minutes Billijae came and took Natalyia into the truck stop. The others had also returned. The man, who sat on her right, leaned into the car and said with an ugly sneer, "Good work Janken, I even got convinced, lookin' over here, that you two had a thing goin'. Don't worry, I won't snitch to the Putin man... that is, for a price!" He bellowed with laughter and the driver joined him as they climbed into the car.

About ten minutes later Janken got out as he saw Natalyia and Billijae approaching. Holding the door open for their captive he said to Billijae, "I'll be right back," and looked into Natalyia's eyes for an instant. She blinked twice with a slight nod, and climbed in. He knew that her blinking was a coded sign that she understood. Natalyia forced herself to begin eating when Janken left, to avoid any interaction with her abductors.

It was close to ten minutes before Janken returned. "Where the hell is he!", cursed the driver.

"There he is!", Billijae retorted, as she saw him approaching. He got in quickly and she turned around, "What in hell took you so long! We're getting late for the pickup." With these words, a cold chill swept over Natalyia.

"I doubt you really want an explanation," he replied dryly.

The man on the right mocked, "Of course not, there's ladies present. Well, at least one anyway!"

"Shut up Damien!", the woman shot back.

It was getting dark as they got underway. They drove exactly a half an hour and by then; it was dark. Janken had kept his hand on his knee so that Natalyia could see the exact time on his watch's face.

They had all forgotten about the blindfold. She looked over at him and he nodded, almost imperceptibly, as she cried out, "I am sorry, but I feel terribly sick; I think I'm going to...please stop!" She cried out again, this time, making a gagging sound.

"Damn it," yelled the driver. Don't we have a bag or something," shouted Billijae.

Natalyia groaned loudly and cried out, "Let me out!"

The driver put on the brakes and pulled off the highway. Janken got out, opening the door for Natalyia, who followed, bending over while making loud retching noises. Her cohort, Janken, climbed back in and shut the door partially.

"I can't stand the smell. It's making me sick!"

"Can you see her?", cried Billijae.

"Of course, she's still bent over," he replied.

"Shit!", shouted the driver, as lights showed behind them. The woman stuck her arm out the window and waved them on. Another car pulled over and stopped behind, its lights blinding them.

"Get her in here!", screamed Billijae in a panic. Janken threw open the door just as he saw Natalyia climb into the car behind them.

"She's gone; she got into the car behind us!" The informer shouted these words as he jumped out of the vehicle.

Chaos broke out and everyone clamored out of his door shouting curses; but the car, carrying their prisoner, had turned around and sped away in the opposite direction!

"Oh, my God, follow them," shouted the hysterical woman. They had already jumped back into the car, barely slamming the doors shut as Max gunned it, did a wheelie, and sped off at a maniacal speed.

"There they are," he wailed, getting as close as he could to the car in front of them. But the other vehicle sped up and drove into the other lane, braked slightly, and leaning out of the window, started shooting at them. They fired several shots in succession as Max pressed on the brakes, but too late. Their car veered dangerously as the front tire was hit hard. He tried to slow down; but the car rumbled and shook as Max turned toward the shoulder and into a pasture, pulling down a barbed wire fence and stalling twenty feet into the field.

# CHAPTER 44

# HOLY VIGILANTE

"The woods are lovely, dark and deep.
But I have promises to keep
And miles to go before I sleep,
And miles to go before I sleep."

Robert Frost

Stian pulled his upper body back into the window and grabbed the wheel from Natalyia. "Thank you!" He glanced at her and saw that she was wringing her hands. He felt them. "Your hands are trembling. I am so sorry Natalyia; are you alright? I regret having to put you through this; but it seemed the only way to avoid a confrontation with them."

Natalyia slumped into her seat saying, "Yes, it would be terrible to have had them catch up onto us. They would kill you."

"They would try," he added quietly. "Thank you again for steering so well."

She looked over at her rescuer. "I am accustomed to driving from this side in my country, but steering wheel is over here also." She spoke in a shaky voice and gave him a nervous smile as he reached over and squeezed her hand, smiling back.

They drove a while, in silence, both recovering from the trauma of her harrowing escape. Natalyia reached over and took his hand from the wheel, lifting it to her cold cheek.

"Thank you, Pastor Stian. I feel you are like Savior tonight risking great danger for me." He looked at her with utter devotion.

"I love you Natalyia Zupancic; I risked my life gladly." She became very quiet at this declaration and released his hand. In about ten minutes he pulled off the highway and drove through a town until they had reached a small café. He parked and said, "Let's go in here and have some coffee and a bit of a reprieve from this ordeal." Stian turned off the ignition, leaning back with a sigh. "I fear you have had a very frightening time and I have been a bit shell-shocked myself ever since you were..., taken."

"Stian," her voice was strained, and she turned a frightened face toward him. "The other car, men...they will follow soon. They will never give up; they are afraid of him, of punishment or death." Stian sat forward and turned, putting his arm around the back of her seat.

"Dear Mrs. Zupancic, those men have to change at least one tire if they didn't crash, which I believe happened. We have passed several towns already that have gas stations. Trust me poor, terrorized lady; we are safe. I would not stop if I weren't certain. Your safety is paramount to me." He paused, "I also would like to live a while longer myself, given my words to you a few moments ago."

Natalyia looked at him. "It too shocked me when I saw it was you out there, Pastor. Perhaps the shell shocking made you say such things." Stian had to laugh outright at her comment.

"Whatever it took, it felt wonderful to say it." She smiled back but then turned around as a headlight passed.

"Be not alarmed, dear lady; I don't believe they can follow. I know of some men, coming on my heels, that planned to deal with your abductors quite effectively."

"Not police," she cried out.

"No, I was instructed by Renuel not to call them. Please, we will go in and talk about it as much as you wish over coffee and a taste of food." Stian suggested this in a kind voice.

"Which 'it' will we speak of? You must choose the topic." She nodded, smiling. He got out and opened her door, offering his hand. As Natalyia climbed out and looked up at Stian, her stoicism as well as her knees gave way. She grabbed onto his coat. Stian took her in his arms and held her tightly as her body relaxed against him.

She began weeping softly and said, "I am sorry have brought trouble onto your house." Not looking up she took out a handkerchief from her pocket as he embraced her more firmly.

"Trouble? I have not known anything but joy and ecstasy since the first moment you entered my home. Dear Natalyia, I thought I had lost you. I would have you never leave my sight again, if I could. I truly do care for you with all my being, lovely lady." They stood together just a few more moments and then he drew her arm through his and entered the café.

Speaking softly Stian said, "We will take this trouble as it comes..., together and rely upon our good and gracious God, no matter the outcome. He is utterly trustworthy." She nodded with a brave smile that endeared her to him even more.

Stian chose a table by a window which afforded a full, lighted view of the front parking area. They ordered coffee and dessert and then, taking her hand he said, "I have some important news to speak of with you. It is good news and I believe you will agree when I explain it all. I wish I could delay telling you; but I think that would not be wise."

At this, Natalyia wondered, *what could be better news beyond Stian's words of love to her. Her heart still pounded from his nearness. Even her present peril could not stifle the feelings welling up within her. She was not alone anymore and the danger to Bella and Renuel seemed cut in half by this goodly man's faith and his love for her.*

Stian got up, excusing himself, to use the restroom. As he walked away a thought suddenly assaulted her. *What if he mistook pity for love? He is such a pitying man. The idea crashed into her mind like a thunderclap!* "Be careful, Natalyia, do not allow him to confuse mercy with passion," she whispered.

Natalyia had often fought feeling like a shell since Galena's death. *Though pursued by admirers, none could measure up to him; Galena, who knew her so well. Being known and being loved, even in that knowing, was a life force not easily duplicated. She knew her weaknesses and so did he; yet he even loved her indulgently because of them. But now this man, would he love her as more than a needed companion? Would he love her active and questioning mind, her weak spirit that often raged at her enemies and mourned for her countrymen? She already found herself homesick in a strange and threatening way, like a nagging guilty conscience. Could she, Natalyia, really be beautiful in his eyes? Yes, men like Boris had called her beautiful, but it was of little matter except it be in the eyes of a godly husband.* These thoughts flashed through her mind, swift and unbidden. *Dear Lord, is it the Accuser trying to steal away a love that's barely begun?* At that moment, Stian was back and it startled her, so deep in thought was she.

He reached for her hand. "Natalyia, I must tell you this as the future is somewhat uncertain." Stian looked into her eyes so intently that she felt barely able to return his gaze as he spoke. "You are so beautiful to me in so many ways. I know our time together has been brief, though I have often longed for it to be a lifetime. On the occasions of our talks and walks, and just being in the same house together, I have had glimpses of your true self, your womanliness, your compassion for others, your godliness, and your cultured mind. I know that I can never truly know the life you and Galena lived, and the bond created by the hardships you both endured. But I hope to show you, in time, that my ardor will keep you always in my heart 'til death will ensue. I pray that this life, with a simple parish priest, will be a life and love that you can come to cherish as I do you. It is only now that I see the depths of the holy vigil that you have been keeping on Bella and Renuel's behalf. But now, here is news that I believe will lift at least some of the heaviness of your heart which you have known because of your son and little Bella."

Stian then briefly told her of Renuel's encounter with God. He also disclosed the bus driver's advice and Renny's bold action; permission to declare his love and marriage proposal to Linnea. He omitted speaking much about Evan Reinholdt, except to say that his false threats of Bella's removal were nearly over. Linney would not be going through any ceremony with the attorney.

Natalyia stared in disbelief at news that went beyond words at this traumatic moment in time. "Oh Stian Johanneson, I am too silent for any words to speak." Her eyes shone with emotion and hope more than he had ever seen.

"You certainly need no words to convince me of your happiness. Your eyes tell me all I need to know."

# Chapter 45

# Renuel's Gang

"And we are here as on a
darkling plain, swept with confused
alarms of struggle and flight,
Where ignorant armies clash by night."
Matthew Arnold

The station wagon carrying Renuel's gang pulled over on the shoulder. Their car shined its lights on the waylaid vehicle which was through a fence and into the brush. The men standing beside the car shielded their eyes to see with whom they were dealing.

Renny rolled down the window and called, "Need some help?"

"No, no", called back one man. "We have it almost taken care of. Just a flat."

From the opposite door of Renuel's vehicle the very large tattooed man, named Pace, emerged. Loudly he piped in, "So, what happened? Looks like a pretty bad blowout to send you sailin' at full speed. Whaddya doin', hittin' land mines on the highway?" He laughed loudly and kept advancing.

The man, Max, got defensive and called out, "We're not interested in your jokes Mister. Why don't you just leave and mind your own d____ business!" But the tattooed man kept coming.

"Heh Damien!", the man shouted. "Help me out here; we have a do-gooder on our hands!" Billijae had stayed in the car and Janken was on the ground replacing the flat. The guy, Damien, whipped out a pistol pointing it at Pace.

"Get lost. We don't like strangers. You're getting in our way, Stupid." Suddenly all the doors of the station wagon flew open and three men jumped out. Pace had already pulled out a small knife and threw it like an arrow, blade in, knocking the pistol from the man's hand!

"Ow!", he shouted, shaking his hand in pain and bending down to retrieve his weapon.

"Don't touch it or this knife is coming, blade out, and you won't even have to see a stranger anymore." Pace had another small knife in his hand, poised slightly above his shoulder.

The abductor straightened up, his eyes darting around; but Billijae's voice came through the window, "Don't be a fool; leave it alone!" By then he saw the others coming on fast.

"Oh, shit, okay, okay!" He continued to rub his bruised hand. Janken had stopped working on the tire and was surveying the scene. He stood up slowly as Billijae climbed out of the car. Walking towards them, his hands raised slightly to show no weapons, he addressed Pace.

"Heh listen, Pal; we don't want any more trouble. Some drunk was firing shots at us from his window, driving in the other lane. My partner here is a little skitsy since our tire got hit."

Pace called to one of the men to check on the tire that was lying on the ground for bullet holes. Renuel strode over and grabbed Janken by the arm.

"Now before that drunk pulled a gun on you thugs, what had you done?" Pace had walked away saying, "I'll check the car." Renuel's blue eyes were steely as he stared first at Billijae and then at Janken. "She's not here," Pace called back.

Renny continued, "You had someone in your car I wanted; she's gone. You best start talking." Janken had put his hands down.

"Sorry, I don't know what you're talking about. You see all of us here, just having a good time. No one else with us."

Renuel called to one of his men, a muscular black man with green eyes that flashed in the car's lights. "Wesley, would you mind keeping an eye on these men of ill-repute, and the lady of the same. They may try to leave our company before we dismiss them."

Billijae folded her arms and turned away saying, "Don't include me with these thugs."

"But Madame, they are the company you keep", Renuel said softly. He could hear her slight accent and was sure she looked familiar. He shook his head and walked away thinking, *what desperate straits could have driven her to this?*

The others in his vigilante gang were milling around, appearing in varying degrees of ominous. One had long black hair with a short beard. Another was bald with a deep scar on his face, tall and thin as a rail, agitated and constantly moving.

· Renuel grabbed Janken's arm again saying loudly, "If you don't start telling me what I need to know, my men will not hesitate to get information from one of your comrades. We are not the police; there are no rules here."

Staring coldly at Billijae he said, "Maybe you need to know, Madame, what it feels like to be a lone woman in bad company with no rules. Fortunately for you, we are gentleman." Pushing Janken forward meanly he barked, "We're going to my car and you'd better talk."

"Janken!", Billijae cried.

"It'll be okay Billi. I can't say what I don't know. I'll be right back." Renuel gave him another hard shove toward the station wagon, talking in threatening tones and words.

When they were in the vehicle Renny sighed and leaned back. He spoke quietly, "Sorry I had to be so rough; but I can't let them suspect you."

"You weren't rough enough," Janken replied sardonically. "First, I didn't know the lady we nabbed was your mother. I was sent on a different search and used this heist as a cover up. Word's out that there might be an heir to the monarchy. Of course, no amount of money is worth betraying that identity. But that was my mission; to find out if there was such a child."

"And what did you find?" "Just a grave with a woman and her deceased child."

"By the way, Billijae doesn't know anything about this," Janken commented.

"I think I know her."

"Yes, it's quite likely. I've worked with her before. Billi's not normally with those types of thugs. She was threatened in some way to do this job."

"I believe you; but you better lay low after this. Political bounty hunting is a killer job, even with a pretty comrade." He smiled grimly but Janken shook his head

"Pretty, but no romance here. She does things I don't agree with."

"Like kidnapping?"

"Let's just say I wasn't told the whole story; but then neither was she. But at least I can report 'no heir'. That was my real purpose in coming. Hope they believe me."

"You don't believe it?"

"Well Renuel Zaplavnov, I know about Isa and Oleksandr's marriage and their child Bella. Of course, 'they' never will, not over my dead body. That's why I took this job. Subterfuge is my game. I'm a double agent. The resistance has plans for a new kind of government one day. It's only in the earliest stages of planning but we are looking to establish a parliament."

Renuel whistled softly and said in a somber tone, "I should have always known Oleksandr's blood was blue. I saw him bleed often enough. I found out about his bloodline shortly before they murdered him. I'm glad you know about Bella. I am committed to her care, along with a girl I am marrying. By the way, you might want to look up Iiulia Putin, Boris's sister. She is of our persuasion, believe it or not. We were well acquainted in London."

Janken finished with, "You mean the spy, Iiulia? I'd heard about her radical, ideological shift, but was dubious. We have since had a few interactions by phone. I want to believe in her credibility. But..., if you know her to be legit...; I had heard she was quite easy to look at. So, you think that report has full credibility?"

They both laughed as Renny replied, "Very definitely!"

Janken continued. "Well anyway, if I didn't know who your father was, I would never have told you all of this. Now, you'd better start shouting and do some damage."

Renuel looked at him "I hate to, but for your safety, I'm going to pistol whip your face and head with surface cuts that bleed a lot but quickly heal. Those hired bullies won't know the difference."

Janken looked down. "One last thing."

"What?"

"This is hard for me to say. When 'they' found Isa's grave, as I had reported, they exhumed the body to make sure there was a dead child with her. The men bribed the caretaker. I know you'll find out when you visit her grave. I'm sorry."

Renuel looked away with dark fury in his eyes. Hatred over his Father's brutal imprisonment and the murder and Oleksandr flooded his mind. And now Isa's desecration; he felt murderous rage. Suddenly Linnea's words at the cemetery played back, *"Isabella is not here...; she and her little baby are alive in their new country with Jesus...; there it is light and life and beauty."*

He stared at Janken for a full minute saying nothing. Renuel wanted to believe that his father was there with them too. It seemed his fury suddenly drained out of him, like pulling the plug in a sink. He quietly said, "It's alright, they're not there anyway."

"Huh? What does that mean, not there? Not where?" asked his faux captive.

Renny smiled slightly, "Maybe we can talk about it another day. I'd like to, but not today."

"Okay, whatever you say, Zaplavnov. I'll stay in touch once Billijae is back in the country and clear of suspicion. Now for God's sake, hit me and get it over with; they're all looking over here!" Renuel gave several loud shouts with angry sounding words and finished his unhappy task.

# PART IV

# CHAPTER 46

# THE WATCH

"Lo! In yon window-niche
How statue-like I see thee stand.
The agate lamp within thy hand!
Ah, Psyche, from the regions which,
Are Holy-Land!"

To Helen: Edgar Allen Poe

Renuel had dropped off Linnea some hours before. He had gone back and picked up Marthe's car which she had generously offered to him a second time, leaving the keys under the seat. It was very late when he drove to Kati's and carefully parked Marthe's 55 Chevrolet on the same side of the street. It was just a house down from her place, well past the tall arc light. Renuel's body was tired but his mind was clear. Sliding to the passenger side, he stretched out his legs. He clasped his hands behind his neck and sat low in the seat, his head against the window. He could see in the rearview mirror and also straight ahead, should anyone approach the house.

He had no plan, except that of marrying Linnea Johanneson and protecting Bella. Of those two things, he was very certain. It was out of character for him. He had always trusted his intellect above everything else, even God. Early in his life his parents had noted his mental prowess and determined that somehow; he would be educated.

Even with Galena's incarceration they trusted that God would enable Renny to study. After another four-year sentence was added onto Galena's imprisonment, they got a word. An unknown benefactor had gifted Renuel with a four-year study program at Oxford, England. The only stipulation was that he could not visit his father during those four years.

Renuel had staunchly refused. But a patriarchal decision was made. In those places and in those times, a father's word was still law in a family. His son had so much respect for his father that this command, even from prison, was honored.

"The gifts and calling of God are irrevocable, my son. Should we, through pity's disguise, oppose the will of our good God? No Renny, to England you shall go. Greet the lions at Trafalgar square for me. I placed my hand in one's mouth, as a boy. He may remember me." His hearty, rousing laugh caused a coughing spasm that terrified Renuel.

"Father!" he exclaimed, as he gripped the iron bars that separated them."

"Don't worry, Son, it's just that old nagging cough. Don't mention it to your mother." His son nodded sadly as he saw a bit of blood on the tattered shirt sleeve.

"Alright."

*"His raiment hung like tattered leaves, thin as a saint, poor as a thief."* It was something he had read during his sojourn at

Oxford that struck him forcibly in that dark moment. It had come back to him again as he recalled his father's appearance that day. Renuel remembered biting his lip 'til it bled to stop the tears.

"Yes Father, I will go to England but when I return, we shall discuss Hamlet; since you are so fond of the play."

"Well Ren," Galena continued, "Something **was** rotten in Denmark. Was Hamlet wrong to try to uncover it?"

"Just like the rottenness you've tried to expose," Renuel replied bitterly.

"Perhaps yes," his father answered. "But, as to the play, I believe it to be the greatest one Shakespeare ever wrote—forsooth!" He smiled. "In any case, study hard Son; Mr. Shakespeare gave us much to ponder. His works have brought me food for thought, even in here, next to the Bible, of course." Now they were both quiet.

Finally, Galena spoke. "But remember Renuel; not all great writers have great thoughts, nor great intentions, no matter how brilliantly expressed. Have a discerning mind." Then staring tenderly, he continued, "And heart, my son." His parent knew of Renny's struggle with faith. The son winced at the memory of his father's sad eyes. For indeed, it also was the last talk he ever had with his father!

All of Galena's written works were destroyed, except some hand-written notebooks Renuel's mother found hidden in their flat. The Red Guards had overlooked them; or was it possible that one of the guards had mercy on his mother and left them? *Well,* thought Renuel, *perhaps "mercy had her sceptered sway", with one of his father's prison guards.*

He heard from his mother of that guard who had spoken secretly with Galena about God and the meaning of life. He also smuggled in food and medicine. When his father's wretched clothes and few personal effects were returned to his mother, the man personally saw to it, through clandestine actions dangerous to himself, that several of Galena's secret prison journals were mailed to Renuel at Oxford. In one of them were the words, "Stone walls do not a prison make, nor iron bars a cage, minds innocent and quiet make that for a hermitage." "God has been my hermitage here Renny. Trust Him utterly."

Renuel spoke softly, "I miss you so much Father; but there is a hope we will meet again." That was all he could muster at that moment. But the memories of his father were both a grief and a tonic to his soul.

After a short pause he looked up and smiled, whispering, "Speaking of heaven, I think you should know that I have met a girl. She would easily woo your heart. Mother is already quite attached to her. I think she might have some Danish blood!" He chuckled just thinking of the smile which that allusion would have brought to his father.

Of course, they never had that chance to discuss the Danish Prince Hamlet; but Renuel had heard a lecturer at Oxford who agreed with his father's preference. What a lecture it was! The entire hall was packed. Renuel often wondered if his benefactor had possibly been the twisted Ambassador Putin. That villain would do anything to keep him distant from his father and mother.

When Renny returned at twenty-one, his degree obtained, he was forced immediately underground. His father was dead, and his mother was imprisoned. She had kept her status from him, for fear he would throw all away and return home. Putin kept her safe there but put out a warrant for Renuel.

Living underground was when Renny met Oleksandr and found that he and his sister, Isabella, had been secretly married. No one knew except Renuel, not even their underground contacts. But Isa knew that her new husband was the last living heir to the throne. Renuel did not know that until later. The couple had separate rooms when the guards captured her that horrible night, guarding their secret.

They came back later and killed Oleksandr, certain that his death had ended the royal line. Isa was already pregnant and that's when he found out about Olek. Renuel helped his sister to escape from the country.

The Red Guard suspected nothing 'untoward' between Oleksandr and her and he'd heard them sneer saying, "Those Christians are such moral fanatics!"

His thoughts turned to happier things. *Olek and Isa, your Bella is already our little queen. I think she suspects her royal bloodline!* He smiled, thinking of the baby's confident personality and beguiling smile.

"Your Bella will be safe with us," he whispered. "Her new mother adores her and I am gladly pledged to both of them."

Instantly Renuel sat up in shock. It was 2:00 a.m. and Evan Reinholdt was striding toward Kati Jo's house!

# Chapter 47

# Renuel's Threat

"Beware of entrance to a quarrel,
But, being in, bear't that th' opposed
May beware of thee."

Hamlet

Sitting in Marthe's car Renuel stared at Evan Reinholdt with narrowed eyes. He whispered, "God, I hate that man!" His body tensed, anger mounting with every step of his enemy. *I should waste him. He doesn't deserve to live. He is a filthy, lying predator!*

Then quietly came a thought, *and what of your sins Renuel? "Forgive them their trespasses as they forgive those that trespass against them." Where did those lines come from?* He raged. *Of course, he knew them from, 'The Lord's Prayer'. Well, what of it?* And yet, its hushed entry into his mind, stopped him cold. *Nothing has changed!* he argued angrily and felt for the knife in his pocket. He never was without one.

Reinholdt was pacing quickly up to the house Linnea was in. Then he would turn and head back toward his car, and then

284

do it again. *It was as though he couldn't decide, or was he, maybe, afraid?* The intruder continued to look furtively around.

Renuel slumped down in his seat, even though it was quite dark. Linnea's follower had turned and walked back the other direction again. Quietly Renuel opened his door and slid out. His fury had subsided to a sullen hardness and his eyes were fixed, unblinkingly, on Evan Reinholdt.

Quickly he moved surreptitiously from the car and onto the grass. He reached his destination before his quarry turned around. Hidden by a tree, Renny glowered in the darkness. His heart was pounding from his anger and the suspense.

*"The wrath of man does not work the righteousness of God, Renny."* The words hit him like a forceful blow. "Mlynets!" he cursed, as his mind reeled. How often had his father quoted that verse behind prison bars, even with a black eye or cuts on his face.

More words flooded in. *"Anger at evil is good Renny; we should expose and defeat it whenever we can. But wrath is God's quarter, not ours. He has perfect wrath; vengeance belongs only to Him. He will repay Renny; there will be a day of reckoning and the evil will feel it."* Renuel shook his head as the thoughts tormented, as well as chastened him. His heart still pounded as his enemy approached again.

Then suddenly a strange calm descended, and with it, a strong impression that he was being addressed, *"Renuel, Renuel"*, but not a sound. He twisted his head around and then looked up, thinking. *Alright God, I hear you; but this man is evil and does evil things. What in the world do you want me to do? Slap him on the hand?*

Renny became very still as he kept his eye on Reinholdt. He whispered, "Okay, okay, I won't kill him. I want to; but I will not. But he has to be stopped." He watched as the man neared the house, paused, stared and then turned around again.

"Coward!", Renuel hissed, thinking, *afraid to tackle a girl and a baby by himself!* The man's indecisiveness rankled him, and he wondered, *could it be something else, like conscience?* He pushed those thoughts away. They didn't serve his purposes.

The sight of him turning back and walking away replayed, *Reinholdt's afraid to...by himself..., of course! Bullies always become cowards if someone or something, bigger or stronger threatens!* This thought overpowered all others and crystallized into a plan of action! It came with absolute clarity. "That's it!", Renuel whispered.

Leaving the cover of the tree, he walked rapidly across the grass, moving as quietly as a cat. Quickly Renuel closed the gap. Stepping onto the sidewalk he called in a steely, but restrained voice, "Reinholdt!" The man spun around, fear on his face which quickly turned to fury.

He spat out, "Breech!"

Renuel stepped rapidly forward, executed a tactical move learned from guerilla training and took Reinholdt completely off guard. With a painful arm twist and a fierce headlock, Evan could offer no defense. Unlike their first meeting, when Renny was a half-starved and grief-crazed stranger, tonight Reinholdt's foe was an angry specimen of strength and prowess.

He tightened his hold and put his mouth near Reinholdt's ear, "Never again side with the strong against the weak, Attorney Reinholdt! I am a man with a cause, but fortunate for you, today it is seasoned with mercy; so, you had better thank God!" Reinholdt was gasping in pain and unable to move.

Renuel now hissed into his ear, "Listen now; this is a threat, little man, not a warning. Make no mistake. I have a band of men who know this punishing move and dozens more. Some can kill a man in seconds. Their leader is of a very powerful order. Are you listening?" He tightened his grip even more.

Reinholdt cried out, "Ow! Yes! Yes!"

"Good, now hear me. If you ever approach Miss Johanneson, the child Bella, Marthe, Pastor Johanneson, or their guest, or anyone connected to that excellent family, whether it be in person, by phone, by mail, by the courtroom or by any other means; we will find you. You cannot hide from or defend yourself against me and my underground brigands. They know no rule of law. What you are feeling now is mercy compared to what they do to abusers of the defenseless."

"Your degrading behavior and your evil misuse of the court system will cease today! It will begin with the Johanneson family and the child. You will be watched by unseen foes as well as foes seen only by you. All are masters of disguise. Our leader is more powerful and dangerous than any of them. It would be a terrible thing if you were to fall into his hands."

"Okay, okay Breech! I get it...; let go! No woman is worth this." Then, in a whining voice, "I was only trying to help the child..."

"Shut up! Not another action against that girl or child will issue from your lying mouth in court or out!" Then there followed another wrench of Reinholdt's arm and neck.

"Got it!" the attorney squealed.

Releasing slightly his hold, Renuel, his voice cold, spoke, "Do not turn around. Walk straight to your vehicle. I will never approach you again; but others will, should you make any attempt to expose me, here or abroad. Leave here and know this; I am the least of your enemies. You will know and see them soon enough. They have no rule of law and now, even in court, you are alone and defenseless!"

Renuel threw off his arms from the man. Reinholdt stumbled, holding his neck and sprinted to his car. Jumping in, he floored the gas pedal and sped away. Renny smiled grimly, but he was also sobered from the encounter.

Now, he would immediately contact Pace and his other 'friends'. He would inform them of his plan to intimidate Evan Reinholdt. He had a feeling they would enjoy this tasking immensely, on the other side of the jail and courtroom.

Their mission: they were to let Reinholdt see each of them, one here, one there; but none was to come into direct contact with him. Their fearsome appearance would unnerve even the bravest of men. Renuel grinned as he recalled his threat to Evan of there being unseen foes.

"Alright God, I did as you asked. The man is not dead; but he is terrorized. I'd like it better if he were dead. I also gave you credit for being our powerful leader."

He looked up and smiled grimly, jammed his hands into his pockets and sauntered back to Marthe's car. Looking back, only once, he settled into his seat until morning, still guarding his precious charges.

About an hour later Linnea arose and checked on Bella. She came back and glanced out of the window. Under the lamplight she saw Renuel's feet sticking out from Marthe's car window. She smiled, sighed and climbed back into bed. In only a moment, she was back asleep.

\* \* \*

## Epilogue I

That very next evening, from out of his window, Evan Reinholdt noticed a large black man strolling in his neighborhood. The man paused, stared hard at Evan's house from across the street, took a picture and walked on. Evan shivered, closed his blinds and poured himself a stiff drink. This scenario of being watched would be often repeated, in different places and with different men (or disguises).

This surveillance had the desired effect. Strangely enough, Evan Reinholdt began to change. An ancient truth was proving true, "No chastisement for the moment seemeth pleasurable, but afterward, it reaps the peaceable fruit of righteousness to those who are trained by it." Attorney Reinholdt was being chastised and trained, and every hour of every day; he was afraid.

"Hear ye, hear ye..." Then came the sharp sound of the judge's mallet on wood. The court proceeded as usual that day; but the prosecuting attorney seemed distracted. After the hearing, Attorney Reinholdt cautiously approached the bailiff.

"Heh Sam, who was that big fellow with the ponytail and tattoos; the one with whom you were just speaking? He sat in the front row during the hearing."

"Don't know Sir; said he likes to observe court cases. Looks like he's known some trouble in the courtroom himself. He said a funny thing."

"What?"

"Well, something like, just wantin' to see if waiting justice still sleeps here too. "Strange words huh? But no matter, it's not a crime to sit in the courtroom."

Reinholdt shook his head saying quietly, "No, I guess not." *'Waiting justice still sleeps,'* assaulted his mind.

"Well, anyway the guy behaved himself and left. Odd type to be sittin' in the court for no good reason I could think of. It'd be kind of like seeing his type in church!" The bailiff thought he had made a good joke and guffawed. Attorney Reinholdt nodded and smiled nervously. He turned and left without another word. The bailiff, Sam, stared after the prosecutor, surprised at his abrupt departure.

"Humph...," *Reinholdt almost acts scared of that weird fella. Well, good thing that guy's not after any of us in the courtroom or I might be a bit scared myself. Yeah, tough lookin' character; wouldn't want to meet him in a dark alley,* he thought.

## Epilogue II

It was noted some years later, by those who knew Attorney Evan Reinholdt before he became judge, that a change had occurred in him, a very significant change. From a cold, hard, unsympathetic lawyer towards the underprivileged and weak, he became their champion. He was known as the 'Just Judge' but very tough on crime. Overturning the vacuous and corrupt years of the former Judge Devant was long in being reversed.

But in time, the new judge's crusade made its mark in the court-room. He was particularly active in speeding up policies on behalf of children locked into the social work system.

In a much-debated interview, he stated, "The earlier we release children for adoption, the better defense against their repeating the pattern of welfare dependency. This court's goal for social workers is to release children available for adoption, not maintain a government system gone afoul. There are 76,000 children available for adoption; "What's the damn hold up Washington? We don't want a trickle; we want a tidal wave!"

No one who had been old cronies of the playboy attorney could account for the lifestyle change. He had become reclusive and withdrawn for a time focusing only on his law practice. Around the age of fifty he married a widow with four young children and later adopted three more. An article in a city paper featuring him read, "Judge Evan, Defender of the Little Man, also a family man with 'born-again' religion who attends the rugged city chapel, downtown..., teaches Sunday school classes to down and outers..."

In a 'letter to the editor', written after the article was published, someone wrote, "There is a tide in the affairs of men when taken at the head, leads on to glory...,' Thanks from the kids, Judge". The letter was anonymous with only a first name given of 'Pace'.

# Chapter 48

# The Beloved Captive

"Love has no limits; love has no bounds..."

"Come, Natalyia; we must go." She glanced at him nervously. "Take courage; God goes before and behind." They stood and he pulled out her chair. His blue eyes were looking down at her and she saw his intensity.

Neither could deny that a pall was threatening to envelop them. He prayed softly, "Father, we know that you are the One who is greater than any darkness; and it is in this One that we put our trust." Natalyia immediately felt God's presence; it was real and palpable, and stilled her pounding heart.

They moved toward the door and she stopped, laying her hand on his arm, "Thank you, Stian," and they walked out into the darkened night. There was a sliver of moon and the sky was filled with stars. Stian pointed up at an angle.

"Look, Natalyia, I believe that is Jupiter with his red eye blinking. I've read that he is a symbol of our salvation."

She tipped her head back and the light fell across her face, making her eyes sparkle. Stian just stared at her, "Dearest

Natalyia." Taking her face in his hands he kissed each cheek with gentle fervor. They were like kisses of farewell that you might give to a dear sister whom you do not expect to see again for a long time. She wiped away a few tears. He spoke fervently, "I know it has been pressing you to speak of love tonight, of all nights. I couldn't risk something happening and you not knowing how I adore you."

She responded, "Oh Stian, if only time was longer, but to be loved by you is great gladness; much is uncertain for us."

He was thrilled by her words "great gladness."

"Natalyia, those kisses were unplanned. I think it was the radiance of your lovely face looking up at the stars. Even God must understand my impulse. After all, he created their beauty. They spark jubilation!" The lady laughed quietly. Stian grew a bit silent. Natalyia kept staring upwards. "By the way, I told Marthe about my feelings for you." Dabbing at her eyes again, she smiled widely.

"Marthe? I am glad for her to know." Glancing up, still feeling the warm press of his lips on her cheeks she said warmly, "You have given me 'jubilation', Stian Johanneson." With a bit of mischief in her eyes she said, "Are you sure it was not planet Venus you saw just then?"

Stian was something of an amateur astronomer and he smiled broadly. "I believe not, Madam. Venus is in an eight o'clock sky this time of year. But perhaps we can try again to see her earlier tomorrow night!?" They laughed.

Though his voice was teasing, his affect was intense. Natalyia felt suddenly self-conscious, having revealed her heart so openly. The pulse of her feelings and the look of love in Stian's eyes made her remember words of her mother, *"You mustn't let your lover know your whole heart, Natty; a lady must retain her reserve, even with such a gentleman as Galena Zaplavnov.*" This old-world standard of behavior made her smile, especially at this moment in which she had declared her heart.

Stian spoke now, in a decided voice, "Natalyia, at least you are smiling. My timing may seem very hasty in what I am about to ask; but please hear me out." She looked calmly at him but spoke with uncertainty.

"What is it Stian?"

"Would you consider becoming my wife within the week?" She gasped slightly, but he continued. "I say this, not only because I deeply love you, but because I feel an urgency, born of your present peril. If we are married, you are in no danger of deportation, extradition and even worse, from foul play. I can't allow what happened tonight to ever endanger you again. I do believe that you care for me; and in time, I may be able to win your whole heart."

Natalyia was very taken aback but thought, *perhaps I haven't been too unguarded after all. Mother would be pleased.* She was very touched by his fervent desire to protect her. She paused, only for a moment. This thrilled his heart.

"Dear Stian, before I respond to your words of such import, I must tell you this whole story of Bella and the dark things that make her life such risk."

He replied quickly, but firmly, "Of course, yes, you must! I feared there was more to this tale of intrigue than I knew. However, I must persist that I would rather risk even more rather than be parted from you again." With a spark in his eye he exclaimed, "Ambassador Putin will just have to step out of line. Pastor Johanneson and friends have handily thrown his thugs into the ditch and stolen his prize."

At first Natalyia looked a bit grave and unsettled. But then she responded, "The Ambassador will be very angry; but Galena would be very glad." They both smiled, stepping to the vehicle. Stian opened her door, looking carefully inside. After helping her in, he made sure the door lock button was down, and then, as the calm Pastor Johanneason looked furtively in both directions, Natalyia felt her heart surge again at his caution.

Walking around the vehicle, still looking all around, he climbed in and turned on the ignition and then the radio. There was soft music coming over the airwaves, playing a popular song, "Love is lovelier the second time around, just as wonderful with both feet on the ground." Johanneson had heard it a few times before. Linnea often chose that station. He turned to Natalyia and took her hand with both of his. He bent and kissed it warmly.

Looking up he said, "I must rewrite one line of that song. Loving you has caused me to sing it this way." His mellow voice sang to her these words, "Love is lovelier, the second time around, just as wonderful again, with both feet off the ground..." "You, Natalyia, lovely and noble, have made my feet, head and heart, and whole self to soar! I am utterly devoted to you. I'm like a schoolboy in love for the first time. After all, I have never loved a Natalyia before."

She laughed that girlish laugh which was so irresistible. Natalyia felt a thrill come over her. "I do have great fondness for you, Pastor Stian Johanneson. My soul also has risen from me and my breath is hard to find. How do you say it, "Taking my breath away?" On impulse she leaned over and kissed him softly on his cheek. "Thank you so again for helping me against much danger."

Stian was so touched by the natural gesture of her affection that he became momentarily choked up. Then, turning toward her, he said quietly, "Thank you Natalyia."

Her brown eyes gazed into his, seeing his tears. She swallowed hard and speaking in a serious tone began, "Now, I must reveal to you about my Bella grandchild. She is granddaughter, yes, but much larger claim is upon her life."

Natalyia explained Isabella's secret marriage to Oleksandr and his royal bloodline. That made Bella the last living heir to the throne. The hopes and future of thousands of her countrymen rested on her infant shoulders. Only those deeply in the Resistance knew this. Whoever would care for Bella must do it in absolute secrecy. Also, their lives would be in constant jeopardy. She must be kept safe; but even more, she must be educated and reared with wisdom and discipline. This was a must, considering her weighty future. Until the despotism and tyranny of her country were over, her existence would continue to be affected.

These words were the essence of Natalyia'a speech to Stian, spoken in her growing command of English. Stian listened in awed silence, a sober look crossing his countenance. This account of their recent foundling, who was no foundling at all, shocked him. Shocked also would be his daughter to find that her fierce devotion to Bella, as well as her strong attachment to her 'Wanderer', was something of a Divine drama. She was intimately connected, but unaware of her role. His heart grew somewhat heavy thinking about Linnea's life with Renuel and Bella.

Oh, but what a lost soul she had seemed to be in recent months! Linney's heart was continuously drawn to both Renuel and the baby. Yes, she was attached to a haunted man and an endangered, royal orphan! How juxtaposed in her love were these two objects of her devotion. And yet, how real and intricate were the workings of Divinity. He alone knows the end from the beginning.

He shook his head and concern played on his features as he thought, *we often do not see the intricacies of God's plan all around us.*

Natalyia's soft voice broke in, "So, I ask you; have you some thoughts of where baby and your daughter would be safe?"

"Oh yes, I'm sorry for my silence. I was just pondering the journey of your granddaughter and son. God is always at work in the world, is He not? Possibly you know of another story of a child born into kingship. He was kept secret and safe, brought up as a royal son, right in the middle of an enemy state." He winked at Natalyia, "Did your mother-in-law teach you that one?"

His companion looked at him, smiling, "Yes Stian, it was boy—Josiah, I think Grandmama said." They were both relieved as they pulled up to the front of the house.

Stian declared, "I must never doubt Grandmama again. Here we are home. We will talk in more detail, my dear lady. It is quite late; and you are very safe here. They cannot look for you now. Please sleep in Linnea's room. It's right between Marthe's and mine. Now, that is especially safe, with Marthe and me, both on the watch!"

She laughed as he turned off the car and, once again, he took both of Natalyia's hands in his. "But lastly, I pray you will say 'yes' to my offer of marriage as soon as we have determined a safe and loving home for our little Bella. I believe I already know of just such a couple, as well as an idyllic place, for the three of them to live."

Natalyia's eyes were shining as tears welled up, "Oh, if only it to be true; but yes, Stian, I will marrywith you; for I wish no other."

He replied with a serious expression, "Do you mean you would be willing to change the saintly name, Zaplavnov, for the mere mortal, Johanneson?" She laughed, with a gay response.

"Oh Stian, you mistake. I never knew any man not strong mortal."

A laugh came from him quickly. Sliding out of his door he went around, opening Natalyia's and offering his hand. "I am so relieved; my theology does not include haunting spirits. If it did, I might fear Galena's ghostly presence!" She smiled, shaking her head. He hugged her shoulders tightly as they walked up to the house. They stopped at the front door.

"We have one final hurdle to overcome."

Natalyia looked up worriedly. "What is hurdle?"

Dodging her question, he replied, "We must get Marthe's blessing on our marriage. She is my last living relative, my third cousin, twice removed!" Natalyia gave Stian a mild push.

"You frighted me!", she whispered, both laughing quietly as they entered the dimly lit dwelling.

## Chapter 49

# White Gloves and Lympa

"...Or watch the things you gave your life to broken,
And stoop and build 'em up with worn-out tools."
Rudyard Kipling

Stian had received the message from Renuel. Marthe would have a meeting place at a bakery she frequented. It was there she would meet up with Janken. They had all agreed it was too risky for Renuel to be in the vicinity of the Johanneson's house.

By now Reinholdt was well under the threatening presence of his 'bodyguards'. The newer and greater threat was those foes who might discover anything that could point to Bella's existence and location, thus endangering her life. Although the coroner's report read 'no living child', these men of power left nothing to chance. Renuel knew them only too well.

Marthe arrived at the bakery and was startled as the screen door shut loudly behind her. The proprieter nodded to her frequent customer who said, "Ja, it's gud to let the air come in. The bakery is varm today, as usual, Mrs. Yonson."

As they conversed Marthe's eyes swept the room and landed on Janken whom she had never met. He was sipping coffee with a large cinnamon roll on a plate before him. She was certain, by Renuel's description, that he was her contact. Marthe held a pair of white gloves in her hand. There were a few non-discriminate people seated at various tables; but that man was alone.

The door slammed behind her again and her heart lurched; but she smiled and calmly spoke, "I vant a loaf of Svedish lympa bread, sliced 't'in please."

"Oh, no kringle today Marthe? You haf found how gud our Svedish bread is, ja?"

"Vell, Norvegian kringle is a favorite; but Svedish Lympa is vat ve vant tis time."

It was a coded message and confirmed the location of the wedding, the Swedish Free Church. Stian, as well as Linnea, knew its location was on Payne Avenue. The pastor was a friend of Stian's. They had chosen the small church for the ceremony as it was more clandestine than their own. Now, all they needed was the day and time. That was where Janken came in.

Marthe waited at the counter as Mrs. Johnson turned to fill her order. She then strolled over to look at the glass case filled with pastries. The man had arisen from his table, requesting a refill for his coffee. Just then Marthe dropped a glove.

Janken, for so he was, walked over slowly. (A small wad of paper was to be inserted into the glove.) He bent over coolie, without notice, picked up the glove and slipped the tiny note into it, all in one motion. Straightening, he handed the glove to Marthe with a smile and tipped his hat saying, "I believe this is yours M'am."

"Oh, vy t'ank you Sir", she replied, smiling back. The 'courier' walked to the counter, retrieved his coffee and returned to his table, continuing to dig into his cinnamon roll with great relish.

Marthe paid for her purchase, turned and left with a whispered, "Humph!", at having to openly purchase Swedish bread instead of Norwegian kringle. She never cast a single other glance at her contact; but had noted he was a nice-looking man, with dark hair and blue eyes.

She put on her gloves and felt the wad beside her palm. Marthe walked home without making any motion to remove the note. Wartime had taught her well the necessity of guarded actions; and she would be careful. After all, this was about Linney's close-hold wedding location.

A distant memory washed over her; and she whispered with a smile, "Ja Per, I remember our secret vedding too."

# Chapter 50

# Marthe's Kitchen

"But one man loved the pilgrim soul in you
And loved the sorrows of your changing face."

W. M. Yeats

It was a sweet coffee hour. Stian and Natalyia had been seated at the breakfast table with Marthe when she arose to answer the doorbell. Natalyia started up and her eyes flew to Stian. He put his hand over hers. Marthe saw her alarm.

"Ve t'ink ve know who is calling", she said, and looked back with a smile.

In a few moments she returned with Renuel. He came into the cozy breakfast nook smelling the coffee and saw a most moving sight. There sat his mother with Pastor Johanneson, his hand over hers. Natalyia's eyes filled with tears at the sight of her son.

"Renuel", she cried, rising quickly and throwing her arms around him. Words in their own language flowed from one to the other.

Marthe dabbed at her eyes with her apron. Stian arose and clapped Renuel affectionately on his back.

"Very good to see you again today, Son." Somewhat puzzled, Natalyia looked at them through her tears.

Renuel responded tenderly, "I had something very important to ask Pastor Johanneson before I could contact you. It was urgent; but don't be alarmed. All is well now, and here you are freed." She nodded and looked at her son.

"Was your savior not a ready comrade-in-arms Mother? Those thugs of Putin felt it; their tire did, I mean!" Renuel and Stian laughed at the image it brought to their minds. Though she smiled, Natalyia still felt a foreboding underneath her relieved demeanor. After a simple breakfast of Swedish lympa, eggs (for which bread Marthe was apologetic!) and coffee, they amended to the living room.

A serious conversation followed. This, of course, would include Marthe who would figure largely into the plans they would discuss. The housekeeper had had much experience with subterfuge, albeit young, during the pre-war and later the occupation.

Her country had stood up to Hitler's Nazism and her parents were active in the Resistance. Marthe's father and brothers were caught and sent to concentration camps. All died there! Unless guests could benefit from the telling of her tales, the war had been a mute subject in the Johanneson household.

"But vone should not vithold from ot'ers, w'at fai't in God's power to help can do," the woman explained.

That morning Marthe shared bits of her history, information crucial to the young couple's new place of residence and her relatives. She had married at thirty. Because of Per's involvement in the underground, they kept their love clandestine lest Marthe be detained to force Per to talk. Her husband had disappeared five years after their marriage. It was not until some time later, that he was finally confirmed dead.

Marthe never remarried. They had only one child who died in infancy. Not once did she waver in believing that her family and husband had died doing what was right. Because of their efforts, many people were saved from the death camps.

As they began their planning meeting Marthe stated, "Free people 'ust must fight for t'e freedom of oters. God vill not close his eyes to evil and neit'er should ve."

Renuel and Natalyia were not aware of Marthe's history. In hearing of her ordeals in the war, they looked upon her with surprise and admiration.

Stian spoke in a noticeably subdued voice, "Thanks to Marthe's relatives we have some plans laid out for the safety of our little Bella. She and I have contacts in another country; and we believe it is the solution we are all seeking. I will inform Linnea of all this as well. Now, let us pray as we go forward in finalizing our plans." They joined hands and Johanneson prayed humble, but strong words of entreaty.

The day before the two elderly ladies of the Parish were out sweeping their sidewalks. They dearly loved to watch all the comings and goings of the good Pastor and his household. Their conversation went something like this, "Did you see them again last night?"

"Yes, of course Berthe, you telephoned me."

"Well Ebb, what did you think?"

"The one with the flaming sword, just like in the Garden of Eden was out there, swinging his weapon in a circle, with the blade held straight out. It seemed to me like it was on fire."

"Yes, yes, and he frightened me standing on the very top of the roof. He was big!"

"Ebbe, they are all big!"

"But are you sure it was a 'he', Berthe?"

"Of course, they are always a 'he'! Have you ever seen a 'she' One?"

"Berthe, you are right. You only see 'she' types on the greeting cards in drug stores."

"Furthermore, why would the female ones scare any devils away?"

"Shhh Berthe, don't say 'devils' out loud. It scares me."

"Me too," shivered Berthe. "Glad it's daytime Ebbe; but come over and keep me company anyway. I made some coffee cake."

"Of course, I'm coming."

Their conversation went on at Berthe's house. "I wonder what the Pastor was praying for and where he was driving away to at that time of night? Those Beings always come when he prays about something that must be big, I guess."

"Yes, it must be true." Ebbe agreed. "You know that tall fellow who was staying with them is back again. I saw him over there this morning. He's kind of a strange one, sort of makes me curious."

"Yes, but he's very gentleman like. Okay, maybe he is somewhat strange; but I hope he'll chase away that horrid lawyer."

"Did you hear him call us 'old cats' and to hurry up and donate our organs," decried Berthe. "What a terrible thing for him to say; but I wouldn't do it no matter who said it! No Sir, not me Eb! They act like it's everyone's sacrificial, patriotic duty. Listen, I've heard they declare you dead long before you breathe your last. And they even help you along without your say so. They get big money for hearts and livers and brains you know."

"No!" Ebbe gasped.

"Yes siree, it's a sign of the times. Well, never you mind dear; stay over; we can have more coffee cake and play some Parchesi."

"Well, I declare Berthe, I'm going to trust the good Lord to help me cross over when He says it's time, and no sooner."

"Amen sister. But still, I wouldn't mind one of those big fellas flying to paradise with me, for a bodyguard." They had a good chuckle over the thought of Ebbe's bodyguard.

Sometime later the two neighbors saw Miss Linnea pull up to her house. They were watching out of the window, as usual.

"There's that sweet Linnea; she's always toting that poor little orphan baby everywhere."

"They've had this one longer than the others."

"Well, I guess someone's got to do it; too bad she and that handsome strange fella can't join up. That way he can carry that baby around some and get rid of the lawyer all at the same time."

It was a hearty, happy group that gathered around the dinner table that evening. Plans were shared and hopes, long laid down, were reborn. Renuel had come back and Natalyia was safe.

If the nosy ladies could have looked through the window of Johanneson's they would have rejoiced at Linnea sitting close to the stranger. His arm was around her and the 'poor' babe was asleep between them.

Nearby, at the fireside, sat the older couple. They were sipping tea while Stian dictated a letter to Marthe who copied it, word for word, in her own language. It went something like this, "Dear friends in Vos, we have a great favor to ask of you concerning the empty 'gaard' of my cousin Marthe Hoyjiem's. There is a young couple that will soon be married, and they also are adopting an orphaned child. I will explain more about this dear family member and her circumstances which are all very proper and right. For now, they just need a fresh, secure place to start their life together."

There was a bit more detail and the proper cordialities. Marthe finished the letter and re-read it to Stian. She smiled with satisfaction, knowing just where to send it and who could be trusted on the other side of the ocean.

# Chapter 51

# The Ruse

"Love, look at the two of us, strangers in many ways...
We'll take a lifetime to say, "I knew you well".

Stian had confirmed arrangements with Pastor C.W., a kindly, but highly vocal old Swedish pastor. He was a widower too. He had snow-white hair and always wore a long black jacket over his tall, stooped frame. He had known hardship and therefore to people enduring hardship, he was undaunted as a shepherd. But then, with their good news, he was ready to jump up and celebrate. C.W. was from the old school and its teachings, where life was lived out with this, "Vell, vat do the Scriptures say? 'Rejoice with those that rejoice and weep with those who weep.'" He was very glad to give Renuel and Linnea his place of worship for their vows.

C.W. teased Stian. "Vell, it is time t'ose 'Luterans' got a bit free in t'ere vorship. Ve vill sing in the Spirit, aye Johanneson?" He laughed boisterously, slapping his friend on the back.

"Mange takk, C.W.", Stian said, "Might even awaken a few of my 'sleepers'. Ja?"

"Ja sure."

The note from Janken confirmed the day and time. Bella and Linnea had remained at Kati Jo's. A couple of days before the wedding there came a loud banging on Kati's front door. She looked down to see a large, tall man, arms tattooed and sporting a ponytail. She and Linnea froze. Bella was asleep.

"What shall I do?" Kati pleaded.

Linney replied firmly, "Let me go down; I think this is possibly a friend of Renny's."

"Some friends," Kati replied cynically. "Talk about scary looking!"

"Ya, some of them are. They might be keeping watch here. Renny told me."

Kati Jo shrugged, "Takes all kinds I guess." Linnea nodded nervously. The pounding continued. Bella still continued to nap as Linney went downstairs.

She saw a note under the door and retrieved it. It read, "I am a friend of Breech's. He wants a disturbance in front of this house so he can see you out back. Bring down your Kati friend so she and I can talk loudly out here on the porch. Tell her you'll be back in two hours." Linney took a deep breath. She was a brave girl but trembled as she opened the door and stepped outside.

In a loud voice she said, "What do you want? We've paid our utilities!"

The big, tattooed man winked at her. He was young, but tough looking, returning her loud demand in kind. "I need to speak with that Kati woman; she holds the contract!" Kati had already come down and read the note. She stepped out of the door and spoke angrily to the man as Linnea stepped inside, and then out through the back door. Renuel was standing there, flat against a tree.

Linney smiled widely, went over and took his hand. They walked into the little garden gazebo. It was well-protected by shrubs and trees, as well as being screened in.

"Oh Renny," and she threw her arms around him. Laying her head against his chest, she sighed deeply, "Is everything alright?" He looked down at her. Linnea wore a blue cotton dress with tiny flowers. It had a lovely lace collar and more lace at the sleeves. It went down just below her knees and was belted at the waist. Her blond hair was hanging down. Although completely enchanted, and wishing to hold her close, Renny held her away and stared, entranced.

"Linney, you are a lovely and winsome thing. Are you sure you want a reclusive life with a wanderer and a baby?" Linnea looked worried but smiled. Her blue eyes shone up at him.

"There is no life for me, other than with you and Bella!" Then, with mischief in her eyes, she said, "Well, maybe if there weren't a baby in the deal I wouldn't be so sure." She laughed gaily as she hugged Renuel and kissed him on the cheek. Then, with her arms outspread, Linnea twirled around. "See, I would marry you today, in this very dress, if I could; and if you didn't look so serious."

"Oh Linnea Johanneson!" Lifting her up, he held her so close that she felt his heart pounding. Setting her down, he brushed back her curls and touched her face. "Well, if not a bride, would you consider being a maid of honor in that dress?"

"What?" She was confused by his smiling but serious affect and question.

"Some things have changed. You and I must leave, with Bella, immediately after our wedding".

"Yes, I knew ours must happen soon, but a maid of honor, today? For whom?"

"For my mother's marriage to your Father." The screen door opened and in stepped Stian. He had been waiting outside listening.

"Father, are you and Natalyia really getting married today?"

He smiled widely, "Yes, dearest Linney, we are! As soon as we have your approval! Marthe has already given hers!"

"Of course, Father, if she'll have you!", she commented laughing. "But what about the sisters?"

"Marthe's approval was enough for them," he added with a twinkle in his eye.

Renuel proceeded to disclose the present safety issues regarding Natalyia and Bella. They told her briefly of the plan concerning her and Renuel's immediate future at the gaard. Linnea embraced her father warmly. She closed with tearful words of gratitude for their planning. In a short time, they all stepped out from the gazebo.

Just outside stood Kati Jo, with the tattooed man by her side and Janken following. Kati had dressed in a yellow shirt-waist dress and her short auburn hair was sprinkled with glitter. She was very attractive and the large, tattooed man, named Pace, stared at her with obvious admiration. She glanced up at him saucily, and turning toward Linnea said, "Bella is still asleep, believe it or not." "The little sweetie. She had a rough night," replied Linney.

"All looks clear, Ren," commented Pace and signaled to a car Janken had walked toward. The door opened and out came Pastor C.W. smiling broadly, attired in his usual black jacket. Stian, walked over, dressed in a blue sweater over a dress shirt and a tie. His light hair and crystal blue eyes made him a striking figure.

The two men shook hands warmly as C.W. remarked, "Vell, I vasn't expecting two veddings t'is veek but the Lord vas!" and chuckled.

"Thank you, friend," Stian replied, but his eyes were now fixed on Natalyia who had just exited Marthe's car.

# PART V

# Chapter 52

## Natalyia's Day

*"O, my luv is like a red, red rose,*
*That's newly sprung in June.*
*O, my luv is like the melodie,*
*That's sweetly played in tune."*
Robert Burns

Natalyia had stepped out of the vehicle first, her eyes scanning the area for Stian. At the same moment they saw one another. Natalyia's dress was linen, a light taupe in color. It was ankle length, with an ornate pattern cut out all around the hemline. On her head was a small cap with a short veil attached. She was stunning and brought admiring glances. She smiled but then looked straight ahead at Stian. He smiled broadly and she blew him a kiss. Her groom was captivated by her loveliness and a huge lump arose in his throat. *Love is just as lovely the second time around,* he thought with great emotion and almost a holy awe at her womanliness.

C.W. had walked up to Marthe. "Ja, I've heard that vone is 'as good as she is beautiful', just like in the fairy tale." He said it in a quiet voice.

Marthe replied, "Vell, I know t'is is true Pastor."

'Ust like you, Marthe Hoyjiem," he added firmly.

"Vell I...I...takk, Pastor," she whispered and walked quickly towards the gazebo. The old widower smiled broadly.

Yes, this bride of fifty should be stunning in the eyes of her groom; but other eyes observed her beauty as well. As she, joined by Marthe, walked towards them, Janken nudged Pace and whispered, "Look at her. Now that is a vision of beauty and grace, passed her flower, but no less fine. I wish Boris Putin could behold it, every day, for ten thousand years in purgatory!" Pace knew first-hand, from the rescue, all about Putin's obsession with Mrs. Zupancic.

He leaned over and said, "Better not tell the Parson. He's not Catholic, might make him want to believe in purgatory."

Katie Jo replied, "No it won't, but it doesn't matter. I happen to know he believes firmly in hell."

"That's even better!", Janken quipped and Pace laughed.

The girl whispered, "Just forget it all guys, cuz Pastor J is into the forgiveness thing."

C.W. and Johanneson walked back to the Gazebo area. Renuel had left Linnea and now approached his mother, offering his arm. Her gloved hand looped through it and she held a single white rose in the other. Marthe stepped away as they moved forward.

At that moment C.W. walked up and offered his arm. "May I escort you as a friend of t'e groom?"

Marthe nodded and said quietly, "Takk Pastor."

Stian observed this with a smile. *I am amazed; seems Marthe has forgiven his being Swedish!* A humorous moment, but his mind quickly shifted back to Marthe's actions the day before.

She had sent the letter off to Vos. It was a real beginning, preparing the way for Renuel and Linnea. She had also telegraphed her cousin, Haakon Alesund, apprising him of the employment needs of Renuel. Because the property legally belonged to Marthe, she would preceed the three of them, lending credibility to their soon arrival there. As their temporary housekeeper, she would assist them in establishing their new home. Marthe would also visit her relatives as a part of the charade. The story was: *she had come to Norway to help a dream come true for a young relative as well as her husband and child.*

Linnea was ecstatic to have Marthe stay with them for a time. She told her father later with tears in her eyes, "It's like Rebecca, whose nurse went with her when she married Isaac. It must have meant so much to have her go too. Rebecca left her family, home and country, like me Father, and her father gave his blessing just as you have."

Stian stood in the front of the gazebo as Renuel stopped with Natalyia, a short distance away. Marthe walked up with C.W. and stood on the opposite side of Stian. The old pastor stood beside the groom. Linnea walked slowly forward, followed by Natalyia, her eyes on Stian. Pace and Janken sat beside Kati Jo and just behind them were Ebbe and Berthe. They had been asked by Stian to help Marthe serve refreshments back at the manse. They were delighted to be included. Ebbe then stood, lifted a flute to her lips and played a beautiful rendition of the Lord's Prayer.

C.W.'s bass voice rang out and his gray eyes danced. "Dearly beloved, ve are gat'ered toget'er, in t'is place, before God and t'ese vitnesses..."; and seldom were those words more truly spoken. He then read almost without accent, "T'rough the glorious and trying years t'at lay before you, may the vows you speak hold you securely in each ot'er's arms. May the memories of your past life enrich you bot and give credence to God's new gift of love."

Stian leaned closer to Natalyia and whispered, "This is our wedding day; I can't believe it!" She smiled in a slightly shy way and he thought. *Here she is beside me, Natalyia Zaplavnov, such a dark-haired beauty, and my very own bride. Queen Esther could not compare in my eyes.* Visions of their life together flashed before him, holding her in the night, walking, talking and living day by day in the brightness of her company. He had relegated those joys to the past but ..., he heard his own voice saying, "For richer or poorer, in sickness and in health, to love and to cherish, til death do us part."

Pace looked at Kati Jo and whispered, "Serious stuff, huh?"

"Shhh, no talking now."

He smiled at her with obvious infatuation, still whispering, "I really mean it; I'm interested; let's talk over a beer, later."

"Champagne," she replied smiling.

He smiled, "Did you hear the guy say, "Before God and these witnesses?" Then, pushing lightly against her, "Heh, that's us, witnesses." Kati just shook her head trying to look indifferent.

"...To keep you from the fowler's snare...", the minister quoted, concluding his homily.

"What the crap is that?", Pace demanded softly.

His pretty, new companion hissed, "I have no idea!", and stepped away slightly, trying not to laugh.

"By the aut'ority...", and C.W. declared those ancient words, "I now pronounce you husband and vife!" A chill ran through Kati Jo; something she had never felt before at a wedding.

"This really must be a holy thing," she remarked to Pace.

"Feels like it, huh?", he agreed, staring at her.

The small group cheered and clapped as Stian kissed Natalyia and then smiling broadly, lifted her in his arms. She laughed, holding on to her hat and bouquet. He held her very tightly and she said, "I love you, my husband, and kissed him on the lips." Ebbe and Berthe dabbed at their eyes, each with a lovely, starched handkerchief.

"Oh Ebb, I'll bet those big ones will be on the roof tonight for sure, chasing the devil away!"

"Bert, don't scare me like that; what if we see the devil? I'm not going to look."

"Oh, don't worry Ebb, he can't trouble us; we're Christians; we have the Holy Ghost, don'tcha know?"

The woman nodded uneasily, whispering. "Don't say, 'ghost' Berthe, it scares me. Say 'Spirit', okay?"

After congratulating her father, Linnea hugged Natalyia. Shortly after, she disappeared to check on Bella. Janken had slipped away earlier and had been pacing the downstairs level. He was armed, in the unlikely instance he would need to defend the child. Linnea came back downstairs, smiling.

"Asleep! Resting up for Renuel and my wedding day!" laughing gaily. Just then Natalyia entered the house and the girl went back outside. Walking over, she placed her hand on Janken's arm.

"Thank you Janken."

"Glad I could be here, Madam." She paused and continued speaking in their language, "Have you heard from Billijae?"

"Not personally, but she is back home living underground, in the protection of a very trusted friend. This friend has defected to the Resistance, at great personal risk; since she is closely connected to the new government."

"The new tyranny, you mean." Natalyia replied darkly, and Janken nodded.

"You know now, Mrs. Zaplavnov, that I did know of Bella's existence and her link to the monarchy. But I did not know it was you whom we were kidnapping."

"Yes, of course I know that Janken. Think no more of it. But who is that 'friend' of whom you speak? I may know her." Natalyia was surprised but not shocked at his revelation.

"It is Iiulia Putin, the Ambassador's sister."

"Oh, of course, I should have known right away," she added quickly. "She is courageous, loyal and... beautiful," he smiled, with a twinkle in his eyes. Then, in a serious tone, "It is she who knew that Billijae was thrown in with those low lifes because of threats against her family by Iiulia's brother. He knew he could force Billi to follow through and bring you back unharmed. Billijae's family has since escaped the country."

Natalyia felt a cold chill come over her. She knew Boris had no intentions of keeping her 'unharmed' once she was his captive. Janken touched her arm gently.

"You are safe from him now. Your name is Mrs. Stian Johanneson and that madman has lost his power over you."

"Yes, of course you are right." She smiled, with a slight shadow crossing her countenance. Then, her eyes began to sparkle again. "Come Janken, you must meet my new husband! By the way, I know Iiulia Putin fairly well. Her mother and I were confidantes. You would do well to get to know her 'fairly well' too."

"Yes Madam, I will try as I am already quite convinced!" He laughed and offered her his arm.

# Chapter 53

# The Wedding the Wanderer and the Wayfarers

"When love with one another so
Interanimates two souls
That abler soul, which thence doth flow,
Defects of loneliness controls."

John Donne

Renuel stared with enraptured eyes at the girl walking the aisle with her parson father. Many images flashed before him; but the recurring one was the first one, when he saw her girlish face under the lamplight on that desperate, winter night. Now here she came, still his 'beatific savior', veiled and lovely, dressed in her mother's ivory lace. Now, she was entrusting herself again and he yet remained, an untried lover. *Why should she or they give such a treasure away, such a girl as Linnea Johanneson. How could he ever deserve her? Only God could know; and He may not tell.* Renuel could feel emotion overcoming him but, other than watery eyes, he gazed ahead and stood straight and tall, awaiting his bride.

Linnea could never forget looking down the aisle as she took her father's arm, a strong steady arm that she had always leaned on so gladly. But now she only had heart for Renuel Breech. That tall frame looking devotedly at her from deeply set eyes. Those same eyes that had haunted her with frightening desire were tender now, tho' still fervent. To be thought beautiful and desired was a sweet potion for Linnea Johanneson. It would always be so. Renny often asked her, in times to come, why did she love him?

"Because there is only one Renuel, otherwise I would be torn apart, having to love two men! But because there is only one you; there is no one else for me to love, silly man!" And that was that. Renny would just smile and shake his head. He really did understand it vaguely, because although there were many beautiful, talented, appealing ladies that crossed his path, none of them was Linnea.

Kati Jo stood to Renny's far left and Pace across the aisle. What strange companions were Renuel the freedom fighter, and tattoo man, Pace, the beer brawler. Pace looked over at Kati and winked. She wore a tea length, green satin gown with cap sleeves just slightly over her tanned shoulders. Her auburn hair and slightly freckled skin were magical to the groomsman. He whispered to the groom as he stared at the bridesmaid, "Damn, I wish I could trade places with you today!"

Pastor C.W. Nelson looked over at Pace with a frown and said quietly, "I'm free next week if you two are saved by t'en," chuckling softly.

Linnea's dress was as breathtaking as on the day her mother was wed. True, the color was more ivory than white, but the bead and lacework were intricate and Linney's fair skin showed off the handiwork beautifully. They had purchased a new shoulder length veil and attached it to the tiara Kristin had worn. Linnea wore her mother's diamond ring on a chain, and it sparkled in the sunlight. Her bouquet was made up of leafy gardenias with ivy flowing down eight inches or so. Kati Jo had a smaller version. The train followed six feet behind, with lace borders, as its satin length traversed down the aisle.

As soon as Lohengrin's Bridal March began, the small audience stood; but the beckoning arms of C.W. lowered the crowd to be seated," At the bride's request," he stated. Still it was a grand moment when they all arose, and it gave Linney the shivers.

"And I saw the new Jerusalem coming down from heaven like a bride adorned for her husband." These were Renuel's thoughts as he saw Linnea coming, replaying ancient words from his grandmother's lessons. "So true Grandmama," he whispered in awe.

Linney felt her father's arm tighten around her hand as they moved slowly forward. She smiled under her veil and looked up at him. A lone tear escaped his eye and he whispered, "All of Kirsten's girls are wed and gone now; but you are going very far away, my dearest child. I will miss you."

"Yes Papa, as will I, but Natalyia and Renny will care for us, and that makes me glad." That was all there was time and place for. Renuel stepped forward and Stian placed Linney's hand in Renuel's with a tender smile.

"She is yours now Son. Guard her well." He lifted her veil slightly and kissed her cheek. Stepping up to the platform alongside of C.W. they began the ceremony.

Renuel and Linnea requested the traditional vows as both parents had emphasized the great thought and effort behind the original writers. C.W. had bellowed them forth at the brief rehearsal time.

Stian added, "Do not say these vows but once…, not today. Those words will run over and over in your minds at crisis times and remind you of your promises. They should not be lightly spoken nor discarded for trite replacements."

Stian was the one that conducted the exchange of vows on their wedding day. "For better or worse, for richer or for poorer, in sickness and in health, to love and to cherish 'til death do us part; and so, I pledge you my troth." Renny and Linnea both later said that they were awed pledging themselves and speaking sacred words countless others had spoken over the years. Those vows had an eternal dimension to them, and indeed replayed themselves during the very hard times that were to come.

C.W. began his marriage homily with, "It vas the best of times, it vas the worst of times" and ended with…,and t'ey lived happily ever after til the trump of God !" The words in between were laced with humor, pathos and wisdom from the book of Proverbs. He was a good man and wanted them to hear truth, and so it was.

Stian stepped forward again. After a few words of charge and counsel he declared, "By the power vested in me…, I now pronounce you husband and wife. You may kiss the bride." Since that afternoon in the sunroom, when Renuel had given in to his passion, he had restrained himself. He had not kissed Linnea on her lips since. Taking her tenderly in his arms he now threw restraint to the wind and kissed her so thoroughly that she broke away laughing, then kissed him back.

The crowd was delighted, except for Pace, who mumbled, "That guy has all the luck today."

Kati Jo whispered, "Not luck Bucko, love!", and laughed grabbing his arm. "Cheer up you can kiss her on the cheek in the receiving line; but you'd better hurry!"

"I'm talkin' about your receiving line, Miss Kati!", he declared.

She smiled cagily and taunted with, "Don't have one...yet!"

Pace pushed against Kati Jo gently as they walked the rest of the way down the aisle together, smiling widely.

"Guess those vows mean 'no backsies,' huh?"

She looked over at him laughing, "Really scary for you, huh Tattoo Man?!"

Marthe had sat with Ebbe and Berthe and all three had their ironed handkerchiefs put to good use. Linnea wanted Marthe to stand up next to her. She could walk down the aisle with C.W. since he was assisting anyway. Marthe would have none of that!

"I would do it," said Ebbe smiling coyly. "After all, he is a widower, poor man."

"Humph!" muttered Marthe and walked away.

At the reception itself, C.W. took Marthe off guard by asking her if she would dance a waltz with him. She politely accepted, eyeing the shocked ladies with an upturned nose. The older parson was quite a leader and light on his feet. He had Marthe smiling in delight, chatting as he led her around the floor.

Afterward, Berthe and Ebbe walked over to their friend and Ebbe said in a teasing tone, "Humph; thought you would have 'none of that', eh Marthe?"

"'Ust being polite," Marthe responded firmly, then gave them a charge. "Now ladies, you know t'at I must leave tomorrow for t'e old country and making t'e gaard gud for t'e new married couple and Bella. So t'en maybe you and Berthe can dance 'vit t'e 'poor widow man' 'vile I'm away. But, 'ust remember, ladies, I **vill** be back." Here she turned and chuckled, leaving a befuddled Ebbe and Berthe to wonder.

* * *

It was two weeks since their wedding. The ocean voyage was a much-needed reprieve as well as their honeymoon of sorts. Standing together, leaning on the ship's railing, Renuel stared down at the deep waves splashing against the ship's side. There was something steadying and reassuring about the sea. No matter how it could rage, it always returned to its oceany self.

"Your proud waves must stop here," his grandmother had loved saying with ardor. "You see Renny, God is in charge."

Linnea had stooped to tuck the blankets around Bella as she lay in her buggy. She kissed the baby and then looked up at him with shining eyes.

Renny thought, *that lady, those blue, blue trusting eyes, blond curls blowing about her face, that darling lady loves me, is really mine.* But instead he declared, "I have two girls now. Both charming. and both all mine." His expression was glad but his voice emotional.

"Yes Renny, but lucky for you, only one is a wife with opinions!" She laughed gaily, mischief in her eyes.

He countered, "Is one of those opinions the reason that baby is tucked up in bed with us half the time, 'wife'?" They both laughed.

"But she is a sweet interloper; isn't she husband?"

He quipped, "Is she always now?" Linnea blushed and Renny pulled her close, kissing her and pinching her waist. Linney jerked away with a squeal, but then came back and kissed his cheek.

"See Bella Rene, your Daddy is a tease." The lady leaned over the railing again and took a deep breath, "Oh Renney, I'm so glad we decided to take the ship, aren't you? Marthe came over this way when she was sixteen you know; and I feel like I am making the voyage with her."

Renuel nodded indulgently, "I know."

Linney chattered on, "She was the dearest thing to my mother and family and now, to us in this new place. I can barely wait to see her there and our little gaard home. Our very own home, Renny. Oh, I am happy beyond words!" She turned and hugged him hard.

He laughed. "I hadn't noticed. You seem to be doing quite well with your words." His voice was playful, and she smiled. "You are truly my little wordsmith, Linnea Breech!" She kissed him again.

Linnea's spontaneous affection always touched Renuel's heart. *She was so unspoiled. He hoped the clandestine circumstances of their life would not chase that spontaneity away. He was accustomed to stealth and caution. She was not. Be that as it may, her carefree ways would help to establish a smokescreen for their real purpose in living there. Of course, any shady characters would have to get passed Marthe first.* That image made him smile.

"What are you secretly smiling about?"

"Oh, just thinking about Marthe's protectiveness.

She is quite a she-bear," Linney replied, frowning slightly. "Are you worried about our safety, Ren? Oh, don't worry, dear love, God is taking care of us. Marthe just thinks she is."

He nodded and chuckled as he bent over and picked up the baby who was scolding them for her perceived 'neglect'. "You see, this child already thinks she is royalty. She says, "Obey my commands, Papa..., and I do!" They laughed as Bella clapped her hands.

The ocean waves, like their honeymooning, were sometimes calm, sometimes quite stormy during their crossing; but they were also calm and dreamy!

They arrived in their new country of residence with anticipation, but also, with some uneasiness about the unknown that lay before them. However, Linnea was awed and full of admiration at the confidence Renuel demonstrated. It was as though he was made for a life of challenge and suspense. "Danger and intrigue must be fulfilling Linney, as so many men have embraced it. Now we will embrace it together." "Hmmm..." she replied, "I think you are just showing your bravado to comfort me. Plus, I only heard you say 'men' have." "Just men have, ocean-crossing lady?" he countered. Stepping off the gang plank Linnea Johanneson Breech smiled, but with a quiver in her stomach.

# PART VI

# CHAPTER 54

# THE GAARD

"A house is built of tiles and wood
Of logs and posts and piers.
A home is built of loving deeds,
That last a thousand years."

Victor Hugo

Linnea was eager to see the inside of the gaard house. She
left Bella outside in the arms of Renny who was perusing
the fields and outbuildings. His eyes also scanned the long view
of where he and Linnea would spend an undetermined length
of time. Though they were not far from town, both had been
city dwellers and this would be new to them. Yet, it felt safe
and peaceful to Renuel not to be under the scrutiny of towns-
people. Still, it could be lonely too, especially for Linney.

He looked into the eyes of the baby who was squirming to
get down. He squeezed her more tightly, kissing her soundly,
which made her protest even more. She reached her arms
towards the house where Linnea had disappeared.

"I will let you down, little one, and you will be safe here; but you must stay close to us. Yes, I know how you love your Mama; how could you not, my Sweet? She is both good and Christian, but not too good, nor too Christian; else how could she love me?" Renuel laughed heartily at this and at Bella's loud cries. Linney appeared at the doorway, hearing the baby's cries.

"Bring her to me Ren, and oh, do come and see our little dwelling. It is so charming!" The house was old but very clean. Little did they know how many hours of labor had been accomplished at Marthe's tireless hands. Yet, it being a place she had lived with her own family, there were many images that had crowded her mind in sweet retrospect. Even some of the same chores had once been hers, like scrubbing the wood floor on her hands and knees. Her brothers had the task of waxing it during the long winter months, which occupied troublesome bouts of boredom for them. She smiled, remembering the testy glares they had directed at her in protest.

A closed, yet unoccupied house falls quickly into entropy. It becomes the haunt of many little creatures. They leave their accoutrements everywhere; like careless, naughty children who leave a trail of toys, crumbs and small debris behind them. In this case, there were shells and hoarded animal 'treasures' in corners and cupboards, not to mention dried insect remains and nastier stuff.

What the young couple saw was a spotless house with a clean wooden floor, scrubbed and waxed. A large braided rug, oval and multicolored, rested in the center of the great room. The furniture was sparse but near the kitchen stood a long, rustic table, with four chairs, crafted of a similar wood variety.

In the center was spread out a white cloth with an empty pitcher placed there.

"Oh Renny, dear Marthe put that pitcher there just for me to fill with wildflowers!" "I do not doubt it." She smiled. "I'll go outside, as soon as we've seen the whole house, and pick some flowers with Bella." Linnea had taken the baby from Renuel and setting her down, took her hand firmly as she was only just beginning to walk and was very tottery.

They drifted slowly past the stone fireplace to a cradle, shaped like a Viking boat. It had a dragon head at the top, curving its neck downward as though guarding some infant of yesteryear. Linney looked down. "See ReyRey," a baby cradle just like the Viking ships. But your Papa will remove that creature head; for we know who really protects our babies. Jesus sends his angels, doesn't he?" She kissed the top of her dark curls.

Renuel smiled. "Well, I do not know 'little one'; perhaps God thinks it best to also have a dragon nearby to help fend off our foes. After all, it's a long way for angels to fly here from heaven!"

The shocked girl chided her husband, "Renny, it's irreverent to talk about God and superstition in the same breath!" But Linnea had to turn away quickly to hide her smile. He loved to tease her about sacred things, just for a reaction. She bent low and spoke to Bella just loud enough for her husband to hear.

"Shhh dearest, don't tell Papa, but you are too big for that cradle. Perhaps a different baby will sleep there one day. I think we should name him Oleksandr Johann. What do you say to that? Then maybe your Papa will change his mind about that scary dragon staring at his baby boy!"

Linnea laughed in delight as Renuel shook his head, smiling, "Very amusing, little wife." They carefully investigated the rest of the gaard cabin. Coming back into the main room, they set Bella on the floor.

Linnea declared, "Oh Ren, isn't this just the most enchanting place!" She threw herself into his arms as the baby clapped in delight. He lifted his wife and held her tightly.

"Yes, it is that. But I especially liked your idea of making a baby to occupy that cradle. Seems like a very enchanting past time to me." With a flush Linney looked into his laughing, dark eyes, kissed him and released her hold as he set her down. Giving Renny a light tap, on his head, she scooped up the baby, grabbed the pitcher and headed for the door.

Looking back, Linnea smiled saying saucily, "Your Daddy has a lot of work to do unloading our things. I think he needs something to do, don't you baby?" She laughed and they went out into the sunlit day.

Renuel carried in several loads from the old 'Woody' automobile Marthe had found for them. Earlier, they had found a note from her attached to the ice box, stating that there was some food in the cupboard and a few things also in the ice box. *How thoughtful of her to give them this time to be in the house on their own. It was so like Marthe. He wondered if she and Per, her husband, had spent much time here at the gaard. Renuel often thought about Marthe's brief, married life and all the subterfuge they lived out during the Nazi invasion. Her countrymen had shown exemplary courage and resourcefulness; but many paid for it with their lives. Just like Oleksandr and Per, now he was living that life too; but he shook off the thoughts of danger and leaving*

*Linnea behind. God had to be trusted completely or not trusted at all. No middle ground was tenable.*

He shook off his dark musings and went upstairs. There was a large, loft bedroom up a wooden spiral staircase. There were two windows, with shutters attached, that blocked out the light and afforded privacy. Attached to that room was a smaller room which held a wooden crib and could also have ample space for another small child's bed.

The other bedroom on the lower level was where Marthe would stay. There was even indoor plumbing and a wringer washing machine, installed within the last decade. All the walls were log and Marthe said the cabin gaard was five hundred years old. Its age was a documented fact; yet engineers were still baffled by the techniques that kept the logs of these cabin homes almost airtight, even after centuries of use.

Renny had looked at Linnea's eyes, filled with wonder, as they surveyed her minimally furnished dwelling. *How many young brides,* he wondered, *would be so taken with such a rustic environment thousands of miles from home? So 'other worldly' was she, yet so real and sturdy and full of anticipation for the challenges which lay before her.*

When she came back from gathering wildflowers, she arranged them in the pitcher and lifted Bella up saying, "Now, doesn't that just look so homey and pretty, Baby?" Bella clapped her hands again, as babies are wont to do, and Linney gave her a tight squeeze and a kiss. Putting her on the floor, with some bowls and wooden spoons, she stated, "I'm hungry ReyRey, and I'll bet Papa is too," as she moved into the kitchen.

Linnea prepared a simple lunch with their provisions and, beside their plates, folded small cloth napkins she had found in a drawer. They had held hands and prayed, about to partake, when something unnerving happened.

There was a loud banging on the front door. They both stared at it wide-eyed. Renuel pointed at Bella in her little highchair and whispered to Linney, "Go to the bedroom with her, just for this once, until I see who it is," as he lifted her out.

Linnea grabbed some cheese from the table to quiet Bella, took her, and hurried to the back room. Renny had placed his loaded pistol in the drawer of a tall wooden cabinet, near the front door, but did not go for it. Looking back, he saw Linnea softly close the door. As he approached the front door, another volley of knocking came, and then a booming voice calling, "Anyvone hjem?" Renuel put his hand on the knob and turned it slowly, wondering why he should be feeling for his pocket-knife. Opening the door, he saw before him a very large, middle-aged man with a red mustache and a broad smile.

"Vell gud, you haf arrifed! Cousin Marthe vill be pleased. I haf t'is soup and also, some fish, canned lingonberries and bread. Ve brought some more chairs too. Oh ja; I brought anot'er bed. A shild vone." Here he winked at Renuel. "You vill need t'at some time fer sure, ja! I'm Haakon Alesund. Velcommen to Norge country!" Renny smiled widely. Relief washed over him and he felt slightly weak.

"Yes, thank you Mr. Alesund, we are grateful for all these items. Come in! Come in!" He extended his hand, "I am Renuel Breech. My wife and daughter are in the back. I'll just go and get them."

Haakon handed Renny the pot of soup and replied, "I haf my 'Lili', Hanne, and my 'holger', Hakkon, vit' me. I vill 'ust go and help t'em bring in t'e ot'er t'ings."

Renuel hurried to the bedroom and opened the door gently. Linney was in the back near an opened window, holding Bella close. He spoke quietly, "I'm sorry I frightened you; it is only Haakon Alesund, Marthe's cousin that she told us about and his children. I just didn't know."

"Oh!" she exclaimed in relief fear still resident in her eyes. She blinked back tears and handed Bella to Renuel whispering, "It's alright. Thank you, Lord." Smiling, she walked confidently out of the room and went to the doorway. Two quite young children were coming in with the food in baskets.

"Why, you must be Hanne and Haakon. Mrs. Hoyjiem has told me all about you and that someday you want to take piano lessons." The children smiled and brought the baskets to the table.

The boy replied quickly, "Vell, my sister vants t'e music lessons and my Mor says I must. But I 'ust vant to go fish at 'Freja's Tears'. T'ere are little white jelly fish that the big fish like to eat and get fat," offered Haakon boldly.

"Ja", said the girl. "T'e jellyfish look 'ust like stars in t'e black vater." Little Hanne's eyes were sparkling.

Linnea replied, "I've heard about that beautiful waterfall. We must visit it sometime soon."

Mr. Alesund had come in with Renuel, both carrying the bed, and had overheard Linney's remark. "It is very beautiful in Juni, springtime,' ven t'e hunks of glacier have fallen into t'e fjords."

"Sounds like an adventure," Linney offered. Alesund cried out with gusto.

"You are in Norvay now and it is t'e Norwegian vay to be hungry for adventure."

Renuel laughed saying, "I believe we have established that my wife is a lover of adventure, Sir."

"Vell t'ats gud, especially ven you are young." They had set the bed down and Alesund clapped Renuel on the back, "Ot'erwise you vill get lasi like me!", laughing with gusto.

Linney entreated, "You have brought us all this food. Please sit down and join us for lunch." Their visitor could see the sparsely set table with only cheese, salami and crackers. The children looked at their father hopefully. Little Hanne was already playing on the floor with Bella.

"Vell, mange takk, but my vife vould haf her lunch spoilt and t'en make me vait too long for supper. Also, cousin Marthe says you need time to settle in," winking again at Renny.

"Hanne gar skolen, goes to school t'at is, but only two days a veek. But may she can come and play vit t'e baby vone day?"

"Oh yes, that would be lovely," voiced Linnea happily.

They visitors were gone as quickly as they had arrived. The bread, soup and lingonberries were a welcome addition to their simple fare. However, the trauma from the knock on their door had taken an edge from their celebration. Such moments would come again. They were fugitives and exiles in a strange land; but it was what they were called to. Like the Jews exiled to Babylon, they were to make a home, plant a field, have children and wait on God's time.

They were not the first, and there is a sweetness that attends living a life of uncertainty, which only those that live it can know. Linnea and Renuel were both 'wanderers' now, but this new place held hope and 'hope deferred makes the heart sick; but when dreams come true at last there is life and peace.'

# CHAPTER 55

# IIULIA'S NOTE

"When we have exhausted our hoarded
resources; the Father's full giving has only begun."
Old Swedish

Natalyia moved close to Stian, put her arm over his chest and hugged him. He sighed, "Ah bedtime, it is such a great thing. But bedtime with my beautiful Natalyia..., now that is the greatest!"

"Shhh Stian, not so loud."

"Why, do you think God might be jealous?" He laughed tiredly.

"Oh no, don't say that Love. I fear Marthe may hear."

"Dearest Lady, she already knows you are beautiful and that we sleep together!"

Natalyia laughed. "I know that, husband, but I do not want her to feel sad or lonely without Linnea."

"You are kind Natty; but she'll get used that, as well as to our laughing and talking. It makes her happy that we are so happy. She hasn't been back long enough to be lonely."

"Yes, we are very happy; but are we too happy? So many others I know are sad. But I feel such gladness when I am close to you as we are right now."

"And when you aren't?"

"I miss my people, though so many were killed, I cannot help to think of the others quite often. Some are alone, in prison and afraid. Some have been released but are still being hunted; they too are afraid. I know all this Stian. It was my life too. Sometimes I feel that I have deserted them; but I know that God is their helper and friend. I would be a prisoner too, but a different kind of prisoner had Boris succeeded. I would be lost to all of you, but perhaps I would have had a way to aid them!" Stian rolled towards Natalyia and held her close. This thought came to him *remember those that are in chains, as though you were there yourself.*

"It is right that you remember them. You have helped me to remember them too, dear lady. I thank you for that; but God has given you and me to one another; let us not doubt Him." She nodded but was quiet.

"There is something more, isn't there Natalyia?"

"I saw someone today." Stian released her slightly and sat up on one elbow.

"Who?"

"I do not know. She looked very familiar. It may have been nothing. I had gone on a short walk to the bakery and she came into the shop just after me. I felt that I knew her from back home."

"Why home and not from a local store or somewhere else right here," he replied.

"It is hard to explain; but when you have lived there, it is certain way people act who are not free."

"Do you mean that they don't swing their arms when they walk?" She smiled as he squeezed her.

"Yes, funny old man, something to be like that." He chuckled. Natalyia liked to call him 'old man' when he irritated her too much with his teasing. Her life with Stian Johanneson was so full of joy. His youthful vigor and confident manner made her feel safe and whole. Often, he truly seemed younger than she was as she struggled to shed the aged skin of her oppression.

The lady felt healing come more and more through her efforts and personal touch at making their home her home too. "Such a wondrous thing to have home, after feeling without such for so long," she told him. Living here in the manse she had spent much time out of doors tending flowers and planting her first summer. What creations of beauty and wonder growing things were! These vibrant reminders of God's renewing force brought hope to her injured heart.

Iiulia had managed to procure a number of Natalyia's watercolors and had sent them by ship under Marthe's name. They were hung in various places in their home. One day she hoped to pick up her brush again; but time was needed to assuage related sorrows.

Natty felt Stian jerk slightly. He had fallen asleep; she patted his head gently. He kissed her cheek and rolled over with a vigorous flop. He was snoring within a minute. Natalyia smiled, in secret delight, at the sound of his 'breathing'. *Sometimes, during the night, she would reach out and touch his foot, just to see if he was still there.*

As she often did, she prayed for Renuel and their little family that no trouble would come to their hideaway. *But who was that woman at the boulangerie?* Suddenly Natalyia sat straight up in bed. *Oh, dear Lord, could it be she?*

Boris had sent his sister to 'study' at Oxford; but she and Renuel knew it was really to spy on him. There, Iiulia fell in love with Renny. She had told Natalyia this herself, later, but also declared she had given that hope up, even if he ever returned her love. Iiulia knew that Boris would kill him and probably her, as well, if he felt betrayed.

Now Natalyia was trembling and wide awake. She was remembering fully the encounter at the bakery. The woman had brushed closely enough to snag Natalyia's coat pocket. She paused, apologized but hurried on out. The stranger's scarf was large and didn't allow for more than a glimpse of her face. Her eyes were crystal blue and stared into Natalyia's. *It must have been Iiulia! Of course, how could she have neglected to see that.*

Natalyia gently climbed out of bed, feeling her way in the dark. Noiselessly descending the stairs, she switched on a light and hurried to the front coat closet. Feeling in her pocket, there it was, a small note folded. Trembling, she opened it and read, "I hoped you would remember my blue eyes, dear Natalyia, as you always remarked about them. You so lovingly cared for me during those months after I left England. I can never thank you enough for your friendship, and your love for my mother during her final months. Without your sharing of spiritual truths, she would have died without hope.

My father had forbidden even the mention of Christ or God in our home. Now, I am endeavoring to share this with our dear countrymen, still in harm's way. Janken and I have teamed together in the underground with many others. He said you suggested he get to 'know me' well! I thank you for introducing this brave, loving man, into my life, dear lady. He is now a believer too and my name will soon to be changed to his!

I am in this country on a brief mission, but I wanted to contact you. Live gladly now and enjoy the love of Pastor Johanneson, this fine man of faith. I have heard much of him from Janken, whom God used to greatly impact Jan. We will continue to care for our people, in the underground, until Boris stops us. Pray that we will go undetected, if God wills. You have done all that you could. Now, stand firm believing this and, "Do not be anxious." Remember, you told my mother that.

"Pray for Boris, he is so lost, and haunted by his past. I tell him I fear he will go to hell, but I tell him he can be forgiven instead. I say he could do much good for so many and go to heaven too. I so wish this for my brother."

But he tells me, "It's too late, and why don't you just go to hell."

One day our little Queen Bella may lead 'our country' in a new way. Your son will soon know all of this. We will all pray and plan together for that day. If the Lord wills, all of us shall meet again, dear and great Lady!" Y.P.

## CHAPTER 56

# THE BOOK AND THE MESSAGE CODE

"O spread thy pure wings o'er them!
Let no ill power find place,
When onward through life's journey
Thy hallowed path they trace."

John Keble

It had been almost eighteen months. Life in the Gaard was 'gud' but Linnea had broken down occasionally with homesickness, since Marthe's departure. At those times, she yearned for her father and the old ways of city life.

"I even miss the neighborhood with Berthe and Ebbe always minding my business; and now Kati says she is their newest cause," she said laughing and sobbing pitifully one day. They were both glad that Kati Jo and Pace were seeing C.W. after their quick nuptials. Kati wrote that C.W. declared, "It's gud since t'ose two are bo't 'saved' now, even tho 't'ey did it 'backvards'. Now t'ey need a church and a Bible pastor!"

After one such crying jag Renuel asked her the obvious question between them, "Are you sure you're not sorry we came here? I knew it would be hard; but is it too hard?" Linney stroked Renny's cheek tenderly.

"No, my husband, I am only a little sad. There is always heartache in life, no matter what. But think how much sadder I would be at home, risking your and our Bella Rene's safety. That in turn would jeopardize your people's future; whatever it holds. No, I will not be sad for long. I won't be melancholy. I love our life together here too much; you'll see."

That was months ago and indeed Linnea had found surcease from sorrow by daily busyness and choosing to be happy. Remembering a catechism verse buoyed her often. 'A cheerful heart does good like medicine.' That Hebrew maxim often made for flowers or holly branches on the table or some kringla, hot from the oven!

Linney smiled and sighed blissfully as she stroked her rounded belly. Bella was two and a half now and such a fascinating creature. Both she and Renny were intrigued with her, as were others, but they were also protective and always on the alert. Linney felt weary of it at times. All parents fear kidnapping of their child; but it was a daily reality for them.

She heard the loud stomping of Renuel's boots on the porch. Her heart beat a little faster and her breaths were a little shorter. That was always the way with Linnea when she heard sounds of his return. *Renuel's home*, she thought happily.

"Who is that ReyRey?"

"Da!", came the excited cry. Linney pondered briefly, *would it always be this way, this love for him, even with too many cross words from her and his silent rebukes, or his pacifying remarks?* A stout blast of cold air came thru the doorway.

"Uff da Renny! Are you the abominable snowman?" He closed the door soundly. She laughed as she took his coat and hung it by the fire. Bella clapped and came running to him and squealed as he rubbed her face with his cold nose and beard. "Brrr, tell Da it's cold out there!"

"Heh, I thought you loved living in a Christmas card," he teased.

"I do love it all—-outside!" They laughed, caught up with their day, and soon sat down to supper. It was a good night for potato sausage and white gravy, on potatoes, and bread with a special treat of lemon curd from home.

Later, Bella was playing on the floor, talking to her dollies at her little tea party table and chairs.

"She loves that so much Ren. Thanks for making it."

"Glad too." Renuel's voice was serious and Linnea looked up quickly from her mending. "I got a letter today from home."

"From your mother?"

"No, not that home." His eyes flashed up at her. "My home." Linnea froze.

"What do you mean? From whom?"

"The postmark is from my city and country."

"Who sent it then?"

"I don't know." His voice was flat. Linney's eyes were wide open as she looked quickly down at their toddler who was still chatting and playing distractedly.

"What does it say," trying to make her voice even.

"It is in a kind of code."

"What code? Why a code?"

"I think in case it got intercepted." His voice was quiet.

"So, did you figure it out?"

"Not yet. I have to study the book that came with it."

"A book? What is it about?" He held it up but didn't hand it to her, though she held out her hand.

"It is just about politics, in my language, of course." He looked cautiously at her.

"The letter reads, "It will be a fine time for a birthday celebration. Prayers that your journey, til then, will be safe and without mishap. Enjoy reading while you plan your trip."

Now Linnea's voice became animated. "What birthday celebration? Whose? Mine was in July and yours is six months away. Bella is only two. Why would we 'journey' anywhere for her birthday or ours? Where would we go?"

Renuel just shook his head. Linnea was very sharp and asked all the logical questions for which he had no answer.

"It's coded Linney. I have to figure it out."

"I'm afraid Ren." She went and scooped up Bella. "Someone knows we're here."

He stood up and put his arms around both and squeezed them tenderly.

"Yes, I know. But it might be a friend giving a warning of some kind."

Tears streamed down Linney's face. "Or someone cruel and vindictive and..." She tossed her head in protest at her own dread. "No I'm so sorry, God doesn't want me think that. Come ReyRey, let's have some cookies and milk with Da." She walked away, wiping her tears on Bella's dress, and humming in a shaky voice, "Leaning on the everlasting arms."

# CHAPTER 57

# FAIRYLAND

෧ஜ෦

"The goodness of the fairy tale was not...
that there might be more dragons than princesses,
It was just good to be
In the fairytale."

G.K. Chesterton

Renuel stared hard as he carefully flipped through the pages of his father's small book. It felt 'other worldly' to hold in his hands a published, first edition copy of 'Living in Fairyland' by Galena Zaplavnov. This was the treatise on freedom that had sealed his eventual fate. The book went rapidly into a second printing and thus had caught the attention of Nietzsche-schooled adherents and fascists who were in power.

Opening it to the foreword he read aloud a quote by G.K. Chesterton, a journalist and writer of the past, whom his father highly regarded. "The things I believed most then, the things I believe now, are the things called 'fairy tales'; in short, they teach that the democratic faith is this: the most terribly important things must be left to ordinary men themselves—mating of the

sexes, rearing of the young, laws of state. This is Democracy....".
Some may call it fairyland, but "In this I have always believed."

Renuel's mind was reeling. *Who could possibly have obtained
this copy or even more incredible, who would have kept it in his
possession and risked being caught with 'subversive material?' It
had obviously been read and reread by its worn condition.*

Renny had not initially told Linnea that it was his father's
book. He feared it would be too distressing and a threat to
their anonymity. He himself was very perplexed and unnerved
in the beginning. Once he followed the code and began to
decipher the imbedded words, he believed that the sender was
no foe. He knew that eventually sharing the author's identity
with Linney was essential, good or bad.

He called to her and told her what he had ascertained. She
paused a moment, quite stunned by the revelation. Then, putting her arms around his neck said, "Oh Renny, how wonderful
for you to be holding such a treasure in your very own hands. It
is almost like your father has made a visit; a touch, a gift from
God to encourage you in this undertaking. It is so like our kind
God; isn't it?"

*How like her it was, to fight her own fears of exposure and be
gracious about his father's book.* Renuel had a lump in his throat
as he smiled and nodded, "Thank you Linnea Zaplavnov. You
are a kind wife and a true friend."

She flushed slightly, and kissing him on the cheek said,
"Varse gud", with a twinkle in her eye. "You see, I am becoming
'bi-lingual' too" and left him to his deciphering.

He studied the sentences, not for content, as much as
to note the tiny pencil dots above certain letters. They were
spelling a message that was intriguing, but also daunting in its

meaning. He would need to share it all with Linnea. So far, the 'Coder' had not identified himself.

"Too risky," Renny mumbled. "Can't blame 'him'— or 'her.'" What had seemed a normal assumption now was charged in another direction entirely! *What had made him even think of the possibility of it being a woman? True, it wasn't uncommon for women to carry secret messages hidden in their routines of going to the bakery or walking their infants in a pram etc. But to be politically active was much riskier. Only two women came to mind. Billijae..., he ruled her out quite quickly and the only other was Boris Putin's sister, Iiulia!* The thought was electrifying! *Iiulia would have access to many documents, confiscated materials and books.*

As a girl, she had been several years ahead of him in school. The girl's family lived in a regal diplomatic residence in his city. Iiulia had insisted on attending the public school because as she told him once, "I can't bear the confinement of that house with my father and brother. If it weren't for my mother and her true views of right and...well, never mind; but I would run away."

Iiulia also knew Renuel's father was in and out of prison, as well as his mother being often detained and interrogated. The girl seemed drawn to Renuel and his family and once even apologized for her father's actions against his parents. She had spoken this in a whisper and begged him not to tell anyone. Of course, it was unthinkable for him to ever betray such a confidence; but she couldn't know that. Iiulia was beautiful and older, yet they were friends and for that he was glad. She left school three or four years before him.

Before leaving she drew him aside and said, "Thank you for not betraying me. I have so few I can trust. I won't forget this." After that, they had no more contact. He missed her.

Renny was greatly surprised when in his second year at Oxford, Iiulia arrived there for studies. He was also quite guarded. Things were very grave at home. By then her brother was even more powerful in the government. He was ten years her senior. *Was Iiulia sent to England to spy on him? It was a likely scheme of Boris's; but would she do it?* He wondered but doubted such a betrayal from her.

As months passed, they were together in various classes, study groups and lectures. Always attending separately, yet Renuel heard her openly share her conservative views. She ranted against the progressives and the evil of tyranny dressed up in socialistic garb.

Iiulia also made pointed statements about the last war and how Winston Churchill had saved Christian Civilization and Great Britain from the Nazis. She wrote a paper on the war and read it in class. Tears filled her eyes as she spoke of Dunkirk and how the Prime Minister's actions had saved nearly 300,000 soldiers' lives.

Renuel clearly remembered much of her concluding statement. *"There are still today despotic men in power who care for no one nor no good thing except their precious oligarchy. They are Liberals who hate true religion and tromp on the people, enslaving them in the labor force, unheralded and impoverished in their souls and bodies."*

Renny had stood and clapped with others, drowning out the boo'ers. If she was putting on an act, it was a good one.

From then on, he banished any suspician of her purpose in attending Oxford and they became friends once again.

Could this package have come from Iiulia? She had told him, one day before she left, that there was important work to do at home and that his father's writings had inspired her greatly. She spoke with emotion about Natalyia's friendship with her own, deathly ill mother. It was with deep admiration that her mother had observed the love his parents had modeled.

"'Don't settle for less my Iily,' my mother had pleaded, said Iiulia sadly. Their eyes met then and Renny knew that she knew of Boris's obsession with his mother and of her brother's philandering lifestyle.

Too soon this friend from home was gone. He missed Iiulia's presence, but mostly her passion for right and the plight of their country.

"Dear Renny, what are you thinking about so deeply?" Looking up at Linney he rubbed his eyes, weary from staring so long at the pages looking for dots which were making words, leading to answers. He realized he had stopped writing and become lost in thought.

"I was thinking about my friendship with Iiulia Putin at Oxford and wondering if she has any connection to this book mystery."

Linnea looked wide-eyed. "Is it from her; do you think? I know she must have loved you so. Poor thing, how could she help herself? Did you not love her back just a little? I know I would have fallen to pieces if you hadn't loved me back."

Renuel drew her down on his lap. "Do you think all the ladies loved me just because you did, beautiful girl?" Hugging her he chuckled. She sat up looking into his laughing eyes.

"Of course, I do, but now you can't love anyone back or I may be very jealous!" She had a serious but loving look in her eyes, with a bit of mischief thrown in.

"Fear not, 'fair lady', but pray for me! I am a man!" Linney jumped off his lap. "Oh, you are such a tease, Ren!" Then, she laughed.

"Now, my wife, let's get back to our cryptic message. Whether we determine the sender or not. Here is what I have deciphered so far."

"In year 10, the tyranny will end,
The path to parliament begin.
On your journey home,
The girl must not roam.
Like young Josiah of old,
Our small Queen must be told.
Make ready for that fray
T'will be her 10th birthday.
This God-fearing monarchy
Brings an end to sad anarchy."

"That is all I have so far. It is a strange rhyming message but surely has a strong theme that involves Bella Rene. If the Resistance can put into place a secret parliament, then the missing piece for the people will be an heir to the monarchy. If it can all be done; then I am glad beyond measure. It is everything my father and mother hoped and worked for."

"And prayed for!" Linney added excitedly.

Renuel agreed firmly. "Yes, that they surely did; and yet a parliament is a step beyond even his dreams of 'Fairyland' for our country. As God 'died to make men holy', Galena Zaplavnov died for the rights of men to **pursue** freedom and holiness.

Renuel blinked away the tears and said with enthusiasm, "Come, let's celebrate with Marthe's excellent cranberry cordial, tart, but delicious."

"What are we celebrating exactly Renuel Breech?"

"Maybe the right to live in Fairyland and call ourselves the Zaplavnov's, not 'Breech', including all our little ones that will follow." Renny bent over and said, "Did you hear that, Baby Isabella Iiulia?"

He stroked Linney's rounded shape. Smiling demurely, she quipped, "I guess that is a good name, if it's a girl, as long as you only loved Iiulia Putin back a little. After all, she is beautiful and brave; and we want our girls to be so also."

"Fear not wife. She was loved only 'a little' as an old friend and is 'a lot' too much like me. But I hear she and Janken are loving each other more than 'a little'!" He smiled, but a grim look overtook his moment of cheer. "I fear they are in constant peril and may never make it to the marriage altar. They live from day to day and I remember it well."

Linnea sat on his lap and hugged his neck. "I pray, one day, they can also live in fairyland as we do, dragons and all."

# CHAPTER 58

# THE TOWN SQUARE

"Should auld acquaintance be forgot
and never brought to mind..."

The girls and ladies were dressed in their traditional bunads. It was a gay and colorful sight. The fiddles were up, and tuned, and the dancers were moving in and out of their steps, with smiles and agility, except for a few young and insecure ones. They too brought youthful charm and a winsomeness in their hesitancy.

"Mother, I so wish I could be part of the dancing. I have my bunad now and so does Hanne, of course. We've practiced the dance steps with Haakon; and he is very good; but he doesn't even want to dance anymore".

"Maybe at seventeen Haakon has other interests. I'm sorry for both you and Hanne; but those are the town square rules in Vinhaven."

"You aren't thirteen, just barely ten, and Hanne doesn't wish to leave you out." The girl let out a sigh. "Come here, little Miss."

Linnea, hugging her, said, "Anyway, someday you will be dancing enough, and in beautiful dresses."

"Is that why you and Papa have taught me different kinds?"

"Yes."

"Why?"

"Because you are musically inclined, so there." And she laughed, hugging her daughter.

"Oh, there is Hanne, Mama! May I go now?"

"Yes, you may; and take this new music I brought for her lessons. You'd better work harder or she still may pass you by!!"

"Mother, so might Haakon or some of your other piano students."

"Haakon? I doubt that; but he and Hanne were my first and they both have talent but in a different way."

"Haakon thinks his talent is for fishing and the sea, Mama. But even Hanne and I would both rather practice singing in the summer musical than practice piano."

"Time enough for both, I think. When you get old and your voice cracks, you will still be able to play the piano and the violin! I'm not so sure about dancing!" She laughed and her daughter ran off but threw her mother a smile over her shoulder.

The girl's tall form skipped away. Linnea sighed and mused a bit sadly. *The Alesunds two oldest children were so dear to Bella. She had always been older for her years than her peers. How Linnea wished she could hold Bella back, keep her as a child, carefree and secure, in the circle of their love. Bella was tall for her age and her maturing was coming early for this beloved daughter. The girl's dark hair was long and thick and stood out amongst the light-haired children in their community. It was obvious to Renuel and Linnea that Haakon Alesund was already very taken with Bella. Would he play a role in her future? Even as a child, her striking beauty was evident; but she was unspoiled in all ways that mattered. Haakon had said casually one day to Linnea that he loved Bella's love of life and of God. Haakon was already a serious Christian, but with a wild side that loved the untamed sea, plus hunting. He was also a keen debater and had a reputation for it in Vinhaven. When visiting, her father loved sparring with Hakkon about theology and apologetics, not to mention hunting debacles and deep-sea fishing, off the coast, with its many perils.*

Linnea smiled and sighed again. Bella Rene had been such a deep soul connection for Linnea. Through her she observed God's benediction on her unusual life with Renuel and all within their family.

Knowing she must lose this girl too soon, their family of five children was a comfort she had not even planned. Their daughter had led a humble, but happy family life.

Renuel earned a very moderate income. He taught classes in English and literature at the Vinhaven Secondary School, but it was little enough pay for an Oxford graduate. Their new little baby was a girl, coming after three brothers. They named her Iiulia Isabella and naturally; she was the love of them all, but especially her big sister.

"Finally, my very own sister. When I grow up, I shall take her with me when I marry Haakon," Bella had declared sincerely.

Linnea's face sobered slightly at her musings. Bella knew something of her destiny. In particular, she knew who her real parents were. On her 10th birthday they had just given her the necklace Renuel had brought for Isa. She wore it daily now.

With it came part of her parent's story. It was only right that she be prepared for what was to come.

But also, they had protected her childhood years, as much as they possibly could. This was kept from the children in the family, for safety reasons, but her seven-year-old brother, Oleksandr Johannes, was somewhat aware. He knew no details but asked Renuel if that was why Bella had to study so many books and learn his father's language.

"Uff da! Sure glad I'm not Bella! When would I have time to go fishing with the Alesunds!?" Olek had learned some of his Father's language by hearing it spoken. But of necessity, English and Norwegian were foremost in the early stages of his reading and writing.

Today Renuel was helping Haakon Alesund and some of the other men set up the outside dining area for the smorgasbord. *It was a good community for them,* Linnea thought. *The Stave church they attended was hundreds of years old and a remnant of superstition still lingered about 'staving' off demons, or 'furies', as some called them. Berthe and Ebbe would have had a few things to say about that.* She smiled. Their pastor was an evangelical man of the Lutheran persuasion and preached with a lot of 'fire in his belly', as C.W had said.

Marthe had finally said 'yes' to the elderly widower's proposal of marriage. (Even though he was Swedish!) But she did have some conditions.

"I vant to help t'e pastor and his lady vit t'e manse, so 'let us all be gud friends toget'er,' C.W. Nelson, but I vill take gud care of our hjem too. My girl Linney is in t'e old country, ja, and you and me can go toget'er t'ere and stay vit t'em a bit too, ja? T'e have lots of t'ings to t'ink about and ve and t'e Lord can help t'em t'ink better." She smiled a tender but quirky smile. "Maybe I can go to Sveden vit' you too."

"Ja, Marthe, t'at vould be a very 'god jul' present for me but you are t'e best gift," and he kissed her cheek.

C.W. was so thrilled to have Marthe accept his offer that he said he would even help her 'clean house'; and he meant it. Come across the sea they did, every year or two, and it was like a double taste of home for Linnea.

Her father and Natalyia came much more often and played a strong role in their family's life. Her grandmother told Bella many stories about her native country. Accounts that were true and even some of the struggles they had been through, but in story form. As the girl grew older, she would understand and recognize them as true facts.

Linnea sat contentedly as she adjusted her blouse to nurse the baby. It was Summer Equinox. This was heralded with feasting and dancing in the town square. Oleksandr was helping the men, along with some of the older boys. Her two little boys were playing with rocks and pinecones close by her.

She chuckled at some of their playtime dialogue, although the younger boy was barely two and spoke in jabberwocky that only his big brother Galena, grasped. Linnea looked toward the road that led up to the town square and saw two people walking toward her, along with Renuel and Oleksandr. *Odd,* she mused. *I thought the men would be working for a while yet.* She adjusted her clothing as they would soon be upon her.

Looking up, even though they were still twenty yards off, she immediately recognized Janken. The beautiful woman by his side could only be Iulia Putin, not Putin any longer, from their incognito letters. It was she who had purchased the piano for their gaard. "Your daughter needs musical accomplishment," she wrote.

Linnea felt a knot tighten in her stomach and a feeling of breathless panic. *Why are they here? Bella is just turned ten years old!* She took in a deep breath and looked up whispering, "Oh God help us." The young woman and mother stood and smiled to welcome the two people on earth whom she feared most to see.

At the same moment, in her happy way, Bella Rene ran past her and up to her father, breathless. Her mother heard her say, "Papa, you should see all the dancers for the festival? How 'gud' they look!"

Almost immediately Linnea heard him say, "This is my daughter, Bella Rene. Greet our visitors Bella." Bella gave a light curtsy and flashing a bright smile said, "Pleased to meet you."

"Now Papa, please come and see the dancing." She turned to Renuel. "Papa, the girl dancers are one short as Siv became sick. They have asked me to dance in the square in her place. Oh, may I please?"

Renuel looked at her with a mischievous smile. "Well I ..." and laughed at her wide eyes. "Yes, you may Bella," and off she ran.

Janken and Iiulia looked at each other and smiled broadly. "You do mean that she is Bella Rene Skoropadskyi?"

Renuel nodded, "Yes, she is Oleksandr Pavlov Skoropadskyi's only living child, heir to the monarchy."

## THE END

# POSTLUDE

"I have no home until I am in the realized
presence of God.
This holy presence is my inward home,
and until I experience it,
I am a homeless wanderer,
a straying sheep
in a waste-howling wilderness."

Anonymous, circa 1841

# Bio –

# Judy R. Carlson.

J udy is a storyteller, a Romancer, a bible scholar, a musician, an enchanting weaver of tales, a colorful intriguing Mor Mor (Norwegian for 'grandmother') and a wife of 50 years with a long-held crush on her teenage boyfriend/now husband. She has been writing and telling tales since the age of ten. Names from stories she has told in the oral tradition like, 'Flighty the flying pony, Abigail the girl heroine, the triplets, Ope, Pahpah and Peterkin, have danced across her children's and grandchildren's imaginations for decades. These unwritten stories and many others, written down in notebooks, some partially begun on random paper are stowed away in folders along with finished files of poetry. She has journals in excess of dozens and dozens.

Judy is a writer and has written hundreds of notes and letters. It is her delight and her commitment. But she is also a storyteller and always will be until the first page of her heavenly story begins. Even she will have to wait to hear that. But, don't miss this newest (or is it?) story!

That's all I have to say folks! Nevertheless, here is a little more pertinent information. Judy Carlson is also the published author of the epic fantasy, "The White Knight, the Lost Kingdom and the Sea Princess", published in 2015, by Nordskog Publishers, Ventura, CA.

She has a B.A. in English and creative writing from Trinity International University, Deerfield, Ill. She largely claims being a professional homemaker, mother of six children and twenty-seven grandchildren. Judy also has an active ministry to military wives.

C.S. Lewis, Sir Walter Scott, George MacDonald, Jane Austin, G.K. Chesterton and the American and English poets of the 18th and 19th centuries are just some of her mentors. She is a storyteller who must and will keep on telling.

Harold T. Carlson, Chaplain (COL)
U.S. Army Retired

CPSIA information can be obtained
at www.ICGtesting.com
Printed in the USA
FSHW011712120620
70796FS

9 781545 677520